THE
ECHOES
OF
L'ARBRE
CROCHE

THE ECHOES OF L'ARBRE CROCHE

Donald A. Johnston

ADAPTED AND UPDATED
BASED ON THE ORIGINAL TEXT OF
The Indian Drum
by William MacHarg and
Edwin Balmer, 1917

The University of Michigan Press | Ann Arbor

This work is based on *The Indian Drum* by William MacHarg and Edwin Balmer,
copyrighted and published in 1917.

U.S. CIP data on file.

ISBN 978-0-472-03396-6

To
My Guiding Light

Contents

Prologue

The State of Michigan consists of two large peninsulas, with extensive shorelines touched by four of the large Great Lakes—Erie, Huron, Superior and Michigan—and by the much smaller Lake St. Clair at Detroit. Across the eastern and northern water boundaries lies another country, Canada. The rich history of Michigan and its growth and development have been shaped by this unique geography, and by the diverse people who found their way into the area before it was a state, and who were attracted to the area after statehood was granted in 1837.

In the 17th century, about the time the Pilgrims landed at Plymouth, Europeans first reached what is now Michigan. Jacques Cartier discovered the St. Lawrence River in the name of the king of France in 1534, but it was not until after 1608, when Quebec was founded, that the French navigator and mapmaker-friend of Henry IV, Samuel de Champlain, moved westward, reaching as far as Lake Huron's Georgian Bay in 1615. He, like other early explorers in North America, thought that by going west he would find a route to the Orient. A few years later, a protege of Champlain's, Etienne Brulé, reached Sault Ste. Marie on the St. Mary's River, and then canoed up the river to Lake Superior. By the mid-1600s, French Jesuits had ventured into the area to establish missions in their efforts to bring Christianity to the Indians. For the rest of the century the French continued to explore and map both upper and lower Michigan, and to develop fur trading with the Indians at Sault Ste. Marie.

Antoine de Mothe Cadillac, in essence, founded Detroit when he strengthened the fort there, and—among others—Father Marquette, Louis Jolliet and LaSalle—played important roles in the early exploration and development of Michigan. The 17th century was clearly the French period of Michigan's history.

The 18th century brought international wars for possession of the North American interior, and Michigan was in the midst of that struggle. Following the fighting between the French and the British, all territory east of the Mississippi was granted to the British by the Paris Peace of 1763. The American Revolution began in 1775, and later the French joined the thirteen colonies against their old enemy, the British, by the 1778 Alliance. After the colonies won independence, the 1783 Treaty, marking the end of the American Revolution, gave the Michigan territory to the new United States, although the British did not evacuate the forts at Detroit and Mackinac until 1796.

During the War of 1812, the British re-took the Fort at Mackinac without firing a shot, and Detroit succumbed after a brief artillery duel. The outcome of the War of 1812 was tipped in our favor when Oliver Hazard Perry, commanding our Navy in Lake Erie, destroyed the entire British Squadron in the devastating battle off Bass Island, which marked one of the greatest naval losses in British history. By winning this battle, the United States gained control of the Great Lakes, and may well have prevented Detroit and the entire State of Michigan from becoming a part of Canada.

The early 19th century saw little change in the Michigan area from when the French first arrived. By Act of Congress in 1805, Michigan became a Territory, and later immigrants began to arrive bringing their skills and trades with them. The British controlled fur trading, but by 1811 John Jacob Astor and his American Fur Company at Mackinac Island began what later gave him control of all fur trade. By 1850 the logging and timber industry was under way and later became a boom in lower Michigan, and in the Upper Peninsula iron and copper mining developed at an active pace.

With construction of the Soo Canal and later the Locks at Sault Ste. Marie in 1855, ships could traverse the St. Mary's River between lakes Huron and Superior despite the 22-foot difference in their levels. The Welland Canal and Locks enabled ships to get around Niagara Falls to Lake Ontario, the St. Lawrence River and the Atlantic Ocean.

Railroads began to reach into Northern Michigan soon after mid-century as commercial activity grew. In the 1880s, in an effort to stimulate passenger traffic as lumbering began to taper off, railroads sponsored construction of hotels in such places as Traverse City, Charlevoix, Petoskey and Harbor Springs. The largest was the Grand Hotel on Mackinac Island. Built in 1887, it became the most fashionable resort in the Midwest. With public transportation and hotels readily available, and the excellent climate and fresh lake air, it was inevitable that Northern Michigan would become a popular resort area.

Summer colonies appeared at Charlevoix, Petoskey and Harbor Springs in the Little Traverse Bay area; Bay View Assembly, a Methodist oriented colony, was established in 1875 just north of Petoskey, and Wequetonsing, a Presbyterian colony, began in 1877. Harbor Point, purchased in 1855 by John Weikamp, a Franciscan Monk from Chicago who had fallen from favor with his church, was sold to the Harbor Point Association in 1878, and it, too, became a summer colony. Roaring Brook resort was opened by a group of Lansing businessmen in 1894. Over on the northern tip of Leelanau

Peninsula on Grand Traverse Bay, Northport Point resort colony got under way in 1899 when Cedar Lodge was built as a social center for the Cottage Owners Association.

Michigan became a state in 1837, and during the next two decades—as the population grew and natural resources were developed—commercial traffic on the Lakes began to emerge. By the end of the Civil War the age of sail was being replaced by steam propulsion. Steel ships carrying freight and passengers were beginning to appear on regular routes connecting Duluth, Chicago, Detroit, Cleveland, Toledo and Buffalo. The railroads joined in building large train-carrying ferries to minimize loading and unloading time and avoid having to run trains all the way around the foot of Lake Michigan to get to Illinois and Wisconsin. These large railroad "car ferries" had rails on their lower decks, onto which yard engines could shuttle entire trains of fully loaded freight and passenger cars. They ran across Lake Michigan between Muskegon, Ludington and Frankfort in Michigan and the Wisconsin ports of Milwaukee, Manitowoc and Kewaunee.

Successful ship owners were becoming a driving force in Great Lakes commerce, and many of them—as in other emerging industries—became wealthy in the process. This narrative of both fantasy and fact involves those associated with, and touched by, the fictional ship-owning firm of Corvet, Sherrill and Spearman during the fading Victorian age of the late nineteenth and early twentieth centuries. While the characters and events are fiction, the locales and the Great Lakes historical references are factual.

A man who has riches without
understanding
is like the beasts that perish.

Psalm 49:20
New International Version

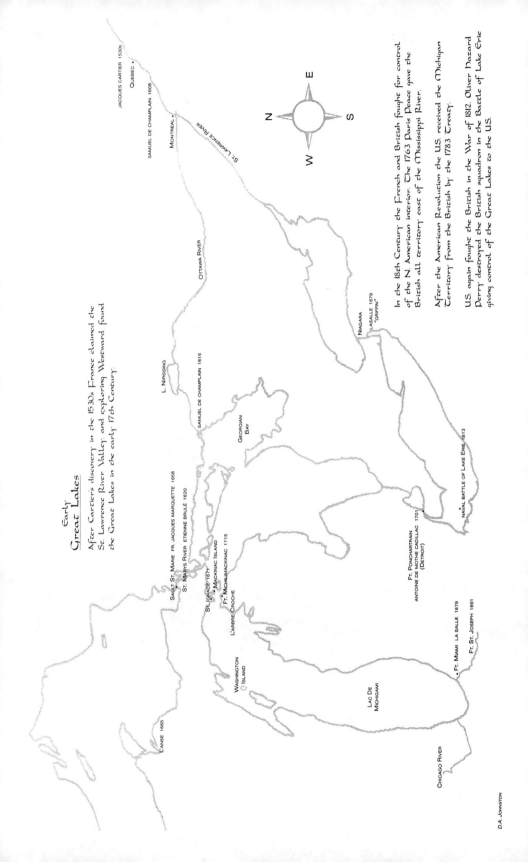

Early
Great Lakes

After Cartier's discovery in the 1530s France claimed the St. Lawrence River Valley, and exploring Westward found the Great Lakes in the early 17th Century.

In the 18th Century the French and British fought for control of the N. American interior. The 1763 Paris Peace gave the British all territory east of the Mississippi River.

After the American Revolution the US. received the Michigan Territory from the British by the 1783 Treaty.

US. again fought the British in the War of 1812. Oliver Hazard Perry destroyed the British squadron in the Battle of Lake Erie giving control of the Great Lakes to the US.

JACQUES CARTIER 1530s
QUEBEC
SAMUEL DE CHAMPLAIN 1608
MONTREAL
ST. LAWRENCE RIVER
OTTAWA RIVER
L. NIPISSING
SAMUEL DE CHAMPLAIN 1615
GEORGIAN BAY
NIAGARA
LASALLE 1679 "GRIFFIN"
NAVAL BATTLE OF LAKE ERIE 1813
SAULT ST. MARIE FR. JACQUES MARQUETTE 1658
ST. MARYS RIVER ETIENNE BRULÉ 1620
ST. IGNACE 1671
MACKINAC ISLAND
FT. MICHILIMACKINAC 1715
L'ARBRE CROCHE
FT. PONCHARTRAIN
ANTOINE DE MOTHE CADILLAC (DETROIT) 1701
WASHINGTON ISLAND
LAC DE MICHIGAMI
FT. MIAMI LA SALLE 1679
FT. ST. JOSEPH 1691
L'ANSE 1665
CHICAGO RIVER

N E S W

D.A. JOHNSTON

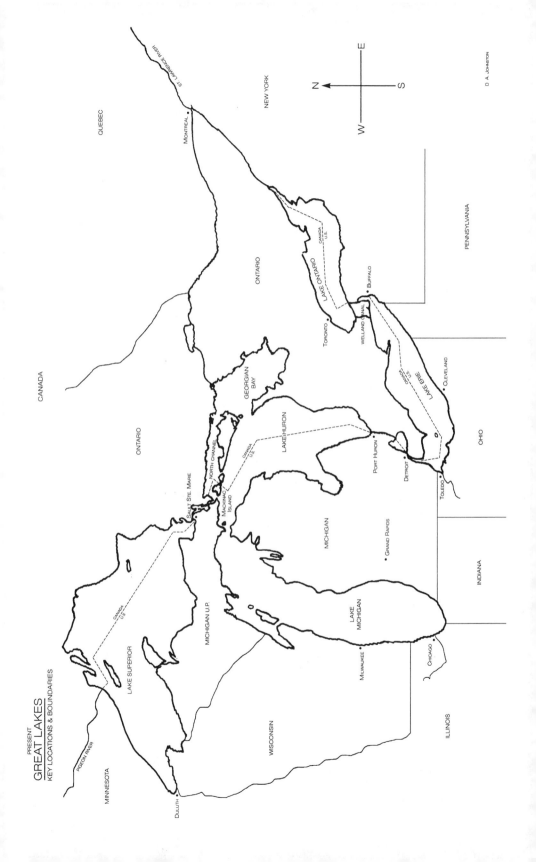

PRESENT
GREAT LAKES
KEY LOCATIONS & BOUNDARIES

D. A. JOHNSTON

N
W — E
S

CANADA

QUEBEC

MONTREAL

ST. LAWRENCE RIVER

NEW YORK

ONTARIO

LAKE ONTARIO

CANADA
U.S.

TORONTO

BUFFALO

WELLAND CANAL

LAKE ERIE

CANADA
U.S.

CLEVELAND

PENNSYLVANIA

OHIO

GEORGIAN BAY

NORTH CHANNEL

SAULT STE. MARIE

MACKINAC ISLAND

LAKE HURON

CANADA
U.S.

PORT HURON

DETROIT

TOLEDO

ONTARIO

MICHIGAN U.P.

CANADA
U.S.

MICHIGAN

GRAND RAPIDS

INDIANA

LAKE SUPERIOR

DULUTH

POGEON RIVER

MINNESOTA

WISCONSIN

MILWAUKEE

LAKE MICHIGAN

CHICAGO

ILLINOIS

Part
One

Questions

I

T he tall, bent, pine tree overhanging a high bluff near the
north end of Lake Michigan marked one of the most important
Indian Villages in the North. This tree, on the northwestern shore
of what is now Emmet County, Michigan, could be seen for a great
distance by occupants of approaching canoes and was always a welcome beacon and happy sight to the Indians, and later to the French
voyageurs who traveled the northern reaches of the lake.

When the French Jesuits arrived in the 17th century they named
this fascinating land of that bent tree, *L'Arbre Croche*. That name
came to mean the entire area running north along Lake Michigan
from Harbor Springs and up through Cross Village. The lore of the
lakes is always present in this land so rich in Indian history and
legend. This beautiful place of pine and hemlock woods, extending
inland from the stony and sometimes sandy beaches near Middle
Village, is silent at most times, as it was when the great Indian spirit,
Manitou, ruled his inland waters. Tradition has it, however, that at
times of storm, whenever the lake claims life, the sound of a drum
can be heard, tolling one beat for every life so lost.

When the large steel steamer *Wenota* sank, those living in the area say the drum tolled to thirty-five upon the hour, the number lost as later learned. They heard the requiems for the five who went down with the schooner *Grant* and the seventeen lost with the *Susan Hart*, and for the twenty-three Irish headed for Beaver Island on the *Elk*. And so with other ships lost over time. Only once, it is said, did the drum count wrong.

That was during the great storm of December, 1895. The drum beat for a sinking ship to the count of twenty-four, time and again. Those who heard the drum waited for a report of a ship lost with twenty-four aboard, but no such news came. A new steel freighter, the *Miwaka,* on her maiden voyage with twenty-five aboard—not twenty-four—never made port. No word was ever heard from her, no wreckage was ever found. Among the families of the officers and crew of the ship, there stirred for a time a desperate belief that one had been saved; that somehow, somewhere one was alive and might return. The day of the loss of the *Miwaka* was fixed as December fifth, after she passed through the Straits of Mackinac, heading west; the hour was set as five o'clock in the morning only by the sounding of the drum.

The region of L'Arbre Croche, alive as it is with Indian history and legend—and memories of shipwrecks—encourages such beliefs as this. Lake Michigan is large, and can be both mysterious and deadly. To the northward and the west, at Ile-aux-Galets— "Skilligalee," as the lakemen call it—at Waugoshance, and at Beaver and Fox Islands, navigation beacons gleam spectrally above the water, or blur ghostlike in the haze. Northward on the dark knolls and sandy bluffs of the mainland, echoes still live of the bloody 1763 massacre at Fort Michilimackinac by the Chippewas. Later the Ottawas, upset because they were not included in the attack, raided the Fort, captured the few surviving British officers and men, and took them back to L'Arbre Croche and then to the British at Montreal for reward. To the southward, where other hills frown down upon Little Traverse Bay, black-robed priests in their chapels

4

still chant the same masses their predecessors chanted to the Indians in earlier times, giving some cause to wonder how close the Indian spirit Manitou might be to the Christian Creator.

Whatever may be the origin of the drum—or whether it even exists—it is not questioned by the descendants of those Indians, who today make baskets, beadwork and other crafts for the summer trade. It is firmly believed by old-time farmers and fishermen—white and Indian—whose word on any other subject is beyond question. In essence, of course, this is only the most absurd of irrational beliefs, and could in no way affect men who, in 1915, carried ore in ships to the mills in Gary, transported grain to the elevators in Chicago, hauled iron and machinery to Detroit. Therefore, it is recorded now only as a superstition which, for twenty years, had been connected with the loss of a great ship in 1895.

*   *   *

A storm of the February, 1915, norther was howling down the ice-jammed length of Lake Michigan and assaulting Chicago with a vengeance. The stinging storm was a whirling maelstrom of sleet and snow, obscuring at mid-afternoon even the lighthouses at the harbor entrance. Foghorns were bellowing blindly from the freighters trying for the harbor entrance, and sirens echoed loudly in the city during lulls in the storm.

Battering against the fronts of the row of fashionable hotels, shops and club buildings which face across the narrow strip of park to the lake front in downtown Chicago, the gale swirled and eddied the sleet and snow until all the wide windows, warm within, were frosted. At the staid Fort Dearborn Club, a much respected downtown club for men, great log fires blazed on the open hearths and reflected from the heavily frosted panes to lend additional warmth to the rooms.

The few members present at this hour of the afternoon showed by their lazy attitudes and the desultory nature of their conversation the dulling of vitality which warmth and shelter bring on a cold and stormy day. On one, however, the storm seemed to have a contrary effect. With swift, uneven steps he paced from one room to another. From time to time he stopped abruptly by a window, scraped the frost from it with fingernail, stared out for an instant through the small opening he had made, then resumed his nervous pacing. His manner had been so uneasy and distraught since his arrival at the club an hour before, that even among those who knew him best none had ventured to speak to him.

In every great city there are a few individuals who, from their fullness of experience in an epoch of the city's life, come to epitomize that epoch in the general mind. When one thinks of a city in more personal terms than its square miles, its towering buildings, and its censused millions, one must think of those individuals. Almost every great industry has one, and seldom more than one, predominant figure. Others of his rivals, or even his partners, may be more powerful than he, but he is the personality. He represents to outsiders the romance and mystery of the secrets and adventures of great achievement. Thus, to think of the great mercantile establishments of State Street is to think immediately of one person; another vivid and picturesque personality stands for the stockyards; another for the exchanges; one rises from banking; another from steel. The man who was pacing restlessly and alone the rooms of the Fort Dearborn Club on this stormy afternoon was Benjamin Corvet, the man who, to most people, embodied the life underlying all other commerce thereabouts, the life and industry of the Lakes.

The Lakes, which mark unmistakably those who get their living from them, had put their marks on him. Though he was slight in frame with a spare, almost ascetic leanness, he had the wiry strength and endurance of a man whose youth had been spent upon the water. He was very close to sixty now, but his thick, straight hair was still jet black except for a slash of pure white above one temple. His brows were black above his deep blue eyes. Unforgettable eyes, they were, that gazed at one directly with surprising, disconcerting intrusion into one's thoughts. Then, before amazement became resentment, one realized that though he was still gazing, his eyes were vacant with speculation; a strange, lonely withdrawal into himself. His acquaintances, in explaining him to strangers, said he had lived too much by himself of late. He and one manservant shared the great house which had been unchanged, and in which nothing appeared to have been worn out or have needed replacing, since his wife left him suddenly and unaccountably some twenty years before. At that time, he had looked much the same as now. Since then, the white at his temple had grown a bit broader perhaps; his nose had become a trifle aquiline, his chin more sensitive, his well formed hands a little more slender. Some said he looked more French, referring to his father who was known to have been a skin-hunter north of Lake Superior in the '50s, and who had married an English girl at Mackinac and settled down to become a trader in the Upper Peninsula woods, where Benjamin Corvet was born.

During his boyhood, men came to the peninsula to cut timber. Young Corvet worked with them and, later, began building ships. Thirty-five years ago, he had been only one of hundreds whose fortunes lay in the fate of a single, small ship. Now in Cleveland, in Duluth, in Chicago, more than a score of great steamers under the names of various independent companies were owned or controlled by him and his two partners, Sherrill and young Spearman.

He was a quiet, gentle-mannered man. At times, however, he suffered from fits of intense irritability, and these had increased in frequency and violence. It had been noticed that these outbursts occurred generally at times of storm upon the Lake. The mere threat of financial loss through destruction of one or even more of his ships was not enough to cause them. Rather it was believed they were the result of some obscure physical reaction to the storm, which had grown upon him as he grew older.

Today his irritability was so marked, his uneasiness so much greater than anyone had seen before, that the attendant whom Corvet had sent a half-hour earlier to reserve his usual table for him in the grill—the table by the second window—had started away without daring to ask whether the table was to be set for one or two. Corvet himself corrected the omission; "For two," he had shot after the man. Now, as his uneven footsteps carried him to the door of the grill and he went in, the steward who started forward on seeing him suddenly stopped, and the waiter assigned to the table stood nervously uncertain, not knowing whether to give his customary greeting or efface himself as much as possible.

The tables at this hour were all unoccupied. Corvet crossed to the one he had reserved and sat down. He turned to the window at his side and scraped a small opening in the frost through which he could see the storm outside. Ten minutes later he looked up sharply but did not rise, as the man he had been awaiting, Spearman, the younger of his two partners, arrived.

Spearman's first words, audible through the big room, made plain that he was late for an appointment asked by Corvet. His acknowledgement took the form of an apology, but one which, in tone different from his usual bluff, hearty manner, seemed almost contemptuous. He seated himself, his big powerful hands clasped on the table, his gray eyes studying Corvet closely. Corvet, without acknowledging the apology, took the check and began to write an order for both. Spearman said he had already lunched and would take only a cigar. The waiter took the order and went away.

When the waiter returned, the two men were obviously in a bitter quarrel. Corvet's tone, low-pitched but violent, sounded steadily in the room, though his words were inaudible. The waiter, as he set the food upon the table, felt relief that Corvet's outburst had fallen on shoulders other than his. It had fallen, in fact, upon the shoulders best able to bear it. Spearman was still called "young Spearman," even though he was slightly over forty now. He was the power in the great ship-owning company of Corvet, Sherrill and Spearman. Corvet, during recent years, had withdrawn almost entirely from active life. Some said the sorrow and mortification of his wife's leaving him had made him choose more and more the seclusion of his library in the big lonely house on the North Shore, and thus had given Spearman the chance to rise to prominence. But those most intimately acquainted with the affairs of the great ship-owning firm maintained that Spearman's rise had not been granted him, but had been forced by Spearman himself. In any event, Spearman was not one to accept Corvet's irritation meekly.

For nearly an hour the quarrel continued, with intermittent periods of silence. The waiter, listening as waiters always do, caught at times single sentences.

"You have had that idea for some time," he heard Corvet say.

"We have had an understanding for more than a month," came the reply.

"How definite?"

Spearman's answer was not audible, but it intensely agitated Corvet, whose lips were set and whose hand clasped and unclasped a fork nervously. He dropped the fork, making no further pretense of eating.

The waiter, following this, caught only single words, "Sherrill"— that, of course, was other partner. "Constance"—that was Sherrill's daughter. The other names he heard were names of ships. As the quarrel went on, the manners of the two men changed. Spearman, who at first had been assailed by Corvet, now was assailing him. Corvet sat back in his chair, while Spearman pulled at his cigar, now and then taking it from his lips, and gestured with it between his fingers, as he spat some angry ejaculation across the table. Corvet leaned over to the frosted window, and looked out. Spearman shot a comment which made Corvet wince and draw back from the window. Then Spearman rose. He delayed, standing, to light another cigar deliberately and with studied slowness. Corvet looked up at him once and asked a question, to which Spearman replied with a snap of a burnt match down on the table, then turned abruptly and strode from the room. Corvet sat motionless.

The reversion to self-control—sometimes even to apology—which usually followed Corvet's bursts of irritation had not come this time.

9

His agitation had plainly increased. He pushed away from his un-eaten luncheon and got up slowly. He went out to the coat room, where the attendant handed him his hat and coat. As he hung the coat on his arm, the doorman, acquainted with him for many years, ventured to suggest a cab. Corvet, staring at him strangely, shook his head.

"At least, sir," the man urged, "put on your coat." Corvet ig-nored him. He seemed to shrink as he stepped out into the smart-ing, blinding swirl of sleet. Rather than physical, however, it was mental—the unconscious reaction to some thought the storm called up. The hour was barely four o'clock, but it was so dark from the storm that the shop windows were lit. Automobiles slipped and skidded up the broad boulevard with headlights on, their drivers blowing horns constantly to alert other drivers blinded by the weather. The sleet-swept sidewalks were almost deserted. Here and there, before a hotel or one of the shops, a car came to the curb, and the alighting passengers dashed swiftly across the walk to shelter.

Corvet, still carrying his coat on his arm, turned northward along Michigan Avenue, facing into the gale. The sleet beat into his face and lodged into the folds of his clothing without his heeding it.

Suddenly he aroused on hearing the four booming blasts of a steam whistle out on the Lake. A ship out in that sleet and snow-shrouded grayness was in distress. The sound ceased, and the gale bore in only the ordinary storm and fog signals. Corvet recognized the foghorn at the lighthouse on the end of the government pier. The light he knew was turning white, red, white, red, white behind the curtain of invisibility. Other vessels, not in distress, blew their blasts, which were interrupted again by the four long blasts of the ship in distress. Corvet stopped, drew up his shoulders, and stood staring out toward the Lake, as the signal blasts of distress cut in again from the ship calling for help. Color came into his pale cheeks now, but only lasted for an instant. A siren swelled and shrieked, then died away wailing, shrieked louder and then stopped. The four blasts blew again, and the siren wailed in answer.

A door opened behind Corvet. Warm air rushed out, laden with the sweet, heavy odors of chocolate and candy. Girls' laughter, exaggerated exclamations, and laughter again came with it as two girls passed by holding muffs before their faces. They hurried to different cars, scurried into them, and the cars drove off.

Corvet turned about to the candy shop and tearoom from which they had come. He could see as the door opened again, a dozen tables with white cloths, shining silver, and steaming porcelain pots. Twenty or more young women and girls were refreshing themselves, pleasantly, after shopping or a concert. A few young men were sitting at the tables with them. The blasts of the distress signal and fog horns must have been audible to them when the door was opened, but if they heard, they gave it no attention. The clatter and laughter and sipping of chocolate and tea was interrupted only by someone's occasionally reaching for a shopping list or some filmy possession threatened by the draft from the icy street through the opened door. The tearoom customers were oblivious to the lake in front of their windows, to the ship struggling for life in the storm. It was as if the snow was a protective screen which shut them off from a distant world.

To Corvet, a lakeman for forty years, there was nothing strange in this. Twenty miles from north to south, the city—its business blocks, hotels and restaurants and homes—faced the water. Except where the piers formed the harbor, all unprotected water was an open sea where, in times of storm, ships sank and grounded, and men fought for their lives against the elements and sometimes drowned and died. Corvet was well aware that it was likely none of those in the tearoom, or in the whole building, knew what four long blasts meant, or what the siren meant that was now answering. But now, as he listened, the blasts seemed to grow more desperate, and they profoundly affected Corvet. As another couple came out of the tearoom, he advanced as if to stop them. They hesitated as he stared at them, then sidestepped. When they had passed him, they glanced back. Corvet shook himself and went on.

He continued to go north. In the beginning, he had not seemed to have made conscious choice of this direction, but now he was following it purposely. He stopped at a shop and requested to use the telephone. When the number answered, he asked if Miss Sherrill were home but said he did not wish to speak to her. He said he merely wanted to be sure she would be there when he stopped in to see her in half an hour. After completing the call, he left the shop and headed north again and crossed the bridge. Now, fifteen minutes later, he came in sight of the Lake once more.

Great houses—the Sherrill house among them—here face the drive, the bridle path, the strip of park, and the wide stone esplanade which edges the lake. Corvet crossed to the esplanade, which was an ice bank now. Hummocks of snow and ice higher than a man shut off view of the floes tossing and crashing on the lake as far out as the blizzard let one see. Some ice along the shore, dislodged and shaken by the buffeting, parted occasionally to let gray water swell up from underneath and wash around his feet as he went on. He did not stop at the Sherrill house or look toward it, but went on a quarter of a mile beyond. Then he came back, and with an oddly strained and queer expression and manner stood staring out into the Lake. He could not hear the distress signals now.

Suddenly he turned. Constance Sherrill, having seen him from a window in her home, had caught up a coat about her, and ran out to him.

"Uncle Benny!" she hailed him, using the affectionate name by which she had called her father's partner since she had been a child. "Uncle Benny, aren't you coming in?"

"Yes," he said vaguely. "Yes, of course." He made no move, but remained staring at her. "Connie! Dear little Connie!"

"Uncle Benny!" she asked, "What's the matter?"

He seemed to pull himself together. "There was a ship out there in trouble," he said in quite a different tone. "They aren't blowing any more. Are they all right?"

"It was one of the M and D ships," she answered. "The *Louisi-*

ana, they told me. She went by here blowing for help, and I called the office to find out. A tug and one other of their line got out to her. She had cracked a cylinder head bucking the ice and was taking on some water. Uncle Benny, you must put on your coat."

She brushed the sleet from his shoulders and collar, and held the coat for him. He put it on obediently.

"Has Spearman been here today?" he asked, not looking at her.

"To see Father?"

"No, to see you."

"No."

He seized her wrist. "Don't see him, when he comes!" he commanded.

"Uncle Benny!"

"Don't see him!" Corvet repeated. "He's asked you to marry him, hasn't he?"

Connie could not deny it. "Yes," she said.

"And you?"

"Why . . . why, Uncle Benny, I haven't answered him yet."

"Then don't . . . don't; do you understand, Connie?"

She hesitated, frightened for him. "I'll . . . I'll tell you before I see him, if you want me to, Uncle Benny," she granted.

"But if you shouldn't be able to tell me then, Connie; if you shouldn't . . . want to then . . . ?"

The humility of his look perplexed her. If he had been any other man—any man except Uncle Benny—she would have thought some shameful and terrifying threat hung over him. He broke in sharply, "I must go home," he said uncertainly, "I must go home, then I'll come back. Connie, you won't give him an answer till I come back, will you?"

"No." He got her promise, half frightened, half bewildered. Then he turned at once and went swiftly away from her.

She ran back to the door of her father's house. From there she saw him reach the corner and turn west to go to Astor Street, where he lived. He was walking rapidly and did not hesitate.

13

The trite truism, that human beings can not know the future, has a counterpart not so often mentioned: We do not always know our own past until the future has made plain what has happened to us. Constance Sherrill, at the close of this, the most important day in her life, did not know at all that it had been important to her. All she felt was a perplexed, indefinite uneasiness about Uncle Benny. How strangely he had acted! Her uneasiness increased when the afternoon and evening passed without his coming back to see her as he had promised, but she reflected he had not set any definite time when she was to expect him. During the night her anxiety grew still more. The next morning she telephoned his house, but the call was unanswered. An hour later, she called again. Still getting no answer, she called her father at his office, and told him of her anxiety about Uncle Benny, but without repeating what he had said to her, or revealing the promise she had made to him. Her father made light of her fears. Uncle Benny, he reminded her, often acted queerly in bad weather. Only partly reassured, she called Uncle Benny's house several more times during the morning, but still got no reply. After lunch she called her father again to tell him she had resolved to get someone to go over to the house with her.

Her father, much to her surprise, forbade this rather sharply. His voice, she realized, was agitated and excited, and she asked him the reason. Instead of answering her, he made her repeat to him her conversation of the afternoon before with Uncle Benny, and now he questioned her closely about it. But when she in her turn tried to question him, he merely put her off and told her not to worry. Later, when she called him again, resolved to make him tell her what was the matter, he had left the office.

In the late afternoon, when dusk was turning into darkness, she stood at the window, watching the storm which still continued, with one of those delusive hopes which come during anxiety. Because it was the same time of day at which she had seen Uncle Benny walking by the Lake the day before, she hoped she would see him there again. As she looked out the window, she saw her father's car approaching, and knew from its direction that he was coming from Uncle Benny's house and not his office or club. The car pulled up to the house, and she ran out into the hall to meet him as he entered.

He came in without taking off his hat or coat. She could see that he was perturbed and greatly agitated.

"What is it, Father?" she demanded. "What has happened?"

"I do not know, my dear."

"Is it something . . . something that has happened to Uncle Benny?"

"I am afraid so, dear . . . yes. But I do not know what it is that has happened, or I would tell you."

He put his arm around her and drew her into a room opening off the hall—his study. He made her repeat again to him the conversation she had had with Uncle Benny, and tell him how he had acted. She saw, however, that what she told him did not help. He seemed to consider it carefully, but in the end to discard or disregard it. Then he drew her to him.

"Tell me, little daughter. You have been with Uncle Benny a great deal, and have talked with him often. I want you to think carefully. Did you ever hear him speak of anyone called Alan Conrad?"

She thought a few moments, then answered, "No, Father."

"No reference made by him at all to either name—Alan, or Conrad?"

"No, Father."

"No reference either to anyone living in Kansas, or to a town there called Blue Rapids?"

"No, Father. Who is Alan Conrad?"

"I do not know, dear. I never heard the name until today, and Henry Spearman had never heard it. It appears to be intimately connected in some way with what was troubling Uncle Benny yesterday. He wrote a letter yesterday to Alan Conrad in Blue Rapids and mailed it himself. Afterward, he tried to get it back, but it had already been taken up and was on its way. I have not been able to learn anything more about the letter than that. He seems to have been excited and troubled all day. He talked queerly to you, and he quarreled with Henry, but apparently not about anything of importance. And today that name, Alan Conrad, came to me in quite another way; in a way which makes it certain that it is closely connected with whatever has happened to Uncle Benny. You are quite sure you never heard him mention it, dear?"

"Very sure, Father."

He released her, still in his hat and coat, and went swiftly up the stairs. She ran after him and found him standing before a highboy in his dressing room. He unlocked a drawer in it, and from within the drawer he took a key. Then, still disregarding her, he hurried back down the stairs.

As she followed him, she caught up a wrap and pulled it around her. He had told his driver, she realized now, to wait. As he reached the door, he turned and stopped her.

"I would rather that you did not come with me, little daughter. I do not have any idea what has happened, but I will let you know as soon as I find out."

The finality in his tone stopped her from argument. As the house door and then the door of the limousine closed after him, she went back to the window, slowly taking off the wrap. She saw the car move swiftly out of the driveway, turn northward in the way it had come, and then turn again, and disappear. She could now only stand and watch for it to come back, and listen for the phone. For the moment she found it difficult to think. Something had obviously happened to Uncle Benny, something terrible, dreadful for those who loved him; that was plain, though only the fact and not its nature was known to her and to her father. That something was connected, intimately connected, her father had said, with a name no one who knew Uncle Benny had ever heard of before; the name of Alan Conrad of Blue Rapids, Kansas. Who was this Alan Conrad, and what could his connection be with Uncle Benny so to precipitate disaster upon him?

2

Two mornings later, the recipient of the letter Benjamin Corvet had written, and later excitedly attempted to recover, was asking himself much the same question Constance Sherrill had asked. He was waiting for the first of the two eastbound trains which stopped every day at the depot in the little Kansas town of Blue Rapids, where he lived. As long as he could remember back in his life, he had wondered who he really was. Who am I, this person they call Alan Conrad? And what am I to the man who writes from Chicago? These questions had framed the enigma of existence for him.

Since he was now twenty-three, as nearly as he had been able to approximate it, and as his distinct recollections of events went back to the time when he was five, it had been some eighteen years since he had first heard the question put to the people who had him in charge: "So this is little Alan Conrad. Who is he?"

Undoubtedly the question had been asked in his presence before; certainly it was asked many times afterwards; but it was since that day—the day he first questioned aloud the absence of a birthday of his own and they told him he was five—that he connected their evasion of the questions with the difference between himself and the other children he saw. This was particularly significant to him when he thought of the difference between himself and the boy and girl who lived in the same house with him. Always, when some one came to visit, it was, "So this is little Jim!" and "This is Betty; she's more of a Welton every day!" But it was always, "So this is Alan Conrad," or, "So this is the child!" or, "This, I suppose, is the boy I have heard about!" Each time he sensed that change in the voice, in the eyes, in the feel of the arms about him—for, though Alan could not feel how the arms hugged Jim and Betty, he knew that for him it was quite different.

At times, there was quite a definite, if not puzzling, advantage in being Alan Conrad. Following the arrival of certain letters—distinguished from most others arriving at the house by being addressed not with handwriting, like most, but in black or purple printing like newspapers—Alan invariably received a dollar to spend in any way he liked. To be sure, unless Papa took him to town, there was nothing for him to spend it on. Most often it went into the square, iron bank to which the key had been lost. Sometimes, he'd spend it according to plans agreed upon among all his friends, and in memory of these occasions and anticipation of the next, "Alan's dollar" became a community institution among the children.

But exhilarating and wonderful as it was to be able of oneself to take three friends to the circus, or to be the purveyor of twenty whole packages, not just sticks, of gum, at the same time the dollar really made all the more clear the boy's difference. The regularity and certainty of its arrival, as Alan's share of some larger sum of money which came to Papa in the letter, never served to make the event ordinary or accepted.

"Who gives it to you, Alan?" was a question more often asked, as time went on. The only answer Alan could give was, "It comes from Chicago." The postmark on the envelope, Alan noticed, was always Chicago. That was all he could ever find out about his dollar.

He was about ten years old when, for a reason as inexplicable as the dollar's coming, the letters with the typewritten addresses and the enclosed money stopped coming.

Except for the loss of the dollar at the end of every second month (a loss much discussed by all the children and not accepted as permanent until more than two years had passed) Alan felt no immediate effect of the cessation of the letters from Chicago.

When the first effects appeared, of course, Jim and Betty felt them just as much as Alan. Papa and Mamma felt them, too, and finally they had to give up the farm. The family moved to town, and Papa went to work in the woolen mill beside the river.

Papa and Mamma, at first surprised and dismayed by the stopping of the letters, still clung to the hope that the familiar, typewritten envelopes would reappear. But slowly resentment set it, and when, after two years, no more money came, resentment began to turn against Alan, and his "parents" finally told him all they knew about him:

In 1896 they had noticed an advertisement for persons to care for a child, and they had answered it to the office of the newspaper which printed it. In response to their letter a man called upon them and, after seeing them and going around to see their friends, had made arrangements with them to take a boy of three, who was in good health and came from good people. He paid a year in advance for room and board, and agreed to send a certain amount of money to them every two months after that time. The man brought the boy, whom he called Alan Conrad, and left him with them. For seven years the money agreed upon came, and now it had ceased, and Papa had no way of finding the man, as the name given by him appeared to be fictitious. He had left no address except "general delivery, Chicago," and Papa knew nothing more than that. He had advertised in the Chicago papers after the money stopped coming, and he had communicated with everyone named Conrad in or near Chicago, but he learned nothing. Thus, at the age of thirteen, Alan now knew definitely what he had already guessed: that he belonged somewhere other than in the little brown house in which he lived.

This knowledge now naturally gave rise to many other internal questions. Where did he belong? Who was he? Who was the man who had brought him here? Had the money stopped coming because the person who sent it was dead? In that case, the connection of Alan with the place where he belonged was permanently broken. Or would some other communication from the source reach him some day? If not money, then something else? Might he be sent for?

He did not resent Papa and Mamma's new attitude. He loved them both because he had no one else to love. He fully sympathized with them. They had struggled hard to keep the farm. They had ambitions for Jim, and were scrimping and saving now so that Jim could go to college, and whatever they might give Alan would be denied Jim, and would diminish by just that much Jim's opportunity.

But when Alan asked Papa to get him a job in the woolen mill at the other side of town where Papa himself worked in some humble and indefinite capacity, the request was refused. Thus, externally at least, Alan's learning the little that was known about himself made no change in his way of living. He had gone, like Jim, to the town school, which combined grammar and high schools under one roof. As he had grown older, he had clerked in one of the town's stores during vacations and in the evenings, as, too, had Jim. The only difference was that money Jim earned was his to keep. Alan carried his pay home to Papa as partial payment of the arrears which had been mounting against him since the letters stopped coming.

At seventeen, when he had finished high school and was working full-time as a clerk at Merrill's general store, the next letter came. It was addressed this time not to Papa, but to Alan. He seized it, tore it open, and out fell a bank draft for fifteen hundred dollars. There was no letter enclosed with the draft, and no other communication. Just the draft, made payable to the order of Alan Conrad.

Alan wrote to the Chicago bank by which the draft had been issued, but the reply said the draft had been purchased with currency, and there was no record of the identity of the person who had sent it. Since the amount due Papa for the seven years' arrears was more than the amount of the draft, even deducting what Alan had earned, he merely endorsed the draft over to his father.

That fall Jim went to college, and when he discovered that it was possible for a boy to work his way through school, he wrote Alan about it, and Alan followed him to the university.

Four wonderful years followed. The family of a physics professor, with whom Alan was brought in contact by his work outside of college, liked him and made it possible for him to live in their home, where he was accepted as one of the family. In the company of these educated people, Alan acquired ideas and manners he could not have learned in Blue Rapids. Athletics straightened and added bearing to his muscular, well formed body, and his pleasant, strong young face reflected new self-reliance and self-control. Life became filled with possibilities for himself which it had never held before. But when he graduated he had to put aside the enterprises he had planned and the dreams he had dreamed. His father's health had failed, and Jim, who had opened a law office in Kansas City, said he was "not in a position" to help. Alan, conscious that his debt to "Father and Mother" remained unpaid, returned to care for them.

No more money—no communicatioon of any kind—had followed the draft from Chicago. Still, receipt of the draft had revived and intensified all of Alan's speculations about himself, along with the vague expectation of his childhood that sometime, in some way, he would be "sent for." That expectation had grown during the last six years to a definite belief. Now the summons had come, and he was on the platform at the depot waiting for the eastbound train.

As he had torn open the envelope, he had seen that it contained not only a check, but also a note, in uneven but plainly legible longhand. It told him, rather than asked him, to come to Chicago. It gave detailed instructions for the journey, and advised him to telegraph when he started. Check and letter were signed by a name completely strange to him: Benjamin Corvet.

Alan was a distinctive, attractive young man as he stood on the station platform fingering the letter from Chicago in his pocket. As the train came to a stop he pushed his suitcase up onto a car platform, climbed to the bottom step, and stood looking back at the little town beyond the railroad station among brown, treeless hills scantily covered with snow. The town was the only home he had ever consciously known, and his eyes dampened. He choked as he looked at it and at the people on the station platform—the stationmaster, the drayman, the man from the post office who would receive the mail bag. These people knew him by his first name, and he called them by theirs. It never occurred to him that he might not see the town and them again. As the train started to move, he picked up his suitcase and carried it into the daycoach.

Finding a seat, he immediately took the letter from his pocket and for the dozenth time he reread it. Was Corvet a relative? Was he the man who had sent the remittances when Alan was a little boy, and the one who later had sent the fifteen hundred dollars? Or, was he merely a go-between, perhaps a lawyer? There was no letterhead to give aid in any of these speculations.

The address to which Alan was to come was on Astor Street. He had never heard the name of the street before. Was it a business street, Benjamin Corvet's address in some great office building, perhaps? He tried by repeating both names over and over to himself to arouse any obscure, obliterated childhood memory he might have had of them, but the repetition brought no result. Memory, when he stretched it back to its furthest, showed him only the Kansas prairie.

Late that afternoon he reached Kansas City, designated in the letter as the point where he would change trains. That night saw him on a transcontinental train with berths nearly all made up, and with people sleeping behind curtains. Alan got into his berth and undressed, but he lay awake most of the night. The late February dawn the next morning showed him the rolling lands of Iowa, which changed while he was at breakfast in the dining car to the snow-covered farm fields of northern Illinois. Toward noon, as the train rounded curves, he could see that the horizon to the east had taken on a murky look. Vast, vague, the shadowy emanations of hundreds of thousands of chimneys thickened and grew more definite as the train sped on. Suburban villages began supplanting country towns, and stations became more imposing. They passed factories, and then hundreds of acres of small houses of factory workers in long rows. Swiftly the buildings became larger and closer together. After passing miles upon miles of streets, the train rolled slowly by a train shed and then stopped under a long covered platform.

Alan, following the porter carrying his suitcase, stepped down among the crowds hurrying to and from the trains. He was not confused, but he was intensely excited. Acting in implicit accord with the instructions in the letter, which he knew by heart, he went to the uniformed attendant and engaged a taxicab, itself no small experience, as there would be no one at the station to meet him, the letter had said. He gave the Astor Street address to the driver and got in. As he leaned forward in his seat, looking to the right and then to the left as he was driven through the city, his first sensation was disappointment. Except that it was larger, with more and bigger buildings and with more people on its streets, Chicago apparently did not differ from Kansas City. In reality, if it was the city of his birth, or if he had ever seen these streets before, they now aroused no memories in him.

It had begun to snow again. For a few blocks the cab drove north past more or less ordinary buildings, then it turned east on a broad boulevard where tall tile and brick and stone structures towered until their roofs were hidden in the snowfall. The large light flakes, falling lazily, were thick enough so that when the cab turned north again, there seemed to Alan only a great vague void to his right. For the hundred yards which he could view clearly, the space appeared to be a park. A huge, granite building, guarded by stone lions, went by, and then more park. But then he felt a strange stir and tingle—quite unlike the excitement of his arrival at the station. It pricked in Alan's veins, and he dropped the window to his right and looked out. The lake, as he had known since his geography lessons, lay east of Chicago. Therefore, he decided, that void out there beyond the park was the lake. A different air and sounds seemed to come from it. Then it was all shut off, as the taxicab, swerving a little, was now dashing between business blocks, and a row of buildings rose again upon the right. They broke abruptly at one point to show him a walled chasm, in which flowed a river full of ice. He saw a tug dropping its smokestack as it went under the bridge as the cab crossed. Then there were buildings again on both sides. Then, suddenly, again, to the right, was a roaring, heaving, crashing expanse.

The sound had been coming to him as an undertone for many minutes. Now it overwhelmed Alan, swallowing all other sound. Even the monstrous city's murmur was insignificant compared with this. He could see but a few hundred yards out over the water as the taxicab ran along the lake drive, but what was before him was a sea. That constant roar came from far beyond the shore—the surge and rise and fall and surge of a sea in motion. Great chunks of ice floated there, tossed up, tumbled, broke, and rose again with the rush of the surf. Spray flew up between the floes; geysers spurted high into the air as the pressure of the water, bearing up against the ice, burst between great ice blocks before the waves cracked them and tumbled them over. And all was happening, he realized, without wind. Over the lake, as over the land, soft snowflakes lazily floated down undeterred in their drifting by the slightest breeze. That roar Alan heard was the voice of the water, that awesome power of its own.

Alan gasped, his pulse pounding in his throat. He had snatched off his hat, and leaning out of the window drew the lake air into his lungs. There had been nothing to make him expect this overwhelming crush of feeling. He had thought of the lake, of course, as a great body of water, an interesting sight for a prairie boy to see. But that was all. No physical experience in all his memory had affected him like this, and it came upon him without warning. The strange feeling that had stirred within him downtown was strengthened a thousandfold. It amazed him—half frightened and half dizzied him.

Then the cab suddenly turned a corner and shut out the view of the lake. Alan sat back breathless.

"Astor Street," he read the marker on the corner lamp post a block back from the lake, and he bent quickly forward to look as the cab swung right, into Astor Street. It was a residential street of handsome mansions built close together. The cab pulled to the curb near the middle of the block and came to a stop outside a large stone house. Of quiet, good design, it appeared to be a generation older than the houses on either side of it, which were brick and terra-cotta of more recent, fashionable architecture. Alan only glanced at them long enough to get that impression before he opened the door and got out. As the cab drove away, he stood beside his suitcase looking up at the old house, which bore the number given in Benjamin Corvet's letter. He glanced around at the other houses, and then back to the Corvet house again.

The nature of the neighborhood obviously precluded the probability of Corvet's being a mere go-between. He must be some relative—a possibility ever present in Alan's thought since the receipt of the latest letter. Alan had held in abeyance any judgment as to the nearness of Corvet's kinship, if any, to him. Now this thought took sharper and more exact form as he dared to again consider it. Was his relationship to Corvet, perhaps, the closest of all relationships? Might Corvet be . . . his father? He checked the thought. The time had passed for mere speculation. Alan was trembling excitedly, for whoever Corvet might be, the enigma of Alan's existence was going to be solved when he entered the house now before him. He was going to know who he was. All of the possibilities, the responsibilities, the attachments, the opportunities, perhaps, of that person who he was, whom, as yet, he did not know, were now before him.

He half expected the heavy, solid oak door at the top of the stone steps to be opened by someone coming out to greet him, as he took up his suitcase, but the gray house, like the brighter mansions on either side of it, remained impassive. If anyone in the house had observed his coming, no sign was given. He went up the steps and, with fingers excitedly unsteady, he pushed the button beside the door.

The door opened almost instantly; so quickly after the ring, that Alan, with throbbing heart, knew that someone must have been awaiting him. The door was opened about half way by a man within who, gazing out at Alan questioningly, was obviously a servant.

"What is it?" he asked, as Alan stood looking at him, and past him to the narrow section of hall which was in sight.

Alan put his hand over the letter in his pocket.

"I've come to see Mr. Corvet," he said, "Mr. Benjamin Corvet."

"What is your name?"

Alan gave his name, and the man repeated it after him quite without inflection, in the manner of a trained servant. Not familiar with such a tone, Alan waited uncertainly. So far as he could tell, the name was entirely strange to the servant, awakening neither welcome nor opposition, but rather indifference. The man stepped back, but not in such a manner as to invite Alan in; on the contrary, he half closed the door as he stepped back, leaving it open only an inch or two; but it was enough so that Alan heard him say to someone within; "He says he's him."

"Ask him in; I will speak to him." It was a girl's voice, this second one, a voice such as Alan had never heard before. It was low and soft but clear and distinct, with youthful, impulsive modulations, and the manner of accent Alan knew must go with the sort of people who lived in houses like those on this street.

The servant, obeying the voice, returned and opened the door wider.

"Will you come in, sir?"

Alan put his suitcase down on the stone porch, and the man made no move to bring it inside. As Alan stepped into the hall, he came face to face with the girl who had come from the large room on the right.

She was quite a young woman of perhaps twenty-one or twenty-

26

two, Alan judged. She seemed to Alan to have gained young womanhood in far greater degree in some respects than the girls he knew. At the same time, in other ways, she seemed to have retained, more than they, some characteristics of a child. Her slender figure had a woman's assurance and grace, and her soft brown hair was dressed like a woman's; her gray eyes, however, had the open directness of a girl's. Her smoothly oval face, with straight brows and skin so delicate that at the temples the veins showed dimly blue, was both womanly and youthful. There was something altogether likable and simple about her, as she studied Alan now. She had on a plain blue dress, and the matching hat in her hand suggested she had just recently arrived. In contrast to this somber and darkened house, her youth and vitality instinctively told Alan this house was not her home. More likely, it was some indefinable, yet convincing expression of her manner that gave him that impression. While he hazarded, with rapidly beating heart, what privilege of acquaintance with her Alan Conrad might have, she moved a little nearer to him. She was slightly pale, he noticed now, and there were lines of strain and trouble about her eyes.

"I am Constance Sherrill," she announced. Her tone implied quite evidently that she expected him to have some knowledge of her, and she seemed surprised to see that her name did not mean more to him.

"Mr. Corvet is not here this morning," she said.

He hesitated but persisted. "I was to see him here today, Miss Sherrill. He wrote to me, and I telegraphed him I would be here today."

"I know," she answered. "We had your telegram. Mr. Corvet was not here when it came, so my father opened it." Her voice broke oddly, and he studied her in indecision, wondering who that father might be that opened Mr. Corvet's telegrams.

"Mr. Corvet went away very suddenly," she explained. She seemed, he thought, to be trying to make something plain to him which might be a shock to him, and yet herself to be uncertain what the

nature of that shock might be. Her look was scrutinizing, questioning, anxious, but not unfriendly.

"After he had written to you, something else happened, I think,
to alarm my father about him. So Father came here to his house to
look in on him. He thought something might have . . . happened to
Mr. Corvet here, in his house, but he was not here."

"You mean he has . . . disappeared?"

"Yes, he has disappeared."

Alan gazed at her dizzily. Benjamin Corvet—whoever he might
be—had disappeared. Did anyone else, then, know about Alan
Conrad?

"No one has seen Mr. Corvet," she said, "since the day he wrote
to you. We know that . . . that he became so disturbed after writing
to you that we thought you must be bringing information with
you."

"Information?"

"So we have been waiting for you to come here and tell us what
you know about him, or . . . or your connection with him."

3

Alan, as he looked confusedly and blankly at her, made no attempt to answer the question she had asked, or to explain. For the moment, as he fought to understand what she had said and its meaning for him, all his thought was lost in mere dismay, and in the denial and checking of what he had been feeling as he entered the house. His silence and confusion, he knew, must seem to Constance Sherrill as unwillingness to answer. She seemed not to suspect that he was unable to answer. But she did not seem to be offended. Rather, it was sympathy that she showed. She seemed to appreciate, without understanding except through her feelings, that for some reason, answering was difficult for him.

"You would rather explain to Father than to me, wouldn't you?" she said.

"Yes; I would rather do that," he replied.

"Will you come over to our house, then, please?" She caught up her fur collar and muff from a chair and spoke a word to the servant. As she went out on the porch, he followed her and stooped to pick up his suitcase.

"Simons will bring that," she said, "unless you would rather have it with you. It is only a short walk."

He was recovering from the first shock of her question now, and reflecting that men who accompanied Constance Sherrill probably did not carry hand baggage, he put the suitcase down and followed her to the walk. As she turned north and he caught up with her, he studied her with quick interested glances, realizing her difference from all other girls he had ever walked with, but he did not speak to her nor she to him. Turning east at the first corner, they came within sight and hearing again of the turmoil of the lake.

"We go south here," she said at the corner of the drive. "Our house is almost back to back with Mr. Corvet's."

Alan, looking up after he had made the turn with her, recognized the block as one he had seen pictured sometimes in magazines and illustrated papers as a row of the city's most beautiful homes. Larger, handsomer and finer than the mansions on Astor Street, each had its lawn or terrace in front and on both sides, where snow-mantled shrubs and straw-bound rosebushes suggested the gardens of spring. They turned in at the entrance of a house in the middle of the block and went up the low, wide stone steps. The door opened to them without ring or knock, and a servant in the hall within took Alan's hat and coat. He followed Constance past a great room on his right to a smaller one further down the hall.

"Will you wait here, please?" she asked.

He sat down, and she left him. When her footsteps had died away, and he could hear no other sounds except the occasional soft tread of some servant, he twisted himself about in his chair and looked around. A door between the room he was in and the large room he had seen on his right as they came in stood open. It was a large drawing room. He could see into it and across, through its large doorway, into the hall. His inspection of these interesting rooms increased his bewilderment.

Who were these Sherrills? Who was Corvet, and what was his relation to the Sherrills? What, beyond all, was their relation—and

Corvet's—to him? The shock and confusion he had felt at the nature of his reception in Corvet's house, and the strangeness of his transition from his little Kansas town to a place and people such as these, had prevented him from inquiring directly of Constance Sherrill. On her part, she had plainly assumed that he already knew the answers and need not be told.

Alan got up and moved about the rooms. They, like all rooms, must tell something about the people who lived in them. The rooms were large and open. In dreaming and fancying to himself the places to which he might some day be summoned, he had never dreamed of entering such a home as this. In its light and furnishings there was nothing of the stiffness and aloofness which Alan, never having seen such rooms except in pictures, had imagined to be necessary evils accompanying riches and luxury. It was not the richness of its furnishings that impressed him first, it was its livableness. Among the more modern pieces in the drawing room and hall were some which were antique. In the part of the hall that he could see, a black and ancient looking chair, lines of which he recognized, stood against the wall. He had seen chairs like this, and knew they must be heirlooms of colonial Massachusetts or Connecticut, cherished in Kansas farmhouses and recalling some family exodus from New England. On the wall in the drawing room, among the beautiful and illusive paintings and etchings, was a picture of a ship, plainly framed. He moved closer to it, and observed that it was a clipper ship under full spread of canvas. Then he drew back into the smaller room where he had been left, and sat down to wait.

A comfortable fire of cannel coal was burning in this smaller room in a black iron basket set back in a white, marble-faced fireplace obviously much older than the house. There were big leather easy chairs before it, and beside it there were bookcases. On one of these stood a two-handled, silver, trophy cup, and hung high upon the wall above the mantel was a long racing sweep with the date "1885" painted in black across the blade. Alan had the feeling that he liked the people who lived in this handsome house.

31

He straightened and looked about, and then got up as Constance Sherrill came back into the room.

"Father is not here just now," she said. "We weren't sure from your telegram just when you would arrive, and that was why I waited at Mr. Corvet's home to be sure we wouldn't miss you. I have telephoned Father, and he is coming home at once."

She hesitated an instant in the doorway, then turned to go out again.

"Miss Sherrill . . ." he said.

She halted. "Yes?"

"You told me you had been waiting for me to come and explain my connection with Mr. Corvet. Well . . . I can't do that. That is what I came here hoping to find out."

She came back toward him slowly. "What do you mean?"

He was forcing himself to disregard the strangeness which his surroundings and all that had happened in the last half hour had made him feel. Leaning his arms on the back of the chair in which he had been sitting, he managed to smile reassuringly, and he fought down and controlled resolutely the excitement in his voice, as he told her rapidly the little he knew about himself.

He could not tell definitely how she was affected by what he said. She flushed slightly, following her first start of surprise after he had begun to speak, and when he had finished, he saw she was a little pale.

"Then you don't know anything about Mr. Corvet at all," she said.

"No. Until I got his letter sending for me, I had never seen or heard his name."

She was thoughtful for a moment. "Thank you for telling me," she said. "I'll tell my father when he comes."

"Your father is . . . ?" he ventured.

She understood now that the name of Sherrill had meant nothing to him. "Father is Mr. Corvet's closest friend, and his business partner as well," she explained.

He thought she was going to tell him something more about them, but she seemed then to decide to leave that for her father.

She crossed to the big chair beside the fireplace and sat down. As she sat looking at him, hands clasped beneath her chin and her elbows resting on the arms of the chair, there was speculation and interest in her gaze. She inquired about the Kansas weather that week in comparison with the recent storm in Chicago, and about Blue Rapids, which she said she had looked up on a map. He took this chat for what it was; an indication she did not want to continue the other topic they had been discussing. She, he saw, was listening, like himself, for the sound of Sherrill's arrival at the house, and when it came, she recognized it first, rose and excused herself. He heard her voice in the hall, then her father's deeper voice which answered. Some ten minutes later, he looked up to see the man they had been awaiting and discussing, Constance Sherrill's father.

He was a tall man, sparely built. His broad shoulders might have been those of an athlete in his youth. Now, at something over fifty, they had taken on a slight, rather studious stoop. The man's hair was thin on his forehead. His eyes, gray like his daughter's, were thoughtful, and they reflected deep trouble. His refined and educated manner and bearing were the air of a gentleman, and kept Alan from taking any offense at the long, inquiring scrutiny to which he subjected Alan as he came into the room.

Alan rose. Constance's father offered his hand and motioned him back to his seat. He himself did not sit down, but instead crossed to the mantel, leaned against it and said, "I am Lawrence Sherrill."

As the tall, graceful man stood looking thoughtfully down at him, Alan could tell nothing of how this friend of Benjamin Corvet's felt towards him. His manner had the same reserve towards Alan—the same questioning consideration—that Constance had had after he told her about himself.

"My daughter has repeated to me what you told her, Mr. Conrad," Sherrill observed. "Is there anything else you can add to what you have already told her?"

"There is nothing I can add," Alan answered. "I told her all that I know about myself."

"And about Mr. Corvet?"

"I know nothing at all about Mr. Corvet."

"I am going to tell you some things about Mr. Corvet," Sherrill said. "I had reason—and I do not want to explain just yet what that reason is—for thinking you could tell us certain things about Mr. Corvet which would perhaps make plainer what has happened to him. When I tell you about him now, it is in the hope that I may awaken in you some forgotten memory of him. If not that, we may discover some coincidence of dates or events in Corvet's life with dates or events in your own. Will you tell me frankly if you do discover anything like that?"

"Yes, certainly."

Alan leaned forward in the big chair, hands clasped between his knees, the blood tingling sharply in his face. So Sherrill expected to make him remember Corvet! There was strange excitement in this, and he waited eagerly for Sherrill to begin. For several moments Sherrill paced up and down before the fire, and then he returned to his place before the mantel.

"I first met Benjamin Corvet," he commenced, "nearly thirty years ago. I had come West for the first time the year before. I was about your age and had been graduated from college only a short time, and a business opening had offered itself here. There was a sentimental reason—I think I must call it that—as well, for my coming to Chicago. Until my generation, the property of my family had always been largely, and in general exclusively—in ships. Mine was a Salem family. To be a Sherrill was to be a sea captain; living in Salem at a time when his neighbors, and he, I suppose—hanged witches. We had privateers in 1812, and our clippers went around the Horn in 1849. The Confederate warship *Alabama* during the Civil War ended our ships in '63, as it ended nearly all of the rest of American shipping on the Atlantic. The *Alabama* was built in England, and was one of a number of ships built, equipped, yes, and even crewed by the British for the South. After the War between the States, the British government expressed regret for ships built and fitted out for the Confederacy, and was obliged to pay reparations for damages so inflicted on Northern shipping. When our share of the *Alabama* claims was paid to us, my mother put it in bonds waiting for me to grow up.

"Sentiment, when I came of age, made me want to put this money back into ships flying the American flag, but there was small chance of my doing so with profit at that time, as far as American ships on the sea. In Boston and New York, I had seen the foreign flags on deep water ships—British, German, French, Norwegian, Swedish and Greek. Our flags flew mostly on ferries and excursion steamers. But times were booming on the Great Lakes. Chicago, which had more than recovered from the fire, was doubling its population every decade, and Cleveland, Duluth and Milwaukee were leaping up as ports. Men were growing millions of bushels of grain which they couldn't ship except by water, and there were tens of millions of feet of pine and hardwood from Michigan forests. Sailing vessels such as the Sherrills had always operated, it is true, had seen their day, and were disappearing from the lakes; many being 'sold' to the insurance companies by deliberate wrecking. Steam ships were taking their place. Towing had come in, and the first whalebacks were built about that time.

"We began to see tugs with two, three and four barges in tow, which the lakemen called the 'sow and her pigs.' Men of all sorts had come forward, of course, and serving the situation more or less accidentally, were making themselves rich.

"It was railroading that brought me West, but I had brought with me the *Alabama* money to put into ships. I have called it sentiment, but it was not merely that. I felt, young man though I was, that this transportation matter was all one thing, and that in the end the railroads would own the ships. I have never engaged very actively in the operation of the ships. My daughter would like me to be more active in it than I have been, but ever since I have been here

I have had money in lake vessels. It was the year that I began that sort of investment that I first met Benjamin Corvet."

Alan looked up quickly. "Mr. Corvet was . . . ?" he asked.

"Corvet was . . . is . . . a lakeman," Sherrill said.

Alan sat motionless as he recollected the strange exultation which had come to him when he saw the lake for the first time. Should he tell Sherrill that? He decided it was too vague and indefinite to mention. No doubt any other man knowing only the prairie would have felt the same.

"He was a ship owner, then," he said.

"Yes, he was a ship owner . . . not, however, on a large scale at that time. He had been a master of sailing ships which belonged to others; then he sailed one of his own. He was operating then, I believe, two vessels, but with the boom times on the lakes, his interests were beginning to expand. I met him frequently in the next few years, and we became close friends."

Sherrill broke off and stared for an instant down at the rug. Alan bent forward. He made no interruption but watched Sherrill attentively.

"It was one of the great advantages of the West, I think—and particularly of Chicago at that time—that it gave opportunity for friendships of that sort," Sherrill said. "Corvet was a man of a sort I would have been far less likely ever to have known intimately in the East. He was both what the lakes had made him and what he had made of himself; a great reader and wholly self-educated, he had many of the attributes of a great man. At the very least, they were those of a man who should have become great. He had both imagination and vision. His whole thought and effort, at that time, were absorbed in furthering and developing the traffic on the lakes, and not at all from mere desire for personal success.

"I met him for the first time one day when I went to his office on some business. He had just opened an office at that time in one of the old ramshackle rows along the river. There was nothing at all pretentious about it, but as I went in and waited with the others who were there to see him, I had the feeling of being in the anteroom of a great man. I do not mean there was any idiotic pomp or lackyism or red tape about it, rather I mean that the others who knew him and were waiting to see him were keyed up by the anticipation, and this keyed me up as well. I saw as much as I could of him after that, and our friendship became very close.

"In 1892," Sherrill continued, "when I married and took my residence here on the lake shore in this house, Corvet bought the house on Astor Street. His only reason for doing so was, I believe, his desire to be near me. The neighborhood was what most refer to as fashionable. Neither Corvet nor Mrs. Corvet, as he had married in 1889, had social ambitions of that sort. Mrs. Corvet came from Detroit and a good family there with a strain of French blood in their veins. She was a school teacher when he married her, and she made a wonderful wife for him—a good woman with very high ideals. It was a great disappointment to both of them that they had no children.

"Between 1886, when I first met him, and 1895, Corvet laid the foundation of a great success. His ships were well-fortuned, men liked to work for him, and he got the best of skippers and crews. A Corvet captain boasted of it, and if he had experienced bad luck on another line, believed his luck changed when he took a Corvet ship. Cargoes in Corvet bottoms somehow always reached port, and there was a saying that in a storm a Corvet ship never asked help, but always gave it. Certainly in twenty years no Corvet ship had suffered disaster. Corvet was not yet rich, but unless accident or undue competition intervened, he was certain to become so. Then something happened."

Sherrill looked away, evidently at a loss as to how to describe it.

"To the ships?" Alan asked.

"No; to him," said Sherrill. "In 1896, for no apparent reason, a great change came over him."

"In 1896!" Alan repeated.

"Yes, that was the year."

Alan bent forward, his heart throbbing. "That was the year when I was brought and left with the Weltons in Kansas," he said.

Sherrill did not speak for a moment. "I thought," he finally said, "it must have been about that time, but you did not tell my daughter the exact date."

"What kind of a change came over him that year?" Alan asked.

Sherrill gazed down at the rug, then at Alan and then past him. "A change in his way of living," he replied.

"The Corvet line boats went on and expanded, interests were acquired in other lines, and Corvet and those allied with him swiftly grew rich. But in all this great development, for which Corvet's genius and ability had laid the foundation, Corvet himself ceased to take active part. I do not mean that he formally retired. He retained his control of the business, but he very seldom went to the office, and except for occasional violent, almost petty interference in the affairs of the company, he left it in the hands of others. He took into partnership, about a year later, Henry Spearman, a young man who had been merely a mate on one of his ships. This proved subsequently to have been a good business move, for Spearman had tremendous energy, daring and enterprise, and seemingly Corvet had recognized these qualities in him before others did. But at the same time it excited considerable comment. It marked certainly, the beginning of Corvet's withdrawal from active management. Since then he has been ostensibly and publicly the head of the firm, but the management of it has been left almost entirely to Spearman. The personal change in Corvet at that time is more difficult for me to describe to you."

Sherrill halted, his eyes dark with thought, his lips pressed closely together; Alan waited.

After a long pause, Sherrill continued.

"When I saw Corvet again, in the summer of '96—I had been South during the latter part of the winter, and East through the spring—I was impressed by the vague, but to me, alarming change in him. I was reminded, I recall, of a classmate of mine in college who had thought he was in perfect health, but when he was examined for life insurance he was refused coverage, and then tried to deny to himself and others that anything could be the matter. But with Corvet I knew the trouble was not physical. The next year his wife left him."

"The year of . . . ?" Alan asked.

"That was 1897. We did not know at first, of course, that the separation was permanent. It proved so, however, and Corvet, I know now, had understood it to be that way from the beginning. Mrs. Corvet went to France. I suppose the French blood in her inspired her to select that country. She lived for a number of years in a cottage near Trouville in Normandy, and was active in church work. I know there was almost no communication between the Corvets during those years, but her leaving him definitely affected Corvet. He had been very fond of her, and proud of her as well. I had seen him sometimes watching her while she talked; he would gaze at her steadily and then look about at other women in the room and back to her, and his head would nod just perceptibly with satisfaction; and she would see it sometimes and smile. There was no question of their understanding and affection up to the very time she so suddenly, and so strangely, left him. She died in Trouville in the spring of 1910, and Corvet's first information of her death came to him through a paragraph in a newspaper."

Alan leaned forward, and Sherrill looked at him questioningly.

"The spring of 1910," Alan explained, "was when I received the bank draft for fifteen hundred dollars."

Sherrill nodded, but did not seemed surprised to hear this. Rather, it appeared to be confirmation of something in his own thought.

"Following his wife's leaving him," Sherrill went on, "Corvet saw very little of anyone. He spent most of his time in his own house. Occasionally he lunched at his club, and at rare intervals, and always unexpectedly, he appeared at his office. I remember that summer he was terribly disturbed because one of his ships had been lost. It was not a bad disaster, for everyone on the ship was saved, and the hull and cargo were fully covered by insurance, but the fine Corvet record had been broken; a Corvet ship had appealed for help and had not reached port. Later in the fall, when two deckhands washed overboard from another of his ships and drowned, he was again greatly wrought up, though his line still had a most favorable record. In 1902, I proposed to him that I buy full ownership in the vessels I partly controlled, and ally them with those he and Spearman operated. It was a time of combination. The railroads and the steel interests were acquiring lake vessels, and though I believed in this, I was not willing to enter any combination which would take the name of Sherrill off the list of ship owners. I did not discuss this with Corvet in any detail, but he made me at that time a very strange counter-proposition, which I have never been able to understand, and which entailed the very obliteration of my name which I was trying to avoid. He proposed that I accept a partnership in his concern on a most generous basis, but that the name of the company remain as it was, Corvet and Spearman. Spearman's influence and mine prevailed upon him to allow my name to appear. Since then, the firm name has been Corvet, Sherrill and Spearman."

Sherrill paused again, as if to collect himself, then went on.

"Our friendship had strengthened and ripened during those years. The intense activity of Corvet's mind, which as a younger man he had directed wholly to the shipping, was directed to other things after he isolated himself. He took up almost feverishly an immense number of studies; diverse studies for a man of his age whose youth had been almost violently active, and who had once been a lake captain.

"I can not tell you what they all were, but among them were geology, ethnology and history. He corresponded with various scientific and educational societies, and has given almost the whole of his attention to such things for about twenty years.

"Corvet became very interested in Great Lakes history, and in particular in the French explorer Robert Cavelier de la Salle."

When Alan seemed a bit puzzled, Sherrill offered explanation.

"In 1679, south of Niagara Falls, LaSalle and his men built the first commercial sailing vessel to navigate the Great Lakes. He named it *Griffin*. They set sail August 12 in that year, crossed the length of Lake Erie, sailed up the Detroit River and across Lake St. Clair and through the St. Clair River to Lake Huron. They continued northward through the Straits of Mackinac into Lake Michigan and crossed to a small Indian village in Green Bay, Wisconsin. After loading a cache of furs aboard, La Salle and some of his men in canoes headed down the western side of Lake Michigan; *Griffin* was to take the furs back to Niagara, and immediately return with supplies to a rendezvous with La Salle at the St. Joseph River in southeastern Lake Michigan. The *Griffin* set sail from Washington Island bound for Niagara September 18, 1679, and was never heard from again.

"Corvet was intrigued with what may have happened to the *Griffin*, and even got me interested in it as well. He discussed it at length with his historical societies, and having been a ship's captain well acquainted with autumnal winds and storms in northern Lake Michigan, came to the opinion that the *Griffin* had sailed east of the Beaver Islands to find favorable winds to the Straits of Mackinac, but probably never reached there.

"Corvet concluded she encountered a storm, probably foundered, and may well have been lost off L'Arbre Croche, where her wreck may still lie. This interest in the *Griffin's* fate and Corvet's thoughts about it, are what first drew me to Harbor Springs, Michigan, where we now have a summer home."

Sherrill paused again, to shift his mind back from the story of the *Griffin* to the matter at hand.

"Since I have known Benjamin Corvet, he has transformed himself from the rather rough, though always spiritually minded man he was when I first met him, into an educated gentleman whom anyone would be glad to know. He has made very few acquaintances over this past many years, and has kept almost none of his old friendships. He has lived all alone in the house on Astor Street with only one servant—the same one all these years.

"The only house he has visited with any frequency has been mine. He has always liked my wife, and he had . . . has . . . a great affection for my daughter, who as a child ran in and out of his house as she pleased. He would take long walks with her, and he'd come here sometimes in the afternoon to have tea with her on stormy days; he liked to hear her play and sing for him. My daughter believes now that his present disappearance, and whatever has happened to him, is in some way connected with herself. I do not believe that is so."

Sherrill broke off and stood in thought for a moment. He seemed to consider, and then to decide that it was not necessary to say anything more on that subject.

"Recently," he continued, "Corvet's moroseness and irritability had very considerably increased, and he had quarreled frequently and bitterly with Spearman over business affairs. He had seemed more than usually eager at times to see me or to see my daughter. At other times he had seemed to avoid us and keep away. I have had the feeling of late, though I could not give any actual reason for it except Corvet's manner and look, that the disturbance which has oppressed him for twenty years was culminating in some way. That culmination seems to have been reached three days ago, when he wrote summoning you here. Henry Spearman, whom I asked about you when I learned you were coming, had never heard of you."

Sherrill's pause this time was longer, and Alan sensed he had come to the end of the exposition. His sense was confirmed when Sherrill took a step in Alan's direction and looked down at him.

"Is there anything . . . ," the older man asked, ". . . anything in what I have told you which makes it possible for you to recollect or to explain?"

Alan shook his head, flushed and then grew a little pale. Some of what Sherrill had told him had excited him, because of a few coincidences between events in Benjamin Corvet's life and in his own, but it had not made him recollect Corvet or explain anything. It had, however, given shape and direction to his speculations on his relationship to Corvet.

Sherrill drew one of the large chairs nearer to Alan and sat down facing him. He felt in an inner pocket and brought out an envelope. From the envelope he took three pictures, and he handed the smallest of them to Alan. As Alan took it, he saw it was a picture of himself as a round-faced boy of seven. "That is of you?" Sherrill asked.

"Yes. It was taken by the photographer in Blue Rapids. We all had our pictures taken on that day—Jim, Betty and I. Mr. Welton sent one of me to the general-delivery address of the person in Chicago." It was the first time in his life that Alan had consciously avoided referring to the man in Kansas as "Father."

"And this?" asked Sherrill, handing Alan another of the pictures.

Alan saw that it was one that had been taken in front of the barn at the farm. It showed Alan at twelve, in overalls and barefooted, holding a stick over his head at which a shepherd dog was jumping.

"Yes. That is Shep and I. She was Jim's and my dog, Mr. Sherrill. It was taken by a man who stopped at the house for dinner one day. He liked Shep and wanted a picture of him, so he got me to make Shep jump, and he took the picture."

"You don't remember anything about the man?"

"Only that he had a camera and wanted a picture of Shep."

"Doesn't it occur to you that it was your picture he wanted, and that he had been sent to get it?"

Sherrill let that question sink in, then went on.

"I wanted your verification that these earlier pictures were of you, but this last one is easily recognizable." He unfolded the third picture. It was larger than the others and had been folded to get it into the envelope. Alan leaned forward to look at it.

"That is the University of Kansas football team," he said. "I am the second one in the front row; I played end my junior year and tackle when I was a senior. Did Mr. Corvet . . . ?"

"Yes," said Sherrill before the question was even formed, "Mr. Corvet had these pictures. They came into my possession day before yesterday, the day after Corvet disappeared. I do not want to tell just yet how they did that."

Alan's face, which had been flushed at first with excitement, had gone quite pale, and his hands were cold as he clenched and unclenched them nervously, and his lips were very dry. He could think of no possible relationship between Benjamin Corvet and himself, except one, which could account for Corvet's obtaining and keeping these pictures of him through the years. As Sherrill put the pictures back in the envelope and the envelope back in to his pocket, Alan felt nearly certain now that it had not been proof of this relationship Sherrill had been trying to establish, but only corroboration of some knowledge which had come to Sherrill in some other way. The existence of this knowledge was implied by Sherrill's withholding of the way he had come into possession of the pictures, and his manner showed now that he had received from Alan the confirmation he had been seeking.

"I think you know who I am," Alan said.

Sherrill had risen and stood looking down at him.

"You have guessed, if I am not mistaken, that you are Corvet's son."

The color flamed to Alan's face for an instant, then left it paler than before. "I thought it must be that way." he answered. "But you said he had no children."

"Benjamin Corvet and his wife had no children."

"I thought that was what you meant." A twinge twisted Alan's face, and he tried to control it, but for a moment he could not.

Sherrill suddenly put his hand on Alan's shoulder. There was something so friendly, so affectionate in the quick, impulsive grasp of Sherrill's fingers, that Alan's heart throbbed to it. For the first time someone had touched him in full, unchecked feeling for him. For the first time, the unknown about him had failed to be a barrier, and instead, it had drawn another to him.

"Do not misapprehend your father," Sherrill said quietly. I cannot prevent what other people may think when they learn this, but I do not share such thoughts with them. There is much in this I cannot understand, but I know that it is not merely the result of what others may think—a wife in more ports than one, as you will hear lakemen put it. What lies under this is some great misadventure which had changed and frustrated all of your father's life."

Sherrill crossed the room and rang for a servant. "I am going to ask you to be my guest for a short time, Alan," he announced. "I have had your bag taken to your room, and the man will show you which one it is."

Alan hesitated. He felt that Sherrill had not told him all he knew—that there were some things Sherrill was purposely withholding—but he could not force Sherrill to tell more that he wished. So, after an instant's irresolution, he accepted the dismissal.

Sherrill walked with him to the door and gave his directions to the servant, and then stood watching as Alan and the man went upstairs. Then he went back and seated himself in the chair Alan had occupied, and sat with hands grasping the arms of the chair as he stared into the fire.

Some minutes later, he heard his daughter's footsteps and looked up. Constance halted in the doorway to assure herself that he was now alone. Then, she came to him and, seating herself on an arm of the chair, she put her hand on his thin hair and smoothed it softly. He reached for her other hand with his, and held it clasped between his palms.

"You've found out who he is, Father?"

"The facts have left me no doubt at all as to that, little daughter."

"No doubt that he is . . . who?"

Sherrill was silent for a moment—not from uncertainty, but because of the effect which what he must say would have upon her. Then he told her in almost the same words he had used to Alan. Constance started, flushed, and her hand stiffened convulsively between her father's.

They said nothing more to one another. Sherrill seemed to be considering and debating something within himself, and presently he seemed to come to a decision. He got up, stooped and touched his daughter's hand, and left the room. He went up the stairs and on the second floor went to a front room and knocked. Alan's voice told him to come in. Sherrill went in and, when he had made sure that the servant was not with Alan, he closed the door carefully behind him.

Then he turned back to Alan and for an instant stood in hesitation, as though he did not know how to begin what he wanted to say. As he glanced down at a key he took from his pocket, his indecision seemed to take direction. He put the key down on Alan's dresser. "I've brought you," he said evenly, "the key to your house."

Alan gazed at him bewildered. "The key to my house?"

"To the house on Astor Street," Sherrill confirmed. "Your father deeded the house and its furniture and all its contents to you the day he disappeared. I do not have the deed here; it came into my hands the day before yesterday at the same time I got possession of the pictures, which at that time for all I knew, might or might not be you. The house is yours in fee simple, given to you by your father, not bequeathed to you by him to become your property after his death. He meant by that, I think, even more than the mere acknowledgement that he is your father."

Sherrill walked to the window and stood as though looking out, but his eyes were blank with thought. "For almost twenty years," he said, "as I have told you, your father lived in that house practically alone, and during all those years a shadow of some sort was over him. I don't know at all, Alan, what that shadow was. But it is certain that whatever it was that had changed him from the man he was when I first knew him culminated three days ago when he wrote to you. It may be that the consequences of his writing to you were such that, after he had sent the letter, he could not bring himself to face them, so he merely . . . went away. In that case, as we stand here talking, he may still be alive. On the other hand, his writing may have precipitated something that I know nothing of. In either case, if he has left any evidence anywhere of what it is that changed and oppressed him all these years, or if there is any evidence of what has happened to him now, it will be found in his house."

Sherrill turned back to Alan. "It is for you, Alan, not me," he said simply, "to make that search. I have thought seriously about it, this last half-hour, and have decided that is as he would want it—perhaps as he did want it—to be. He could have told me what his trouble was any time in these twenty years, if he had been willing I should know, but he never did."

Sherrill was silent for a moment.

"There are some things your father did just before he disappeared that I have not told you about," he continued. "The reason I have not told them is that I have not yet fully decided in my own mind what action they call for from me. I can assure you, however, that it would not help you now in any way to know them." He thought again, and then glanced to the key on the dresser and seemed to recollect.

"That key," he said, "is the one I made your father give me some time ago; he was at home alone so much that I was afraid something might happen to him there. He gave it to me because he knew I would not misuse it. I used it for the first time three days ago, when, after becoming certain something had gone wrong with him, I went to the house to search for him. My daughter used it this morning when she went there to wait for you.

"Your father, of course, had a key to the front door like this one, and his servant has a key to the servant's entrance. I do not know of any other keys."

"The servant is in charge there now?" Alan asked.

"Just now there is no one in the house. The servant, after your father disappeared, thought that if he had merely gone away, he might have gone back to his birthplace near Manistique, and he went up there to look for him. I had a wire from him today that he has not found him and is coming back."

Sherrill waited a moment to see whether there was anything more Alan wanted to ask, and then he went out.

4

As the door closed behind Sherrill, Alan went over to the dresser and picked up the key which Sherrill had left. It was, he saw, a flat key of a sort common twenty years before, not of the more recent corrugated shape. As he looked at it and then away from it, thoughtfully turning it over and over in his fingers, it brought no sense of possession to him. Sherrill had said the house was his, having been given him by his father, but that fact could not actually make it his in his realization. He could not imagine himself owning such a house or what he would do with it if it were his. After a few moments, he put the key on the ring with two or three other keys he had, and dropped them into his pocket; then he crossed to a chair and sat down.

As he tried now to untangle the events of the afternoon he found that from them, and especially from his last interview with Sherrill, two facts stood out most clearly. The first of these related more directly to his father, Benjamin Corvet. When such an unusual man disappears, when he vanishes without warning and without leaving any account of himself, it is only natural that those most closely interested in him would pass through a number of stages of anxiety. They would first doubt whether the disappearance is real and whether inquiry on their part is appropriate and will not be resented. They awaken next to the realization that the man is actually gone, and that something must be done, and finally that the disappearance must be accepted and made open to public inquiry. Whatever might be the nature of the information Sherrill was withholding from him, Alan saw that its effect on Sherrill had been to shorten very greatly Sherrill's time of doubt as to Corvet's actual disappearance. The Sherrills, particularly Lawrence Sherrill himself, had been in the second stage of anxiety when Alan came. They had been awaiting his arrival in the belief that he could give them information which would show them what, if anything, must be done about Corvet. Alan had not been able to give them this information, but his coming, and his interview with Sherrill, had strongly influenced Sherrill's attitude. Sherrill had shrunk, still more definitely and consciously after that, from prying into the affairs of his friend. He had now, strangely, almost withdrawn himself from the inquiry, and had given it over to Alan.

Sherrill had spoken of the possibility that something might have "happened" to Corvet, but it was plain he did not believe he had met with violence. He had left it to Alan to examine Corvet's house, but he had not urged Alan to examine it at once. Rather, he had left the time of examination to be determined by Alan. This showed clearly that Sherrill believed, perhaps had sufficient reason for believing, that Corvet had simply "gone away." The second of Alan's two facts related even more closely and personally to Alan himself. Corvet, Sherrill had said, had married in 1889. But Sherrill had shown firm conviction that there had been no mere extramarital liaison in Corvet's life. Did this mean that there might have been some previous marriage, some marriage which had strangely overlapped and nullified his public marriage? In that case, Alan could be Corvet's son, not only in fact but legally as well. Alan knew such things had sometimes happened, by a strange combination of events, innocently for all parties. Corvet's public separation from his wife, Sherrill had said, had taken place in 1897, but the actual separation between them might possibly have taken place long before that.

Alan resolved to hold these questions in abeyance. He would not accept or grant the stigma which his relationship to Corvet seemed to attach to himself until it had been proven to him. He had come to Chicago expecting not to find there had been anything wrong, but to find that the wrong had been righted in some way at last. But what was most plain of all to him, from what Sherrill had told him, was that the wrong—whatever it might be—had not been righted; it still existed.

The afternoon had changed swiftly into night. Dusk had been gathering during his last talk with Sherrill, so he had hardly been able to see Sherrill's face, and just after Sherrill had left him, full darkness had come. Alan did not know how long he had been sitting in the darkness thinking over these things, but now a little clock which had been ticking steadily in the darkness chimed six o'clock. Alan heard a knock at the door, and when it was repeated, he called, "Come in."

The light which came in from the hall as the door opened showed a manservant. After a respectful inquiry, the man switched on a light and crossed into the adjoining room—a bedroom. The room where Alan was, he thought, must be a dressing room, and there was a bathroom between. Presently the man reappeared and moved quietly about the room as he unpacked Alan's suitcase. He hung Alan's other suit in the closet on hangers, and put the linen—except for one shirt—in the dresser drawers. He put Alan's shaving things with the ivory-backed brushes and comb on the dressing table.

Alan watched him queerly. No one except himself had ever unpacked his suitcase before. When he first had gone away to college, when the suitcase was brand new, "Mother" had packed it. After that first time, Alan had packed it and unpacked it himself. It gave him an odd feeling now to see some one else unpacking his things.

51

The man, having finished and taken everything out, continued to look in the suitcase for something else.

"I beg your pardon, sir," he said finally, "but I cannot find your buttons."

"I've got them on," Alan said. He took them out and gave them to the valet with a smile. It was good to have something to smile about, even if it was only the realization that it never occurred to him that anyone might have more than one set of cuff links for ordinary shirts. Alan found himself wondering with a sort of trepidation whether the man was going to stay and help him dress. But he merely put the buttons in the clean shirt. Then he reopened the dresser drawers and laid out a change of things.

"Is there anything else, sir?" he asked.

"Nothing, thank you," Alan replied.

"I was to tell you, sir, Mr. Sherrill is sorry he cannot be home for dinner tonight. Mrs. Sherrill and Miss Sherrill will be, however. Dinner is at seven, sir."

Alan dressed slowly, after the man had gone, and at one minute before seven he went downstairs.

There was no one in the lower hall, and after an instant of irresolution and a glance into the empty drawing room, he turned into the small room at the opposite side of the hall. A handsome, stately, rather large woman he found there introduced herself as Mrs. Sherrill.

He knew from Sherrill's mention of the year of their marriage that Mrs. Sherrill must be about forty-five. Had he not known this, he would have thought her ten years younger. In her dark eyes and her carefully dressed, coal-black hair, and in the contour of her youthful looking, attractive face, he could not find any such pronounced resemblance to her daughter as he had seen in Lawrence Sherrill. Her reserved, and almost too casual acceptance of Alan's presence, told him that she knew all the particulars about himself which Sherrill had been able to give to her. When Constance came down the stairs and joined them a few moments later, Alan was certain that she also knew.

There was something in Constance's manner toward her mother's reaction to Alan which seemed almost like opposition. Not that Mrs. Sherrill was unfriendly or critical. Rather she was kind with the sort of reserved kindness which told Alan, almost as plainly as words, that she had not been able to hold so charitable a conviction in regards to Corvet's relationship with Alan as her husband held, but that she would be all the more considerate to Alan for that. It was this kindness which Constance set herself to oppose, and which she opposed as reservedly and as subtly as it was expressed. It gave Alan a strange, exhilarating sensation to realize that as the three of them conversed, this girl was defending him. Not him alone, of course, or him chiefly. It was Benjamin Corvet, her friend, whom she was defending primarily, and yet it was Alan too; and all this went on without a word about Benjamin Corvet or his affairs.

Dinner was announced, and they went into the great dining-room, where the table with its fine linen, silver and china gleamed under shaded lights. The oldest and most dignified of the three men who waited upon them in the dining room, Alan thought, must be a butler. He'd heard of them, but never seen one. The other servants received things from him, and handed them back to him, and were directed by his orders. As the servants moved silently about, Alan kept up a somewhat strained conversation with Mrs. Sherrill—a conversation in which no reference was made to his own affairs. He wondered whether Constance and her mother always dressed for dinner in full evening dress as now, or whether they were going out. A word from Constance to her mother told him this latter was the case, and while it did not completely satisfy his curiosity, it offered him his first glimpse of a world in which social engagements are a part of the business of life. In spite of the fact that Benjamin Corvet, Sherrill's close friend, had disappeared, the Sherrills' engagements had to be fulfilled. Or perhaps, Alan silently speculated, it was because his disappearance was not as yet publicly known, and to cancel an engagement would betray the fact.

Alan surmised from some of the dinner conversation that Mrs.

Sherrill kept busy with many charitable and social activities, and that Lawrence Sherrill was content to have her so involved as he had neither the time nor the desire to participate in them.

What Sherrill had told Alan about his father had been iterating itself again and again in Alan's thoughts, and now he recalled that Sherrill had said his daughter believed that Corvet's disappearance had something to do with her. Alan had wondered at the moment how that could be, and as he watched her across the table during the dinner conversation, it puzzled him still more. He had the opportunity to ask her when she waited with him in the library after dinner was finished and her mother had gone upstairs, but he did not know then just how to go about it.

"I'm sorry," she said to him, "that we can't be home tonight, but perhaps you would rather be alone anyway."

He did not reply to her statement, but instead asked, "Have you a picture here, Miss Sherrill, of . . . my father?"

"Uncle Benny had very few pictures taken, but there is one here."

She went into the study, and then came back with a book open at a picture of Benjamin Corvet. She gave it to Alan and he took it over to a table lamp. The face that looked up to him from the heavily glazed page was regular of feature, handsome in a way, and forceful. There was imagination and vigor of thought in the broad, smooth forehead; the eyes were strangely moody and brooding; the mouth was gentle and rather kindly. It was a queerly impelling, haunting face. This was his father! But as Alan held the picture and gazed down upon it, the only emotion which came to him was the realization that he felt none. He had not expected to know his father from strangers on the street, but he had expected, when told his father was before him, to feel the call of common blood. Now, except for consternation at his lack of feeling, he had no emotion of any sort. He could not attach to this man the passions he had always hoped, when dreaming of his father, that he would feel.

As he looked up from the picture to the girl who had given it to him, startled at himself and believing she must think his lack of feeling strange and unnatural, he surprised her gazing at him with tears in her eyes. He fancied at first it must be for his father, and that the picture had brought back poignantly her fears. Then he realized she was not looking at the picture but at him, and when his eyes met hers, she quickly turned away.

His own eyes filled, and he choked. He wanted to thank her for her manner toward him in the afternoon, for defending his father and him, as she had at the dinner table, and now for this unplanned, impulsive sympathy when she saw how he had not been able to feel for this man who was his father, and how he was dismayed by it. But he could not put his gratitude into words.

A servant's voice came from the door, startling him. "Mrs. Sherrill wishes you told she is waiting, Miss Sherrill."

"I'll be there at once." Constance, also, seemed startled and confused, but she delayed and looked back to Alan.

"If . . . if we fail to find your father," she said, "I want to tell you what a wonderful man he was."

"Thank you . . . thank you so very much."

She left him swiftly, and he heard her mother's voice in the hall. After a minute or so he heard the house door closed, followed by the sound of an automobile driving away from the house. Alan stood still a moment longer, then remembering the book which he held, he drew a chair up to the light, and began to read the short biography of his father printed on the page opposite the portrait.

It summarized in a few hundred words his father's life. He turned to the cover of the book and read its title, *Year Book of the Great Lakes - 1910.* He turned back again to the book's contents. They consisted in large part, he saw, of mere lists of ships—their kind and size, dates when they were built, names of their owners. Under this last heading, he saw many times the name "Corvet, Sherrill and Spearman." There was a separate list of engines and boilers, and when they had been built and by whom. There was a chronological table of events during the year on the lakes. Then he came to a part headed "Disasters of the Year," and he read some of them. They were short accounts, dryly and unfeelingly put, but his blood thrilled to these stories of drowning, freezing, blinded men struggling against storm and ice and water, and conquering or being conquered by them.

Then he came to the five-year-old biography and picture of his father again, and to pictures and biographies of other lakemen. He turned to the index and looked for Sherrill's name, and then for Spearman's, and on finding they were not in the book, he read some of the others.

There was a strange similarity, he found, in these biographies. For the most part, these men—like his father—had no family seafaring tradition, such as Sherrill had told him he himself had. They had been sons of lumbermen, of farmers, of mill hands, of miners, of fishermen. They had been very young for the most part when they had heard and answered the call of the lakes, the excitement of fierce and swelling demand for lumber, grain and ore. They had lived hard; life had been violent, raw and brutal for them. They had sailed and built ships, owned and lost ships. They had fought against nature and man to keep their ships, to make them profitable, and to get more of them. In the end, a few—a very few—had survived. By daring, by enterprise, by taking great chances, they had pulled themselves above their fellows. These giants had come to own fleets—a half dozen, a dozen, perhaps a score of ships—and incomes in six figures or more.

Alan shut the book and sat in thought. He felt strongly the immensity, the power and the grandeur of all this, and he also felt its violence and its fierceness. What might there have been in the life of his father who had fought his way up and made a way for himself through such things?

The tall clock in the hall struck nine. He got up and went out into the hall and asked for his hat and coat. When they had been given him, he put them on and went out.

The snow had stopped some time before, and the wind had risen—a powerful wind which Alan, who knew about the wind across his prairies, recognized. It was the aftermath of the great storm that had produced it, and was from the opposite direction, from the west. From the Sherrills' doorway, as he looked toward the lighthouse at the harbor mouth, he could see the flashing red-white-red-white-red-white light. He could see, too, that this westerly, offshore wind was causing new commotion and upheaval among the ice floes, which groaned and labored and fought against the opposite pressure of the waves surging underneath them.

He went down the steps and to the corner and then turned west to Astor Street. When he reached the house of his father he stopped under a street-lamp, and looked up at the big, stern old mansion questioningly. It had taken on a different look for him since he had heard Sherrill's account of his father, and there was an appeal to him now that made his throat grow tight; its look of being unoccupied, in the blank stare of its unlighted windows which contrasted with the lighted windows in the houses on either side, and in the slight evidences of disrepair about it. He waited some minutes, his hand on the key in his pocket. He could not yet go in, but instead walked on down the street, his thoughts and feelings in a turmoil.

He could not call up any sense that the house was his, any more than he been able to when Sherrill first told him about it. He own a house on that street! Was that in itself any more remarkable than that he should be the guest, the friend of such people as the Sherrills? No one as yet, since Sherrill had told him he was Corvet's son, had called him by name. When they did, what would they call him? Alan Conrad still, or Alan Corvet?

He noticed up a street to the west the lighted sign of a drug store and turned up that way. He had promised to write to those in Kansas, he remembered now, and tell them what he had discovered as soon as he arrived. He could not tell them that, but he could write them at least that he had arrived safely and was well; he could not call them "Father" and "Mother" any more. He bought a postcard in the drug store and wrote just, "Arrived safely and am well." This he addressed to John Welton in Kansas. He bought a box of matches from the clerk and put them in his pocket.

He mailed the card and then turned back to Astor Street. He walked more swiftly now, having come to a decision, and only shot one quick look up at the house as he approached it. With what had his father shut himself up within that house for twenty years? And was it still there? Was it from that Benjamin Corvet had fled? He saw no one on the street and was certain no one was observing him as, taking the key from his pocket, he went up the steps and unlocked the door. Holding the door open to get the light from the street lamp, he fitted the key into the inner door; then he closed the outer door. For fully a minute, with fast beating heart and a sense of expectation of he knew not what, he kept his hand on the key before he turned it, and then he opened the door and stepped into the dark and silent house.

5

Standing in the darkness of the hall, Alan felt in his pocket for the matches and struck one on the box. The light showed the hall in front of him reaching back into some vague, distant darkness, and great rooms with wide portiered doorways on both sides. He turned into the room on his right, glanced to see that the shades were drawn on the windows toward the street, then found the switch and turned on the light.

As he looked around, he fought against his excitement and feeling of expectancy. It was after all, he told himself, merely a vacant house, though bigger and more expensively furnished than any he had ever been in, that is, except the Sherrills'. He had been told by Sherrill that, hopefully, there might be something in the house which would give the reason for his father's disappearance; probably only a paper, or perhaps a record of some kind. It seemed unlikely to him that something of this nature, so easily concealed, could be found by him on his first examination of the place. What he had come here for now, he tried to make himself believe, was merely to obtain whatever other information he could find about his father, and the way his father lived; this, before he and Sherrill had any further conversation.

When Alan stepped into the house in the morning, he had not noticed whether the house had been heated. Now he could feel that it was quite cold, and probably had been for the three days his father had been gone, as Sherrill had said the servant had left to look for him. Coming from the street, it was not the coldness of the house he felt as much as the stillness of the dead air. When a house is heated there is always some motion of the air, but this air was stagnant. Alan had dropped his hat on a chair in the hall, and now he unbuttoned his overcoat, but left it on, and stuffed his gloves into a pocket.

A light in a single room, he thought, would not excite curiosity or attract attention from the neighbors or anyone passing on the street, but lights in more than one room might do that. He resolved to turn off the light in each room as he left it before lighting the next one.

It had been a pleasant as well as a handsome house, if he could judge by the little of it he could see, before the change had come over his father. The rooms were large with high ceilings. The one in which he stood was obviously a library. Bookshelves reached almost to the ceiling on three of its walls, except where they were broken in two places by doorways, and in one place on the south wall by an open fireplace. There was a large library table-desk in the center of the room, and a stand with a shaded lamp upon it nearer the fireplace. A leather chair—a lonely, meditative-looking chair—was by the stand at an angle toward the hearth. The rug in front of it was quite worn through and showed the floor underneath. A sympathy toward his father, which Sherrill had not been able to make him feel, came to Alan as he reflected on how many days and nights Benjamin Corvet must have passed reading or thinking in that chair before his restless feet could have worn away the tough, oriental fabric of the rug.

There were several magazines on the top of the large desk, some unwrapped and some still in their wrappers. Alan glanced at them and saw that they all related to technical and scientific subjects. The desk evidently had been much used and had many drawers. He pulled one open and saw that it was full of papers, and his sensation as he touched the top one made him close the drawer again and postpone prying of that sort until he had looked more thoroughly about the house.

He went to the door of the connecting room and looked into it. This room, dusky in spite of the light which shone past him through the wide doorway, was evidently another library. It appeared to have been the original library, and the room he had just left had apparently been converted into a library to supplement it. The bookcases here were built so high that a little ladder on wheels was required for access to the top shelves. Alan located the switch in the room, and then returned and turned off the light in the front room. He crossed in the darkness into the second room and pressed the switch. A weird, uncanny, half wail, half moan coming from the upper hall suddenly filled the house. Its unexpectedness and the nature of the sound stirred the hair on his head. When he collected his wits, he pressed the switch again, and the noise stopped. He lighted another match, found the right switch, and turned on the light. Only then did Alan discover the two long tiers of black and white keys of an organ against the north wall, and knew the first switch must control its motor working the bellows and pipes in the upper hall. It was the sort of organ that could be played either by hand or mechanical means, and a book of music had fallen upon the keys, pressing one down and causing the note to sound when Alan inadvertently switched on the bellows pump.

Having accounted for the sound did not immediately end the start that it had given Alan. He had the feeling, which can come to one in an unfamiliar and vacant house, that there was someone in the house with him. He listened and seemed to hear another sound in the upper hall: a footstep. He went out quickly to the foot of the stairs and looked up them.

"Is anyone there?" he called. "Is there anyone here?"

His voice brought no response. He went half way up the curve of the wide stairway, and called again, and listened, and then he fought down the uncertain feeling he had. Sherrill had said there would be no one in the house, and having reassured himself, Alan now felt he was the only one there. So, he went back down to the room he had left lighted.

The center of the room, like the room next to it, was occupied by a library table-desk. He pulled out some of the drawers in it, and one or two had blueprints and technical drawings in them. The others had only the miscellany which accumulates in a room much used. There were drawers also under the bookcases all around the room. When Alan opened some of them, they appeared to contain pamphlets of various societies, and scientific correspondence of which Sherrill had told him. He looked over the titles of some of the books on the shelves covering a multitude of subjects, among them, anthropology, history, ship-building, astronomy and exploration. The books in each section of the shelves seemed to correspond in subject with the pamphlets and correspondence in the drawer beneath, and these, by their dates, to divide themselves into different periods during the twenty years that Benjamin Corvet had lived alone in the house.

Alan felt that seeing these things was bringing his father closer to him, and they gave him a little of the feeling he had been unable to get when he looked at his father's picture. He could realize better now the lonely, restless man, pursued by some ghost he could not kill, taking up for distraction one subject of study after another, exhausting each in turn until he could no longer make it engross him, and then absorbing himself in the next.

These two rooms evidently had been the ones most used by his father. As Alan went into the other rooms on this floor, one by one, he found they spoke far less intimately of Benjamin Corvet. A dining room was in the front of the house to the north side of the hall with a service room opening from it, and on the other side of the service room was what appeared to be a smaller dining room. The service room communicated both by dumbwaiter and stairway with rooms below. Alan went down the stairway only far enough to see that the rooms below were servants' quarters; then he came back, turned out the light on the first floor, struck another match, and went up to the second floor.

The rooms opening on to the upper hall, it was apparent to him though their doors were closed, were mostly bedrooms. He hazarded to put his hand on the nearest door and opened it. As he caught the smell and taste of the air in the room—heavy, colder and deader even than the air in the rest of the house—he hesitated; then with his match he found the light switch.

The room and the next one to it evidently were, or had been, a woman's bedroom and boudoir.

The hangings, which were still swaying from the opening of the door, had taken permanently the folds in which they had hung for many years, and there were obvious signs of idleness, not of use, in the rugs and in the upholstery of the chairs. The bed, however, was freshly made up, as if the bed linen had been changed occasionally. Alan went through the bedroom to the door of the boudoir and saw that it, too, had the same look of disuse. On the low dressing table were scattered such articles that a woman starting on a journey might think it not worthwhile taking with her. There was no doubt that these were the rooms of his father's wife.

Had his father preserved these rooms as she had left them, in the hope that she might come back—fixing no time when he might abandon that hope? Had he not changed them after he learned that she was dead? Alan thought not, as Sherrill had told him that Corvet had known from the start that his separation from his wife was permanent. The bed made up, the other things neglected and looked after and cleaned only periodically. It seemed more likely to Alan that Corvet had simply shrunk from seeing them—or even thinking of them—and had left them to be looked after wholly by the servant without ever being able to bring himself to give instructions that this situation should in any way be changed. Alan felt that he would not be surprised if he learned that his father had not entered these vacant rooms since the day his wife had left.

On the top of a chest of drawers in a corner near the dressing table were some papers. Alan went over to look at them, and found they were invitations and notices of concerts and of plays twenty years old. They appeared to be mail received the morning she had gone away—left where she or her maid had laid them, and picked up and put back there only at the times since when the room was dusted. As Alan touched them, he saw that his fingers left marks in the dust on the smooth top of the chest. And then, he noticed, someone else had touched the things and made marks of the same sort as he had made. The freshness of these marks startled him. They had obviously been made within a day or so. They could not have been made by Sherrill, for Alan had noticed that Sherrill's hands were slender and delicately formed. Corvet, too, was not a large man. Alan's own hands were of good size and quite powerful, but when he put his fingers over the other marks, he found that the other hand must have been larger and more powerful than his own.

Had it been Corvet's servant? It might have been, though the marks seemed too fresh for that, since the servant, Sherrill had said, had left the day Corvet's disappearance had been discovered.

Alan pulled open the drawers to see if he might deduce what someone had been after. He discovered it had not been the servant, for the contents of the drawers—woman's clothing and old brittle lace—were tumbled as though they had been pulled out and then roughly and inexpertly pushed back. The clothing still showed the folds in which they had lain for years, and quite obviously had been very recently disarranged.

This proof that someone else had been prying about in the house—his house—since Corvet had gone both startled Alan and angered him. It brought him suddenly a sense of possession which he had not been able to feel when Sherrill had told him the house was his; it brought him an impulse of protection of these things about him.

Who had been searching in Benjamin Corvet's . . . his . . . house? He pushed the drawers closed hastily and hurried across the hall to the room opposite. In this room, which was plainly Benjamin Corvet's bedroom, there were no signs of intrusion. He went to the door of the room adjoining, turned on the light, and looked in. It was a smaller room than the others and contained a roll-top desk and a cabinet. The cover of the desk was closed, and the drawers of the cabinet were also closed and apparently undisturbed. Alan recognized that quite probably in this room he would find the most personal and intimate things relating to his father, but before examining it, he turned back to the bedroom.

It was a carefully arranged and well-cared-for room, plainly in constant use. A reading stand with a lamp was beside the bed, and a book on the stand top was marked about in its middle. On a chest of drawers were hairbrushes and a comb, and a box of razors, none of which was missing. When Benjamin Corvet had gone away, Alan realized, he had not even taken his shaving articles with him. Among other things on the chest was a silver frame, with a cover closed and fastened over. As Alan picked up and opened it, the stiffness of the hinges and the edges of the lid sticking to the frame by disuse showed that it had not been opened in a very long time. The photograph within was of a woman, perhaps in her thirties; a beautiful woman, dark hair with dark eyes, and a refined, sensitive, spiritual face. Alan suddenly recognized the dress she wore as one he had seen and touched in the drawers across the hall. It gave him a queer feeling. Instinctively, as he held the picture and studied it, he now felt that it could have been no ordinary bickering between husband and wife, nor any caprice of a dissatisfied woman, that had made her separate herself from her husband. The photographer's name was printed in one corner, and the date shown was 1894—the year after Alan had been born.

Alan felt that the picture and the condition of her rooms across the hall did not shed any light on the relations between Benjamin Corvet and his wife; rather they obscured them. His father had neither put the picture away from him and devoted her rooms to other uses, nor had he kept the rooms arranged and ready for her return, and her picture uncovered so he would see it. He would have done one or the other of these things, Alan thought, if it were she his father had wronged, or at least, if it were only she.

Alan reclosed the case and put the picture down, and then he went into the room with the desk. He tried the cover of the desk, but it appeared to be locked. After looking around vainly for a key, he tried again, exerting a little more force, and this time the top went up easily, tearing away the metal plate into which the claws of the lock clasped and the two long screws which had held it. Surprised, he examined the lock and saw that the screws must have been merely set into the holes. Scars showed where a chisel or some metal implement had been thrust in under the top to force it up. The pigeonholes and small drawers in the upper part of the desk, as he swiftly opened them, he found entirely empty. He hurried to the cabinet, and found the drawers there, too, had been forced very recently as the scars and the splinters of wood were clean and fresh. These drawers and the ones in the lower part of the desk were either empty, or the papers in them had been disarranged and tumbled in confusion, as though someone had examined them hastily and tossed them back.

Sherrill had not done this, nor had anyone else who was authorized to be in the house. If Benjamin Corvet had emptied some of those drawers before he went away, he would not have relocked the empty drawers. To Alan, the marks of violence and roughnesss were unmistakably the work of the man with the big hands who had left marks on the top of the chest of drawers, and the feeling he had been in the house very recently was stronger than ever.

Alan ran out into the hall and listened. He heard no sound, but went back to the little room more excited than before. For what had the man been searching? For the same things as Alan? And had the other man found them? Who might the other be? And what might be his connection with Benjamin Corvet? Alan had no doubt now that everything of importance had been taken away, but he would now somehow have to make sure of that. He took some of the papers from the drawers and began to examine them. After nearly an hour of this, he had found only one article which appeared connected in any way with him, or with what Sherrill had told him. In one of the small drawers of the desk he found several little books, much worn as though from being carried in a pocket, and one of them contained a series of entries extending over several years. These listed an amount of $150.00 opposite each of a series of dates for which only the year and month were given. There was an entry for every second month.

Alan felt his fingers trembling as he turned the pages of the little book and found at the end of the list a blank, and below—in the same hand but in writing which had changed slightly with the passage of years—another date with the confirming entry of $1,500.00. The other papers and books were only such things as might accumulate during a lifetime on the water and in business—government certificates, manifests, boat schedules of times long gone by, and similar papers. Alan looked through the little book again and then put it in his pocket. Beyond doubt, this was his father's memorandum of the sums sent to Blue Rapids for his support. It told him that here he had been in his father's thoughts; in this small room within a few steps from the deserted apartments of his wife, Benjamin Corvet had sent "Alan's dollar"—that dollar which had been such a subject of speculation in his childhood. He felt a warm glow at the thought as he began putting the other things back into the drawers.

Alan started and straightened suddenly. He listened attentively, and his skin, warm an instant before, turned cold. Somewhere within the house, unmistakably on the floor below him, a door had slammed. The wind, which had grown much stronger in the last hour, was now battering the windows and whining around the corners of the building. The house was tightly closed, so it could not be the wind that had blown the door shut. It was beyond question now that someone was in the house with him.

This realization was quite different from the feeling he had experienced earlier. Had his father's servant come back? That was impossible, as Sherrill had received a wire from the man that very day, and he could not possibly get back to Chicago before the following morning at the earliest. Sherrill had said this man was the only one other than himself and his father who had a key. Was it his father who had come back? That, though not impossible, seemed improbable.

Alan bent over quickly and took off his shoes, and then moved quickly into the hall to the head of the stairs where he looked down and listened. From there the sound of someone's moving about came to him distinctly. He could see no light below, but when he worked himself slowly down to the turn of the stairs, he could see a very dim and flickering light in the library. As he crept further on down the stairs, his hands were cold and moist from his excitement, and his body was hot and trembling.

Whoever it was that was moving about in the library, even if it was not one who had a right to be there, at least felt secure from interruption. He was going with heavy step from window to window, and wherever he found a shade up, he pulled it down brusquely with a violence that suggested great strength under a nervous strain. One shade which had been pulled down flew up, and the man damned it as it startled him, and then he pulled it down again.

Alan crept still farther down and at last caught sight of him. The man was not his father, and he was not a servant. It was equally sure at the same time that he was not anyone who had any business being in the house, and that he was not any common housebreaker.

He was a big, young-looking man with broad shoulders, and very evident vigor. Alan guessed his age at thirty-five. He had a straight forehead over daring, deep-set eyes; his nose, lips and chin were powerfully formed, and he was expensively and very carefully dressed. The light by which Alan saw these things came from a flat little pocket flashlight the man carried in his hand, which threw a brilliant circle of light as he directed it. Now, as the light chanced to fall on his other hand, powerful and heavy muscled, Alan recollected the look and size of the finger prints on the chest of drawers upstairs. He did not doubt that this was the same man who had gone through the desk, but since he had already rifled the desks and drawers above, what did he want here now? As the man moved out of sight, Alan went on down as far as the door to the library. The man had gone on into the rear room, and Alan went far enough into the library so he could see him.

He had pulled open one of the drawers in the big table in the rear room—the room where the organ was and where the shelves reached to the ceiling—and with his light held so as to show what was in it, he was tumbling over its contents and examining them. He went through one after another of the drawers of the table like this, and after examining them, he rose and kicked the last one shut disgustedly. He stood looking about the room questioningly, and then started toward the front room.

He cast the light of his flashlight ahead of him, and Alan had time to anticipate his action and to retreat to the hall. He held the hangings a little way from the door jamb so he could see into the room. If this man were the same one who had looted the desk upstairs, it was plain he had not found there what he wanted, or all that he wanted, and now he did not know where next to look.

As yet, the man had neither seen or heard anything to alarm him, and as he went to the desk in the front room and peered impatiently into the drawers, he slammed them shut, one after another. "Damn Ben! Damn Ben!" he ejaculated violently, and he returned to the rear room.

Alan, again following him, found him on his knees in front of one of the drawers under the bookcases. As he continued searching through the drawers, his irritation became greater and greater. He jerked one drawer entirely out of its case, and the contents flew in every direction; swearing at it, and damning "Ben" again, he gathered up the letters. One suddenly caught his attention, and he began reading it closely, then snapped it back into the drawer, crammed the rest on top of it, and went to the next of the files. He searched in this manner through half a dozen drawers, plainly finding nothing that he wanted. He dragged some of the books from their cases, felt behind them and then shoved some of them back, but dropped others on the floor, all the while swearing incessantly.

He cursed "Ben" again and again, and himself, and God. He damned men by name, but so violently and incoherently that Alan could not make out the names. Terribly he swore at men living and men "rotting in hell."

The beam of light from his searchlight swayed from side to side, and up and down. Without warning, the beam suddenly caught Alan as he stood in the dark of the front room. As the dim white circle of light gleamed into Alan's face, the man looked that way and saw him.

The effect of this upon the man was so strange and so bewildering to Alan that Alan could only stare at him. The big man seemed to shrink into himself, and then to shrink back and away from Alan. He roared out something in a bellow thick with fear and horror, and he seemed to choke with terror. There was nothing in his look akin to mere surprise or alarm at realizing that another was there, and had been seeing and overhearing him.

The light which he still gripped swayed back and forth showing him Alan again, and he raised his arm before his face and recoiled. The consternation of the man was so complete that it checked Alan's rush toward him. He halted, and then advanced silently and watchfully. As he went forward, and the light shined upon his face again, the big man cried out hoarsely:

"Damn you . . . damn you, with the hole above your eye! The bullet got you! And now you've got Ben! But you can't get me! Go back to hell! You can't get me! I'll get you . . . I'll get you! You . . . you can't save the *Miwaka!*"

He drew back his arm and with all his might hurled the flashlight at Alan. It missed and crashed somewhere behind him, but it did not go out.

The beam of light shot back, wavering and flickering over both of them as it struck the floor. Alan rushed forward and aiming through the dark, his hand struck the man's chest, and he seized his coat. The man caught at and grasped Alan's arm. He seemed to feel it and assure himself of its reality.

"You're alive!" he roared in relief, and with that his big arms grappled Alan. As they struggled, they stumbled and fell to the floor, the big man underneath. His hand shifted its hold and caught Alan's throat. Alan got an arm free and, with all his force, he struck the man's face. The man struck back—a heavy blow on the side of Alan's head which dizzied him but left him strength to strike again. His knuckles reached the man's face once more, but he got another heavy blow in return. The man was grappling no longer. He swung Alan to one side and off of him, and rolled himself away. He scrambled to his feet and dashed out through the library, across the hall, and into the service room. Alan heard his feet clattering down the stairway to the floor beneath. Alan got to his feet. Dizzied and not yet familiar with the house, he blundered against a wall and had to feel his way along it to the service room. As he slipped and stumbled down the stairway, a door closed loudly at the end of the corridor he had seen at the foot of the stairs. He ran along the corridor to the door. It had closed with a spring lock, and seconds passed while he felt in the dark for the catch. He found it and tore the door open, and came out suddenly into the cold air of the night in a paved passageway beside the house which let in one direction to the street, and in the other to a gate opening on the alley. He ran forward to the street and looked up and down, but found it empty; then he ran back to the alley. At the end of the alley, where it inter-sected the street, the figure of the man running away appeared out of the shadows, then disappeared. Alan, following as far as the street, could see nothing more of him. This street, too, was empty.

He ran a little farther, and seeing nothing, he went back to the house. The side door had swung shut again and latched. He felt in his pocket for his key and went around to the front door. The snow on the steps had been swept away, probably by the servant who had come to the house earlier in the day with Constance Sherrill, but some had fallen since. The footsteps made in the early afternoon had been obliterated by it, but Alan could see those he had made that evening, as well as those made by someone else who had gone into the house and not come out again. It was clear what had happened. The man had come from the south, and had obviously not seen the light Alan had on at the rear of the house on its north side. Believing no one was in the house, the man had gone in through the front door with a key. He had been someone familiar with the house, for he had known about the side door and how to reach it, and how to get out that way. This appeared to indicate he was the same one who had searched the house before.

Alan let himself in at the front door and turned on the library reading lamp. The flashlight was still glowing on the floor, and he picked it up and extinguished it. He went upstairs for his shoes and brought them back down to the library. He had seen that wood was set in the fireplace, and now he lighted it and sat before the warming fire drying his wet socks. Alan was still shaking and breathing fast from his struggle with the man and his chase after him, and from the strangeness and excitement of what had taken place.

When the shaft of light had flashed across Alan's face in the dark library, the man had not taken him for what he was—a living person; he had taken him for a specter. His terror and the things he had cried out could mean only that. The specter of whom? Not of Benjamin Corvet; for one of the things Alan had remarked when he saw Benjamin Corvet's picture was that he did not look at all like his father. Besides, what the man had said made it certain that he did not think the specter *was* Ben; for the specter had "got Ben." Did Alan look like someone else then? Like whom? Evidently like the man, now dead, who had "got" Ben, in the man's opinion. Who could that be? No answer, as yet, was possible to that. But if he did look like someone, then that someone was, or had been, dreaded not only by the big man who had entered the house, but by Benjamin Corvet as well. "You got Ben!" the man had cried out. Got him? How? "But you can't get me!" he had said. "You . . . with bullet hole above your eye!" What did that mean?

Alan got up and went to look at himself in the mirror in the hall. He was white, now that the flush of the fighting was gone; he had probably been pale before the excitement, and over his right eye there was a round, black mark. Alan looked down at his hands. A little skin was off one knuckle where he had struck the man, and his fingers were smudged with a black and sooty dust. He had smudged them on the papers upstairs or in feeling his way around the dark house, and at some time he touched his forehead which left a black mark. This was the "bullet hole" the man had seen.

In the rest the man had said had been a reference to some name. Alan had no trouble recollecting the name—*Miwaka*—and while he did not understand it at all, it stirred him strangely. *Miwaka.* What was that? The strange excitement and questioning the name brought, when he repeated it to himself, was not recollection, for he could not recall ever having heard it before. But the name in a way seemed not completely strange to him. He could define the excitement it stirred in him only in that way.

He went back to the chair, and finding his socks nearly dry, he put on his shoes. As he moved about in front of the fireplace, he recalled Sherrill's believing that here in this house Benjamin Corvet had left, or might have left, a memorandum, a record, or an account of some sort which would explain to Alan, his son, the blight which had hung over his life.

It was very clear to Alan now that whatever might be hidden in the house involved someone else deeply—perhaps desperately. There was no other way to explain the intrusion of the sort of man whom Alan had surprised there an hour earlier. The events of the night had made this very certain.

The fact that the intruder was also looking for something did not prove that Benjamin Corvet had left anything of importance in the house, as Sherrill believed, but it did establish that another person knew there must be documentation of some sort, and he desperately feared it. Whether or not it had been guilt that had sent Benjamin Corvet away four days ago, whether or not guilt had been suggested by the apparition which had "got Ben," there was guilt in the big man's terror when he had seen Alan. So bold and powerful a man as the intruder, when his conscience is clear, does not see apparitions. And the one he *had* seen had a bullet hole above his brow!

Alan did not flatter himself that in any physical way he had triumphed over the man. So far as it had gone, his adversary had rather the better of the battle. He had endeavored to stun Alan, or perhaps worse, but after the opening encounter, his prime purpose had been to get away. But he had not fled from Alan; he had fled from the discovery of who he was.

Sherrill had not mentioned anyone in their conversations Alan could identify with this man, but he could most certainly describe him to Sherrill.

Alan found a lavatory, washed, straightened his collar and tie, and brushed his clothes. There was a bruise on the side of his head, and though it throbbed painfully, it did not have any visible mark. He could return now to the Sherrills'. While the hour was late, he believed by this time Sherrill was probably home; he may possibly have already gone to bed.

As Alan put on his hat and coat, he knew he was going to return and sleep here, as he was not going to leave the house unguarded for any length of time after what had happened. He felt he could leave the house safely for half an hour, particularly if he left a light on within. When he stepped outside and closed the front door, the wind from the west was blowing ferociously now, and the night had become bitter cold. When he reached the drive as he went toward the Sherrills', he looked out over the stormy water and could see, far out, the lights of a ship. He knew that his father must have battled such weather as this on many similar nights.

The man who answered his ring at the Sherrills' recognized him at once and admitted him, and in reply to Alan's question, said that Mr. Sherrill had not yet returned. When Alan went to his room to get his things, the valet appeared and offered his services. As an automobile had just driven up the crescent driveway, Alan let him pack and went downstairs.

The car was bringing Constance and her mother home. After telling Alan that Mr. Sherrill might not be home until some time later, Mrs. Sherrill went upstairs and did not appear again. Constance followed her mother, but in about ten minutes came down again.

"You're not staying here tonight?" she said, evidently having learned as much from the valet.

"I thought it best that I go over to the other house, and I wanted to tell you and your father," Alan explained.

She came a little closer to him in her concern. "Nothing has happened . . . here?"

"Here? You mean in this house?" Alan smiled. "No; nothing."

She seemed relieved. Alan, remembering her mother's manner, thought he understood. She knew that remarks may have been made which, repeated by a servant, might have offended him.

"I'm afraid it's been a hard day for you," she said.

"It's certainly been unusual," Alan admitted.

It had been a hard day for her, too, he observed. Not only this day, but the recent days since her own good friend, and her father's, had gone.

She was tired now but nervously excited as well over the possibility that Alan might shed light on Uncle Benny's disappearance. She was so young that the little signs of strain and worry of these trying days, instead of making her seem older, made her youth more apparent. The curves of her neck and shoulders were as soft as before; her lustrous brown hair seemed more beautiful, and a slight flush colored her attractive face.

It seemed to Alan that when Mrs. Sherrill had spoken to him a few minutes before, her manner toward him had been more reserved and constrained than earlier in the evening. He had attributed this to the lateness of the hour, but now he realized that she had probably been discussing him with Constance, and that it was perhaps in defiance of her mother that Constance had come to speak with him again.

"Are you taking anyone over to the other house with you?" she inquired.

"Anyone?"

"A servant, I mean."

"No."

"Then let us lend you a man from here."

"You're awfully good, but I don't think I will need anyone to-night. Mr. Corvet's . . . my father's . . . man is coming back tomor-row, I understand. I'll get along very well until then."

She was silent a moment as she looked away. Her shoulders sud-denly jerked a little. "I wish you'd take someone with you," she persisted. "I don't like to think of you alone over there."

"My father must have been often alone there."

"Yes," she said. "Yes." She looked at him quickly, then away, check-ing a question. She wanted to ask, he knew, what he had discovered in that lonely house which had so agitated him, as she had noticed agitation in him. And he had intended to tell her and her father. He had been rehearsing to himself the description of the man he had met there in order to ask Sherrill about him. But now Alan knew that he was not going to discuss the matter even with Sherrill just yet.

Sherrill had believed that Benjamin Corvet's disappearance was from circumstances too personal and intimate to be made a subject of public inquiry, and what Alan had encountered in Corvet's house had confirmed that belief. Sherrill had further said that Benjamin Corvet, if he had wanted Sherrill to know those circumstances, would have told him. But Corvet had not done that. Instead, he had sent for Alan, his son.

Sherrill had admitted he was withholding from Alan, for the time being, something that he knew about Benjamin Corvet, but he said that it was nothing that would help Alan to learn about his father or what became of him. Alan determined to ask Sherrill what he had been withholding before he told him all of what had happened in Corvet's house. There was one other circumstance which Sherrill had mentioned but had not explained. It occurred to Alan now.

"Miss Sherrill . . . ," he checked himself.

"What is it?"

"This afternoon your father said that you believed that Mr. Corvet's disappearance was in some way connected with you. He said that he did not believe that was so, but do you want to tell me why you thought that?"

"Yes. I will tell you." She colored slightly. "One of the last things Mr. Corvet did—in fact, the last thing we know of his doing before he sent for you—was to come to me and warn me against one of my friends."

"Warn you, Miss Sherrill? How? I mean warn you against what?"

"Against thinking too much of him." She turned away.

Alan saw in the rear of the hall the man who had been waiting with his suitcase. It was now after midnight, and for far more than the intended half hour Alan had left his father's house unwatched; the house had been exposed to entry through the front door by the intruder if he again chose to use his key.

"I think I'll come to see your father in the morning," Alan said, when Constance looked back at him.

"You won't borrow Simons?" she asked again.

"Thank you, no."

"But you'll come over for breakfast in the morning?"

"You want me to come?"

"Certainly."

"I would like that very much."

"Then I will expect you."

She followed him to the door when he put on his things, and he made no objection when she asked that the man be allowed to carry his bag around to the other house. When he glanced back after reaching the walk, he saw her standing inside the door watching him through the glass.

When he had dismissed Simons and re-entered the house on Astor Street, he found no evidence of any disturbance while he had been gone. On the second floor, to the east of his father's rooms, was a bedroom which evidently had been kept as a guest room. Alan carried his suitcase there and made ready for bed.

The sight of Constance Sherrill standing and watching after him in concern as he started back to the Corvet house came to him again and again, as did also her expression when she had spoken of the friend against whom Benjamin Corvet had warned her. Who was he? It had been impossible at that moment for Alan to ask her more. Besides, if he had asked and she had told him, he would only have learned a name that would be meaningless to him. Whoever it was, it was plain that Constance Sherrill "thought of him." *Lucky man*, Alan said to himself. Yet, why had Corvet warned her not to think of him . . . ?

Alan turned back his bed. It had been for him a momentous day. Barely twelve hours before, he, Alan Conrad from Blue Rapids, Kansas, had come to that house. Now, phrases from what Lawrence Sherrill had told him were running through his mind, as he opened the door of the room in order to be able to hear any noise in Benjamin Corvet's house—a house of which he was now the sole protector. The emotion roused by his first sight of the lake went through him again as he opened the window to the east.

Now, as he lay in bed, Alan seemed to be standing, again a specter before a man blaspheming Benjamin Corvet and the souls of men dead. *And the hole above the eye! . . . The bullet got you!. . . So it's you that got Ben! . . . I'll get you! . . . You can't save the* Miwaka!

The *Miwaka!* The stir of that was even stronger now than it had been before. It had been running through his mind almost constantly since he had first heard it. He sat up and turned on the light, and found a note pad and pencil in the bedside stand. He did not know how to spell the word, but he wanted to be sure he wouldn't forget it. Not that he ever could! But once written down, he would be sure to remember. As he wrote, he guessed at the spelling—*Miwaka.*

It was a name, of course, but the name of what? It repeated and repeated itself to him after he got back in bed, until the very repetition made him drowsy.

Outside, the gale whistled and shrieked. The wind, passing its last resistance after its sweep across the prairies before it leaped upon the lake, battered and clamored in its assault about the house. As Alan became sleepier, it rattled the windows and howled under the eaves and over the roof. So, with the roar of the gale in his ears and the fading image of struggling, ice-shrouded ships, he went to sleep with the sole conscious connection in his mind between himself and these people among whom Benjamin Corvet's summons had brought him—and the name *Miwaka.*

Part
Two

Violence

6

In the morning a great change had come over the lake. The wind still blew freshly from the west, but no longer fiercely, and the ice had departed from the beach beyond the drive, from the piers and breakwaters at the harbor mouth—indeed, from all the western shore. Far out in the lake a nearly indiscernible white line marked the edge of the floes where they were retreating eastward on the offshore wind. Only a gleaming, crystal fringe of frozen snow clung to the shore, and the water sparkled blue and dimpling, under the morning sun. Multitudes of gulls, hungry after the storm, called to one another and circled over the breakwaters and piers, and out over the water as far as the eye could see. Some half a mile offshore a small work boat—a shallop perhaps twenty feet long—was chugging along where, twelve hours before, no amount of horsepower created by man could have taken the hugest steamer.

Constance Sherrill, awakened by the sunlight reflecting from the water onto her ceiling, found nothing unusual in this change. It excited her but did not surprise her. Except for short visits, she had lived all of her life on the shore of the lake. The water, wonderful and ever changing, was the first thing she saw each morning. Just as it made the desolation of a stormy day wilder and more grim, it also could brighten the splendor of sunshine, happily influencing her feelings.

Constance held by preference to the seagoing traditions of her family. Since she had been a child, the lake and the ships had delighted and fascinated her. Very early she had discovered that upon the lake she was permitted privileges sternly denied upon land. This was an arbitrary distinction which led her to designate water, when she was a little girl, as her family's "respectable element." While her father's investments were, in part, on the water, her mother's property was all on the land. Her mother, who was a Seaton, owned property somewhere in the city in common with Constance's uncles. As a child, Constance had learned that the Seaton property consisted mostly of large, wholesale-grocery buildings. They and "The Brand" had been in the possession of the Seaton family for years. Both of her uncles worked in the big buildings where the canning was done, and when she was taken to visit them, she found the place most interesting—the berries and fruit coming up in great steaming cauldrons; the machines pushing the cans under the enormous faucets where the preserves ran out, then sealing the cans and attaching the bright Seaton labels on them. The people there were interesting, too—girls with flying fingers sorting fruit and men pounding big boxes together. The great, shaggy-hoofed horses which pulled the huge, groaning wagons were most fascinating of all. She wanted to ride on the wagons, but her requests were always promptly and completely squashed. It was not "done." Nothing about the groceries and the canning was ever to be mentioned before visitors, as Constance learned painfully the one time she brought up the subject.

It was different with her father's ships. She could talk about them when she wanted to, and her father often spoke about them. Anyone who came to the house could speak about them. Ships, apparently, were respectable.

When she went down to the docks with her father, she could climb all over them if she were careful of her clothes. She could spend a day watching one of her father's boats discharging grain, or another unloading ore. When she was twelve, for a great treat, her father took her on one of the freighters to Duluth, and for one delightful, wonderful week she chummed with the captain and mates and wheelsmen, and she learned all the pilot signals and the way the different lighthouses winked.

Mr. Spearman, who had recently become a partner of her father's, was also aboard on that trip. He had no particular duty, as he was just an owner like her father. But Constance observed that while the captain and the mates and engineers were always polite and respectful to her father, they asked Mr. Spearman's opinion about things in a very different way, and paid real attention when he talked. He was a most desirable sort of an acquaintance; for he was a friend who could come to the house at any time, and he had done all sorts of exciting things. He had not just gone to Harvard and then become an owner, as Constance's father had. At fifteen, he had run away from his father's farm behind the east shore of Little Traverse Bay, near the northern end of Lake Michigan. At eighteen, after all sorts of adventures, he had become a mate of a lumber schooner, and shortly after that he had "taken to steam" and had been an officer on many kinds of ships. Then Uncle Benny had taken him into partnership.

The twelve-year-old Constance had had a most exciting example of what he could do when the ship ran into a big storm on Lake Superior. Coming into Whitefish Bay, a barge had blundered against the vessel and the impact had opened a seam. Water had come in so fast that it gained on the pumps. Instantly, Mr Spearman, not the captain, had been in command and had handled the ship to protect the damaged seam and devised a scheme to stay the in-rush of the water. The pumps had begun to gain at once, and the ship had gone into Duluth safe and dry. Constance—and everyone else aboard— had been impressed.

Spearman was the most active partner in Corvet, Sherrill and Spearman, and almost everyone in Chicago knew him. A bachelor, he lived in one of the most fashionable apartment buildings in the city, facing the lake just north of Downtown. He had become a member of the best clubs and was welcomed along the Drive, where the Sherrills' mansion was considered an "old Chicago" home.

Now, at forty-two—and he looked younger—Spearman was distinctly of the new generation. Constance Sherrill was but one of many of younger girls who found him an exciting, refreshing relief from youths who were the sons of men but who would never become men themselves. These nice, earnest boys had all sorts of serious, Marxist ideas about establishing "social justice" in the plants their fathers had built and plans for carrying their idealism into local and national politics. But these reformers, Constance was quite certain, could never have built the industries with which they so blithely found fault, and most either failed at election or, if elected, seemed to leave things pretty much unchanged.

As Constance grew to womanhood, the image of Spearman as someone always instantly in charge remained—became more vivid— if only because she never saw him except when he dominated. Ten years before, an abyss had separated Constance, at twelve, from Spearman at thirty-two. Now, at twenty-two, she found the forty-two-year-old Henry the most vital and interesting of the men who moved socially within the restricted ellipse curving down the lake shore south of the park and up Astor Street.

He had recognized very early that he possessed the vigor and courage to go far, and he had disciplined away almost all the coarseness and roughness which had sometimes offended the little girl of ten years before. What crudeness still came out she regarded romantically, as reminders of his hard, early life on the lakes.

Uncle Benny's troubling warning seemed odd, indeed. Had there been anything in Henry's early life about which he had not told her—something worse than merely rough and rugged, which might strike at her, injure her? Uncle Benny's last, dramatic appeal certainly suggested that. But even as he was speaking to her, any fright she had felt was for Uncle Benny, not at the possibility that there had been something "wrong" in Henry's life. It was very evident that Uncle Benny had not been himself.

As long as Constance could remember, he and Henry had quarreled. Uncle Benny's antagonism to Henry had become almost an obsession, and her father had told her that most of the time Uncle Benny had no just ground for these quarrels with Henry. A most violent quarrel had occurred on that last day, and undoubtedly its fury had carried Uncle Benny to the length of going to Constance as he did.

Constance had come to this conclusion during the last gloomy and stormy days. This morning as she gazed out upon the shining lake, clear blue under the wintry sun, she was more satisfied than ever that her conclusion was well drawn. Summoning her maid, she inquired first whether anything had been heard since last night of Mr. Corvet. She was quite certain, if her father had learned anything, he would have awakened her. There was no news. She suddenly remembered that Alan Conrad was coming to breakfast.

Uncle Benny's son! To Constance's mother, that only suggested something unpleasant, something to be avoided and considered as little as possible. But Alan Conrad—Uncle Benny's son—was not unpleasant at all. Quite the reverse, in fact. Constance had liked him from the moment when, confused by Benjamin Corvet's absence and Simons' manner in greeting him, he had turned to her for explanation. She had liked the way he had told her of himself, and the fact that he knew nothing of the man who proved to be his father. She remembered how he had looked at her, openly amazed at himself for not feeling. And she had liked most of all his refusal—for himself and his father—to accept stigma until it should be proved.

She had not designated an hour for breakfast, and she supposed that coming from the country he would believe breakfast to be early. But when she got downstairs, though it was nearly nine o'clock, he had not come. She went to the front window to watch for him, and after a few minutes she saw him approaching, looking often at the lake as though amazed by the change in it. She went to the door and let him in.

"Father has gone to the office," she told him, as he took off his things. Mr. Spearman is returning from Duluth this morning, and Father wanted to tell him about you as soon as possible. I told Father you had come to see him last night, and he told me to bring you down to the office."

"I overslept, I am afraid."

"You slept well, then?"

"Very well . . . after a while."

"I'll take you downtown myself after breakfast."

She said no more but led him into the breakfast room. It was a delightful, cozy little room, Dutch furnished, with a single wide window to the east. An enormous hooded fireplace took up half the north wall, and blue Delft tiles were set above it and into the walls all about the room. There were the quaint blue windmills; fishing boats; baggy breeked, wood-shod folk; the canals and barges; the dikes and their guardians, and the fishing ship on the Zuider Zee.

Alan, Constance saw, gazed about at these with quick and appreciative interest. It was one of his pleasantest and most interesting characteristics—that quality of instantly noticing and appreciating anything unusual.

"I like those, too," she said. "I selected them in Holland."

She took her place beside the coffee pot, and when he remained standing, she indicated the chair opposite her and said, "Mother always has her breakfast in bed; that's your place."

He took the chair. There was fruit upon the table, and Constance took an orange; then passed the little silver basket across to him.

"This is such a little table; we never use it if there are more than two or three of us. And we like to help ourselves here."

"I like it very much," Alan said.

"Coffee right away, or later?"

"Whenever you do," he said. "You see," he explained, smiling in a way that pleased her, "I haven't the slightest idea what else is coming, or whether anything else is coming."

A servant entered, bringing cereal and cream. He removed the fruit plates, put the cereal dish and two bowls before Constance, and went out.

"And if anyone in Blue Rapids," Alan went on, "had a man waiting in the dining room, and at least one other in the kitchen, they would not speak of our activities here as 'helping ourselves.' I'm not sure just how they would speak of them. We had a maid servant at one time when we were on the farm, and when we engaged her, she asked, 'Do you do your own stretching?' That meant serving from the stove to the table, usually."

She laughed, and he was silent for a few moments, and when she looked at him again across the table, he seemed about to speak seriously.

"Miss Sherrill," he said gravely, "what is—or was—the *Miwaka*? A ship?"

He made no attempt to put the question casually; rather he made it evident by the change in his manner that it was of considerable concern to him.

"The *Miwaka*?" Constance asked.

"Do you know what it was?"

"Yes, I know, and it was a ship."

"You mean it doesn't exist any more?"

"No. It was lost a long time ago on Lake Michigan."

"You mean by 'lost' that it was sunk?"

"Yes, it was sunk, but no one knows what happened to it; whether it was wrecked, or burned or possibly foundered."

The thought of the mystery set her blood tingling as it had ever since she first heard of it and the superstition surrounding it—the unknown fate of the ship and crew; the ship which had sailed and never reached port and of which nothing had ever been heard but the beating of the native drum. It was clear that Alan Conrad had not asked about it idly.

Something about the *Miwaka* had come to him recently, and had excited his intense concern.

"Whose ship was it?" he asked. "My father's?"

"No. It belonged to Stafford and Ramsdell. They were two of the big men of their time in the carrying trade on the lakes. Both Mr. Stafford and Mr. Ramsdell were lost with the *Miwaka*."

"Will you tell me about it—and them—please?"

"I've told you almost all I can about Stafford and Ramsdell, I'm afraid. I have heard Father say that they were men who could have amounted to a great deal on the lakes, if they had lived—especially Mr. Stafford, who was very young. The *Miwaka* was a great, new, steel ship, built the year after I was born, and it was the first of nearly a dozen that Stafford and Ramsdell had planned to build. There was some doubt among lakemen about steel boats at the time because there had been some serious losses. Whether it was because they were steel, or were built on models not fitted for the lakes, no one knew. But several of them had broken in two and had sunk, and a good many men were talking about going back to wood. Stafford and Ramsdell firmly believed in steel, and had finished this first one of their new fleet.

"The *Miwaka*," Constance continued, "left Duluth for Chicago loaded with ore on the first day of December in 1895 with both the owners and part of their families on board. She passed the Soo on the third and went through the Straits of Mackinac on the fourth into Lake Michigan. After that, nothing was ever heard of her."

"So probably she broke in two like the others?" Alan asked.

"Mr. Spearman and your father both thought so, but nobody ever knew. No wreckage came ashore, and no message of any kind ever came from anyone on board. A very sudden winter storm had come up and was at its worst on the morning of the fifth. Uncle Benny . . . your father . . . told me once when I asked him about it that it was as severe a storm for a time as any he had ever experienced. He very nearly lost his own life in it. He had just finished laying up one of his boats, the *Martha Corvet*, at Manistee for the

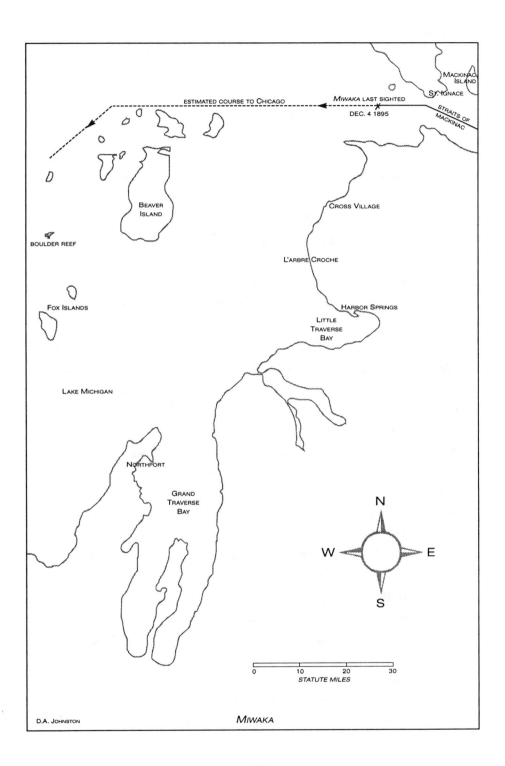

ESTIMATED COURSE TO CHICAGO

MIWAKA LAST SIGHTED
DEC. 4 1895

STRAITS OF MACKINAC

MACKINAC ISLAND

ST. IGNACE

BEAVER ISLAND

CROSS VILLAGE

L'ARBRE CROCHE

HARBOR SPRINGS

LITTLE TRAVERSE BAY

BOULDER REEF

FOX ISLANDS

LAKE MICHIGAN

NORTHPORT

GRAND TRAVERSE BAY

N

W   E

S

0   10   20   30
STATUTE MILES

D.A. JOHNSTON

MIWAKA

winter, and he and Mr. Spearman, who was then mate of the *Martha Corvet*, were crossing the lake in a tug with a crew of four men to Manitowoc, where they were going to lay up more ships.

"The captain and one of the deck hands of the tug were washed overboard in the storm, and the engineer was lost trying to save them. Uncle Benny and Mr. Spearman and the stoker brought the tug in. The storm was worst about five in the morning, which is when the *Miwaka* went down."

"How do you know that the *Miwaka* sank at five o'clock," Alan asked, "if no one ever heard from the ship?"

"Oh; that was told by the drum!"

"The drum?"

"Yes; the drum! I forgot, of course you wouldn't know. It's a superstition that some of the lakemen have, particularly those who come from the north end of the lake. The native drum is in the woods there, they say. No one has seen it, but many say they have heard it. It's a spirit drum which beats, they say, whenever a ship is lost on the lake. It beats once for every life lost. There's a particular superstition about it for the *Miwaka,* because the drum supposedly beat incorrectly. You see, the people up there swear that about five o'clock in the morning on the fifth, when the storm was at its worst, they heard the drum beating and knew that a ship was going down. They counted the sound to twenty-four before it stopped. This was repeated again and again. Everyone knew it had been beating for the *Miwaka,* for every other ship on the lake that night got to port. But there had been twenty-five on the *Miwaka,* so either the drum beat wrong, or . . . ," she hesitated.

"Or what?"

"Or the drum was right, and someone was saved. Many people believe that. It was years before the families of those on board who were lost gave up hope, because of the drum. There may be some who haven't given up hope yet."

Alan made no comment for a moment. Constance had seen the blood flush to his face and then leave it, and her own pulse had beat as swiftly as she related the superstition. As he looked at her and then away, it was plain that he had heard something additional about the *Miwaka*—something which he was trying to fit into what she had told him.

"That's all anybody knows?" His gaze came back to her at last.

"Yes. Why did you ask about it . . . the *Miwaka*? I mean, how did you hear about it so you wanted to know?"

He considered an instant before replying. "I encountered a reference to the *Miwaka*—I supposed it to be a ship—in my father's house last night."

His manner, as he looked down at his coffee cup, toying with it, prevented her then from asking more. He seemed to know she wanted to press it; he looked up quickly and changed the subject.

"I met my . . . I mean, my father's servant this morning," he said.

"Yes, I know. He got back this morning, and he came here early to report to Father that he had no news of Uncle Benny. Father told him you were at the house, and sent him over."

Alan was studying the coffee cup again, a queer expression on his face which she could not read.

"He was there when I woke up this morning, Miss Sherrill. I hadn't heard anybody in the house, but I found a small table on wheels in the hall outside my door with a coffee pot on it, and he was bending over it. His back was toward me, and seeing his straight black hair, at first I though he was an Oriental, but when he turned around, I saw he was an American Indian."

"Yes, that was Wassaquam."

"Is that his name? He told me it was Judah."

"Yes . . . Judah Wassaquam. He's a Chippewa from the north end of the lake. They are very religious there, and many of them have a Biblical name which they use for a first name, and use their Indian name for a last one."

"He called me 'Alan' and my father 'Ben.' "

"The Indians almost always call people by their first names."

"He said that he always served Ben his coffee that way before he got up, and so he had supposed he was to do the same for me. He also said that long ago, he used to be a deckhand on one of my father's ships."

"Yes," said Constance. "When Uncle Benny began to operate ships of his own, many of the ships on the lakes had Indians among the deckhands; some had all Indians for crews and white men only for officers. Wassaquam was on the first freighter Uncle Benny ever owned a share in, and afterwards he came here to Chicago with Uncle Benny. He's been looking after Uncle Benny all alone now for more than ten years; he's very much devoted to him, and is fully trustworthy. Besides, he is a wonderful cook. I've wondered sometimes whether Uncle Benny wasn't the only city man in the world who had an Indian servant. Wassaquam's nephew, Paul Red Hawk, has a log cabin a few miles north of our place at Harbor Point. Both Paul and his wife, Mary, work for my father during the summer months—Paul on Father's power cruiser, the *Salem,* and Mary in the house for my mother. Mary is also an excellent cook."

"You know a good deal about Indians."

"A little about the lake Indians, the Chippewas and the Pottawatomies in Northern Michigan."

"Recollection's a funny thing," Alan said, after considering a moment. "This morning, after seeing Judah and talking to him—or rather hearing him talk—somehow a story got running through my head. I can't exactly make out what it was . . . about a lot of animals on a raft, and there was someone with them . . . I don't know who. I can't fit any name to him, but he had a name."

Constance bent forward quickly. "Was the name Michabou?" she asked.

He returned her look, surprised. "That's it. How did you know?"

"I believe I know the story, and Wassaquam would have known it too, I think, if you had asked him. But, he might have thought it impious to tell it, because he and his people are great Christians now. Michabou is one of the Indian names for Manitou. What else to you remember of the story?"

94

"Not much, I'm afraid . . . just sort of scenes here and there, but I can remember the beginning now that you have given me the name. In the beginning of all things there was only water, and Michabou was floating on the raft with all the animals. Michabou, it seemed, wanted the land brought up so that men and animals could live on it, and he asked one of the animals to go down and bring it up . . . "

"The beaver," Constance supplied.

"Was the beaver the first one? The beaver dived and stayed down a long time, so long that when he came up he was breathless and completely exhausted, but he had not been able to reach the bottom. Then Michabou sent down . . . "

"The otter."

"And he stayed down much longer than the beaver, and when he came up at last, they dragged him onto the raft quite senseless, but he had not been able to reach the bottom either. So the animals and Michabou himself were ready to give it up, but then the little muskrat spoke up . . . am I right? Was it the muskrat?"

"Yes."

"Then you can finish it for me?"

"He dived and he stayed down, the little muskrat," Constance continued, "longer than the beaver and the otter both together. Michabou and the animals waited all day for him to come up, and they watched all through the night, so then they knew he must be dead. And, sure enough, they came across the body floating on the water and apparently lifeless. They dragged him onto the raft, and found that his small paws were all tight shut. They forced open three of the paws and found nothing in them, but when they opened the last one, they found one grain of sand clutched in it; he'd reached the bottom. And out of that one grain of sand, Michabou made the world."

"That's it," he said. "Now what is it?"

"The Indian story of creation . . . or one of them."

"Not a story of the Plains Indians surely."

"No; of the Indians who live about the lakes and so got the idea that everything was water in the first place . . . the Indians who live on the islands and peninsulas. That's how I came to know it."

"I thought that must be it," Alan said. His hand trembled a little as he lifted his coffee cup to his lips.

Constance, too, flushed a little with excitement. It was a surprisingly close and intimate thing to have explored with another back into the concealments of his first childhood consciousness, and to have aided another in the sensitive task of revealing himself to himself. This which she had helped to bring back to him must have been one of the first stories told him. He had been a very little boy when he had been taken to Kansas, away from the place where he must have heard the story—the lakes.

She was also a little nervous from watching the time as told by the tiny watch on her wrist. Henry's train from Duluth must be in now, and he had not yet called her, as had been his custom recently when he returned to town after a trip. But just then, a servant entered to inform her that Mr. Spearman wished to speak to her. She excused herself and hurried out. Henry was calling her from the railroad station, and, he said, from a most stuffy booth, and besides having a poor connection, there was any amount of noise about him. He was very anxious to see Constance as soon as possible. Could she be in town that morning and have lunch with him? Yes; she was going into town very soon, and after luncheon, he could go home with her, if he wished. He certainly did wish, but he couldn't say yet what he might have to do in the afternoon, but please, he asked, would she save the evening for him? She promised and started telling him about Alan, then recollected that Henry was going to see her father immediately at the office, so she did not continue.

Alan was standing, waiting for her, when she returned to the breakfast room.

"Ready to go into town?"

"Whenever you are."

"I'll be ready in a minute. I'm planning to drive; are you afraid?"

He smiled in his pleasant way as he glanced at her; she had become conscious of saying that sort of thing to tempt his smile. "Oh, I'll take the risk."

7

Her little gasoline-driven car, delicate as though a jeweler had made it, was waiting for them under the porte cochere beside the house when they went out. She delayed a moment to ask Alan to let down the windows. The sky was clear and the sunshine had become almost warm, although the breeze was sharp and cold. As the car rolled down the drive, and he turned for a long look past her toward the lake, she watched his expression.

"It's like a great shuttle, the ice out there," she commented, "a monster shuttle nearly three hundred miles long. All winter it moves back and forth across the lake, from east to west and from west to east as the winds change, blocking each shore half the time and forcing the winter boats to fight it always."

"The gulls go opposite to it, I suppose, sticking to open water."

"The gulls? That depends on the weather.

" 'Seagull, seagull,' " she quoted, " 'sit on the sand; It's never fair weather when you're on the land.' "

Alan looked at her. "What was that?" he asked.

"That rhyme? It's one the wives of lakemen teach their children. Did you remember that, too?"

"After you said it."

"Can you remember the rest of it?"

" 'Green to green . . . Red to red,' " Alan said, almost to himself. " 'Green to green . . .' and then something about . . . how is it? 'Back her . . . back and stopper.' "

"That's from a lake rhyme too, but another one!" she said. "And that's quite a good one. It's one of the pilot rules that every lake person knows. Some skipper and wheelsman set them to rhyme years ago, and the lakemen teach them to their children so they'll never go wrong with a ship. It keeps them clearer in their heads than any amount of government printing. Uncle Benny used to say the rhyme has saved any number of collisions."

Almost without pause, she began reciting the familiar rhyme.

> *Meeting steamers, do not dread*
> *When you see three lights ahead!*
> *Port your helm and show your red.*
> *For passing steamers you should try*
> *To keep this maxim in your eye,*
> *Green to Green or Red to Red,*
> *Perfect safety; go ahead.*
> *Both in safety and in doubt,*
> *Always keep a good lookout;*
> *Should there be no room to turn,*
> *Stop your ship and go to stern . . .*

"Now," said Constance, interrupting herself. "Now we're coming to your 'back and stopper'. . . .

> *If to starboard, red appear,*
> *'Tis your duty to keep clear;*
> *Act as judgment says is proper.*
> *Port or starboard—back or stop her!*
> *But when on your port is seen*
> *A steamer with a light of Green,*

There's not much for you to do.
The green light must look out for you.

She had driven the car swiftly along the boulevard to the turn
where the motorway bears west to Rush Street, then turned south
again toward the bridge. As they reached the approach to the bridge
and the cars congested there, Constance was required to give all her
attention to driving, and not until they were crossing the bridge at
a slower pace was she able to glance at her companion's face. She
found him gazing out the window.

To the westward, on both sides of the river, summer boats were
laid up, their decks covered with snow. On the other side, still nearer
to the bridge, were some winter vessels. While the car was on the
span, bells began ringing the alarm to clear the bridge so it could
turn to let through a large ship just in from the lake. The sun glis-
tened on the ice that covered the huge vessel's bows and sides as far
back as Alan could see.

Forward of the big, red-banded black funnel, a cloud of steam
bellowed up and floated back, followed by another. Two deep and
imperious blasts rumbled majestically up the river and reverberated
on the frigid air. The shrill little alarm bells on the bridge jangled
more nervously and excitedly, and the policeman at the south end
hastily signaled the approaching automobiles to stop while he urged
those still on the bridge to scurry off as the freighter slowly approached.

"Can we stop and see it?" Alan appealed. Constance drove the car
from the bridge just before it began to turn, then swung to the
curb and stopped. He gazed back, and she knew he was seeing not
only his first great ship close by, but was also having his first view of
the lakemen from whom he had come. He was beginning to find
his identity and feel his origins.

The ship was sheathed in ice from stem to stern; tons of the gleaming crystal covered the forecastle; the rails all round were a frozen
bulwark; the boats in the davits were hummocks of ice; the bridge
was encased, and from the top of the pilot house hung giant stalac-

tites, at which an axman was chopping away. Alan could see the officers on the bridge, the wheelsman, the lookout. He could see the spurt of water from the ship's side as it was expelled with each thrust of the pumps, and he could see the whirlpool about the screw as, with signals clanging clearly from somewhere below, the vessel slowly and steadily steamed past the open bridge. From up the river ahead of it came the jangling of bells and the blowing of alarm whistles as other bridges were cleared to let the freighter through. It showed its stern now; Alan read the name and registry aloud: "*Groton* of Escanaba."

"Is that one of yours? Miss Sherrill; is that one of yours and my . . . Mr. Corvet's?"

She shook her head. "No, that's a Nicholson ship. But the lake ships do look alike," she said, somewhat surprised to find that she was sorry she had had to tell him it was not one of "theirs."

"You see," she went on aloud, "on lake ships, because of their length, the pilot house and bridge deck are located high near the bow, and on this ship, quarters for the captain and officers are just below. The crew's quarters and galley are aft below the funnel, and the engine rooms are on the decks located below that area."

The bridge was swinging shut again, and the long line of automobiles was beginning to move slowly. Constance turned the car down the narrow street fronted by warehouses which Alan had passed the morning before. They came to Michigan Avenue, with the park and harbor on their left. When she glanced at Alan now, he seemed oddly sad following his excitement at seeing the ship pass close by.

A strange depression had overcome him. Memory, if he could call it that, had given him a feeling for ships and for the lake—a single word, *Miwaka*, a childish rhyme and story which he might have heard repeated and have asked for a hundred times as a small child. But these were only the dim recollections of a three-year-old child. Not only did they refuse to connect themselves with anything else, but by the very finality of their isolation, they warned him that they, and perhaps a few more equally vague memories, would be all the recollection he would ever have. He pulled himself together and turned his thoughts to the approaching visit to Sherrill's—and his father's—offices.

Observing the towering buildings to his right, he was able to identify some of the more prominent structures, familiar to him from photographs of the city. Constance drove swiftly a few blocks down this boulevard, then with a sudden, "Here we are!" she shot the car to the curb and stopped. She led Alan into one of tallest and best looking of the buildings, where they took an elevator marked "Express" to the fifteenth floor.

On several of the doors opening on to the wide marble hall where the elevator left them, Alan saw the names, "Corvet, Sherrill and Spearman." As they passed one of these doors which was propped open, he looked in and was surprised to see how little office space was required by a great business conducted upon the water. What he saw was only one large room with hardly more than a dozen desks in it. Nearly all of the desks were closed, and there were not more that three or four people in the room, who were apparently stenographers. Doors of several smaller offices opened into the larger room, and bore names, among which he saw "Benjamin Corvet" and "Henry Spearman."

"It won't look this way a month from now," Constance said, catching his expression. "Just now, you know, the straits and all the northern lakes are locked fast with ice. There's nothing going on now except the winter traffic on Lake Michigan, and to a much smaller extent, on Lakes Ontario and Erie. We have an interest in some winter boats, but we don't operate them from here. Next month we will be busy fitting out, and the month after that all of the ships we have will be on the water."

She led the way to a door farther down the corridor, which bore merely the name, "Lawrence Sherrill." Evidently Sherrill, who had interests aside from the shipping business, had offices connected with but not actually a part of Corvet, Sherrill and Spearman. A girl just inside the door immediately recognized Constance and said that Mr. Sherrill had been waiting for Mr. Conrad. She opened an inner door and led them into a large, many-windowed room, where Sherrill was sitting before a large table-desk. He arose, a moment after the door opened, and spoke a few words to his daughter after greeting Alan. Constance withdrew, and the girl from the outer office followed her, closing the door behind her. Sherrill pulled a chair rather close to his desk and to his own large chair before asking Alan to be seated.

"Constance has told me the you wanted to tell me—or ask me—something last night," Sherrill said cordially. "I'm sorry I wasn't home when you returned from Corvet's house."

"I wanted to ask you," Alan said, "about those facts in regard to Mr. Corvet which you mentioned yesterday but did not explain. You said it would not aid me to know them, but I found certain things in Mr. Corvet's house last night which made me want to know, if I could, everything you can tell me."

Sherrill opened a drawer and took out a large, plain envelope.

"I did not tell you about these yesterday, Alan," he said, "not only because I had not decided how to act in regard to these matters, but because I had not said anything to Mr. Spearman about them previously, as I had expected to get some additional information from you. After seeing you, I was obliged to wait for Spearman to get back to town. The circumstances are such that I felt myself obliged to talk them over with him first. I have done that this morning, and I was going to send for you, if you had not come down."

Sherrill thought a minute, still holding the envelope closed in his hand.

"On the day after your father disappeared," he went on, "but before I knew he was gone—or before anyone except my daughter felt any alarm about him—I received a short note from him. I will show it to you later, if you wish; its exact wording, however, is unimportant. It had been mailed very late the night before, and apparently at the mail box near his house, or at least, by the postmark, somewhere in the neighborhood.

"For that reason it had not been taken up before the morning collection, and so did not reach the office until I had been here and gone away again about eleven o'clock. I did not get it, therefore, until after lunch. The note was agitated, and almost incoherent. It told me he had sent for you, Alan Conrad, of Blue Rapids, Kansas, and spoke of you as though you were someone I ought to have known about, and it commended you to my care. The remainder of it was merely an agitated, almost indecipherable farewell to me. When I opened the envelope, a key fell out which I identified as being to a safe deposit box in the vaults of a company where we both had boxes.

"The note, taken in connection with my daughter's concern about him, made it so plain that something serious had happened to Corvet, that my first thought was solely for him. He was not a man of whom one would expect suicide, Alan, but that was the first thought I had. I hurried at once to his home, but the bell was not answered. His servant, Wassaquam, has very few friends, and the few times he has been away from home in recent years have been when he visited an acquaintance of his who is the head porter in a South Side Hotel. I telephoned the hotel from the house next door and found Wassaquam there. I asked him about the letter to 'Alan Conrad,' and Wassaquam said Corvet had given it to him to mail early in the evening. Several hours later, Corvet had sent him out to wait for the mail collector to get the letter back, and then had come outside to wait, too. When the mail collector came, of course, he told them he could not return the letter, but he did let Corvet look through the letters. They discovered the letter was not there. It had been collected previously, obviously almost immediately after it had been mailed. Corvet became very excited over this when he discovered the letter was not there, and became more so on learning from the mailman that the letter was probably already on its way west. He controlled himself later enough to at least reassure Wassaquam, and shortly after this he sent Wassaquam away from the house. Wassaquam had gone without feeling any anxiety about him.

"On the telephone I told Wassaquam only that something was wrong, and then hurried to my own home to get the key to the Corvet house. When I came back and let myself into the house, I found it empty and with no sign of anything having happened.

"The next morning, Alan, I went to the safe deposit vaults as soon as they were open. I presented the key and was told it was to a box rented by Corvet, and that he had arranged three days before for me to have access to the box if I presented the key. I had only to sign my name in their register, and was then given the box to open. In it, Alan, I found the pictures which I showed to you yesterday, and the very strange communications that I am now going to show you."

Sherrill opened the long envelope from which several thin, folded papers fell out. He picked up the largest of these, which consisted of several sheets fastened together with a clip, and handed it to Alan without comment. Alan, as he looked at it and turned the pages, saw that it contained two columns of typewriting carried from page to page in the manner of an account.

The column to the left was an inventory of property and profits and income by months and years, and the one to the right was a list of losses and expenditures. Beginning at an indefinite day or month in the year 1895, there was set down in a lump sum what was indicated as the total of Benjamin Corvet's holdings at that time. To this, in sometimes undated items, the increase had been added. In the opposite column, beginning apparently at the same date in 1895, were shown expenditures. The painstaking exactness of these left no doubt of their correctness. They included items for depreciation of perishable properties, and it appeared they had been worked on quite recently. On the last sheet, the second column had been deducted from the first, and an apparently purely arbitrary sum of two hundred thousand dollars had been taken away. From the remainder there had been taken away approximately one hundred fifty thousand dollars more.

Alan, having ascertained that the papers contained only this accounting, looked up questioningly to Sherrill, who without speaking, merely handed him the second of the papers. This, Alan saw, had evidently been folded to fit in a smaller envelope. He unfolded it and saw that it was a letter written in the same hand which had written his summons from Blue Rapids—the same that made the entries in the little memorandum book of remittances that had been sent to John Welton. It read:

Lawrence:

This will come to you in the event that I am not able to carry out the plan upon which I am now, at last, determined. You will find with this a list of my possessions which, except for two hundred thousand dollars settled upon my wife which was hers absolutely to dispose of as she desired, and a further sum of approximately one hundred fifty thousand dollars presented in memory of her to the Hospital Service in France, have been transferred to you without reservation.

You will find deeds of all real estate executed and complete except for recording of the transfer at the county office; bonds, certificates, and other documents representing my ownership of properties, together with signed forms for their legal transfer to you, are in the box.

These properties, in their entirety, I give to you in trust to hold for the young man now known as Alan Conrad of Blue Rapids, Kansas, to deliver any part or all over to him, or to continue to hold it all in trust for him, as you shall consider to be to his greatest advantage.

This, for reasons which I shall have told to you or him—I cannot know which one of you now, nor do I know how I shall tell it—but when you learn, Lawrence, think as well of me as you can and help him to be charitable to me.

With the greatest affection,

Benjamin Corvet

As Alan finished reading, he looked up to Sherrill bewildered and dazed.

"What does it mean, Mr. Sherrill? Does it mean that he has gone away and left everything he had—everything—to me?"

"The properties listed here," Sherrill touched the pages Alan had first looked at, "are in the box at the vault with the executed forms of their transfer to me. If Mr. Corvet does not return, and I do not receive any other instructions, I shall take over his estate as he has instructed for your advantage."

"And, Mr. Sherrill, he didn't tell you why? This is all you know?"

"Yes; you have everything now. The fact that he did not give his reasons for this, either to you or me, made me think at first that he may have made his plan known to someone else who opposed his plan—to the extent even of inflicting violence upon him to prevent him from carrying it out. But the more I have considered this, the less likely it has seemed to me.

"Whatever happened to Corvet that so much disturbed and excited him lately seems to have precipitated his plan, rather than to have deterred him in it. He may have determined after he had written this that his actions and the plain indication of his relationship to you, gave all the explanation he wanted to make. All we can do is to search for him in every way we can. There will be others searching for him too, now, as information of his disappearance has got out. There have been reporters at the office this morning making inquiries, and his disappearance will be in this afternoon papers."

Sherrill put the papers back in their envelope, and the envelope back into the drawer, which he locked.

"I went over all this with Mr. Spearman this morning," he said. "He is as much at a loss to explain it as I am." He was silent for a few moments.

"The transfer of the Corvet properties to me for you," he said, "includes, as you have seen, Corvet's interest in the firm of Corvet, Sherrill and Spearman. I went very carefully through the deeds and transfers in the deposit box, and it is plain that, while he had taken great care with the forms of transfer for all properties, he had taken particular pains with whatever related to his holdings in this company and to his shipping interests. If I make over the properties to you, Alan, I shall begin with those for it seems to me that your father was particularly interested that you should take a personal, as well as a financial place among the men who control the traffic of the lakes. I have told Spearman that this is my intention. He has not been able to see it my way as yet, but he may change his views, I think, after meeting you."

Sherrill got up. Alan arose a little unsteadily. The list of properties he had read and the letter and Sherrill's statement portended so much that its meaning could not all be absorbed by him at once. He followed Sherrill through a short private corridor, flanked with company filing cabinets, into the large room he had seen when he came in with Constance. They crossed this, and Sherrill, without knocking, opened the door marked "Henry Spearman." Alan, looking on past Sherrill as the door opened, saw that there were some half dozen men in the room, smoking and talking. They were big men mostly, ruddy-skinned and weather-beaten in appearance, and he judged from their appearance and from the pile of their hats and coats on a chair, that they were officers of the company's ships; idle while the ships were laid up, but reporting now at the offices and receiving instructions as the time for fitting out approached.

His gaze went swiftly on past these men to the one who, half seated on the top of the flat desk, had been talking to them, and he felt his heart throb. He started, choked with astonishment, and then swiftly forced himself under control. For this was the man he had met, and with whom he had fought, in Benjamin Corvet's house the night before—the big man Alan had surprised in his blasphemy of Corvet and of souls "in hell"; the powerful man who, at sight of an apparition with a bullet hole above its eye, had cried out in fright, "You got Ben! But you won't get me . . . damn you! Damn you!"

Alan's shoulders drew up slightly, and the muscles of his hand tightened as Sherrill led him to this man. Sherrill put his hand on the man's shoulder; his other hand was still on Alan's arm.

"Henry," he said to the man, "this is Alan Conrad. Alan, I want you to know my partner, Mr. Spearman."

Spearman nodded an acknowledgement, but did not put out his hand. His eyes—steady, bold, watchful eyes—seemed to measure Alan attentively, as Alan in return, with his direct stare, was measuring him.

8

The instant of meeting, when Alan recognized in Sherrill's partner the man whom he had fought in Corvet's house, was one of swift readjustment of all his thought; adjustment to a situation of which he could not even have dreamed, and which made him breathless. But for Spearman, obviously, this was not the case. Following his noncommittal nod of acknowledgement of Sherrill's introduction and his first steady scrutiny of Alan, the big, handsome man swung himself off the desk on which he sat and leaned against it, facing them more directly.

"Oh, yes . . . Conrad," he said. His tone was hearty. In it Alan could recognize only so much of reserve as might be expected from Sherrill's partner who had taken an attitude of opposition. The shipmasters, who were looking on, were not aware of this attitude, and except for the excitement which Alan himself could not conceal, to them it must have appeared to be just an ordinary introduction.

Alan fought the swift rush of blood to his face and the tightening of his muscles.

"I can say truly that I'm glad to meet you, Mr. Spearman," he managed to reply.

There was no recognition in Spearman's words or his slow smile of acknowledgment as he turned from Alan to face Sherrill.

"I'm afraid you've caught me at rather a bad time, Lawrence."

"I can see that you're busy. This can wait, Henry, if what you're doing is immediate."

"I want some of these men to be back in Michigan tonight. Can we get together later . . . this afternoon?" Then, looking at Alan, he said, "Will you be here this afternoon?" His manner was not casual; Alan doubted that any expression that man might have could be casual. But this, he thought, came as near to it as Spearman could come.

"I think I can be here this afternoon," Alan replied.

"Would two-thirty be agreeable?"

"As well as any other time."

"Let's say two-thirty, then." Spearman turned and noted the hour almost solicitously among the scrawled appointments on his desk pad. Straightening, after this act of dismissal, he walked with them to the door, his hand on Sherrill's shoulder.

"Circumstances have put us . . . Mr. Sherrill and myself . . . in a very difficult position, Conrad," he remarked. "We want very much to be fair to all concerned . . ."

He did not finish the sentence, but halted at the door. Sherrill went out, and Alan followed him.

Exasperation at Spearman's bearing, half outrage yet half admiration, held Alan speechless. His blood rushed hotly to his face as the door closed behind them, his hands clenched, and he turned back to the closed door. Then he checked himself and followed Sherrill, who, oblivious to Alan's excitement, led the way to the door which bore Corvet's name. He opened it, disclosing an empty room, somewhat larger than Spearman's and similar to it, except that it lacked the marks of constant use. It was clear that, since Spearman had chosen to put off discussion of Alan's status, Sherrill did not know

what to do next. He stood an instant in thought, and then content-
ing himself with inviting Alan to lunch, he excused himself and returned to his office. When he had gone after closing the door behind him, Alan began to pace up and down the room.

What had just passed had left him still breathless; he felt bewildered. If every movement of Spearman's great, handsome body had
not recalled to him their struggle of the night before—if, as
Spearman's hand had rested on Sherrill's shoulder, Alan had not
seemed to feel again that big hand at his throat—he would almost
have been ready to believe that this was not the man with whom he
had fought. But he could not doubt that, because he had recognized Spearman beyond question, and Spearman had recognized
him. Of this he was sure. He was also convinced that Spearman had
known it was Alan whom he had fought in Corvet's house even
before Sherrill had brought them together. Was there not further
proof of that in Spearman's subsequent manner toward him? For
what was all this cordiality except defiance? Undoubtedly Spearman
had acted just as he had to show how undisturbed he was, and how
indifferent he might be to any accusation Alan could make. Not
having told Sherrill of the encounter in the house, and not having
told anyone else, Alan could not tell it now, after Sherrill had informed him that Spearman opposed his accession to Corvet's estate. Certainly, he could not identify the man.

In the face of Spearman's manner toward him today, if Alan told
Sherrill what had actually happened, Sherrill would not believe it. If
Spearman denied it—and the story of his return to town that morning made it perfectly certain that he would deny it—it would only
be Alan's word against Spearman's, the word of a stranger unknown
to Sherrill except for Alan's own account of himself and the infer-
ences from Corvet's acts, against the word of his business partner
of many years. Spearman had nothing to fear if Alan blurted out an
accusation against him. Perhaps, he even wanted Alan to do just
that. Nothing could more discredit Alan than such an unsustainable
accusation against the partner who was opposing Alan's taking his

father's place in the firm. It had been apparent to Alan that Spearman dominated Sherrill, and that Sherrill admired and felt confidence in his partner.

Alan grew hot with the realization that, in the interview just past, Spearman had also dominated him. He had been unable to find anything adequate to do, anything adequate to answer this man more than fifteen years older than he who had a lifelong experience in dealing with all kinds of men. He would not yield to Spearman like that again. It was the bewilderment of his recognition of Spearman that had made him do it. Alan stopped his pacing and threw himself down on Corvet's leather desk chair. He could hear Spearman's heavy, genial voice addressing the shipping men in his adjoining office; its tones—half comradeship, half command—spoke plainly of his dominance of those men also. He heard Spearman's office door open as some of the men left, and after a few minutes it opened again when the rest of them went out. He heard Spearman's voice in the outer office, and then heard it again as Spearman returned alone into his private office.

There was a house phone on Corvet's desk which undoubtedly connected with the switchboard in the general office. Alan picked up the phone and asked for "Mr. Spearman." At once the hearty voice answered:

"Yes."

"This is Conrad."

"I thought I told you I was busy, Conrad!" The phone clicked as Spearman hung up. The quality of the voice at the other end of the wire had altered. It had suddenly again become the harsh voice of the man who had called down curses upon "Ben" and on the men "in hell" in Corvet's library.

Alan sat back in his chair, smiling a little. It had not been for him, then, that pretense of almost mocking cordiality. Spearman was not trying to deceive or to influence Alan. It had been merely for Sherrill's benefit—the most effective weapon against Alan which Spearman could employ in Sherrill's presence. Spearman might still try to deny to Alan that it was he whom Alan had fought, but now, at least between themselves, there was to be no pretense about the antagonism and opposition they felt toward one another.

Prickling thrills of excitement were leaping through Alan, as he got up and moved about the room again. The room was on a corner, and there were two windows, one looking to the east over the white and blue expanse of the harbor and the lake; the other showing the roofs and chimneys, towers and domes of Chicago, reaching away block after block, mile after mile to the south and west, until they dimmed and blurred in the brown haze of the sunlit smoke. Power and possession, both far exceeding Alan's most extravagant dreams, were promised him by those papers which Sherrill had shown him. When he had read down the list of properties, he had no more feeling that such things could be his than he had at first that Corvet's house could be his. Relative to the house, this feeling changed when he had heard the intruder moving about in that house. And now, it was the sense that another was going to make him fight for those properties that was bringing to him the realization of his new power. He "had" something on that man—on Spearman. He did not know what that something was; no stretch of his thought, nothing that he knew about himself or others, could tell him. But, at the sight of him in the dark of Corvet's house, Spearman had cried out in horror, he had screamed at him the name of a sunken ship, and in terror had hurled his flashlight. It was true that Spearman's terror had not been at Alan Conrad. Rather it had been because Spearman had mistaken him for someone else—for an apparition. Then after learning that Alan was not an apparition, Spearman's attitude had not very greatly changed. He had fought and had been willing to kill rather than to be caught there.

Alan thought for a few moments. He would make sure he still "had" that something on Spearman, and would learn how far it went. He took up the telephone and asked for Spearman again. Again the voice answered: "Yes."

"I don't care whether you're busy," Alan said evenly. "I think you and I had better have a talk before we meet with Mr. Sherrill this afternoon. I am here in Mr. Corvet's office now and will be here for half an hour; then I'm going out."

Spearman made no reply but again hung up. Alan sat waiting, his watch upon the desk before him—tense, expectant, flashes of hot and cold passing through him. Ten minutes passed; then twenty. The telephone on Corvet's desk buzzed.

"Mr. Spearman says he will give you five minutes now," the switchboard girl said.

Alan breathed deeply with relief. Spearman had wanted to refuse to see him, but he had not refused. He had sent for him within the time Alan had appointed, waiting until just before it expired.

Alan picked up his watch, and after crossing to the other office, found Spearman alone. There was no pretense of courtesy now in Spearman's manner. He sat motionless at his desk, his bold eyes fixed on Alan intently. Alan closed the door behind him and advanced toward the desk.

"I thought we'd better have some explanation," he said, "about our meeting last night."

"Our meeting?" Spearman repeated. His eyes had narrowed watchfully.

"You told Mr. Sherrill that you were in Duluth and that you only arrived back in Chicago this morning. Of course, you don't really mean to stick to that story with me!"

"What are you talking about?" Spearman demanded.

"I know exactly where you were a part of last evening, and you know that I know. I only want to know what explanation you have to offer."

Spearman leaned forward and growled, "Talk sense and talk it fast, if you have anything to say to me!"

"I haven't told Mr. Sherrill that I found you at the Corvet house last night, but I don't want you to doubt for a minute that I know you . . . and about your damning of Benjamin Corvet, and your cry about saving the *Miwaka*!"

A flash of blood came to Spearman's face, but it was just one flash—no more. Yet Alan, in his excitement, was sure of it. He turned and, while Spearman sat chewing his cigar and staring at him, went out and partly closed the door. Then, suddenly, he reopened it and looked back in and reclosed it sharply. Shaking a little, went on his way. As he had looked back that second time at the determined, powerful man at his desk, what he had seen in Spearman's face was fear—fear of himself and fear of Alan Conrad of Blue Rapids, Kansas. Yet it was not the sort of fear that weakens or dismays; it was the sort which, merely warning of danger close at hand, leads one to use every means within his power to save himself.

Alan, still trembling excitedly, returned to his chair in Benjamin Corvet's office to await Sherrill. He felt sure now that it was not Alan Conrad that Spearman was opposing, not even as the apparent successor to the controlling stock of Corvet, Sherrill and Spearman. Rather it was that Alan resembled someone—someone whose apparition had seemed to come to Spearman. It might also, Alan thought, have come to Corvet.

With this resemblance in his mind, Alan reasoned, Spearman seemed to have felt a threat in Alan's presence—an active, present threat. Alan could not imagine what the nature of that threat could be. Was something still concealed in Corvet's house which Spearman feared Alan would find? Or was it merely that Alan resembled someone—his mother, perhaps? In what had been told him, and in all that he had been able to learn about himself, Alan had found no mention of his mother. No mention, indeed, of any woman. There had been definite mention of but one thing which seemed to connect him with all of these new experiences: the mention of a lost ship, the *Miwaka*.

That name had stirred Alan as soon as he had heard it, the first feeling he had been able to get of any possible connection between himself and these people here. Spoken by himself just now it had stirred—queerly stirred—Spearman. What was it, then, that he, Alan Conrad, had to do with the *Miwaka?* Spearman might . . . must have had something to do with it. So must Corvet. But for himself—he was not even three years old when the *Miwaka* was lost! Beyond and above all other questions, what did Constance Sherrill have to do with it?

She had continued to believe that Corvet's disappearance was in some way related to her. Alan would rather trust her intuition as to this than to believe Sherrill's contrary opinion. Yet she, certainly, could have had no direct connection with a ship lost at about the time she was born, and before the time her father had allied himself with the firm of Corvet, Sherrill and Spearman. In the misty warp and question of these events, Alan could find nothing which could have involved her . . . .

Suddenly, he realized that he was thinking about her more than he was thinking about Spearman—more, at that moment, than about the mystery which surrounded himself.

*　*　*

Constance Sherrill, going about her shopping at Field's, was feeling the strangeness of the experience she had shared that morning with Alan when she had completed for him the Indian creation legend, and had repeated the ship rhymes of his boyhood. But now her more active thought was about Henry Spearman, for she had a luncheon engagement with him at one o'clock. He always liked one to be prompt at appointments; he either did not keep an engagement at all, or he was on the minute, neither early nor late, except for very unusual circumstance. Constance could never achieve such accurate punctuality, so several minutes before the appointed hour she went to the agreed corner of the silverware department.

She absorbed herself intently with the selection of her purchase as one o'clock approached. She was sure that after his three days absence he would be a moment early rather than late. But after selecting what she wanted, she monopolized several minutes more of the salesman's time in showing her what she had no intention of purchasing, before she picked out Henry's vigorous step from the confusion of ordinary footfalls in the aisle behind her. Though she had determined, a few moments before, to punish him a little, she turned quickly.

"Sorry I'm late, Connie." That meant that it was no ordinary business matter that had detained him; however, there was nothing else unusual in his tone.

"It's certainly your turn to be the tardy one," she admitted.

"I'd never take my turn if I could help it, particularly just after being away; you know that."

She turned carelessly to the clerk. "I'll take that too . . . ." She indicated the trinket she had examined last. "Send it please. I've finished here now, Henry."

"I thought you didn't like that sort of thing." His glance had gone to the bit of frippery in the clerk's hand.

"I don't," she confessed.

"Then don't buy it. She doesn't want that; don't send it," he commanded the salesman.

"Very well, sir."

Henry touched her arm and turned her away. She flushed a little, but she was not displeased. She didn't really want to buy anything more; she just did not want to be seen waiting. Any of the other men she knew would have let her waste the twenty dollars; they would not have admitted that such a sum made the slightest difference to her or, by inference, to them. But Henry was always willing to admit that there had been a time when money meant much to him, and he gained respect from that admission.

The tea room at such a department store as Field's offered to young people opportunities for dining together without furnishing reason for even connecting their names too intimately, if one was not seen there with the same man too often. There was something essentially casual and unpremeditated about it, as if the man and the woman, both shopping and both hungry, had just happened to meet and go to lunch together.

As Constance had grown closer to Henry Spearman in her thought, and particularly since she had been considering marrying him, she had clung deliberately to this unplanned appearance about their meetings. She felt something thrilling in this casualness too. Spearman's bigness, which always attracted eyes to him in a crowd, was merely the first and most obvious of the things which kept attention on him. There were few women who, having caught sight of the big, handsome, decisive, carefully groomed man, could look away at once. Constance suspected that ten years before it might have been the eyes of shop-girls that followed Spearman with the greatest interest, and she was certain no one could find anything flashy about him now. What he compelled now was admiration and respect alike for his good looks and his appearance of personal achievement. This tribute was very different from the tolerance granted those boys brought up as irresponsible inheritors of privilege like herself.

As they reached the restaurant and passed between the rows of tables, women looked up at him. Oblivious apparently to their gaze, he chose a table a little removed and away from the others, where waitresses hurried to take his order, recognizing one whose time was important. She glanced across at him when she had settled herself and the first polite exchanges of their being together were finished.

"I took a visitor down to your office this morning."

Constance was aware that she had really taken Alan Conrad down to confer with her father. She also knew, since Henry was there, that her father would not act without his agreement on any disposition made regarding Alan. She wondered what that disposition had been.

"Did you like him, Henry?"

"Like him?" She would have thought that the reply was merely inattentive, but Henry was never merely that.

"I hoped you would."

He did not answer at once. The waitress brought their order, and served them. Then, as the waitress moved away, he looked across at Constance with a long scrutiny.

"You hoped I would." he repeated, with his slow smile. "Why?"

"He seemed to be in a difficult position and to be bearing himself well, but Mother was horrid to him."

"How was she horrid?"

"About the one thing which, most of all, could hardly be called his fault . . . about his relationship to . . . Mr. Corvet. But he stood up to her!"

Spearman's eyes were intense as he gazed at her.

"You've seen a great deal of him, yesterday and today, your father tells me," he observed.

"Yes." As she put her cup down, she told him about her first meeting with Alan and about their conversation of the morning and the queer awakening in him of those half memories which seemed to connect him in some way with the lakes.

She felt the glow in her face now and then with feeling, and once she was surprised at finding her eyes wet with emotion when she had finished telling Henry about showing Alan the picture of his father. Henry listened intently, eating slowly. When she stopped, he appeared to be considering something.

"That's all he told you about himself?" he inquired.

"Yes."

"And all you told him?"

"He asked me some things about the lakes and about the *Miwaka*, which was lost so long ago . . . he said he'd found reference to that and wanted to know whether it was a ship. I told him about it and the drum which made people think that the crew were not all lost."

"The drum! What made you speak of that?" Irritation in his tone startled her, and she looked quickly up at him.

"I mean," he offered, moderating his voice, "why did you drag in a crazy superstition like that? You don't believe in the drum, do you, Connie?"

"It would be so interesting if someone really had been saved and if the drum had told the truth, that sometimes I think I'd like to believe in it. Wouldn't you Henry?"

"No," he said abruptly. "No!" Then quickly:

"It's plain enough that you like him," he remarked.

She reflected seriously. "Yes, I do; though I hadn't thought of it just that way, because I was thinking most about the position he was in and about . . . Uncle Benny. But I do like him."

"So do I," Spearman said with a seeming heartiness that pleased her. He broke a piece of bread on the tablecloth, and began to roll it into little balls with his well-shaped fingers. "At least I should like him, Connie, if I had the sort of privilege you have, to think whether I liked or disliked him. I've had to consider him from another point of view—whether I could trust him, or must distrust him."

"Distrust?" Constance bent toward him impulsively in her surprise. "Distrust him? In relation to what? Why?"

"In relation to Corvet, Sherrill and Spearman, Connie, the company that involves your interests and your father's and mine, and the interests of many other people—small stockholders who have no influence in its management, and whose interests I have to look after for them. A good many of them, as you know, are our own men—our old skippers and mates and families of men who have died in our service, and who have left their savings in stock in our ships."

"I don't understand, Henry."

"I've had to think of Conrad this morning in the same way as I've had to think of Ben Corvet in recent years . . . as a threat against the interests of those people."

Her color rose, and her pulse quickened. Henry had never talked to her, except in the merest references, about his relations with Uncle Benny. She had recognized this was a subject on which they were opposed. Since the quarrels between the old friend whom she had loved from childhood and Henry, who wished to become more than a mere friend to her now, had grown more violent, she had purposely avoided mentioning Uncle Benny to Henry, and he, quite as consciously, had avoided the subject as well.

"I've known for a good many years," Spearman said reluctantly, "that Ben Corvet's brain was seriously affected. He recognized that himself even earlier, and admitted it to himself when he took me off my ship to take charge of the company. I might have gone with other people then, or started in as a ship owner myself. But in view of his condition, Ben made me promises that offered me most.

"Afterwards his malady progressed so that his mental qualities were affected. His judgment was impaired, and he planned and would have carried out many things which would have been disastrous for the company. I had to fight him, for the company's sake and for my own sake, and that of the others whose interests were at stake. Your father came to see that what I was doing was for the company's good, and he has learned to trust me. But you . . . you couldn't see that quite so directly, of course, and you thought that I didn't . . . like Ben, that there was some lack in me which made me fail to appreciate him."

"No, not that," Constance denied quickly. "Not that, Henry."

"What was it then, Connie? You thought me ungrateful to him? I realized that I owed a great deal to him, and the only way I could pay that debt was to do exactly what I did—oppose him and seem to push into his place and appear to be an ingrate. Because I did that, Ben's been a respected and honored man in this town all these last years, which he couldn't have remained if I'd let him have his way, or if I told others why I had to do what I did. I didn't care what others thought about me, but I did care what you thought. If you couldn't see what I was up against because of your affection for him, why . . . that was all right too."

"No, it wasn't all right," she denied most fiercely, her cheeks reddening. A throbbing was in her throat, which for an instant stopped her. "You should have told me, Henry, or . . . I should have been able to see."

"I couldn't tell you . . . dear," he said the last word very distinctly, but so low that she could scarcely hear. "I couldn't tell now . . . if

Ben hadn't gone away as he has and this other fellow come. I couldn't tell you when you wanted me to keep caring so much for your uncle Benny, and he was trying to hurt me with you."

She bent toward him, her lips parted, but now she did not speak. She had never really known Henry until this moment. She felt she had thought of him always as strong, almost brutal, fighting down fiercely, mercilessly, his opponents and welcoming contest for the joy of overwhelming by his own decisive strength and power. And she had been almost ready to marry this man for his strength and dominance from those qualities. Now she knew that he was merciful too—indeed, more than merciful. In the very contest where she had thought of him as most selfish and regardless of another, she had most completely misapprehended.

"I ought to have seen!" she rebuked herself to him. "Surely, I should have seen that was it!" Her hand, in reproach of her feeling, reached toward him across the table. He grasped it and held it in his large, strong hand, which in its touch, was very tender too. She had never allowed any such demonstration as this before, but now she let her hand remain in his.

"How could you see?" he defended her. "He never showed to you the side he showed to me and—in these last years, anyway— never to me the side he showed to you." But after what has happened this week, you can understand now, and you can see why I have to distrust the young fellow who's come to claim Ben Corvet's palace."

"Claim!" Constance repeated. She drew her hand quietly away from his now. "Why, Henry, I did not know he claimed anything; he didn't even know when he came here . . . "

"He seems, like Ben Corvet," Henry said slowly, "to have the characteristic of showing one side to you, another to me, Connie. With you, of course, he claimed nothing; but at the office . . . your father showed him this morning the instruments of transfer that Ben seems to have left conveying to him all Ben had, his other properties and his interest in Corvet, Sherrill and Spearman. I very naturally objected to the execution of those transfers, without considerable examination, in view of Corvet's mental condition and the fact that they put the controlling stock of our firm in the hands of a youth no one ever heard of and who, by his own story, had never seen a ship until yesterday. And when I didn't dismiss my business with a dozen men this morning to take him into the company, he claimed occasion to see me alone to threaten me."

"Threaten you, Henry? How? With what?"

"I couldn't quite make out myself, but that was his tone. He demanded an 'explanation,' but of exactly what, he didn't make clear. Ben apparently has given him the technical control of Corvet, Sherrill and Spearman. His idea, if I oppose him, evidently is to turn me out and take over the management himself."

Constance leaned back, confused. "He . . . Alan Conrad?" she questioned. "He can't have done that, Henry! Oh, he can't have meant that!"

"Maybe he didn't. I said I couldn't make out what he did mean," Spearman said. "Things have come upon him with rather a rush, of course, and you couldn't expect a country boy to get so many things straight. He's acting, I suppose, only in the way one might expect a boy to act who had been brought up in poverty on a Kansas prairie, and was handed the possible possession of a good many millions of dollars. It's better to believe that he's only lost his head. I haven't had the opportunity to tell your father these things yet, but I wanted you to understand why Conrad will hardly consider me a friend."

"I'll understand you now, Henry," she promised.

He gazed at her and started to speak. Then, as though postponing it on account of the place, he glanced around and took out his watch.

"You must go back?" she asked.

"No; I'm not going back to the office this afternoon, Connie, but I must call your father." He excused himself, and went to the nearest telephone.

9

At half-past three, Alan left the office. Sherrill had told him an hour earlier that Spearman had telephoned he would not be able to get back for a conference that afternoon, and Alan was certain now that in Spearman's absence Sherrill would do nothing further with respect to his affairs.

He stopped on the ground floor of the office building and bought copies of each of the afternoon papers. A line completely across the front page of one announced "Millionaire Ship Owner Missing!" The other papers printed at the same hour, did not display the story prominently, and even the one which did failed to make it the most conspicuous sensation. A line of larger and blacker type told of President Wilson's calling a special cabinet meeting, and as much space was given a bulletin about a local divorce suit. Alan was some time in finding the small print with the heading about a millionaire ship owner, and when he found it, he discovered that most of the space was devoted to a description of Corvet's share in the development of shipping on the lakes and the details of his past life, rather than any definite news concerning his fate.

The other papers printed almost identical items under small headlines at the bottom of their first pages. One's account was typical of what the others also published—that Benjamin Corvet, the senior but inactive partner of the great shipping firm of Corvet, Sherrill and Spearman, whose "disappearance" had been made the subject of sensational rumor, was "believed by his partner, Mr. Henry Spearman, to have simply gone away for a rest," and no anxiety was felt concerning him. Alan found no reference to himself nor any of the circumstances connected with Corvet's disappearance of which Sherrill had told him.

Alan threw the papers away. There was a car line two blocks west, which Sherrill had said would take him within a short distance of the house on Astor Street. But the fashionable neighborhood where the Sherrills—and now Alan himself—lived was less than half an hour's walk from the downtown district, and in the present turmoil of his thoughts, he wanted to walk.

Spearman, he reflected as he went, must have dictated the paragraphs he had just read in the papers. Sherrill, Alan knew, had wanted to keep the circumstances regarding Corvet from becoming public. But it was Spearman who, by speaking to the reporters, had determined what they must believe. And by so doing he had made it impossible for Alan to enroll aid from the newspapers or the police. Alan did not know whether he might have found it expedient to seek publicity, but should he decide to, he had not a single proof of anything he could tell. Sherrill, naturally, had retained the papers Corvet had left. Alan could not hope that Sherrill would believe him, and without Sherrill's aid he could not obtain credence from anyone else.

Was there, then, no one whom Alan could tell of his encounter with Spearman in Corvet's house, with probability of receiving belief? Alan had not been thinking directly of Constance Sherrill as he walked north to the Drive, but she was, in a way, present in all of his thoughts. She had shown interest in him, or at least in the position he was in, and sympathy. He had even begun to tell her about these things when he had spoken to her of some event in Corvet's house which had given him the name "*Miwaka*," and he had asked her if it was a ship. And there could be no possible consequent peril to her in telling her. The peril, if there was any, would be only to himself.

His step quickened. As he approached the Sherrill house, he saw an open roadster on the driveway with liveried chauffeur. He had seen that roadster, he recognized with a start, in front of the office building that morning when Constance had taken him into town. He turned into the walk and rang the bell.

The servant who opened the door knew him and accepted his right of entry to the house by asking Alan to enter. Alan went into the hall and waited for the servant to follow. "Is Miss Sherrill home?" he asked.

"I'll see, sir." The man disappeared.

Alan did not hear Constance's voice in reply to the servant's message, but he did hear Spearman's unmistakably vigorous tones. The servant returned. "Miss Sherrill will see you in a minute, sir."

Through the wide doorway to the drawing room, Alan could see the smaller, portiered entrance to the room beyond—Sherrill's study. The curtains parted, and Constance and Spearman came into this inner doorway; they stood there an instant talking. As Constance started away, Spearman drew her back to him and kissed her, then returned to the drawing room. Alan's shoulders spontaneously straightened, and his hands clenched. He did not look away, and as she approached, she became aware that he had seen.

She came to him, very quiet and very flushed; then she was quite pale as she asked him, "You wanted to see me?"

He was as white as she and could not speak at once. When he composed himself, he said, "You told me last night, Miss Sherrill," he said, "that the last thing that Mr. Corvet did—the last that you know of—was to warn you against one of your friends. Who was that?"

She reddened uneasily. "You mustn't attach any importance to that; I didn't mean you to. There was no reason for what Mr. Corvet said, except in Mr. Corvet's own mind. He had a quite unreasonable animosity . . ."

"Against Mr. Spearman, you mean."

She did not answer.

"His animosity *was* against Mr. Spearman, Miss Sherrill, wasn't it? That is the only animosity of Mr. Corvet's that anyone has told me about."

"Yes."

"Thank you." He turned, and not waiting for the man, let himself out. He should have known, when learning that Spearman had announced he would be unable to get back to the office, that he was with Constance.

He walked swiftly around the block to his own house and let himself in at the front door with his key. The house was warm; a shaded lamp on the table in the larger library was lighted, a fire was burning in the fireplace, and the rooms had been swept and dusted. The Indian came into the hall to take his coat and hat.

"Dinner is at seven," Wassaquam announced. "You want some change about that?"

"No; seven is all right."

Alan went upstairs to his room—the room next to Corvet's that he had appropriated for his own use the night before—and found it now prepared for his occupancy. His suitcase, unpacked, had been put away in the closet; the clothing it had contained had been put in the dresser drawers, and the shaving articles were arranged on top of the dresser and in the cabinet of the connecting bath. So, clearly, Wassaquam had accepted him as an occupant of the house, though upon what status Alan could not guess. He had spoken of Wassaquam to Constance as his servant; but Wassaquam was not that; he was Corvet's servant—faithful and devoted to Corvet, Constance had said—and Alan could not think of Wassaquam as the sort of man that "went with the house." The Indian's manner toward Alan had been noncommittal, even stolid.

When Alan came down again to the first floor, Wassaquam was nowhere about, but he heard sounds on the basement floor. He went part way down the service stairs and saw the Indian in the kitchen preparing dinner. Wassaquam had not heard his approach, and Alan stood an instant watching the Indian's tall, thin figure and quick movements of his disproportionately small, well-shaped hands, almost like a woman's; then he scuffed his foot on the stair, and Wassaquam turned swiftly about.

"Anybody been here today, Judah?" Alan asked.

"No, Alan. I called tradesmen; they came. There were young men from the newspapers."

"They came here, did they? Then why did you say no one came?"

"I did not let them in."

"What did you tell them?"

"Nothing."

"Why not?"

"Henry telephoned I was to tell them nothing."

"You mean Henry Spearman?"

"Yes."

"Do you take orders from him, Judah?"

"I took that order, Alan."

Alan hesitated. "You've been here in the house all day?"

"Yes, Alan."

Alan went back to the first floor and into the smaller library. The room was dark with the early winter dusk, and he switched on the light; then he knelt and pulled out one of the drawers he had seen Spearman searching through the night before. He carefully examined the papers in it one by one, but found nothing of importance. He pulled the drawer completely out and sounded the wall behind it and the partitions on both sides, but they appeared solid. He put the drawer back in and went on to examine the next one, and after that, the others. The clocks in the house had been wound, as presently the clock in the library struck six, and another in the hall chimed the same hour.

An hour later, when the clocks sounded again, Alan looked up and saw Wassaquam's small black eyes, deep in their large eye sockets, fixed on him intently through the doorway. How long the Indian had been there, Alan could not guess; he had not heard his step.

"What are you looking for, Alan?" the Indian asked.

Alan reflected a moment. "Mr. Sherrill thought that Mr. Corvet might have left a record of some sort here for me, Judah. Do you know of anything like that?"

"Ben put papers in all these drawers; he put them upstairs, too, where you have seen."

"Nowhere else, Judah?"

"If he put things anywhere else, Alan, I have not seen. Dinner is served, Alan."

Alan went to the lavatory on the first floor and washed the dust from his hands and face; then he went into the dining room. A place had been set at the dining room table around the corner from the place where, as the rug showed, the lonely occupant of the house had been accustomed to sit. Benjamin Corvet's armchair, with its worn leather back, had been left against the wall; so had another unworn armchair which Alan thought must have been Mrs. Corvet's. An armless chair had been set for Alan between their places. Wassaquam, having served the dinner, took his place behind Alan's chair, ready to pass him what he needed; but the Indian's silent, watchful presence there behind him where he could not see his face disturbed Alan, and he twisted himself around to look at him.

"Would you mind, Judah," he inquired, "if I asked you to stand over there instead of where you are?"

The Indian, without answering, moved around to the other side of the table, where he stood facing Alan.

"You're a Chippewa, aren't you, Judah?" Alan asked.

"Yes, Alan."

"Have you ever heard of the drum they talk about up there, the one they say sounds when a ship goes down on the lake?"

The Indian's eyes sparkled excitedly. "Yes," he said.

"That is old Indian country up there, Alan. L'Arbre Croche—Cross Village. A big town of Ottawas was there in the old days; Pottawatomies too, and Chippewas. Indians now are all Christians; Catholics and Methodists who hold camp meetings and speak beautifully. But some things of the old days are left. The drum is like that. Everybody knows that it sounds for those who die on the lake."

"How do they know, Judah? How do you yourself know?"

"I have heard it. It sounded for my father."

"How was that?"

"Like this. My father sold some bullocks to a man who kept a store on Beaver Island, Alan. No Indian liked him. He would not hand anything to an Indian, or wrap anything in paper for an Indian. Say it was like this: An Indian comes in to buy salt pork. First the man would get the money. Then, Alan, he would take his hook and pull the pork up out of the barrel and throw it on the dirty floor for the Indian to pick up. He said the Indians must take their food off the floor, like dogs.

"My father had to take the bullocks to the man, across to Beaver Island. He had a Mackinaw boat, very little, with a sail made brown by boiling it with tanbark, so that it would not wear out. At first the Indians did not know who the bullocks were for, so they helped him. He tied the legs of the bullocks, the front legs and the back legs together, and the Indians helped him put them in the boat. When they found out the bullocks were for the man on Beaver Island, the Indians would not help him any longer. He had to take them across alone. Besides, it was bad weather, the beginning of a storm.

"He went away, and my mother went to pick berries . . . I was small then. Pretty soon I saw my mother coming back. She had no berries, and her hair was hanging down, and she was wailing. She took me in her arms and said my father was dead. Other Indians came around and asked her how she knew, and she said she had heard the drum. The Indians went out to listen."

"Did you go?"

"Yes; I went."

"How old were you, Judah?"

"Five years."

"That was the time you heard it?"

"Yes; it would beat once, then there would be silence; then it would beat again. It frightened us to hear it. The Indians would scream and beat their bodies with their hands when the sound came. We listened until night; there was storm all the time growing greater in the dark, but no rain. The drum would beat once; then nothing; then it would beat again once . . . never two or more times. So we knew it was for my father. It is supposed the bullocks came untied and tipped the boat over. They found the body of one of the bullocks in the water near the island, and its feet were untied. My father's body was on the beach near there."

"Did you ever hear of a ship called the *Miwaka*, Judah?"

"That was long ago," the Indian answered.

"They say that the drum beat wrong when the *Miwaka* went down, that it was one beat short of the right number."

"That was long ago," Wassaquam merely repeated.

"Did Mr. Corvet ever speak to you about the *Miwaka*?"

"No; he asked me once if I had ever heard the drum. I told him."

Wassaquam removed the dinner and brought Alan a dessert. He returned to stand in the place across the table Alan had assigned to him, and stood looking down at Alan, steadily and thoughtfully.

"Do I look like anyone you ever saw before, Judah?" Alan inquired of him.

"No."

"Is that what you were thinking, that I do not resemble anyone you have ever seen?"

"That is what I was thinking. Coffee will be served in the library, Alan."

Alan crossed to the library and seated himself in the chair where his father had been accustomed to sit. Wassaquam brought him the single small cup of coffee, lit the small spirit lamp on the smoking stand, and moved that over; then he went away. When he had finished his coffee, Alan went into the smaller connecting room and recommenced his examination of the drawers under the bookshelves. He could hear the Indian moving about his tasks, and twice Wassaquam came to the door of the room and looked in on him. He did not offer to say anything, and Alan did not speak to him. At ten o'clock, Alan stopped his search and went back to his chair in the library. He dozed off, but awoke with a start and a feeling that someone had been bending over him and looked up. He found himself gazing into Wassaquam's face. The Indian had been scrutinizing him with intent, anxious curiosity. He moved away, but Alan called him back.

"When Mr. Corvet disappeared, Judah, you went to look for him up at Manistique, where he was born—at least Mr. Sherrill said that was where you went. Why did you think you would find him there?"

"In the end, I think, a man maybe goes back to the place where he began. That's all, Alan."

"In the end! What do you mean by that? What do you think has become of Mr. Corvet?"

"I think now . . . Ben's dead."

"What makes you think that?"

"Nothing makes me think; I think it myself."

"I see. You mean you have no reason more than others for thinking it, but that is what you believe."

"Yes." Wassaquam went away, and Alan heard him on the back stairs, ascending to his room.

When Alan went to his own room, after making the rounds to see that the house was locked, a droning chant came to him from the third floor. He paused in the hall and listened, then went up to the floor above.

A flickering light came to him through the half-open door of a room at the front of the house, and he went a little way toward it and looked in. Two thick candles were burning before a crucifix, below which the Indian knelt, prayer book in hand and rocking to and fro as he droned his supplications.

A word or two came to Alan, but without them Wassaquam's occupation was plain: He was praying for the repose of the dead—the Catholic chant taught to him, as it had undoubtedly been taught to his fathers, by the French Jesuits of the lakes. The intoned chant for Corvet's soul, by a man who had heard the drum, followed Alan as he returned to his room.

During the evening, he had not been able to determine Wassaquam's attitude toward him. Having no one else, Alan had been obliged to put a certain amount of trust in the Indian. This was why he had explained to Wassaquam that morning that the desk and the drawers in the little room off Corvet's bedroom had been forced. It was also why he had warned him to see that no one without proper business there be allowed in the house. Wassaquam had appeared to accept this order, but now Wassaquam had implied that it was not because of Alan's order that he had refused reporters admission to the house. The developments of the day had tremendously altered things in one respect: The night before, Alan had not thought of the intruder in the house as one who ordinarily claimed any right of entrance there. But now he knew it to be the one person who, except for Sherrill, might most naturally come to the house—and one to whom Wassaquam appeared to grant a certain right of direction of affairs there.

At this thought, Alan became angry; the house was his—Alan's. Alan noted particularly that when Sherrill had showed him the list of properties whose transfer had been left to Sherrill's discretion, the house was not among them. Corvet, he understood now, had left Sherrill no discretion as to the house. Corvet's direct, unconditional gift of the house by deed to Alan had been one of Sherrill's reasons for believing that if Corvet had left anything which could explain his disappearance, it would be found in the house.

Unless Spearman had visited the house during the day and obtained what he had been looking for the night before—and Alan believed he had not done this—it was still in the house. Alan's hands clenched; he would not give Spearman such a chance as that again, and he himself would continue his search of the house—exhaustively, room by room, article of furniture by article of furniture.

Alan started and went quickly to the open door of his room, as he heard voices somewhere within the house. One of the voices he recognized as Wassaquam's; the other—indistinct, thick, accusing—was unknown to him; it certainly was not Spearman's. He had not heard Wassaquam go downstairs, and he had not heard the doorbell, so he ran first to the third floor, but the room where he had seen Wassaquam was empty. He descended again swiftly to the first floor, and found Wassaquam standing in the front hall alone.

"Who was here, Judah?" Alan demanded.

"A man," the Indian answered stolidly. "He was drunk; I put him out."

"What did he come for?"

"He came to see Ben. I put him out; he is gone, Alan."

Alan flung open the front door and looked out, but saw no one.

"What did he want of Mr. Corvet, Judah?"

"I do not know. I told him Ben was not here; he was angry, but he went away."

"Has he ever come here before?"

"Yes; he comes twice."

"He has been here twice?"

"More than that. Every year he comes twice, Alan. Once he came oftener."

"How long has he been doing that?"

"Since I can remember."

"Is he a friend of Mr. Corvet?"

"No friend . . . no!"

"But Mr. Corvet saw him when he came here?"

"Always, Alan."

"And you don't know at all what he came about?"

"How should I know? No; I do not."

Alan got his hat and coat. The disappearance of the man might mean only that he had hurried away, but it might mean too that he was still lurking near the house. Alan had decided to make the circuit of the house to determine that. But as he came out on to the porch, a figure more than a block away to the south strode with uncertain step out into the light of a street lamp, halted, faced about and shook his fist back at the house. Alan pulled the Indian out on to the porch.

"Is that the man, Judah?"

"Yes, Alan."

Alan ran down the steps and at full speed after the man. The other had turned west at the corner where Alan had seen him, and even though Alan slipped as he tried to run on the snowy walks, he must be gaining fast on him. He saw him again, when he had reached the corner where the man had turned, traveling westward with that quick uncertain step toward Clark Street, and at that corner the man turned south. But when Alan reached the corner, he was nowhere in sight. To the south, Clark Street reached away, garish with electric signs and with a dozen saloons to every block. That the man was drunk made it probable he had turned into one of those places. Alan went into every one of them for fully a half mile and looked about, but found no one even resembling the man he had been following. He retraced his steps for several blocks, still looking; then he gave it up and returned eastward toward the Drive.

The side street leading to the Drive was less well lighted; dark entry ways and alleys opened on it, but the night was clear. The stars, with the shining sword of Orion almost overhead, gleamed with midwinter brightness, and to the west the crescent of the moon was hanging and throwing faint shadows over the snow. Alan could see the end of the street and, beyond the yellow glow of the distant boulevard lights, the smooth, chill surface of the lake. A white light rode above it, and below the white light, he saw a red speck—the masthead and port lights of a steamer, northward bound. Farther out, a second white glow appeared, and below it a green speck—a starboard light. The rhyme he had learned that day enabled him to recognize in these lights two ships passing one another at the harbor mouth.

"Green to green . . . ," Alan murmured to himself. "Green to green . . . red to red, perfect safety, go ahead!" he repeated.

It brought him, with marvelous vividness, back to Constance Sherrill. Events since he had talked with her that morning had put them far apart once more, but in another way, they were being drawn closer together. For he knew now that she was caught as well as he in the mesh of consequences of acts not their own. Benjamin Corvet, in the anguish of the last hours before fear of those consequences had driven him away, had given her a warning against Spearman so wild that it had defeated itself. For Alan merely to repeat that warning, with no more than he yet knew, would be equally futile. But into the contest between Spearman and himself—a contest, he had begun to feel, which threatened to destroy either Spearman or him—she had entered. Her happiness and her future were at stake. Her fate, he was certain now, depended upon his discovering the events tied tightly in the mystery of Alan's own identity—which Spearman knew—and the threat of which at moments appalled him. Alan winced as there came to him, in the darkness of the street, a vision of Constance in Spearman's arms and of the kiss he had seen that afternoon.

At that moment he staggered, slipped, and fell suddenly forward onto his knees under a stunning, crushing blow on his head from behind. On the edge of consciousness, he struggled, twisting himself about to grasp his assailant. He caught the man's clothing and tried to drag himself up, fighting blindly, dazed, unable to see or think. He shouted aloud. He shouted again, and seemed to hear answering cries in the distance. But the weight and strength of the other was bearing him down again to his knees. He tried to slip aside from it, to rise. Then another blow, crushing and sickening, descended on his head, and now even hearing left him. Unconscious, he fell forward onto the snow and lay still.

IO

"The name seems like 'Sherrill,' " the intern agreed. "He said it before when we had him on the table upstairs, and he has said it now twice distinctly . . . 'Sherrill.' "

"Do you think that's his name?"

"I wouldn't say so; he seems to be trying to speak to someone named Sherrill."

The nurse waited a few minutes. "Yes, that's how it seems to me, sir. He said something that sounded like 'Connie' a while ago, and once he said 'Jim.' There are only four Sherrills in the telephone book, two of them in Evanston and one way out in Minooka."

"The other?"

"They're only about six blocks away from where he was picked up. They are on the Drive . . . the Lawrence Sherrills."

The intern whistled softly and looked more interestedly at his patient's features. He glanced at his watch, which showed the hour of the morning to be half past four. "You'd better make a note of it," he said. "He's not a Chicagoan; his clothes have Kansas store markings on them. He'll be conscious sometime during the day;

there's only a slight fracture, and . . . perhaps you'd better call the Sherrill house, anyway. If he's not known there, then no harm is done, and if he is one of their friends . . . ."

The nurse nodded and moved off.

Thus it was that at quarter to five Constance Sherrill was awakened by the knocking of one of the servants at her father's door. Lawrence Sherrill went downstairs to take the call where he could talk without disturbing Mrs. Sherrill. Constance, a robe over her shoulders, stood at the top of the stairs and waited. It became plain to her that whatever had happened had been to Alan Conrad.

"Yes . . . Yes . . . You are giving him every possible care? . . . At once."

Constance ran part way down the stairs and met her father as he came up. He told her of the situation briefly.

"He was attacked on the street late last night. He was unconscious when they found him and took him to the hospital, and has been unconscious ever since. They say it was apparently an ordinary street robbery. I shall go at once, of course, but you can do nothing. He would not know you if you came, and of course he is in competent hands. They do not know as yet how seriously he may be injured."

She waited in the hall while her father dressed, after calling the garage on the house telephone to have a car brought around for him.

When her father had gone, Constance returned anxiously to her own rooms. He had promised to call her after reaching the hospital as soon as he had learned the particulars of Alan's condition. It was ridiculous, of course, to attach any responsibility to either her father or herself for what might have happened to Alan. An attack such as this might have happened to anyone, yet she felt that they were in part responsible.

Alan Conrad had come to Chicago not by their direction, but by Benjamin Corvet's, and with Uncle Benny gone they had been the ones who met him and received him into their own home. But they had not thought to warn him of the dangers of the city, and then they had let him go to live alone in the house on Astor Street with no better advisor than Wassaquam. Now, perhaps because they had not warned him, he had met injury, and it might be more than just injury; he might be dying.

She walked anxiously up and down in her room, clutching her robe about her, as she knew it might be some time before she would hear from her father. She went to the telephone on the stand beside her bed and called Henry Spearman at his apartment. His house-man answered, and after an interval, Henry's voice came to her. She told him all that she knew of what had occurred.

"Do you want me to go over to the hospital?" he asked at once.

"No; Father has gone. There is nothing anyone can do. I'll call you again as soon as I hear from Father."

He seemed to appreciate from her tone the anxiety she felt, and he tried to quiet and encourage her. She listened to what he said, replied to him, and then got off the telephone so as not to interfere with the expected call from her father. She moved about the room again, oppressed by the long wait, until the phone rang, and she sprang to answer. It was her father calling from the hospital. Alan apparently had had a few moments of consciousness, but Sherrill had not been allowed to see him, and now Alan was sleeping. As Alan was reacting well, the doctors said there was no reason for anxiety, but Sherrill would wait at the hospital a little longer to make sure. Constance's breath caught at this news, and her eyes filled with tears of relief. She called Henry again, and he evidently had been waiting, for he answered at once. He listened without comment as she repeated her father's report.

"All right," he said, when she had finished. "I'm coming over, Connie."

"Now?"

"Yes, right away."

"You must give me time to dress!" His assumption of the right to come to her at this early hour recalled to her forcibly the closer relationship which Henry now assumed to exist between them. Indeed, he assumed it was not just existing, but progressing. And had not she acknowledged that relationship by telephoning him during her anxiety? She had not thought how that must appear to him; she had not thought about it at all; she had just done it.

Constance had been one of those who think of the decision to marry in terms of question and answer, a moment when decision is formulated and spoken. She had supposed that by withholding reply to Henry's question—put even before Uncle Benny went away—she was maintaining the same relation between Henry and herself. But now she was discovering that this was not so, that Henry had not required formal answer because he considered that answer superfluous. Were she to accept him now, it would not establish a new bond but would merely acknowledge what was already understood. She had accepted that, had she not, when in the rush of her feeling the day before, she had thrust her hand into his, and she accepted it more undeniably when he seized and kissed her and she did not resist or object.

Not that she had sought or even consciously permitted his public embrace and kiss. Actually, it had surprised her. She and Henry had been alone together when Alan Conrad had been announced, and when she had arisen to go Henry had tried to detain her. Then, as he looked at her, impulse seemed to conquer him, and he caught her, irresistibly. Amazed, bewildered, she had looked up at him, and he bent and kissed her. The power of his arms around her—she could feel them yet—frightened her yet enthralled her at the same time. But his lips against her cheek . . . she had turned her lips away from him! She had been quite unable to know how she had felt then, because at that instant she realized that she had been seen. So she had disengaged herself as quickly as possible, and after Alan was gone, she had fled to her room without going back to Henry at all.

How could she have expected Henry to have interpreted that flight from him as disapproval when she had not meant it as that?

She did not know herself what led her to leave him as she did, and this did not mean she had disavowed the new relationship Henry now felt established. Did she wish to disavow it now? What had happened had come sooner than she had wished, and with less will on her part than she had expected, but she knew it was only what she anticipated would eventually happen. The pride she had felt in being with Henry, she realized, was only in anticipation of the pride she would experience as his wife. When she considered the feelings of her family and her friends, she knew that some would deplore Henry's simple background, but most would be more than satisfied. They would even boast about Henry, entertain him in her honor, and show him off. There was no one—now that poor Uncle Benny was gone—who would seriously deplore it all.

Constance thought she had recognized no relic of uneasiness from Uncle Benny's last appeal to her. At least, she thought she had understood that. But now there seemed to be a change in the circumstances of that understanding; because of what had happened to Alan, she found that she was redefining to herself her relationship with Henry . . . .

. . . No. It had nothing to do with Henry, of course. It referred only to Benjamin Corvet. Uncle Benny had "gone away" from his house on Astor Street, leaving his place there to his son, Alan Conrad. Something which had disturbed and excited Alan had happened to him on the first night he stayed in the house, and now it appeared he had been prevented from passing a second night there. What had prevented him had been an attempted robbery on the street, her father had said. But suppose it had been something other than robbery? She could not formulate more definitely this thought, but it persisted, and she could not deny it entirely and shake it off.

In the late afternoon of that day, this same thought was becoming far more definite and persistent to Alan Conrad. He had been awake and lucid since shortly after noon, but he was still bruised and sore, and the throbbing headache was beginning to give way to a lassitude, a languor which revisited incoherence upon him whenever he tried to think. He shifted himself on his bed and called the nurse.

"How long is it likely I will have to stay here?" he asked her.

"The doctors think not less than two weeks, Mr. Conrad."

Two weeks! He realized as he lay silent that he must put out of his head now all expectation of ever finding in Corvet's house any such record as he had been looking for. If there had been any record, it unquestionably would be gone before he could get about again to seek it. If he had been hopeless of receiving credence for any accusation he might make against Spearman while he was in good health, how much more hopeless was it now, when everything he might say could be attributed to his injury and to his delirium! He could not even give orders for the safeguarding of the house and its contents—his own property—with assurance that they would be carried out.

The police and hospital attendants, he had learned, had no suspicion of anything but that he had been the victim of one of the footpads who had been attacking and robbing nightly during recent weeks. Sherrill, who had visited him about two o'clock, had showed that he suspected no other possibility. Alan could not prove otherwise. He had not seen the assailant's face, and it was most probable that if he had seen it, he would not have recognized it. But the man who had assailed him meant to kill, and he was no ordinary robber. That purpose, blindly recognized and fought by Alan in their struggle, had been unmistakable. Only the chance passers-by who had responded to Alan's shouts had prevented the execution of the assailant's purpose and driven the man to swift flight.

During his struggle with Spearman in Corvet's library, Alan had believed that Spearman might have killed him rather than be discovered there. Were there others to whom Alan's presence had become a threat so serious that they would proceed even to the length of calculated murder? He could not know that. The only safe plan was to assume that persons, in number unknown, had definite, vital interest in his removal, by violence or otherwise. Among them he must reckon Henry Spearman. And he would have to fight them alone. Sherrill's liking for him, and even Constance Sherrill's interest and sympathy, were nullified in practical intent by their admiration for, and complete confidence in, Spearman. It did not matter that Alan might believe that, in fighting Spearman, he was not only fighting for himself but for her. He knew now certainly that he must count her as belonging to Spearman. Things swam before him again dizzily as he thought of her, and he sank back and closed his eyes.

A little before six Constance Sherrill and Spearman called to inquire after him and were admitted for a few minutes to his room. She came to him, and bent over him while she spoke the few words of sympathy the nurse allowed, and then she stood back while Spearman spoke to him.

In the succeeding days, he saw her nearly every day, accompanied by either her father or Spearman. It was the full two weeks the nurse had allotted for his remaining in the hospital before he saw her alone.

They had brought him home the day before—she and her father in their car—to the house on Astor Street. He had insisted on returning there, refusing to come to their house as they offered. The doctor had prescribed outdoors and moderate exercise for him, and she made him promise to come and walk with her. He had gone to the Sherrill house about ten o'clock, and now they walked northward toward the park.

It was a mild and sunny morning with warm wind from the south which dried the last patches of snow from the lawns and the trickles of water across the walks. Looking to the land, one might say that spring would soon be on the way, but looking to the lake, midwinter still held. The counter of concrete, beyond the withered sod that edged the Drive, was sheathed in ice, and frozen-spray hummocks beyond steamed in the sun. Out as far as one could see, ice floes drifted close together, exposing here and there a bit of blue.

Wind, cold and chilling, blew across this ice field, absorbing the warm south breeze upon its flanks.

Glancing up at her companion from time to time, Constance saw color returning to his face, and he strode beside her quite steadily. Whatever was his inheritance, he certainly possessed stamina and vitality. A little less of either and he might not have recovered at all, much less have leaped back to strength as he had done. Since yesterday, she realized, the languor which held him was gone.

They halted a minute near the south entrance of the park at the St. Gaudens' statue of Lincoln, which he had not previously seen. The gaunt, sad figure, in ill-fitting clothes, seemed to recall something to him; for he glanced swiftly at her as they turned away.

"Miss Sherrill," he asked, "have you ever stayed out in the country?"

"I go to Northern Michigan, up by the Straits, almost every summer for part of the time, at least, and once in a while we open the house in the winter for a week or so. It's quite wild—trees and sand and shore, and the water. I've had some of my best times up in that beautiful country."

"You've never been out on the plains?"

"Just to pass through them on the train on the way to the West Coast."

"That would be in winter and spring; I was thinking more about the plains in late summer, when we—Jim and Betty, the children of the people I was with in Kansas . . ."

"I remember them."

"When we used to play at being pioneers in our sunflower shacks."

"Sunflower shacks?" she questioned.

"I was dreaming we were building them again when I was delirious just after I was hurt, it seems. I thought I was back in Kansas and was little again. The prairie was all brown as it is in late summer; brown billows of dried grass which let you see the chips of limestone and flint scattered on the ground beneath. And in the hollows there were acres and acres of sunflowers, three times as tall as either Jim or me and with stalks as thick as a man's wrist, where Jim and Betty and I—and you, Miss Sherrill—were playing."

"I?"

"Yes. We cut paths through the sunflowers with a corn knife," Alan continued, not looking at her, "and built houses in them by twining the cut stalks in and out among those still standing. I'd wondered, you see, what you must have been like when you were a little girl, so I suppose, when I was delirious, I saw you that way."

She had looked at him a little apprehensively, afraid that he was going to say something more, but his look reassured her.

"Then that," she hazarded, "must have been how the hospital people learned our name. I'd wondered about that. They said you were unconscious first, and then delirious, and that when you spoke you said, among other names, 'Connie' and 'Sherrill.' "

He colored and glanced away. "I thought they might have told you that, so I wanted you to know. They say that in a dream, or in delirium, after your brain establishes the first absurdity—like your playing out among the sunflowers with me when we were little— everything else is consistent. I wouldn't call a little girl 'Miss Sherrill,' of course. Ever since I've known you, I couldn't help thinking a great deal about you. You are not like anyone else I've ever known. But I didn't want you to think I thought of you . . . familiarly."

"I speak of you always as Alan to Father," she said.

He was silent for a moment. "They lasted hardly for a day, those sunflower houses, Miss Sherrill," he said quietly. "They withered almost as soon as they were made. Castles in Kansas, one might say! No one could live in them."

Apprehensive again, she colored. He had recalled to her, without meaning to do so, she thought, that he had seen her in Spearman's arms; she was quite sure that recollection was in his mind. But in spite of this—or rather because of it—she understood that he had formed his own impression of the relation between Henry and herself, and that consequently he was not likely to say anything more like this.

They had walked east, across the damp, dead turf to where the Drive leaves the shore and is built out into the lake. As they crossed to it on the smooth ice of the lagoon between, he took her arm to steady her.

"There is something I have been wanting to ask you," she said.

"Yes."

"That night when you were hurt . . . it was for robbery, they said. What do you think about it?" She watched him as he looked at her and then away, but his face was completely expressionless.

"The proceedings were a little too rapid for me to judge."

"But there was no demand upon you to give over your money before you were attacked?"

"No."

She breathed a little more quickly. "It must be a strange sensation," she observed, "to know that someone has tried to kill you."

"It must, indeed."

"You mean you don't think that he tried to kill you?"

"The police captain doesn't think so. He says it was the work of a man new to the blackjack, and he hit harder and oftener that he needed. He says that sort are the dangerous ones—that one's more safe in the hands of an experienced slugger, as would be the case with a skillful man in any line. I never thought of it that way before. He almost made it seem like it might be better to leave the experienced thugs loose on the streets for the safety of the public, instead of turning the business over to those less educated in the trade."

"What do think about the man yourself?" Constance persisted.

"The apprentice who practiced on me?"

She waited, watching his eyes. "I was hardly in a condition to appreciate anything about the man at all. Why do ask?"

"Because . . . ." She hesitated an instant. "If you were attacked to be killed, it meant that you must have been attacked as the son of . . . Mr. Corvet. Then that meant . . . at least it implied . . . that Mr. Corvet was killed; that he did not go away. You see that, I am sure."

"Were you the only one who thought that? Or did someone speak to you about it?"

"No one did; I spoke to Father. He thought . . ."

"Yes?"

"He thought that if Mr. Corvet was murdered—I'm following what Father thought, you understand—it involved something a good deal worse than anything that could have been involved if he had only gone away. The facts we had almost made it certain that if death had come to him by the hands of another, he must have foreseen that death. And seeking no protection for himself implied that he preferred to die rather than ask for protection. This would also imply that there was something he was concealing that mattered even more to him than life. It . . . it might have meant that he considered his life was . . . due to whomever may have taken it." Her voice, which had become very low, now ceased as she realized she was speaking to Alan of his father. Granted, it was a father he had never known and whom he would not have recognized by sight until she showed him a picture a few weeks before; but she was speaking of his father, nonetheless.

"Mr. Sherrill didn't feel," Alan asked, "that it was necessary for him to do anything, even though he thought that?"

"If Benjamin Corvet was dead," said Constance, "we could do him no good, surely, by going to the police. If the police succeeded in finding out all the facts, we would be doing only what Uncle Benny did not wish—that to which he preferred death. We could not tell the police about it without telling them all about Uncle Benny too. So Father would not let himself believe that you had been attacked to be killed. He had to believe the police theory was sufficient."

Alan made no comment at once. "Wassaquam believes Mr. Corvet is dead," he said finally. "He told me so. Does your father believe that?"

"I think he is beginning to believe it."

They had reached the little bridge that breaks the Drive and spans the channel through which small boats reach the harbor and lagoon. Alan rested his arms on the rail of the bridge and looked down into the channel, now frozen. It seemed to Constance that he was trying to decide something.

"I've not told anyone," he said, now watching her, "how I happened to be out of the house that night. I followed a man who came there to the house. Wassaquam did not know his name. The man did not know that Mr. Corvet was gone, and he had come to see him. He was not an ordinary friend of Mr. Corvet's, but he had come there often; Wassaquam did not know why. Wassaquam had sent the man away, and I ran out after him, but I could not find him."

He stopped an instant, studying her. "That was not the first man who came to the house," he went on quickly, as she was about to speak to him. "I found a man in Mr. Corvet's house the first night that I spent there. Wassaquam was away, you remember, and I was alone in the house."

"A man there in the house?" she repeated.

"He wasn't there when I entered the house . . . at least I don't think he was. I heard him below, after I had gone upstairs. I came down then and saw him. He was going through Mr. Corvet's things—not the silver and all that, but through his desks and files and cases. He was looking for something—something which he seemed to want very much. When I interfered, it greatly excited him."

"What happened when you 'interfered'?"

"A queer thing."

"What?"

"I frightened him."

"Frightened him?" She had perceived in his tone more significance than casual meaning of the words.

"He thought I was a ghost."

"A ghost? Whose ghost?"

He shrugged. "I don't know . . . someone whom he seemed to

have known pretty well . . . and whom Mr. Corvet knew, he thought."

"Why didn't you tell us before this?"

"At least . . . I am telling you now. I frightened him, and he got away. But I had seen him plainly, and I can describe him. You've talked with your father of the possibility that something might 'happen' to me, perhaps, such as happened to Mr. Corvet. If anything does happen to me, a description of the man may . . . prove useful."

He saw the color leave her face, and her eyes brighten, which he accepted as agreement on her part. Then clearly and definitely as he could, he described Spearman to her. She did not recognize the description; he had thought she would not. Had not Spearman been in Duluth? Beyond that, was not connection of Spearman to the prowler in the Corvet's house the one connection she would find it almost impossible to recognize? But he saw her fixing and recording the description in her mind.

They were silent as they went on toward her home. He had said all he could, or dared, to say. To tell her the man had been Spearman would not merely have awakened her incredulity, it would have destroyed credence completely. A definite change in their relation to one another had taken place during their walk. The fullness, frankness of the sympathy there had been between them almost from their first meeting had gone. She was quite aware, he saw, that he had not frankly answered her questions. She was aware that in some way he had drawn back from her and shut her out from his thoughts about his own position here. But this had to be. It had been his first realization after regaining consciousness in the hospital when, newly aware of her relation to Spearman, he had found all questions which concerned his relations with these people made immeasurably more acute by the attack upon him.

When they reached her home, Constance asked Alan to come in and stay for luncheon, but at his refusal she did not urge him further, and moved slowly up the steps. When she saw he did not go on, she stopped.

"Miss Sherrill," he said, looking up at her, "how much money is there in your house?"

She smiled, amused and a little perplexed, then sobered as she saw his intentness on her answer.

"What do you mean?"

"I mean . . . how much is ordinarily kept there?"

"Why, very little in actual cash. We pay everything by check—tradesmen, help . . . . Even if we happen not to have a charge account where we make a purchase, they know who we are, and are always willing to charge it to us."

"Thank you. It would be rather unusual then for you—or your neighbors—to have currency at hand exceeding the hundreds?"

"Exceeding the hundreds? That means in the thousands—or at least one thousand. Yes, for us, it would be very unusual."

She waited for him to explain why he had asked, as she could not think of a reason for his query. But he only thanked her again and moved away. Looking after him from the window after she had entered the house, she saw him turn the corner in the direction of Astor Street.

Part
Three

Strange Caller

II

As the first of the month was approaching, Wassaquam had brought his household bills and budget to Alan that morning directly after breakfast. The accounts, which covered expenses for the month just ending and a small amount of cash to be carried for the month beginning, were written on a sheet of foolscap in neat, unshaded writing exactly like models in a copy book—each letter formed as carefully and precisely as in the work done upon an Indian basket. The statement accounted accurately for a sum of cash in hand on the first of February, itemized charged expenses, and showed a total of all bills. For March, Wassaquam evidently proposed a continuance of the establishment along the present lines. To provide for this, and to furnish Alan with whatever sums he needed, Sherrill had made a considerable deposit in Alan's name in the bank where he carried his own account. Alan had accompanied Sherrill to the bank to be introduced, and signed the necessary cards in order to write checks against the deposit, but as yet, he had withdrawn nothing.

Alan had required barely half of the money which Benjamin Corvet had sent to Blue Rapids to cover the expenses for his trip to Chicago, and he brought with him from "home" a hundred dollars of his own. He had used that for his personal expenses since. The amount which Wassaquam now desired to pay the bills was much more than Alan had on hand, but the amount was also much less than the eleven hundred dollars listed as cash on hand. This, Wassaquam had stated, was in currency and kept by him.

Benjamin Corvet always had him keep that much in the house, and Wassaquam told Alan he would not touch that sum now for payment of current expenses.

This sum of money kept inviolate troubled Alan. Constance Sherrill's statement that, for her family at least, to keep such a sum would have been unusual, increased this troubled thought. However, it did not preclude the possibility that others than the Sherrills might keep such amounts of cash on hand. On the first of the month, therefore, Alan drew against his new bank account to Wassaquam's order, and in the early afternoon Wassaquam went to the bank to cash his check. This was one of the very few occasions when Alan had been left alone in the house; Wassaquam's habit, it appeared, was to go about on the first of the month and pay the tradesmen in person.

Some two hours later, and before Wassaquam could have been expected back, Alan, in the room which had now become his, was startled by a sound of heavy pounding which suddenly came to him from down below. Shouts, heavy, thick and unintelligible, mingled with the pounding. He ran quickly down the stairs to the first floor, and then on down the service stairs to the basement. The door to the house from the areaway was shaking to irregular, heavy blows, which stopped as Alan reached the lower hallway, but the shouts continued still a moment more. Now that the noise of the pounding did not interfere, Alan could make out what the man was saying: "Ben Corvet!"—the name was almost unintelligible—"Ben Corvet! Ben!" Then the shouts stopped too.

Alan sped to the door and turned back the latch. The door bore back at him, not from a push, but from a weight outside which had fallen against it. A big, heavy man, with a rough cap and mackinaw coat, would have fallen to the floor, if Alan had not caught him. His weight in Alan's arms was so dull, so inert, that if violence had been his intention, there was nothing to be feared from him now. Alan looked outside to see if anyone had come with him, and saw that the alley and street were clear. The snow in the areaway showed that the man had come alone and with great difficulty, as it was apparent he had fallen once on the walk. Alan dragged the man into the house and went back and closed the door.

Alan returned to look at the man. He was like, very much like, the one whom Alan had followed from the house on the night he was attacked; certainty that this was the same man came quickly to him. He seized the fellow again and dragged him up the stairs to the lounge in the library. The warmth was beginning to revive him. He sat up, coughing and breathing heavily, and with a loud, rasping wheeze. The smell of liquor was strong from him, and his clothes reeked with the unclean smell of barrel-houses.

He was, or had been, a very powerful man, broad and thick, with overdeveloped—almost distorting—muscles in his shoulders. But his body had become fat and soft. His face was puffed, and his eyes watery and vague. His brown hair, which was shot through with gray, was dirty and matted, and he had three or four days' growth of beard. He was clothed as Alan had seen deckhands on the ships attired, and appeared, Alan judged, to be fifty or more, though his condition made estimate difficult. When he sat up and looked around, it was plain that whiskey was only one of the forces working upon him. The other was fever which burned up and sustained him intermittently.

"Lo!" He greeted Alan. "Where's shat damn Injin, hey? I knew Ben Corvet was shere . . . knew he was shere all time. 'Course e's shere; he got to be shere. That's shright. You go git 'im!"

"Who are you?" Alan asked.

"Say, who'r *you*? What t'hell's you doin' here? Never see you before . . . go . . . go get Ben Corvet'll know Lu . . . Luke, all right . . . alwaysh, alwaysh knows . . . Luke."

"What's the matter with you?" Alan had drawn back, but now went back to the man again. The first idea that this might have been merely some old sailor who had served Benjamin Corvet, or perhaps had been a comrade in the earlier days, had been banished by the confident arrogance of the man's tone . . . an arrogance not to be explained entirely by whiskey, or by fever.

"How long have you been this way?" Alan demanded. "Where did you come from?" He put his hand on the man's wrist; it was very hot and dry; the pulse was racing, irregular; at seconds it seemed to stop, and some seconds later it was continuous. The fellow bent forward. "What is it? Pneumonia?" Alan tried to straighten him up.

"Gi' me drink! . . . Go get Ben Corvet, I tell you! . . . Get Ben Corvet quick! Say . . . yous shere? You get Ben Corvet . . . you tell him Lu . . . uke's here. Won't wait any more . . . goin' t'have my money now . . . sright away, youshere? Kick me out s'loon . . . I guess not no more. Ben Corvet give me all money I want or I talk!"

"Talk?"

"S'you know it! I ain't goin' . . . ." He choked and fell back. Alan, supporting him, laid him down and stayed beside him until his coughing and choking ceased, and there was only the rattling rasp of his breathing.

When Alan spoke to him again, Luke's eyes opened, and he narrated recent experiences bitterly, and all were blamed to Ben Corvet's absence. He had been drinking heavily a few nights before, and had been thrown out when the saloon closed. That was Ben Corvet's fault. If Ben Corvet had been around, Luke would have had money— all the money he wanted, and no one would have thrown Luke out then. Luke slept in the snow, all wet.

When he awakened, the saloon was open again, and he got more whiskey, but not enough to get him warm. He hadn't been warm since. That was Ben Corvet's fault. Ben Corvet better be 'round now; Luke wouldn't stand any more.

Alan felt the pulse again, and opened the coat and under-flannels and felt the heaving chest. He went to the hall and looked in the telephone directory. Remembering the name of the druggist on the corner of Clark Street he telephoned him, and gave him the number on Astor Street.

"I need a doctor right away," he said. "Any good doctor; the one you can get the quickest." The druggist promised that a physician would be there within a quarter-hour. Alan went back to Luke, who was silent now except for the gasp of his breath; he did not answer when Alan spoke to him, except to ask for whiskey. Alan, gazing down at him, felt that the man was dying; liquor and his fever had sustained him only long enough to bring him to the Corvet house, but now the collapse had come, and the doctor, even if he arrived very soon, could do no more than perhaps delay the end. Alan went upstairs and brought down blankets and put them over Luke. He cut the knotted laces of the soaked shoes and pulled them off, and took off the mackinaw and the undercoat.

The fellow, apparently appreciating that care was being given him, relaxed. He slept deeply for short periods, stirred and started up, and then slept again. Alan stood watching, a strange, sinking tremor shaking him. This man had come there to make a claim . . . a claim which many times before, apparently, Ben Corvet had acknowledged. Luke came to Ben Corvet for money, which he always got—all he wanted—the alternative to giving being that Luke would "talk." That meant blackmail, of course; blackmail which not only Luke had told of, but which Wassaquam, too, had implied, as Alan now realized. Money for blackmail—that had to be the reason for the thousand dollars in cash which Benjamin Corvet always kept in the house.

Alan turned, with a sudden shiver of revulsion, toward his father's chair in place before the hearth. There for hours each day his father had sat with a book or staring into the fire, always with what this man knew hanging over him, always arming himself against it with the thousand dollars ready for him, whenever he came. Meeting blackmail, paying blackmail for as long as Wassaquam had been in the house, for as long as it had taken to make the once muscular, powerful figure of the sailor who threatened to "talk," into the swollen, whiskey-soaked hulk of the man dying now on the lounge.

In his state that day, the man blamed Benjamin Corvet. Alan, forcing himself to touch the swollen face, shuddered at the thought of the truth underlying that accusation. Benjamin Corvet's act—whatever it might be that this man might know—had undoubtedly not only destroyed him who paid the blackmail, but him who received it as well; the effect of that act was still going on, destroying, blighting. Its threat of shame was not only against Benjamin Corvet, it threatened also all whose names must be connected with Corvet's. Alan had refused to accept any stigma in his relationship with Corvet, but could he now refuse to accept it?

This shame threatened Alan; it threatened also the Sherrills. Was it because of this that Benjamin Corvet had objected to Sherrill's name's appearing with his own in the title of the ship-owning firm? And was it because of this that Corvet's closeness with Sherrill and his comradeship with Constance had been alternated by times in which he had avoided them both? What Sherrill had told Alan, and even Corvet's gifts to him, had not been able to make Alan feel without question that Corvet was his father, but now shame and horror were making him feel it. In horror at Corvet's act, whatever it might be, and in shame at Corvet's cowardice, Alan was now thinking of Benjamin Corvet as his father. This shame, this horror, were his inheritance.

He left Luke and went to the window to see if the doctor was coming. He had called the doctor because in his first sight of Luke he had not recognized that Luke was beyond the aid of doctors, and because to summon a doctor under such circumstances was the right thing to do. He had also thought of the doctor as a witness to anything Luke might say. But now . . . did he want a witness? He had no thought of concealing anything for his own sake or for his father's, but he would, at least, want the chance to determine the circumstances under which it was to be made public.

He hurried back to Luke. "What is it, Luke?" he said to him. "What can you tell? Listen! Luke . . . Luke, is it about the *Miwaka?* . . . Luke . . . !"

Luke had sunk into a stupor; Alan shook him and shouted in his ear without awakening a response. As Alan straightened and stood hopelessly looking down at him, the telephone rang sharply. Thinking it might be something about the doctor, he went to it and answered. Constance Sherrill's voice came to him, and her first words made it clear that she was at home and had just arrived.

"The servants tell me someone was making a disturbance beside your house a while ago," she excitedly said, "and shouting something about Mr. Corvet. Is there something wrong there? Have you discovered something?"

He held his shaking hand over the telephone in case Luke should break out again and she should hear it, and wondered what he should say to her. In his excitement, he could think of nothing which would reassure her and merely put her off, and at that moment he was not capable of controlling his voice so as to do that.

"Please don't ask me just now, Miss Sherrill," he said. "I'll tell you what I can . . . later."

His reply, he recognized, only made her more certain that there was something the matter, but he could not add anything to it. He found Luke, when he went back to him, still in a coma; the blood-shot veins stood out against the ghastly grayness of his face, and his stertorous breathing sounded through the rooms.

Constance Sherrill had come in a few minutes before from an afternoon reception. Simons had told her at once that something was happening at the Corvet house. They had heard shouts and had seen a man pounding on the door there, but they had not taken it upon themselves to go over there. She had told the chauffeur to wait with the car, and had run at once to the telephone and called Alan. His attempt to put her off had made her certain that what had happened was not finished and was still continuing. Her anxiety and the sense of their responsibility for Alan overrode at once all other thought. She told Simons to call her father at the office and tell him something was wrong at Mr. Corvet's, then called her maid and hurried out to the car.

"To Mr. Corvet's, and hurry!" she directed.

Looking through the front windows of her car as it turned into Astor Street, she saw a young man, carrying a doctor's case, run up the steps of the Corvet house. This, quite unreasonably since she had just talked with Alan, added to her alarm. She put her hand on the catch of the door and opened it slightly so as to leave the car as soon as it stopped.

As the car drew to the curb, she sprang out, pausing only long enough to tell the chauffeur to be attentive and to wait ready to come into the house if he was called.

The man with the bag—Constance recognized him as a young doctor who was starting a practice in the neighborhood—was just being admitted as she and her maid reached the steps. Alan stood holding the door open and yet blocking the entrance when she came up. The sight of him told her that he appeared to be all right, but his face showed her there was basis for her fright.

"You must not come in!" he denied her, but she followed closely behind the doctor so that Alan could not close the door on her. He yielded then, and she and her maid went on into the hall.

She started as she saw the figure on the couch in the library. As the sound of the man's heavy, labored breathing reached her, the wild fancy which had come when Simons told her of what was going on—a fancy that Uncle Benny had come back—was banished instantly.

Alan led her into the room across from the library.

"You shouldn't have come here," he said "I shouldn't have let you in. But . . . you saw him."

"Yes."

"Do you know him?"

"Know him?" She shook her head.

"I mean, you've never seen him before?"

"No."

"His name is Luke . . . he speaks of himself by that name. Did you ever hear my father mention a man named Luke?"

"No; never."

Luke's voice cut suddenly their conversation; the doctor may have given him a stimulant.

"Where'sh Ben Corvet?" Luke demanded arrogantly of the doctor.

"You go get Ben Corvet! Tell Ben Corvet I wan' drink right away. Tell Ben Corvet I want my thousan' dollar . . . !"

Constance turned swiftly to her maid. "Go out to the car and wait for me," she commanded.

Luke's muffled, heavy voice went on, interrupted by moments when he fought for breath.

"You hear me, you damn Injin . . . ! You go tell Ben Corvet I want my thousan' dollars, or I make it two nex' time! You hear me? you go tell Ben Corvet . . . You let me go, you damn Injin . . . !"

Through the doorway to the library they could see the doctor force Luke back on to the couch; Luke fought him furiously, then, as suddenly as he had stirred to strength and fury, he collapsed again. His voice went on a moment more, rapidly growing weaker:

"You tell Ben Corvet I want my money, or I'll tell. He knows what I'll tell . . . You don't know, you Injin devil . . . Ben Corvet knows, and I know . . . Tell him I'll tell . . . I'll tell . . . I'll tell!" The threatening voice stopped suddenly.

Constance, very pale, again faced Alan. "Of course, I understand," she said. "Uncle Benny had been paying blackmail to this man. For years, perhaps . . . ." After an instant, in a frightened voice, she repeated the word: ". . . Blackmail!"

"Won't you please go, Miss Sherrill?" Alan urged her. "It was good of you to come, but you mustn't stay now. He's . . . dying, of course."

She seated herself on a chair. "I'm going to stay with you," she said simply. It was not to share the waiting for the man in the next room to die; in that of itself, there could be nothing for him to feel. It was to be with Alan while the realization which had come to her was settling upon him too—realization of what this meant to him. He was realizing that, she thought. He had realized it, and at moments, it made him forget her. As he listened for sounds from the next room, he paced back and forth beside the table or stood staring away, clinging to the portieres. He left her presently, and went across the hall to the doctor. The man on the couch had stirred as though to start up again, and the voice began once more, but now its words were wholly indistinguishable, meaningless, incoherent. They stopped, and Luke lay still. The doctor and Alan arranged the quite inert form upon the couch. The doctor bent over him.

"Is he dead?"

"Not yet," the doctor answered, "but it won't be long, now."

"There's nothing you can do for him?"

The doctor shook his head.

"There is nothing you can do to make him talk—bring him to himself enough so that he will tell what he keeps threatening to tell?"

The doctor shrugged. "How many times, do you suppose, he's been drunk and still not told? Concealment is his established habit now. It's an inhibition; even in wandering, he stops short of actually telling anything."

Alan briefly told the doctor the circumstances of the man's coming.

The doctor moved back from the couch to a chair and sat down. "I'll wait, of course," he said, "until it's over." He seemed to want to say something else, and after a moment he came out with it. "You needn't be afraid of my talking outside . . . professional secrecy, of course."

Alan came back to Constance. Outside, the gray dusk was spreading, and within the house it had grown dark. Constance heard the doctor turn on a light, and the shadowy glow of a desk lamp came from the library. Alan walked to and fro with uneven steps; he did not speak to her, nor she to him. It was very quiet in the library, and she could not even hear Luke's breathing now. Then she heard the doctor moving. Alan went to the light and turned it on as the doctor came out to them.

"It's over," he said to Alan. "There's a law covering these cases; you may be familiar with it. I'll make out the certificate of death . . . pneumonia and a weak heart with alcoholism. But the police will have to be notified at once; you have no choice as to that. I'll look after those things for you, if you want."

"Thank you, doctor; if you will." Alan went with the doctor to the door and saw him drive away. Returning, he drew the library portieres. Then coming back to Constance, he picked up her coat from the chair where she had thrown it, and held it out for her.

"You must go now, Miss Sherrill," he said. "Indeed, you mustn't stay here now . . . in this house!"

He was standing, waiting to open the door for her, almost where he had stood that morning a few weeks ago, when he had first come to the house in answer to Benjamin Corvet's summons, and where she had stood to receive him. Memory of how he had looked then—eager, trembling a little with excitement and expecting only to find his father and happiness. This came to her, and it contrasted with the way she saw him now. She choked queerly as she tried to speak. He was very white, but quite controlled, and lines not on his face before were now visible.

"Won't you come over home with me," she said, "and wait for Father there until we can think this thing out together?"

Her sweetness almost broke him down. "This . . . together! Think this out! Oh, it's plain enough, isn't it? For years—for as long as Wassaquam has been here—my father has been seeing that man and paying blackmail to him twice a year, at least! He's lived in that man's power. He kept money in the house for him always! It wasn't anything imaginary that hung over my father, or anything created in his own mind. It was something real . . . real, and a disgrace . . . disgrace and worse . . . something he deserved. And he fought it with blackmail money, like a coward! Dishonor . . . cowardice . . . blackmail!"

She moved a little closer to him. "You didn't want me to know," she said. "You tried to put me off when I called you on the telephone, and when I came here, you wanted me to go away before I heard. Why didn't you want me to know? Yes, he was your father, but wasn't he our friend? Mine and my father's? You must let us help you."

As she approached, he had drawn back from her. "No, this is my problem!" he denied her. "Not yours or your father's. You have nothing to do with this. Didn't he try in little cowardly ways to keep you out of it? But he couldn't do that, because your friendship meant too much to him; he couldn't keep away from you. But I can . . . I can do that! You must go out of this house, and you must never come in here again!"

Her eyes filled, as she watched him. Never had she liked him so much as now, as he moved to open the door for her.

"I thought . . . ," he said almost wistfully, ". . . it seemed to me that, whatever he had done, it must have been mostly against me. His leaving everything to me seemed to mean that I was the one that he had wronged, and that he was trying to make it up to me. But it isn't that; it can't be that! It is something much worse . . . . Oh, I'm glad I haven't used much of his money! It wasn't the money and the house he left me that mattered. What he really left me was just this . . . dishonor, shame . . . ."

The doorbell rang, and Alan turned to the door and opened it. In the dusk the figure of the man outside was not recognizable, but as he entered with heavy and deliberate steps, passing Alan without greeting and going straight to Constance, Alan saw by the light in the hall that it was Spearman.

"What's up?" Spearman asked. "They tried to get your father at the office and then me, but neither of us was there. They got me afterwards at the club. They said you'd come over here, but that must have been more than two hours ago."

His gaze went on past her to the drawn hangings of the room to the right, and he seemed to appreciate their significance. His face whitened under its tan, and an odd hush came suddenly upon him.

"Is it Ben, Connie?" he whispered. "Ben . . . come back?"

He drew the drapes partly open. The light in the library had been extinguished, and the light from the hall swayed about the room with the movement of the drapes and gave a momentary semblance of life to the face of the man on the couch.

Spearman drew the drapes quickly together again, still holding to them and seeming for an instant to cling to them; then he shook himself together, threw the drapes wide apart, and strode into the room. He switched on the light and went directly to the couch. Alan followed him.

"He's . . . dead?" Spearman asked.

"Who is he?" Alan demanded.

Spearman seemed intent on satisfying himself that the man was dead, and until he had done so he ignored Alan's question. Finally he turned to Alan and answered.

"How should I know who he is?" Spearman asked. "There used to be a wheelsman on the *Martha Corvet* years ago who looked like him, or looked like this fellow may have looked once. I can't be sure."

He turned to Constance, "You're going home, Connie. I'll see you over there. I'll come back about this afterwards, Conrad."

Alan followed them to the door and closed it after them. He spread the blankets over Luke. Luke's coats which Alan had removed were on a chair, and he looked them over for marks of identification. The mackinaw bore a label of a store in Manitowoc—wherever that might be; Alan did not know. A side pocket produced an old briar, but there was nothing else. Then Alan walked around restlessly, awaiting Spearman. He believed Spearman knew this man, but he had not even ventured modified denial until he was certain the man was dead. Even then he had answered so as not to commit himself, pending learning from Constance what Luke had said.

But Luke had said nothing about Spearman. It had been Corvet, and Corvet alone, of whom Luke had spoken and Corvet he had accused. It was only Corvet who had given him money. Was it conceivable then, that there had been two such events in Corvet's life? That one of these events concerned the *Miwaka* and Spearman and someone "with a bullet hole above his eye" who had "got" Corvet; and that the other event had concerned Luke and something else? No, Alan felt sure, it was not conceivable. It was all one event. If Corvet had to do with the *Miwaka*, then Luke had to do with it too. And Spearman? But if Spearman had been involved in the guilty event, had not Luke known it? Then why had not Luke mentioned Spearman? Or had Spearman really not been involved? Had it been, perhaps, only evidence of knowledge of what Corvet had done that Spearman had tried to discover and destroy?

Alan went to the door and opened it, as he heard Spearman on the steps again. Spearman waited only until the door had been reclosed behind him. "Well, Conrad, what was the idea of bringing Miss Sherrill into this?"

"I didn't bring her in; I tried the best I could to keep her out."

"Out of what . . . exactly?"

"You know better than I do. You know exactly what it is. You know that man, Spearman, and you know what he came here for. I don't mean money; I mean you know why he came here for money, and why he got it. I tried, as well as I could, to make him tell me, but he wouldn't do it.

"There's disgrace of some sort here—disgrace that involves my father, and I think you too. If you're not guilty with my father, you'll help me now. If you are guilty, then at least, your refusal to help will let me know that."

"I don't know what you're talking about."

"Then why did you come back here? You came back here to protect yourself in some way."

"I came back, you young fool, to say something to you which I didn't want Miss Sherrill to hear. I didn't know, when I took her away, how completely you had taken her into . . . your father's affairs. I told you this man may have been a wheelsman on the *Corvet*. I don't know any more about him than that. I don't even know that for certain. Of course, I knew Ben Corvet was paying blackmail. I've known for years that he was giving up money to someone. I don't know who he paid it to, or for what."

The strain of the last few hours was telling on Alan; he turned hot and cold by turns. He paced up and down while he controlled himself.

"That's not enough, Spearman," he finally said. "I . . . I've felt from the beginning that you were involved in this whole situation. The first time I saw you, you were in this house doing something you ought not to have been doing. You fought me then, and would have killed me rather than not get away. Two weeks ago, someone attacked me on the street—for robbery they said, but I know it wasn't robbery . . . ."

"You're not so crazy as to be trying to involve me in *that* . . . ."

A sound came to them from the hall, unmistakably denoting some presence. Spearman jerked up suddenly as Alan went to the doorway. It was Wassaquam, who had evidently returned to the house some time before and now was bringing Alan the accounts he had settled. He seemed to have been standing in the hall for some time, listening, but he came in now and looked inquiringly from one to the other of them.

"Not friends?" he inquired. "You and Henry?"

Alan's passion broke out suddenly. "We're anything but that, Judah. I found him, the first night I was here while you were away, going through my father's things. I fought with him, and he ran away. He was the one who broke into my father's desks; maybe you'll believe that, even if no one else will."

"Yes?" the Indian questioned. "Yes?" It was plain that he not only believed, but believing gave him immense satisfaction. He took

Alan's arm and led him into the smaller library. He knelt before one of the drawers under the bookshelves—the drawer, Alan recalled, which he himself had been examining when he had found Wassaquam watching him. He drew out the drawer and dumped the contents out on the floor. He turned the drawer over then, and pulled the bottom out of it. Beneath this bottom he removed, appeared another bottom and a few sheets of paper scrawled in an uneven hand, and with different colored inks.

At the sight of them, Spearman, who had followed them into the room, uttered an oath and sprang forward. The Indian's small dark hand grasped Spearman's wrist, and his face twitched itself into a fierce grin which showed how little civilization had modified his native passions. But Spearman did not try to force his way. Instead, he drew back suddenly.

Alan stooped and picked up the papers and put them in his pocket. If the Indian had not been there, it would not have been so easy for him to do that, he thought.

12

Alan went with Wassaquam into the front library, after the Indian had shown Spearman out.

"Is this Luke the man, Judah, who came for Mr. Corvet that night I was hurt?"

"Yes, Alan," Wassaquam replied.

"He was the man, then, who came here twice a year, at least, to see Mr. Corvet?"

"Yes."

"I was sure of it," Alan said.

Wassaquam had made no demonstration of any sort since he had snatched at Spearman's wrist to hold him back when Alan had bent over to the drawer. Alan could define no real change now in the Indian's manner, but he knew that since Wassaquam had found him quarreling with Spearman, the Indian somehow had accepted him more favorably. The reserve bordering on distrust with which Wassaquam had first viewed Alan certainly was lessened. In recognition of this, Alan now asked, "Can you tell me now why he came here, Judah?"

"I have told you I do not know," Wassaquam replied.

"Ben always saw him, and gave him money. I do not know why."

Alan had been holding his hand over the papers which he thrust into his pocket, and now he went back into the smaller library and spread them under the reading lamp to examine them. Sherrill had assumed that Corvet had left a record in the house which would fully explain what had thwarted his life, and which would hopefully shed light on what had happened to him and why he had disappeared. And Alan had accepted this assumption. The careful and secret manner in which these pages had been kept, and the importance Wassaquam plainly attached to them—and which must have been a result of his knowing Corvet regarded them of the utmost importance—made Alan certain that he had found the record which Sherrill had believed must be there. Spearman's manner at the moment of discovery showed, too, that this had been what he had been searching for in his secret visit to the house.

But, as Alan looked over the pages now, he felt a chill of disappointment and chagrin. They did not contain any narrative concerning Benjamin Corvet's life, nor did they relate to a single event which could be of help. In his first examination of them, he could not even tell what they were. They consisted in all of some dozen sheets of irregular size, some of which had been kept longer than others, and a few of them even appeared to be fresh and new. The three pages which Alan thought, from their yellowed and worn look, must be the oldest, and which must have been kept for years, contained only a list of names and addresses. Having assured himself that there was nothing else on them, he laid them aside. The remaining pages, which he counted as ten in number, contained many brief clippings from newspapers, which had been very carefully cut out, and had been pasted with painful regularity on the sheets. Each had been dated across its face, and the dates were made with many different pens and many different inks. All were in the same irregular handwriting as the letter which Alan had received from Benjamin Corvet.

Alan, his fingers numb in disappointment, turned and examined all of these papers, but they contained nothing else. He read one of the clippings, which was dated February, 1912:

> The passing away of one of the oldest residents of Emmet County occurred at the farm for the poor on Thursday of last week. Mr. Fred Westhouse was one of four brothers brought by their parents into Emmet County in 1856. He established himself here as a farmer and was well known by our people for many years. He was nearly the last of his family, which was quite well off at one time, Mr. Westhouse's three brothers and his father having perished in various disasters upon the lake. His wife died two years ago. He is survived by a daughter, Mrs. Arthur Pearl of Flint.

He read another:

> Hallford-Spens. On Tuesday last Miss Audrey Hallford, daughter of Mr. and Mrs. Bert Hallford of this place, was united in the bonds of holy matrimony with Mr. Robert Spens, of Escanaba. Miss Audrey is one of our most popular young ladies and was valedictorian of her class at the high school graduation last year. All wish the couple well.

Yet another read:

> Born to Mr. and Mrs. Hal French, a daughter, Saturday afternoon last. Miss Vera Arabella French, at her arrival, weighed seven and a half pounds.

This last clipping was dated—in Benjamin Corvet's hand—"Sturgeon Bay, Wisc., Aug. 1914." Alan put the clippings aside in bewilderment, and picked up again the first sheets he had looked at.

The names and addresses on these oldest, yellowed pages had apparently first been written all at the same time with the same pen and ink, and each sheet in the beginning had contained seven or eight names. Some of these original names and even the addresses had been left unchanged, but most of them had been scratched out and altered many times. Other and quite different names had been substituted. The pages had become finally almost illegible with crowded scrawls, rewritten again and again in Corvet's cramped hand.

Alan again picked up the clippings he had looked at before and compared them swiftly with the page he had just read. Two of the names, Westhouse and French, were the same as those on the yellowed list. Then suddenly he grasped the other pages of the list and looked them through for his own name, but it was not there. He dropped the sheets on the table in frustration and began to pace about the room.

He felt that in this list and in these clippings there must somehow be one general meaning, some relation to, or connection with Benjamin Corvet's disappearance and his present fate. Whatever that might be, the answers must concern Alan Conrad's fate as well. But in their disconnection, their incoherence, he could discern no common thread. What conceivable bond could there have been uniting Benjamin Corvet with an old man dying in Emmet County, wherever that might be, and with a marriage in Escanaba, and with a baby girl in Sturgeon Bay, Wisconsin? He suddenly swept the pages into the drawer of the table and reclosed the drawer, as he heard the doorbell ring and Wassaquam went to answer it. It was the police, Wassaquam came to tell him, who had come for Luke's body.

Alan went out into the hall to meet them. The coroner's crew had either come with them, or had arrived at the same time. They introduced themselves to Alan, and their inquiries indicated that the young doctor whom Alan had called for Luke had fully carried out his offer to look after these things, as the coroner was already supplied with a complete account of what had taken place. A sailor formerly employed on the Corvet ships, the coroner's office had been told, had come to the Corvet house, ill and seeking aid. Mr. Corvet not being at home, the people of the house had taken the man in and called the doctor, but the man had already been beyond doctors' help, and died in a few hours of pneumonia and alcoholism. In Mr. Corvet's absence it had been impossible to learn the sailor's full name.

Alan left corroboration of this story mostly to Wassaquam, the servant's position in the house being more easily explicable than his own. He found that Wassaquam's right there was not questioned, and the police fully accepted him as a member of the household. It was obvious that the police did not think it necessary to push inquiry very actively in such a home as this.

After the police had gone, Alan called Wassaquam into the library and brought out the lists and clippings again.

"Do you have any idea at all what these are, Judah?" he asked.

"No, Alan. I have seen Ben have them, and take them out and put them back. That is all I know."

"My father never spoke to you about them?"

"Once he spoke to me. He said I was not to tell or speak to anyone about them, or even to him."

"Do you know any of these people?" He gave the lists to Wassaquam, who studied them under the lamp.

"No, Alan."

"Have you ever heard any of their names before?"

"That may be. I do not know. They are common names."

"Do you know the places?"

"Yes . . . the places. They are lake ports or little villages on the lakes. I have been in most of them, Alan. Emmet County, Alan; I came from there. Henry comes from there, too."

"Henry Spearman?"

"Yes."

"Then that is where they hear the drum?"

"Yes, Alan."

"My father took newspapers from those places, did he not?"

Wassaquam looked over the addresses again. "Yes, from all. He took them for the shipping news, and sometimes he cut pieces out of them—these pieces, I see now—and afterward I burned the papers. He would not let me throw them away."

"That's all you know about them, Judah?"

Alan dismissed the Indian, who—stolidly methodical in the midst of these events—went downstairs and commenced to prepare a dinner Alan knew he would not eat. Alan got up and moved about the rooms and then went back and looked at the lists and clippings once more. Then he moved about again. How strange a picture of his father did these things call up to him! When he had thought of Ben Corvet before, it had been as Sherrill had described him—pursued by some thought he could not conquer, seeking relief in study, in corresponding with scientific and historical societies, in anything which could engross him and shut out memory. But now he must think of him not merely as someone who was trying to forget. What had thwarted Corvet's life was not only in the past, it was something that was still going on.

It had amazed Sherrill to learn that Corvet had kept track of Alan, but he had, and with the same secrecy he employed in following many other people, as Alan was now learning. When Alan thought of Corvet, alone in his silent house, he must think of him as being solicitous about these people; as seeking for their names in the newspapers which he took for that purpose, and as recording the changes in their lives. The deaths, the births, the marriages among these people had been of intense interest to Corvet.

It was possible that none of these people knew about Corvet. Alan had not known about him in Kansas, but had known only that some unknown person had sent money for his support. But he appreciated that it did not matter whether they knew about him or not, because at some point common to all of them, the lives of these people must have touched Corvet's life. If Alan could only identify that point of contact, he would know about Corvet, and he would know about himself.

Alan had seen among Corvet's books, one lying open with a book mark separating its two sides, and near it a large portfolio containing a set of charts of the Great Lakes standing against the wall. He moved the book and the charts over to the lamp, laying the charts on the floor, and found an atlas which he also brought over to the table. He sat down in the chair and picked up the rather thin open book which he found to be a history of Beaver Island. He immediately thought of Michabou and the animals on the raft, and most important, he thought of Constance Sherrill.

The book's being open and marked indicated that it may have been referred to recently by Corvet. Could there be something in this book that related to the names on the list, or perhaps to himself? He started to read the chapter marked. It told about Joseph Smith's founding the Mormon Church of Latter Day Saints at Fayette, N.Y. in 1830; how the movement grew rapidly, and how Smith moved his followers first to Missouri and then to Illinois . . .

After some stormy years there, Smith was killed by a mob in 1844, and the leadership of the Mormons went to Brigham Young, and to a lesser extent, James Strang. In 1846, Brigham Young moved his followers to Utah, and a year or two later Strang moved his group to Beaver Island. James Strang was a lawyer by education, a strong leader, and a harsh disciplinarian.

In 1852 Strang was elected to the Michigan State Assembly in Lansing with his solid bloc of some 2500 votes, and he was courted by Democrats and Whigs alike because of his political leverage and abilities. Some of the best laws in Michigan were passed while he was in Lansing, among them strong liquor and crime laws. However, he was never liked by the Irish fishermen on Beaver Island, nor by many on the mainland who objected to his harsh punishment of offenders, which drove many of the younger Mormons away from the island. Still more turned against him when he allowed the practice of polygamy and acquired four "additional wives" himself.

While most of the Mormons were peace-loving farmers, enmity grew and charges of piracy and plundering arose. There were raids on Northport, but it appeared that some such incidents were provoked by ruffians to incriminate the Mormons. At the "Battle" of

Pine River on the mainland, shots were exchanged as some of the Strang people were leaving for the Island with supplies.

In 1856, some twenty-five men chartered a schooner and sailed from Cross Village to Beaver Island and assassinated Strang. His followers were attacked by mobs from the mainland and were obliged to flee from the Island . . . .

Alan pulled the chart of Lake Michigan out of the portfolio, laid it on top of the others on the floor and soon located Beaver Island. With the chart and the atlas, he looked up the addresses given on Corvet's lists. He found that most of them were towns around the northern end of the lake. A very few were on Lakes Superior and Huron, but most were on or very close to Lake Michigan. These people lived by means of the lake and got their sustenance from it, as Corvet had lived and derived his. Alan was beginning to feel like one bound who has suddenly been released. From the time he had come to see Corvet, it had been impossible for him to solve the mystery which had surrounded himself and that which had surrounded Corvet. But these names and addresses! They at least now offered something to go on.

He found Emmet County on the map and put his finger on it. Wassaquam had said that he and Spearman had come from there. "The land of the drum!" Alan said aloud, astonished to realize that deep feeling had suddenly stirred within him as he traced out this land on the chart—the little towns and villages, the islands and headlands, their lights and their uneven shores. He felt a sense of familiarity—of "home"—that he had not felt on arriving in Chicago. There were Indian names and French up there where the great waters meet. Beaver Island! He thought of Michabou and the raft again. The sense that he was of these lakes, that surge of feeling which he had felt first in conversation with Constance Sherrill, was strengthened a hundredfold, and he found himself humming a tune. He did not know where he had heard it. Indeed, it was not the sort of tune which one knows from having heard; rather it was the sort which one just knows. A rhyme fitted itself to the hum,

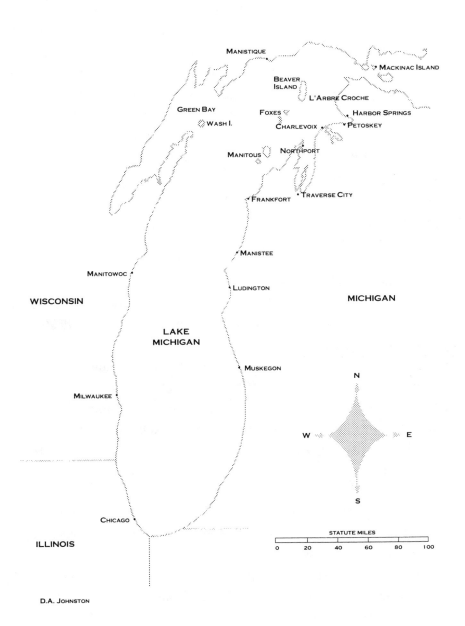

MANISTIQUE

MACKINAC ISLAND

BEAVER
ISLAND

L'ARBRE CROCHE

GREEN BAY

FOXES

HARBOR SPRINGS

WASH I.

CHARLEVOIX

PETOSKEY

NORTHPORT

MANITOUS

MANITOWOC

MANISTEE

WISCONSIN

LUDINGTON

MICHIGAN

LAKE
MICHIGAN

MUSKEGON

N

MILWAUKEE

W

E

S

CHICAGO

STATUTE MILES

ILLINOIS

0   20   40   60   80   100

TRAVERSE CITY

FRANKFORT

D.A. JOHNSTON

181

Seagull, seagull sit on the sand,
It's never fair weather when you're on the land.

He gazed down at the lists of names which Benjamin Corvet had kept so carefully and so secretly. These were his father's people. These ragged shores and the islands studding the channels were the lands where his father had spent the most active years of his life. Here also was where an event had occurred by which that life had been blighted. Chicago and this house here had been for his father only the abode of memory and retribution. North, there by the meeting of the waters, was the region of the wrong which had been done.

"There's where I must go!" he said aloud.

*   *   *

On the following afternoon Constance Sherrill received a telephone call from her father. He was coming home earlier than usual, he said, and if she planned on going out, would she wait until after he got there?

She had, indeed, just come in and had been intending to go out again at once, but she took off her wraps and waited for him. The afternoon's mail was on the hall table. She went through it, and from among the letters, picked an envelope addressed to herself in a firm, clear hand, which was unfamiliar to her. Somehow this queerly startled her, as she tore it open and began to read . . . .

Dear Miss Sherrill,

I am closing for the time being, the house which for default of other ownership, I must call mine. The possibility that what has occurred here would cause you and your father anxiety about me in case I went away without telling you of my intention is the reason for this note. But it is not the only reason.

I could not go away without telling you how deeply I appreciate the generosity and delicacy you and your father have shown me in spite of my position here and of the fact that I had no claim at all upon you. I shall not forget those even though what happened here last night makes it impossible for me to try to see you again, or even write to you.

Alan Conrad

She heard her father's car enter the drive and ran out to him, still holding the letter.

"He's written to you, then," her father said at sight of the letter in her hand.

"Yes."

"I had a note from him this afternoon at the office, asking me to hold in abeyance for the time being the trust that Ben had left me, and returning the key to the house to me for safekeeping."

"Has he already gone?"

"I suppose so; I don't know."

"We must find out."

She picked up her coat and began to put it on. Sherrill hesitated, then assented, and they went around the block together to the Corvet house. As they approached, Constance saw the shades were drawn, and their rings at the doorbell brought no response. Sherrill, after a few instants' hesitation, took the key from his pocket and unlocked the door, and they went in. They saw that the rooms were all in perfect order. Summer covers had been put over the furniture, and protecting cloths had been spread over the beds upstairs. Sherrill tried the water and the gas, and found they had been turned off. After their inspection, they came out again after closing the front door and locking it with the spring latch.

As they walked away, Constance turned and looked at the old house, gloomy and dark among its newer, fresher-looking neighbors, and suddenly she choked and her eyes grew wet. That feeling was not for Uncle Benny. The drain of the days past had exhausted such a surge of feeling for him. The emotion she now felt was for the boy who had come to that house a few weeks ago, and for the man who just now had gone.

Part
Four

Harbor Springs Package

13

Miss Constance Sherrill, Harbor Springs, Michigan. The address, in large scrawling letters, was written across the brown paper of a package which had been brought only a few minutes before from the post office in the little resort village in Emmet County to the Sherrills' summer cottage on the Point. It was postmarked "Manitowoc, Wisc."

Knowing no one in Manitowoc, and surprised at the nature of the package, Constance could only guess what was inside. She cut the strings around the box and took off the wrapping. The paper covered an old and crushed shoe box bearing the name of S. Krug, Dealer in Fine Shoes, Manitowoc, Wisconsin. The box, like the wrapping, was carefully tied with string.

Inside, she found a black and brown, dotted silk cloth filling the box. Seeing it, Constance caught her breath. It was—or at least it was very like—the muffler Uncle Benny used to wear in winter. Remembering him most vividly as she had seen him last on that stormy afternoon when he had wandered beside the lake, carrying his coat until she had made him put it on, she distinctly recalled taking this same silk muffler—or one just like it—from his coat pocket and putting it around his neck.

With trembling fingers she started to take the muffler from the box. Then, realizing from the weight of the box that the silk muffler was only a wrapping around other contents, she hesitated and looked around for her mother. But her mother had gone out. Her father and Henry were both in Chicago. Except for the help, she was alone in the big summer cottage.

Constance picked up the box and ran up to her room. She locked the door and put the box on her bed, and then carefully lifted out the muffler. As she began to unroll it, a paper fluttered out—a little cross-lined leaf evidently torn from a pocket memorandum book and then folded and rolled up. She spread it out, and immediately recognized the small irregular letters of Uncle Benny's handwriting. Her heart was beginning to race.

"Send to Alan Conrad," she read, and there followed the Chicago address of Uncle Benny's house on Astor Street. Below this was another line: "Better care of Constance Sherrill (Miss)." There followed the Sherrills' address on the Drive in Chicago. And to this was another correction: "Not after June 12th; then to Miss Sherrill, Harbor Springs, Michigan. Ask someone of that, and be sure of the June 12th date—this is important."

Indeed, the scarf was a wrapping, and the heavier things came out with it. As she unfolded the muffler, she knew beyond question that it was Uncle Benny's scarf. Her hands trembled as she unrolled it. Some coins appeared from a fold, and then a pocket knife, ruined and rusty. Next, a watch—a large, gold, man's watch, its case queerly pitted and worn completely through in places. And then, last, a plain little band of gold the size of a woman's finger—a wedding ring.

Constance, gasping and with fingers shaking so from excitement that she could scarcely hold these objects, picked them up and examined them. She looked first at the ring. She immediately recognized it was a wedding ring that once fitted a finger only a trifle less slender that her own. One side of the gold band was very much worn, not with the sort of wear which a ring gets on a hand, but by some different sort of abrasion. The other side of the band was roughened and pitted but not so much worn. The inside still bore the traces of an inscription:

"As long as we bo . . . all live," Constance could read, and the date was "June 2, 1891."

It was in January, 1896, Constance remembered, that Alan Conrad had been brought to the people in Kansas, and he was then about three years old. If this wedding ring was his mother's, the date would be about right, being probably something more than a year before Alan was born.

Constance put down the ring and picked up the watch. Wherever it had lain, it had been less protected than the ring. The covers of the case had been almost eroded away, and whatever initialing or other marks there might have been on the outside were gone. But it was like Uncle Benny's watch, or like one of his watches. He had several, she knew, which had been presented to him at different times. Watches almost always were the testimonials given to seamen for acts of sacrifice and bravery. She remembered finding some of those testimonials in a drawer at his house once where she was rummaging when she was a child. One of them had been a watch just like this, large and heavy.

The spring which opened the cover would not work, but Constance forced the cover open. There inside the cover, as she thought it would be, was engraved writing. Sand had seeped into the case, and the inscription was obliterated in part.

"For his courage and skill in seam. . . master of. . .which he brought to the rescue of the passengers and crew of the steamer *Winnebago* foundering. . . Point, Lake Erie, November 26th, 1890, this watch is given by the Buffalo Merchant's Exchange."

Uncle Benny's name had probably been engraved on the outside. Constance had no recollection of the rescue of the people of the

Winnebago. After all, 1890 was years before she was born, and Uncle Benny did not tell her of that sort of thing about himself.

The watch, she saw now, must have lain in water, as the hands under the crystal were rusted away, and the face was all streaked and cracked. She opened the back of the watch and exposed the works, and they too were rusted and filled with sand. Constance left the watch open and, shivering a little, she gently laid it down on her bed. The pocket knife had no distinguishing mark of any kind, and it appeared to be just a man's ordinary knife with the steel turned to rust, and with sand in it too. The coins were abraded and pitted discs—a silver dollar, a half dollar, and three quarters. Not so abraded were three nickels and two pennies.

Constance choked, and her eyes filled with tears. These things—plainly the things found in Uncle Benny's pockets—corroborated only too fully what Wassaquam believed and what her father had been coming to believe: that Uncle Benny was dead. The muffler and the scrap of paper had not been in the water or in sand. The paper was written in pencil, and it had not been moistened or it would have blurred.

There was nothing on it to tell how long ago it had been written, but it certainly had been before June twelfth. "After June 12th . . . ," it said. The day was August the eighteenth.

It had been seven months since Uncle Benny had gone away. After his strange interview with her that day and his going home, had Uncle Benny gone out directly to his death? There was nothing to show that he had, or had not. The watch and coins must have lain for many weeks, even months, in water and in sand to become eroded in this way. And, aside from this, there was nothing that could be inferred regarding the time or place of Uncle Benny's death. That the package had been mailed from Manitowoc meant nothing definite. Someone—Constance could not know who—had had the muffler and the scrawled memo page of directions. At some time— later, perhaps—these things had been given to someone else for mailing, along with the coins, knife, watch and ring which had lain in water and sand so long. Most probably this had been someone who was going about on ships, and when his ship had touched Manitowoc, he had executed his charge.

Constance left the articles on her bed and opened the window more widely. She still trembled and felt faint as she leaned against the window, breathing deeply the crisp fresh air, full of life and with the scent of the evergreen trees around the house.

The cottage with its many rooms stood among the pines and hemlocks interspersed with hardwood on the Point, among the other large, fine summer homes of wealthy resorters. The sound of the breeze rustling through the pine needles and leaves was mingled with the soft lapping of the water against the shore.

Southward and to the east from her stretched Little Traverse Bay, one of the most beautiful expanses of water on the lakes. Across from her, beyond the wrinkling water of the bay, lay the larger town of Petoskey with its hilly streets pitching down steeply to the water's edge and the docks, and with its great resort hotels plainly visible. To westward, from the white life-saving station and the lighthouse, the spit that is the Point ran out in shingled, bone white, outcropping above the water; then for miles away the shallow water was treacherous green and white to where to the north, around the bend of the shore, it deepened and grew blue again, and a single white tower, the Ile-aux-Galets Light, kept watch above it.

This was Uncle Benny's country. Here, twenty-five years before, he had first met Henry, whose birthplace, a deserted farm now, was only a few miles back among the hills. Here, before that, Uncle Benny had been a young man, active, vigorous, ambitious. He had loved this country for itself and for its traditions, its Indian legends and fantastic stories. Since childhood it had been to her a region of delight, and half her love for it was due to him and to the things he had told her about it.

Distinct and definite memories of that companionship came to her. This beautiful bay, which had become now for the most part only a summer playground for such as she, had once been a place where he and other men had struggled to grow rich swiftly. He had outlined for her the ruined lumber docks, and had pointed out to her the locations of the dismantled sawmills. It was he who had told her the names of the freighters passing far out, and the names of the lighthouses, and something about each. He had told her, too, about the Indians. She remembered one starry night when he had pointed out to her in the sky the Indian "Way of the Ghosts," the Milky Way, along which by ancient Indian belief, the souls of Indians traveled up to heaven. And how, later, lying on the recessed seat beside the fireplace where she could touch the dogs upon the hearth, he had pointed out to her through the window the Indian "Way of Dogs" among the constellations, by which the dogs, too, could make that journey. It was he who had told her about Michabou and the animals, and he had been the first to tell her of the drum and the meaning of its beat.

The disgrace, unhappiness, the threat of something worse, which must have made death a relief to Uncle Benny, she had seen now passed on to Alan. What more had come to Alan since she had last heard of him? Had he discovered some terrible substance to his fancies, which would assail him again as she had seen him assailed after Luke had come? Might another attack have been made upon him similar to that which he had met in Chicago?

Word had reached her father through shipping circles in May and again in July which told of inquiries regarding Uncle Benny. This made both of the Sherrills believe that Alan was searching for his father on the lakes. Now, these articles she had received from Manitowoc made plain to her that he would never find Uncle Benny. He would learn through others or through themselves, that Uncle Benny was dead. Would he remain away because of that, not letting her see or hear from him again?

She went back and picked up the wedding ring. The thought which had come to her, that this was Alan's mother's wedding ring, had now become a sense of certainty. The ring defended that unknown mother. It freed her, at least, from the stigma which

Constance's own mother had been so ready to cast. Constance could not yet begin to place Uncle Benny in relation to that ring, but she was beginning to be able to think of Alan and his mother. She held the little band of gold very tenderly in her hand, and she was glad that, as accusation against his mother had come through her people, she could tell him soon of this. She could not send the ring to him, not knowing where he was, and even if she knew where to send it, that would be too much risk. But she could ask him to come to her, as the ring now gave her that right.

She sat thoughtfully for several minutes, the ring clasped tightly in her hand. Then she went to her desk and began to write:

> *Mr. John Welton,*
> *Blue Rapids, Kansas*
>
> *Dear Mr. Welton:*
> *It is possible that Alan Conrad has mentioned me, or at least told you of my father, in connection with his stay in Chicago. After Alan left Chicago, my father wrote twice to his Blue Rapids address, but evidently he had instructed the postmaster there not to forward his mail and has not made any change in those instructions, for the letters were returned to Alan's address, and in that way came back to us. We did not like to press inquiries further than that, as of course, he could have communicated with us if he felt there was some reason for doing so. Now, however, something of such supreme importance to him has come to us that it is necessary for us to get word to him at once. If you can tell me of any address at which he can be reached by telegraph or mail, or where a messenger can find him, it will oblige us very much and will be to his interest.*

She hesitated, about to sign it, and then impulsively she added:

> *I trust you know that we have Alan's interest at heart, and that you can safely tell us anything you may know as to where*

he is or what he may be doing. We all liked him here so very
much . . .

She signed her name. There were still two other letters to write.

The only clues to the identity of the sender of the ring and the watch and the other things lay in the handwriting of the address on the package, the Manitowoc postmark, and the shoe box. Constance herself could not trace those clues, but Henry and her father could. She wrote to both of them, therefore, describing the articles which had come and what she had done. Then she rang for a servant and sent the letters to the post office in time to catch the "Dummy," the train around the bay to Petoskey, where they would get into the afternoon mail. The two for Chicago would be delivered the next day, so she might expect replies from Henry and her father on the day after. The letter to Kansas, of course, would take much longer than that.

The next noon she received a wire from Henry, saying that he was "coming up." It did not surprise her, as she had expected him at the end of the week in any event.

Two evenings later she sat with her mother on the screened veranda. The breeze among the pines had died away, and the bay was calm. A half moon hung midway in the sky showing the hills in the distance and casting a broadening way of silver on the mirror surface of the water. The running lights of a boat caught her eye, bearing around the Point and into Harbor Springs. As it crossed the moonlight's path it looked so much like Henry's power yacht that she arose, startled. She had not expected him until the next morning, but as the boat drew nearer she knew it was indeed Henry's *Chippewa*. He must have left Chicago shortly after receiving her letter, and with the fair weather and by forcing his engines, he was able to arrive this soon.

He had done this partly, perhaps, for the sheer sport of speed, but also partly because he wanted to be with her sooner. It was his way, as soon as he had decided to leave his business and go to her, to arrive as soon as possible. So the sight of the yacht stirred her warmly as she watched while it ran in close and dropped a dinghy from the davits even before anchoring.

She saw Henry in the stern of the little boat as it approached the landing, and a few minutes later she heard the gravel of the walk crunch under his hurried steps. Then she saw him in the moonlight shining through the trees. The impetuousness, almost the violence of his arrival, sent a thrill through her as she went down the path to meet him.

"How quickly you came!"

"The urgency of your letter . . . I thought you needed me, Connie."

"I did . . . "

He had caught her hand in his and held it while they came to the porch and he exchanged greetings with her mother. Then he led her on past and into the house.

When she saw his face in the light, there were signs of strain in it, and she could feel strain now in his fingers which held her hand strongly and tensely.

"You're tired, Henry!"

He shook his head. "It's been rotten hot in Chicago, and then I guess I was mentally stoking all the way up here, Connie. When I got started, I wanted to see you as soon as possible . . . but first, where are the things you wanted me to see?"

She ran upstairs and brought them down to him. Her hands were shaking now as she gave them to him.

Her tremor increased as she saw his big hands fumbling as he unwrapped the muffler and shook out the things it enclosed. He took them up one by one and looked at them, as she had done. His fingers were steady now by only mastering control, the effort for which amazed her.

He had the watch in his hands.

"The inscription is inside the front," she said.

She pried open the cover again and began to read aloud with him the engraved words within.

" 'As master of . . . .' What ship was he master of then, Henry, and how did he rescue the *Winnebago's* people?"

"He never talked to me about things like that, Connie. This is all?"

"Yes."

"And nothing since to show who sent them?"

"No, Henry."

"Corvet, Sherrill and Spearman will send someone to Manitowoc to make inquires," Henry said, putting the things back in the box. "But of course. this is the end of Benjamin Corvet."

"Of course," Constance replied. She was shaking again, and without willing it she withdrew a little from Henry. He caught her hand again and drew her back toward him. His hand was quite steady.

"You know why I came to you as fast as I could? You know why . . . why my mind was behind every thrust of the engines?"

"No."

"You don't? Oh, you must know now!"

"Yes, Henry," she said.

"I've been patient, Connie. Till I got your letter telling me about Ben, I'd waited for your sake—for our sakes—though it seemed at times to be impossible. You haven't known quite what's been the matter between us these last months, little girl, but I . . . I've known. We've been engaged, but that's about all there's been to it. Don't think I make little of that; you know what I mean. You've been mine, but . . . you haven't let me realize it, you see. And I've been patient, for I knew the reason. It was Ben poisoning your mind against me."

"No! No, Henry!"

"You've denied it, and I've recognized that you've denied it, not only to me and to your people, but to yourself as well. I, of course, knew, as I know that I am here now with your hand in mine, and as we will stand before the altar together, that he had no cause to speak against me. I've waited, Connie, to give him a chance to say to you what he had to say. I wanted you to hear it before making you wholly mine. But now there's no need to wait any longer, you and I. Ben's gone, never to come back . . . I was sure of that by what you wrote me, so this time when I started to you I brought with me . . . this."

He felt in his pocket and brought out a ring of plain gold. He held it before her so that she could see within it her own initials and his, and a blank left for the date. Her gaze went from it for an instant to the box where he had put back the other ring—Alan's mother's. Feeling for her long ago gazing thus, as she must have done, at that ring, held her for a moment. Was it because of that Constance found herself cold now?

"You mean you want me to marry you . . . at once, Henry?"

He drew her to him powerfully, and she felt him warm, almost rough with passion. Since that day in Alan's presence when he grasped and kissed her, she had not let him "realize" their engagement, as he had put it.

"Why not?" He turned her face up to his now. "Your mother's here, and your father will follow soon. Or, if you prefer, we'll run away . . . Constance! You've kept me off so long! You don't believe there's anything against me, dear? Do you? Do you?"

"No, no! Of course not!"

"Then we're going to be married . . . . We're going to be married, aren't we? Aren't we, Constance?"

"Yes . . . yes, of course."

"Right away, we'll have it then. Up here; now!"

"No; not now, Henry. Not up here!"

"Not here? Why not?"

She could give no answer. He held her and commanded her again; only when he realized he had frightened her did he cease.

"Why must it be at once, Henry? I don't understand!"

"It's not 'must,' dear," he denied. "It's just that I want you so!"

When would it be, he demanded then. Before spring, she promised him at last. But that was all he could make her say. And so he let her go.

The next evening, in the moonlight, she drove him to Petoskey. He had messages to send and preferred to go to the telegraph office in the larger town. Returning, they swung out along the country roads. The night was cool here on the hills, under the stars. The fan shaped glare from their headlights, blurring the radiance of the moon, sent distorted shadows of the dusty bushes beside the road dancing before them. Topping a rise, they came suddenly upon his birthplace. She had not designed coming to that place, but she had taken a turn at his direction, and now he asked her to stop the car. He got out and paced about, calling to her and pointing out the desirableness of the spot as the site for their country home. She sat in the car, watching him and calling back to him.

The house was small, log built, the chinks between the logs stopped with clay. Across the road from it, the silver birch trees gleamed white among the black barked timber. Smells of rank vegetation came to her from these woods and from the weed-grown fields about and beyond the house. There had been a small garden beside the house once. Now neglected strawberry vines ran riot among the weed stems, and clumps of sunflowers stood with hanging, full-blown heads under the August moon.

She gazed proudly at Henry's strong, well proportioned figure moving about in the moonlight, and was glad to think that a boy from this house had become the man that he was. But when she tried to think of him as a child here, her mind somehow showed her Alan playing about the sunflowers—and the place was not here; it was the brown, Kansas prairie of which he had told her.

"Sunflower houses," she murmured to herself. "Sunflower houses. They used to cut the stalks and build shacks with them."

"What's that?" Henry said as he came back near her.

The warm blood rushed to her face. "Nothing," she said, a little ashamed. She opened the door beside her. "Come, we'll go home now."

Coming from that poor little place, and having made of himself what he had, Henry was such a man as she would be proud to have for a husband; there was no man whom she had known who had proved himself to be as much of a man as he. Yet now, as she turned towards the Point, she was thinking of this lake country not only as Henry's land, but as Alan Conrad's too. In some such place he had also been born—born to the mother whose ring waited for him in the box in her room.

*   *   *

Alan, on the morning of the second of these days, was driving along the long, sandy peninsula which separates the blue waters of Grand Traverse Bay from Lake Michigan, and he was thinking of Constance Sherrill, as he knew that she was near. He had not only remembered that she would be north at Harbor Point this month, but he had seen in the Petoskey paper that she and her mother were at the Sherrill summer home. His business was now taking him nearer them than he had been at any time before, and if he wished to weaken, he might convince himself that he might learn from her circumstances which would aid him in his task. But he was not going to go to her for help. That would be following in his father's footsteps. When he knew everything, then, and not until then, he could go to her; for then he would know exactly what was upon him, and what he should do.

His visits to the people named on those sheets written by his father had been confusing at first. He had had great difficulty in tracing some of them, and afterwards he had been unable to uncover any certain connection, either between themselves or between them and Benjamin Corvet. But recently, he had been succeeding better in the former, and had found things the people on the list might have in common.

He had seen—he counted them over again—fourteen of the twenty-one named originally on Benjamin Corvet's lists. That is, he had seen either the individual originally named, or the surviving relative written in below the name crossed off. He had found that the crossing out of the name meant that the person was dead, except in the case of two who had left the country and whose where-abouts were as unknown to their present relatives as they had been to Benjamin Corvet, and the case of one other who was in an insane asylum.

He had found that not one of the persons whom he saw had known Benjamin Corvet personally. Many of them did not know him at all, and the others knew him only as a name. But as Alan proceeded, he found there was always one thing that linked the original names—always one circumstance that bound all together. When he established that circumstance as common to the first two on his lists, the blood pricked queerly under his skin. But, he had said to himself, the fact might be a mere coincidence. When he established it as also affecting the fate of the third and fourth, and of the fifth, such explanation no longer sufficed. Indeed, he had found it to be true of all fourteen. Sometimes it was the factor that had decided their fate, and sometimes it had affected them only slightly. But it was always there.

In how many different ways, and in what strange, diverse mani-festations had that single circumstance spread to those people whom Alan had interviewed! No two of them had been affected alike, he found, as he went over his notes on them. Now he was going to trace those consequences to another. To what sort of place would it bring him today, and what would he find there? He knew only that it would be quite distinct from the others.

The driver beside whom he sat on the front seat of the small automobile was an Indian, and an Indian woman and two silent, round-faced children occupied the seat behind. He had met these people in the early morning on the road, bound, he discovered, to the annual camp meeting of the Methodist Indians at Northport. It was a place he had never been, but he immediately remembered reading of the raid on Northport that was briefly mentioned in the Beaver Island book he had read in Benjamin Corvet's library. This family was going his way, and as they knew the man he was in search of, he had hired a ride of them.

The region through which they were traveling now was farm land, and interspersed among the farms were desolate, waste fields where blackened stumps and rotting windfalls remained after the lumberers had left. The hills and many of the hollows were wooded, and there were even a few places where lumbering was still going on. To his left across the water of Lake Michigan, the twin Manitou Islands broke the horizon, high and round and blue with haze. To his right, from the higher hilltops, he caught glimpses of Grand Traverse Bay. Looking out on this broad expanse of water, while he could not see its eastern shore, he knew, from the chart and Lake Bulletins he had seen, the higher hills south of Charlevoix broke into Little Traverse Bay to the east where Constance Sherrill was, only some two hours away across the water. But right now he had to shut his mind to that thought.

The driver turned now into a rougher road bearing to the east. They passed people more frequently now—groups in farm wagons, and groups and single individuals walking beside the road. All were going in the same direction as themselves, and nearly all were Indians, drab-dressed figures obviously attired in their best clothes. Some walked barefoot, carrying new shoes in their hands so as to preserve them from the dust. They waved gravely at Alan's driver, who returned their salutes—"B'jou!" "B'jou!"

Traveling eastward, they had lost sight of Lake Michigan, and then suddenly the wrinkled blueness of Grand Traverse Bay appeared quite close to them. The driver turned from the road and drove across a cleared field where ruts showed the passing of many previous vehicles. Beyond the field, in some woods, little fires for cooking burned all about. Nearby in the field were parked an immense number of farm wagons and buggies, with horses unharnessed and munching grain. Alan's guide found a place among these for his automobile, and they got out and went forward on foot to the woods. All about them, seated on the moss or walking about, were Indians, and children played among the family groups. A platform had been built under the trees, and on it some thirty Indians, all men, sat on straight-backed chairs. Around the platform, an audience of several hundred occupied benches. Others gathered around the border of the meeting, simply observing. A very old Indian, with inordinately wrinkled skin and dressed in a frock coat, was addressing these people in the Indian tongue.

Alan stopped beside his guide. Among the drab-clad figures looking on, he saw the brighter clothing of summer visitors who had come to watch. The figure of a girl among these caught his attention, and he straightened, then he swiftly told himself that it was only his thinking of Constance Sherrill that made him believe this was she. But now she had seen him. She paled, then as quickly flushed, and leaving the group she was with, she came toward him.

He had no choice now as to whether he would avoid her or not, and his happiness at seeing her held him spellbound as he watched her approach. Her eyes were very bright, and, it seemed, with something more than friendly greeting. There was happiness in them too. He was ecstatic at recognizing this, and his hand closed warmly over the small, trembling hand which she put out to him. All his conscious thought was lost for the moment in the mere realization of her presence. He stood, holding her hand, oblivious to the possibility that other people were about. She, too, seemed unaware that anyone else was present. Then she whitened momentarily and withdrew her hand. She seemed slightly embarrassed, as did he. This was not the way he had meant to greet her. Quickly he pulled himself together and stood beside her trying to look as any ordinary acquaintance of hers would have looked.

"How is it that you are here?" he asked.

"We always try to come over for this camp meeting. Our Indian friends in Emmet County first told us about it. They come over every year for it. So do many of our friends at Harbor Point, mostly because the Indians from all over bring their best craftwork to display and sell here. Besides, the whole event is very colorful and interesting."

14

Constance quickly changed the subject to what was really on her mind at suddenly finding Alan again.

"So they got word to you!" she exclaimed. Then a confusion seemed to come over her. "Oh, no . . . ," she said. "Of course they couldn't have done that! They've hardly had time to receive my letter yet."

"Your letter?" Alan asked.

"I wrote to Blue Rapids," she explained. "Some things came . . . they were sent to me. Some things of Uncle Benny's which were meant for you instead of me."

"You mean you've heard from him?"

"No . . . not that."

"What things, Miss Sherrill?"

"A watch of his and some coins and . . . a ring." She did not explain the significance of those things, and he could not tell from her mere enumeration of them, and without seeing them, that they furnished proof that his father was dead. She could not inform him of that until later.

"I'll tell you about that later. You . . . you were coming to Harbor Point to see us?"

He colored. "I'm afraid not. I got as near as this to you because there is a man—an Indian—I have to see."

"An Indian? What is his name? You see, I know quite a lot of them."

"Jo Papo."

She shook her head. "No; I don't know him."

She had drawn him a little away from the crowd at the meeting. His heart was beating hard with recognition of her manner toward him. Whatever he was, whatever the disgrace might be that his father had left to him, she was resolute to share in it. He had known she would do so. She found a spot where the moss was covered with soft pine needles and sat down on the ground.

"Sit down," she invited. "I want you to tell me what you have been doing."

"I've been on the boats." He dropped down on the ground beside her. "It's a . . . wonderful business, Miss Sherrill. I'll never be able to go away from the water again. I've been working rather hard at my new profession—studying it, I mean. Until yesterday I was not a very highly honored member of the crew of the package freighter *Oscoda*. I left her at Frankfort and came up here."

"Is Wassaquam with you?"

"He wasn't on the *Oscoda*, but he was with me at first. Now, I believe, he has gone back to his own people; I think to visit his nephew . . . near Middle Village."

"You mean you've been looking for your father in that way?"

"To a degree, yes." He hesitated, but he could see no reason for not telling what he had been doing. He had not so much hidden from the Sherrills what he had found in Benjamin Corvet's house; rather, he had refrained from mentioning it in his notes to them when he left Chicago because he had thought the lists would lead to an immediate explanation, which they had not. He had known that if his search finally developed nothing more than it had, then he would have to consult with Lawrence Sherrill and enlist his aid.

"We found some writing, Miss Sherrill," he said, "in the house on Astor Street that night after Luke came."

"What writing?"

He took the lists from his pocket and showed them to her. She separated and looked through the sheets and read the names written in the same hand that had written the directions on the slip of paper that came to her four days before, with the things from Uncle Benny's pockets.

"My father had kept these very secretly," he explained. "He had them hidden. Wassaquam knew where they were, and that night after Luke died and you had gone home, he gave them to me."

"After I had gone home Henry went back to see you that night. He had said he was going back, and afterwards when I asked him, he told me he had seen you again. Did you show him these?"

"He saw them . . . yes."

"He was there when Wassaquam showed you where they were?"

"Yes."

A little line deepened between her brows, and she seemed somewhat disturbed. "So you have been going about seeing these people," she said. "What have you found out?"

"Nothing at all definite. None of them knew my father. They were amazed to find that anyone in Chicago had known their names."

She got up suddenly. "You don't mind if I am with you when you talk with this Indian?"

He arose and looked around for the guide who had brought him. The man had been standing nearby, evidently waiting until Alan's attention turned his way. He gestured now toward a man, a woman and several children who were lunching around a basket on the ground. The man was thin, and of medium size, and like so many Indians was taciturn and of indefinite age—neither still young nor yet old. It was evident that life had been hard for the man, however, for he looked worn and undernourished, and he was attired in a cast-off suit of someone much larger which had been inexpertly altered to make it fit him. As Alan and Constance approached, the group turned their dark, inexpressive eyes on them, and the woman got up while the man remained seated on the ground.

"I'm looking for Jo Papo," Alan explained.

"What you want?" the squaw asked. "You got work?" The words were pronounced with difficulty and evidently composed most of her English vocabulary.

"I want to see him, that's all." Alan turned to the man. "You're Jo Papo, aren't you?"

The Indian assented by an almost imperceptible nod.

"You used to live near Escanaba, didn't you?"

Jo Papo considered before replying. Either his scrutiny of Alan reassured him, or he recalled nothing having to do with his residence near Escanaba which disturbed him. "Yes; once," he said.

"Your father was Azen Papo?"

"He's dead," the Indian replied. "Not my father, anyway. Grandfather. What about him?"

"That's what I want to ask you," Alan said. "When did he die and how?"

Jo Papo got up and stood leaning his back against a tree. So far from being one who was merely curious about Indians, this stranger perhaps was coming about an Indian claim—to give money, maybe, for injustices done in the past. "My grandfather die fifteen years ago," he informed them. "From cough, I think."

"Where was that?" Alan asked.

"Escanaba . . . near there. Take people to shoot deer . . . fish . . . a guide. I think he plant a little too."

"He didn't work on the boats?"

"No. My father, he work on the boats."

"What was his name?"

"Like me; Jo Papo, too. He's dead."

"What is your name?"

"Flying Eagle."

"What boats did your father work on?"

"Many boats."

"What did he do?"

"Deck hand."

"What boat did he work on last?"

"Last? How do I know? He went away one year and didn't come back. I suppose he was drowned from a boat."

"What year was that?"

"I was little then. I don't know."

"How old were you?"

"Maybe eight years; maybe nine or ten."

"How old are you now?"

"Thirty, maybe."

"Did you ever hear of Benjamin Corvet?"

"Who?"

"Benjamin Corvet."

"No."

Alan turned to Constance. She had been listening intently, but she made no comment.

"That is all, then," Alan said to Papo; "if I find out anything to your advantage, I'll let you know." He understood that he had aroused expectations of benefit in these poor Indians. Something rose in Alan's throat and choked him.

Those of whom Benjamin had so laboriously kept track were, very many of them, of the same sort. What conceivable bond could there have been between Alan's father and such poor people as these? Had his father wronged these people? Had he owed them something? This thought, which had been growing stronger with each succeeding step of Alan's investigation, chilled and horrified him now. Revolt against his father more active than ever before seized him, revolt stirring stronger with each recollection of his interviews with the people on his list As they walked away, Constance appreciated that he was feeling something deeply, and she too was stirred.

"They all . . . all I have talked to . . . are like that," he said to her. "They all have lost someone on the lakes."

In her feeling for him, she had laid her hand upon his arm. Now her fingers tightened to sudden tension. "What do you mean?" she asked.

"Oh, it's not definite yet . . . not clear!" She felt the bitterness in his tone. "They have not any of them been able to make it wholly clear to me. It is like a record that has been blurred. These original names must have been written down by my father many years ago. Many—most of those people, I think—are dead, and some are nearly forgotten. The only thing that is fully plain is that in every case my inquiries have led me to those who have lost one, and sometimes more than one relative on the lakes."

Constance thrilled to a great horror, and it was not anything to which she could give definite reason. His tone, quite as much as what he said, was its cause. His experience clearly had been forcing him to bitterness against his father, and he did not know with certainty yet that his father was dead.

She had not found it possible to tell him that yet, and now she consciously deferred telling him until she could take him to her home and show him what had come. The shrill whistle of her father's yacht, *Salem*, in which she and her party had come, recalled to her that all were to return aboard for luncheon, and that they must be waiting for her.

"You'll lunch with us, of course," she said to Alan, "and then go back with us to Harbor Point. It's a day's journey around the two bays by car, but *Salem* will take us back in about two hours."

He assented, and they walked down to the water where the white *Salem*, with its long, graceful lines and sparkling mahogany bright work, lay somnolently in the sunlight. A small boat took them out over the shimmering, smooth surface to the anchored yacht. Swells from the outer bay swept under the beautiful, burnished power craft, causing it to roll lazily as they boarded it. A party of some dozen young men and women, and an older woman, the mother of one of them, lounged in the shade of the awning covering the after deck. They greeted Constance gaily and looked curiously at Alan as she introduced him.

As he returned their rather formal acknowledgments and afterward fell into general conversation with them, she became for the first time fully aware of how greatly he had changed from what he had been when he had come to them six months before in Chicago. These gay, wealthy loungers could have dismayed him then, and he would have been equally dismayed by the luxury of the carefully appointed yacht. Now he was not thinking at all about what these people might think of him. In return, they granted him consideration. She saw it was not that they accepted him as one of their own sort, or as some ordinary acquaintance of hers. If they accounted for him to themselves at all, they must believe him to be some officer employed on her father's ships. His face was darkened and reddened by the summer sun, and in his clothing he resembled a ship's officer ashore. He had not weakened under the disgrace which Benjamin Corvet had left to him, whatever that might be. Rather he had grown stronger facing it. Pride arose within her as she realized that the lakes had been setting their seal upon him, as they had upon the man whose strength and resourcefulness she was about to marry.

"While I'm up here I will try to reach a man on the list living in Petoskey, who used to live on Beaver Island," Alan said.

"Perhaps our captain, Tim Sullivan, who greeted us when we came aboard, can help you," she replied. "He grew up on Beaver Island. Let's go talk to him."

As they walked up the few steps to the bridge deck, Sullivan turned, and said, "Do you want a turn at the wheel, Miss Sherrill?"

"No, thank you, but Mr. Corvet here is inquiring about a man who used to live on Beaver Island. I suggested you might be able to help him."

"Do you know a man named Dan Hogan?" Alan interjected.

"Yes," Sullivan replied. "Dan and his twin brother Harry were bachelors, and were the sole survivors of their family. They lived together in the old family farmhouse on the Island for years. Before his brother was lost in a shipwreck, he moved to Petoskey and went to work for the Woodland Avenue House in Bayview Assembly when it opened in '86 or '87. He took care of their horses, and ferried the guests around in the house carriage. He died of pneumonia some years ago."

"You said his brother was lost in a shipwreck. Do you know the name of the ship?" Alan asked.

"Never did know, but the ship was lost during a storm in December, 1895. I remember the date because we moved back to the mainland a few days after that storm. I was ten years old then."

* * *

As they left the bridge deck, Alan looked at Constance appreciatively. "Thanks to you, it appears I have found another piece in my jig-saw puzzle. Tim Sullivan has saved me a lot of time in my search."

"Have you worked on any of our boats?" Constance asked.

A queer expression appeared on his face. "I've thought it best not to do that, Miss Sherrill," he replied.

"Alan, will you please stop calling me 'Miss Sherrill?' " she said, grasping his hand. "I'm not a schoolmarm, you know."

The tone of her request, with its spark of humor, and the touch of her hand made his heart beat a little faster as he assented—" 'Constance!' What a beautiful name it is!" His usual captivating smile this time had a new and special meaning which made her glow with a warmth she had never felt before.

She did not know why the next moment she should think of Henry. Could it be because, by contrast, Henry lacked the understanding that was so very natural and pleasing in Alan?

"Henry was going to bring us over in his *Chippewa*," she said. "But he was called away suddenly yesterday on business to St. Ignace and used his boat to go over there."

"He's at Harbor Point, then."

"He arrived a couple of nights ago and will be back again to-night, or tomorrow morning."

The *Salem* was pushing along swiftly and smoothly, with hardly a hum from her engines. Alan watched intently the rolling, wooded hills and the ragged little bays and inlets. His work and his investigatings had not brought him into this area before, but Constance found she did not have to name the places to him, as he knew them from the charts.

"Grand Traverse Light," he said to her as a white tower showed up on their left. Then, leaving the shore, they pushed out across the wide mouth of the larger bay toward Little Traverse. He grew more silent as they approached it, and looking off the port side to the north, he asked, pointing:

"It is up there, isn't it, that they hear the drum?"

"Yes; how did you know the place?"

"I don't know it exactly, but I want you to show me."

She pointed out to him the copse, dark, primeval and blue in its contrast with the lighter green of the trees about it and the glisten-ing white of the beaches and more distant sand bluffs. He leaned forward staring at it until the changed course of the yacht, as it swung about toward the entrance to the bay, obscured it.

They were meeting other power boats now, some of their own size and many smaller, and they passed several almost becalmed sail-boats apparently participating in a race, as the sloops were bunched in one cluster and the cat-boats in another. As they neared the Point, this panorama of play, which Constance knew so well but was some-thing Alan had never seen before, was spread before them. The sun gleamed back from the white sides, the varnished mahogany top-sides and shining brasswork of a score or more cruising yachts and smaller boats lying in the anchorage.

"The Chicago to Mackinac sail yacht race starts this week, and the cruiser fleet is working north to be in at the finish," Constance offered. Then she saw Alan was not looking at these things. He was studying with a strange expression the dark, uneven hills which shut in the two towns and the bay.

"You remember how the ship rhymes you told me, and how the story about Michabou and seeing the ships made me feel like I belonged here on the lakes," he reminded her. "I have felt something many times this summer when I saw certain places . . . . Not recognition exactly, but something that was like the beginning of recognition. It's like one of those dreams, you know, in which you are conscious of having had the same dream before. I feel like I ought to know this place. Perhaps I feel this way because your cottage is near here . . . because . . . because I am here with you. Since being on the boats I have had a lot of time to reflect on what has happened to me since being away from Blue Rapids. I know now that not only is this lake country my home, but more important, I know that when I am with you I am more comfortable and happy than at any other time—like I am right now."

Constance tried to hold back the tears she knew were welling in her eyes as she placed her hand over his on the *Salem's* rail.

15

They landed not far from the cottage, and after parting from her friends, they went on up to it together through the trees. There was a small sun room, rather shut off from the rest of the house, to which she led him.

Leaving him there, she ran upstairs to get the things.

She paused an instant in the hallway with the box in her hands, thinking how she could prepare him against the significance of these relics of his father. She need not prepare him against the mere fact of his father's death; he had been beginning to believe that already. But these things must have far more meaning for him than just that. They would frustrate one course of inquiry for him at the same time they opened another.

They would close for him forever the possibility of ever learning anything about himself from his father, and they would introduce into his problem some new, some unknown person—the sender of these things.

She went into the sun room and put the box down on the card table.

"The muffler in the box was your father's," she told him. "He had it on the day he disappeared. The other things he must have had in his pockets. They've been lying in water and sand . . ."

He gazed at her. "I understand," he said after an instant. "You mean that they prove his death."

She assented gently, without speaking. As he approached the box, she drew back from it and quietly slipped into the next room. She walked up and down there, pressing her hands together. He must be looking at the things now, unrolling the muffler . . . . What would he be feeling as he saw them? Would he be glad, with that same gladness which had mingled with her own sorrow over Uncle Benny, knowing that his father was gone—gone from his guilt and his fear and his disgrace? Or would he resent that death which would now leave everything unexplained to him? He would be looking at the ring. That, at least, must bring more joy than grief to him. He would recognize that it must be his mother's wedding ring. If it told him she must be dead, it would tell him that she had been married, or had believed that she was married!

Then she heard him calling her. His voice had a sharp thrill of excitement. She hurried toward the sun room. She could see him through the doorway, bending over the card table with the things spread out upon its top in front of him.

"Yes."

He straightened up, and was very pale. "Would coins that my father had in his pocket all have been more than twenty years old?"

She bent beside him over the coins. "Twenty years!" she repeated. She was making out the dates of the coins now herself. The markings were eroded, nearly gone in some instances, but in every case enough remained to plainly show the date. "Eighteen-ninety . . . 1893 . . . 1894," she made them out. Her voice faltered queerly. "What does it mean?" she whispered.

He turned over and again examined the articles with his hands now steadying. "There are two sets of things here," he concluded. "The muffler and paper of directions . . . they belonged to my father. The other things . . . it isn't six months or less than six months that they've lain in sand and water to become like this. It's twenty years. My father can't have had these things. They were somewhere else, or someone else had them. He wrote his directions to that person. 'After June twelfth,' the note said, so it was before that date when he wrote it, but we can't tell how long before. It might have been in February, when he disappeared, or it might have been any time after that. But if the directions were written so long ago, why weren't the things sent to you before this? Didn't the person have the things then? Did he have to wait to get them? Or . . . was it the instructions to send them that he didn't have? Or, if he had the instructions, was he waiting to receive word when they were to be sent?"

"To receive word?" she echoed.

"Word from my father! You thought these things proved my father was dead. I think they may prove that he is alive! Oh, we must think this out!"

He paced up and down the room, and she sank into a chair, watching him. "The first thing we must do," he said suddenly, "is to find out about the watch. What is the telephone number of the telegraph office?"

She told him, and he went out to the telephone. She sprang up to follow him, but checked herself and waited until he came back.

"I've wired to Buffalo," he announced on returning. "The Merchants' Exchange, if it is still in existence, must have a record of the presentation of the watch. At any rate, the wreck of the *Winnebago* and the name of the skipper of the other ship must be in the files of the newspapers of that time."

"Then you'll stay with us until an answer comes."

"If we get a reply by tomorrow morning; I'll wait until then. If not, I'll ask you to forward it to me. I must see about the trains and get back to Frankfort. I can cross by boat from there to Manitowoc . . . that will be the quickest. We must begin there, by trying to find out who sent the package."

215

"Henry Spearman's already sent to have that investigated."

Alan made no reply, but she saw his lips tighten quickly. "I must go myself as soon as I can," he said, after a moment.

She helped him put the muffler and the other articles back into the box, and she noticed that the wedding ring was no longer with them. He had taken that, then. It had meant to him all that she had known it must mean . . . .

In the morning she was up very early, but Alan, the servants told her, had risen before she had and had gone out. The morning, after the cool northern night, was chill. She slipped on a sweater and went out on the veranda to look for him. An iridescent haze shrouded the hills and the bay. She heard a ship's bell strike twice . . .then another . . . and another . . . and another. The haze thinned as the sun grew warmer, showing the placid water of the bay on which the boats stood double—a real one and a mirrored one. She saw Alan returning, and from his direction knew he must be returning from the Harbor Springs telegraph office. She ran to meet him.

"Was there an answer?" she eagerly inquired.

He took a yellow telegram from his pocket and held it for her to read.

WATCH PRESENTED CAPTAIN CALEB STAFFORD, MASTER OF PROPELLER FREIGHTER *MARVIN HALCH* FOR RESCUE OF CREW AND PASSENGERS OF SINKING STEAMER *WINNEBAGO* OFF LONG POINT, LAKE ERIE.

She was breathing quickly in her excitement. "Caleb Stafford!" she exclaimed. "Why, that was Captain Stafford of Stafford and Ramsdell! They owned the *Miwaka*!"

"Yes," Alan replied.

"You asked me about that ship—the *Miwaka*—that first morning at breakfast."

"Yes."

A great change had come over him since last night. He was under emotion so strong that he seemed scarcely to speak lest it master him—a leaping, exultant impulse it was, which he fought to keep down.

"What is it, Alan?" she asked. "What is it about the *Miwaka*? You said you'd found some reference to it in Uncle Benny's house. What was it? What did you find there?"

"The man . . . ." Alan swallowed and steadied himself and repeated, "The man I met in the house that night mentioned it."

"The man who thought you were a ghost?"

"Yes."

"How . . . how did he mention it?"

"He seemed to think I was a ghost that had haunted my father . . . a ghost from the *Miwaka*. At least he shouted out to me that I couldn't save the *Miwaka*!"

"Save the *Miwaka*! What do you mean, Alan? The *Miwaka* was lost years ago with all her people—officers and crew—no one knows how or where!"

"All except the one for whom the drum didn't toll."

"What do you mean?" she replied, excitedly.

"I don't know yet, but I think I will soon find out!"

"Can't you tell me more now, Alan? Surely you can. I must know. I have the right to know. Yesterday, even before you found out about this, you knew things you weren't telling me . . . things about the people you'd been seeing. They'd all lost people on the lakes, you said, but you found out more than that."

"They'd all lost people on the *Miwaka*!" he said. "That is, all who could tell me where their people were lost. A few were like Jo Papo, whom we saw yesterday, who knew only the year his father was lost. But the time always was about the time the *Miwaka* disappeared!"

"Disappeared!" she repeated. She felt a cold chill. What did he know, what could anyone know of the *Miwaka*, the ship of which nothing was ever heard except the beating of the legendary drum? She tried to get him say more, but he only looked out on the bay.

"The *Chippewa* must have come in early this morning," he said. "She's anchored in town near the Station; I saw her on my way to the telegraph office. If Mr. Spearman has come back with her, tell him I'm sorry I can't wait to see him."

"When are you going?"

"Now."

She offered to drive him to Petoskey, but he had already arranged for a man to take him there to the train.

She went to her room after he was gone and spread out again on her bed the watch—now the watch of Captain Stafford of the *Miwaka*—with the knife and coins of more than twenty years ago which came with it. The meaning of them now was all changed. She felt that, but what the new meaning might be, she could not even guess. Something of it had come to Alan, of that she was sure. That, undoubtedly, was what had so greatly excited him, but she could not yet reassemble her own ideas, even though a few new facts had become known.

A maid came to say that Mr. Spearman had come up from his boat for breakfast with her and was downstairs. She went down to find Henry lounging in one of the great wicker chairs in the living room. He arose and came toward her quickly, but she stopped before he could embrace her.

"I got back, Connie . . ."

"Yes, I heard you did."

"What's wrong, dear?"

"Alan Conrad has been here, Henry."

"He has? How was that?"

She told him while he watched her intently. "He wired Buffalo about the watch, and brought the reply to me half an hour ago."

"Yes."

"The watch belonged to Captain Stafford, who was lost with the *Miwaka*, Henry."

He made no reply, but waited for her to continue.

"You may not have known that it was his. I mean you may not

have known that it was he who rescued the people of the *Winnebago*, but you must have known that it was not Uncle Benny."

"Yes, I knew that, Connie," he answered evenly.

"Then why did you let me think the watch belonged to Uncle Benny, and that he must be . . . dead?"

"That's all's the matter? You had thought he was dead. I believed it was better for you—for everyone—to believe that."

She drew a little away from him, with hands clasped behind her back, gazing intently at him. "There was some writing found in Uncle Benny's house in Astor Street—a list of names of relatives of people who lost their lives on the lake. Wassaquam knew where those things were. Alan says they were given to him in your presence."

She saw the blood rise to his face. "That is true, Connie."

"Why didn't you tell me about that?"

He straightened as if with anger. "Why should I? Because he thought that I should? What did he tell you about those lists?"

"I asked you if anything else had happened after you went back, Henry, and you said, 'Nothing.' I should not have considered the finding of those lists 'nothing.' "

"Why not? What were they but names? What has he told you they were? What has he said to you, Connie?"

"Nothing—except that his father had kept them very secretly, and he found out they were the names of people who had relatives on the *Miwaka!*"

"What?"

Recalling how her blood had run when Alan had told her that, Henry's whiteness and the following expression on his face did not surprise her. He turned away a moment and considered. "Where is Conrad now, Connie?"

"He's gone to Frankfort to cross to Manitowoc."

"To get deeper into that mess, I suppose. He'll only be sorry."

"Sorry?"

"I told that fellow long ago not to start stirring up these matters about Ben Corvet, and particularly I told him that he was not to bring any of it to you. It's not . . . a thing, that a man like Ben Corvet covered up for twenty years till it drove him crazy, that a girl should know about. Conrad seems to have paid no attention to me. But I should think by this time he ought to begin to suspect what sort of thing he's going to turn up. I don't know, but I certainly suspect . . . Ben leaving everything to that boy whom no one had heard of . . . . The sort of thing he may discover won't be nice. It's certainly not going to be anything pleasant for any of us, Connie— for you, or your father, or for me, or for anybody who cared for Ben, or has been associated with him. Least of all, I should say, would it prove anything pleasant for Conrad. Ben ran away from it, because he knew what it was. Why doesn't this fellow stay away from it?"

"He—I mean Alan, Henry—isn't thinking about himself in this, and he isn't thinking about his father. He believes—he is certain now—that whatever his father did, he injured someone. His idea in going ahead . . . he hasn't told it to me in that way, but I know. His idea is to find out the whole matter in order that he may make recompense. It's a terrible thing, whatever happened. He knows that, and I know. But he wants—and I want him for his sake, even for Uncle Benny's sake—to see it through."

"Then it's a queer concern you've got for Ben! Let it alone, I say."

She stood flushed and perplexed, gazing at him. She had never seen him under stronger emotion.

"You misunderstood me once, Connie!" he appealed. "You'll understand me now!"

She had been thinking about that injustice she had done him in her thought—about his chivalry to his partner and former benefactor, when Uncle Benny was still keeping his place among men. Was Henry now moved, in a way which she could not understand, by some other obligation to the man who long ago had aided him?

Had Henry hazarded more than he had told her of the nature of the thing hidden which, if she could guess it, would justify what he said?

In the confusion of her thought, one thing came clearly which troubled her and of which she could not speak. The watch of Captain Stafford's and the ring and the coins, which had made her believe that Uncle Benny was dead, had not been proof of that to Henry. Yet he had taken advantage of her belief, by omission of facts, to urge her to marry him at once.

She knew of the ruthlessness of Henry's business life. He had forced down and overcome all who opposed him, and he had made full use for his own advantage of other men's mistakes and erroneous beliefs and opinions.

If he had used her belief in Uncle Benny's death to hasten their marriage, it was something which others—particularly she—could pardon and accept. If she was drawn to him for his strength and dominance, which sometimes ran into ruthlessness, she had no right to complain if he turned it thus upon her.

She had made Alan promise to write her, if he was not to return, regarding what he learned, and a letter came to her on the fourth day from him in Manitowoc. The post office employees had no recollection, he said, of the person who had mailed the package, as it had simply been dropped by someone into the receptacle for mailing packages of that sort. They did not know the handwriting on the wrapper, which he had taken with him, nor was it known at the bank or in any of the stores where he had shown it. The shoe dealer had no recollection of that particular box. Alan, however, was continuing his inquiries as he went about the lakes on the boats.

In September he reported in a brief, totally impersonal note from Sarnia, Ontario, on speaking there with someone from the list. In October he sent a different address where he could be found in case anything more came, such as the box Constance had received in August.

She wrote to him in reply each time, and in lack of anything more important to tell him, she related some of her activities and inquired about his. After she had written in this way, he replied describing his life on the boats pleasantly and humorously; then, though she immediately replied, she did not hear from him again.

She had returned to Chicago late in September and soon was very busy with social affairs, benefits and bazaars which were given that fall for the Red Cross and different Allied causes. A little later came a series of more personal and absorbing luncheons, and dances and dinners for her and for Henry, as their engagement, which had long been taken for granted by everyone who knew them, had now been announced. So the days drifted into December and winter again.

The lake, beating against the esplanade across The Drive before Constance's windows, had changed its color. It no longer showed its autumn blue and silver but was now gray, and sluggish with floating needle-points of ice. The floes had not yet begun to form, but the piers and breakwaters had white caps of ice from frozen spray— harbingers of the closing of navigation. The summer boats—those of Corvet, Sherrill and Spearman with the rest—were being tied up. The birds were gone, and only the gulls remained, their gray, clamorous shapes circling and calling to one another across the water. Early in December the newspapers announced the closing of the locks at the "Soo" by the ice.

That she had not heard from Alan was beginning to recur to Constance with strange consistency. He must have left the boats by now, unless he had found work on one of those few which ran through the winter.

He and his occupation, instead of slipping from her thoughts with time, absorbed her more and more. Soon after he had gone to Manitowoc and he had written that he had discovered nothing, she had gone to the Petoskey paper, and looking back over the twenty-year-old files, she had read the account of the loss of the *Miwaka*, with all on board. No mention was made of the legendary, missing drum beat, but the paper had reported that many believed there might be a survivor. Alan's reference to the ship's having "disappeared" went through her with a chill. Who knew what had happened to the *Miwaka*?

She thought of the names on the list again. If there was meaning in the drum, who was the man who survived and visited that fate on Benjamin Corvet? Was it Luke? There was no Luke named among the crew, but such men often went by many names. If Luke had been among the crew of the *Miwaka* and had brought from that lost ship something which threatened Uncle Benny, that, at least, explained Luke. Then another idea occurred to her. Captain Caleb Stafford was named among the lost, and with him, of course, had perished his three-year-old son.

Alan had been three then. This was wild, crazy speculation. The ship was lost with all hands. Only the drum denied that, and it was but a superstition. How could a child of three have been saved, when strong men, to the last one, had perished? And, if he had been saved, he was not Uncle Benny's son. He was Stafford's son. Why should Uncle Benny have sent him away and cared for him, and then have sent for him? Most of all, why should Uncle Benny disappear and leave all he had to . . . Stafford's son?

Or was he Stafford's son? Her thoughts went back to the things which had been sent—the things from a man's pockets with a wedding ring among them. She had believed that the ring had cleared the mother's name. Might it in reality only involve it more? Why had it come back like this to the man by whom, perhaps, it had been given? Henry's words came again and again to Constance: "It's a queer concern you've got for Ben. Leave it alone, I tell you!"

Alan knew, then, something about Uncle Benny, something which might have brought on some terrible consequence Henry did not know of but might have guessed! Constance went weak within. Uncle Benny's wife had left him, she remembered. Was it better, after all, to "leave it alone"?

But this was not something which one could command one's mind to leave alone, and Constance could not make herself try to, as long as it concerned Alan. Coming home late one afternoon toward the middle of December, she dismissed the car and stood gazing at the gulls. The day was chill and gray. The air had the feel, and the voices of the gulls had the sound to her, which precede the coming of a severe storm. The gulls recalled to her sharply the day when Alan had first come to them, and how she had been the first to meet him, and the child's verse which had told him that he, too, was of the lakes.

She went on into the house. A telegraph envelope addressed to her father was on the table in the hall. Simons told her the message had come an hour before, and that he had telephoned Mr. Sherrill's office, but he was not in. There was no reason for her thinking the message might be from Alan, except that his presence was in her thoughts, but she went at once and called her father. He was back in his office, and he directed her to open the telegram and read it to him.

" 'Have someone who knew Mr. Corvet' . . . ," she read aloud before she choked in her excitement at what came next. She had to collect herself and start over. " 'Have someone who knew Mr. Corvet well enough to recognize him, even if greatly changed, meet carferry *Number 25* Manitowoc Wednesday this week.' It's signed by Alan Conrad."

There was no immediate response from her father, and she felt her heart, beating fast. "Are you there?" she said into the phone.

"Yes."

"Whom will you send?"

There was an instant's silence. "I shall go myself," her father answered.

She hung up the receiver. Had Alan found Uncle Benny? He had apparently found someone whose resemblance to the picture she had shown him was enough to make him believe that person might be Benjamin Corvet, or he had heard of someone he thought might be him.

She read the words of the telegram again. ". . . even if greatly changed"! and she felt startling and terrifying warning in that phrase.

Part
Five

Stormy Waters

16

It had been late in November on Lake Superior, where Alan was serving as a lookout aboard the coal carrier, *Pontiac*, that Alan first heard of Jim Burr. This name, spoken among some other names in casual conversation with another crew member, aroused his attention. The name James Burr was on Benjamin Corvet's list. It had opposite it the notation, "All disappeared—no trace." When Alan had investigated this name, he had been able only to verify the fact that at the address given no one of this name was to be found.

He questioned the oiler who had mentioned Burr. The man had met Burr one night in Manitowoc with other men, and something about the old man had impressed both his name and image on him, but he knew no more than that. At Manitowoc!—the place from which Captain Stafford's watch had been sent to Constance Sherrill, and where Alan had sought for, but had failed to find, the sender! Had Alan stumbled by chance upon the one whom Benjamin Corvet had been unable to trace?

Had Corvet, after his disappearance, found Burr? Had Burr been the sender, under Corvet's direction, of those things? The man might well, of course, be some other Jim Burr. There were probably many men by that name. Yet the James Burr of Corvet's list must have been such a one as the oiler described—a white-haired old man.

Alan could not leave the *Pontiac* and go at once to Manitowoc to look for Burr, because he was needed where he was. The navigation season on Lake Superior was near its close. In Duluth, skippers were clamoring for cargoes, and ships were lading in haste for a last trip before the ice closed the lake's outlet at the Soo against all ships.

It was fully a week later and after the *Pontiac* had been laden again and repassed the length of Lake Superior that Alan left the vessel at Sault Ste. Marie and took the train for Manitowoc.

The little lake port of Manitowoc, which he reached in the late afternoon, was turbulent with the lake's approaching close. Long lines of bulk freighters, loaded and tied up to wait for spring, filled the river; their released crews boisterously filling the town. Alan inquired for the seamen's drinking place where his informant had met Jim Burr, and following directions he received, he made his way along the river until he found it.

The place was neat and immaculate, and a score of lakemen sat talking at little tables or leaned against the bar. Alan inquired of the proprietor for Jim Burr.

The proprietor knew old Jim Burr . . . yes. Burr was a wheelsman on carferry *Number 25*. He was a lakeman, experienced and capable, and that fact, some months before, had served as introduction for him to the frequenters of this place. When the ferry was in harbor and his duties left him idle, Burr came up and waited there, occupying always the same chair. He never drank, and never spoke to others unless they spoke first to him, but then he talked freely about old days on the lakes; about ships which had been lost and about men long dead.

Alan decided there could be no better place to interview old Burr than here, so he waited therefore, and in the early evening the old man came in.

Alan watched him curiously as, without speaking to anyone, he went to the chair recognized as his and sat down. He was a slender but muscularly built man seeming about sixty-five, but he might be younger or older than that. His hair was completely white; his nose was thin and sensitive; his face was smoothly placid, emotionless, contented; his eyes queerly clouded, deep set and intent.

Those whose names Alan had found on Corvet's list had been of all ages, young and old, but Burr might well have been a contemporary of Corvet on the lakes. Alan moved over and took a seat beside the old man.

"You're from *Number 25?*" he asked, to draw him into conversation.

"Yes."

"I've been working on the carrier *Pontiac* as lookout. She's on her way to tie up at Cleveland, so I left her and came here. Would you know whether there's a chance for me to get a place through the winter on *Number 25?*"

Old Burr reflected. "One of our boys has been talking about leaving. I don't know when he expects to go. You might ask."

"Thank you, I will. My name's Conrad—Alan Conrad."

He saw no recognition of the name in Burr's reception of it, but he had expected that. None of those on Benjamin Corvet's list had any knowledge of Alan Conrad or had heard the name before.

Alan was silent, watching the old man. Burr, silent too, seemed to be listening to the conversation which came from the tables nearby, where men were talking of cargoes, and of ships and of men who worked and sailed upon them.

"How long have you been on the lakes?" Alan inquired.

"All my life." The question awakened reminiscence in the old man. "My father had a farm. I didn't like farming. The schooners—they were almost always schooners in those days—came in to load with lumber. When I was nine years old, I ran away and got on board a schooner. I've been at it, sail or steam, ever since."

"Do you remember the *Miwaka?*"

"The *Miwaka?*"

Old Burr turned abruptly and studied Alan with a slow scrutiny which seemed to look him through and through. Yet while his eyes remained fixed on Alan suddenly they grew blank. He was not thinking now of Alan, but had turned his thoughts within himself.

"I remember her . . . yes. She was lost in '95," he said. "In '95," he repeated.

"You lost a nephew with her, didn't you?"

"A nephew . . . no. That is a mistake. I lost a brother."

"Where were you living then?"

"In Emmet County, Michigan."

"When did you move to Point Corbay, Ontario?"

"I never lived at Point Corbay."

"Did any of your family live there?"

"No." Old Burr looked away from Alan, and the queer cloudiness of his eyes became more evident.

"Why do you ask all this?" he said irritably. "What have they been telling you about me? I told you about myself; our farm was in Emmet County, but we had a liking for the lake. One of my brothers was lost in '95 on the *Miwaka* and another in '99 on the *Susan Hart.*"

"Did you know Benjamin Corvet?" Alan asked.

Old Burr stared at him uncertainly. "I know who he is, of course."

"You never met him?"

"No."

"Did you receive a communication from him some time this year?"

"From him? From Benjamin Corvet? No." Old Burr's uneasiness seemed to increase. "What sort of communication?"

"A request to send some things to Miss Constance Sherrill at Harbor Point."

"I never heard of Miss Constance Sherrill. To send what things?"

"Several things . . . among them a watch which had belonged to Captain Stafford of the *Miwaka.*"

Burr got up suddenly and stood gazing down at Alan. "A watch of Captain Stafford's? . . . No," he said agitatedly. "No!"

He moved away and left the place, and Alan sprang up and followed him.

Alan thought now it was improbable this man could be the James Burr on Corvet's list. Among the names of the crew of the *Miwaka* Alan had found that of a Frank Burr, and his inquiries had informed him that this man was a nephew of the James Burr who had lived near Port Corbay. Frank Burr had "disappeared" with all his family. Burr had not lived at Port Corbay—at least, he claimed not to have lived there, and he gave another address and assigned to himself quite different connections. For every member of the crew of the *Miwaka* there had been a corresponding, but different name on Corvet's list—the name of a relative. If old Burr was not related to the Burr on Corvet's list, what connection could he have with the *Miwaka*, and why should Alan's questions have agitated him so? Alan would not lose sight of Burr until he had learned the reason for that.

He followed, as the old man crossed the bridge and turned to his left among the buildings on the river front. Burr's figure, vague in the dusk, crossed the railroad yards and made its way to where a huge black bulk, which Alan recognized as the ferry, loomed at the waterside. He disappeared aboard it. Alan, following him, gazed about.

A long, broad, black ship the ferry was, about four hundred feet to the tall, bluff bow. Seen from the stem, the ship seemed only an unusually rugged and powerful steam freighter. Viewed from the beam, the vessel appeared short for its freeboard. Only when observed from the stern did its distinguishing peculiarity become plain, for a few feet only above the waterline, the stern was all cut away, and the long, low cavern of the deck gleamed with rails upon which the electric lights glinted. Save for the supports of the superstructure and where the funnels and ventilator pipes passed up from below, that whole strata of the ship was a vast car shed, its tracks, running to the edge of the stern, touched tracks on the dock. A yard engine was backing loaded cars from a train of sixteen cars upon the rails on the starboard side; another train of sixteen big box cars waited to go aboard on the tracks to the port of the center stanchions. When the two trains were aboard, the great vessel— "No. 25" in big white stencil on her black sides were her distinguishing marks—would thrust out into the ice and gale for the Michigan shore nearly eighty miles away.

Alan thrilled a little at his inspection of the ferry. He had not seen close at hand before one of these great craft, which throughout the winter brave ice and storm after nearly all other lake boats are tied up for the winter. He had not meant to apply for work there when he questioned old Burr about a berth on the ferry; he had used that merely as a means of getting into conversation with the old man. But now he meant to apply, as it would enable him to find out more about old Burr.

He went forward between the tracks on the deck to the companionway and ascended and found the skipper, and presented his credentials. No berth on the ferry was vacant yet but one soon would be, and Alan was accepted in lieu of the man who was about to leave. His wages would not begin until the other man left, but in the meantime he could remain aboard the ferry if he wished. Alan elected to remain aboard. The captain called a man to assign quarters to Alan, and going with him when he came, Alan questioned him about Burr.

All that was known definitely about old Burr on the ferry, it appeared, was that he had joined the vessel in the early spring. Before that, they did not know; he might be an old lakeman, who after spending years ashore, had returned to the lakes for a livelihood. He had represented himself as experienced and trained on the lakes, and he had been able to demonstrate his fitness. In spite of his age, he was one of the most capable of the crew.

The next morning, Alan approached old Burr in the crew's quarters and tried to draw him into conversation again about himself, but Burr only stared at him with his intent and oddly introspective eyes, and would not talk. A week passed. Alan, established now as a lookout, saw Burr almost every hour since his watch coincided with Burr's watch at the wheel, and they went on duty together and were relieved together. But better acquaintance did not make the old man more communicative. Many times Alan attempted to get him to tell more about himself, but he avoided Alan's questions, and if Alan insisted, he avoided him. Then, on an evening bitter cold with the coming of winter, clear and filled with stars, Alan, just relieved from watch, stood by the pilothouse as Burr was also relieved. The old man paused beside him, looking to the west.

"Have you ever been in Sturgeon's Bay?" Burr asked.

"In Wisconsin? No."

"There is a small house there . . . and a child, born," he seemed to be figuring the date, "February 12, 1914."

"A relative of yours?" Alan asked.

"Yes."

"One of your brothers' children or grandchildren?"

"I had no brothers," old Burr said quietly.

Alan stared at him, amazed. "But you told me about your brothers and about their being lost in wrecks on the lake, and about your home in Emmet County."

"I never lived in Emmet County," old Burr replied. "Someone else must have told you that about me. I come from Canada—of French-Canadian descent. My family were of the Hudson Bay people. I was a guide and hunter until recently. Only a few years ago I came onto the lakes, but my cousin came here before I did. It is his child."

Burr moved away and Alan turned to the mate and asked. "What do you make of old Burr?"

"He's a romancer. We get 'em that way once in a while—old liars! He'll give you twenty different accounts of himself—twenty different lives. None of them is true. I don't know who he is or where he came from, but it's sure he isn't any of things he says he is."

Alan turned away, chilled with disappointment. It was only that, then; old Burr was a dreamer after the manner of other old seamen. He constructed for his own amusement these "lives." Not only was he not the Burr of Corvet's list, he was not in any way connected with the *Miwaka* or with Corvet.

Yet, on reflecting, Alan could not believe this. Burr might have merely simulated agitation when Alan questioned him about the *Miwaka*, but why should he have even wished to simulate it? Alan could conceive of no reason, no possible reason why such simulation might have suggested itself to the old man.

Alan ceased questioning Burr now, as either his questions had no result at all or they led the old man to weave obvious fictions. In response, the old man by degrees became more communicative. He told Alan at different times about a number of other "lives" which he claimed as his own. In only a few had he been a seaman. In some he had been a farmer, in others a lumberjack or a fisherman. He told of having been born in a half-dozen different places, and came from different sorts of people.

On deck, one night, listening as old Burr related his sixth or seventh life, excitement suddenly seized Alan. In this latest "life" of which Burr was telling, the old man claimed to be an Englishman born in Liverpool. He had been, he said, a seaman in the British navy; he had been present at the shelling of Alexandria; later, because of some difficulty which he glossed over, he had deserted and come to the States; he had first been a deckhand then the mate of a tramp schooner on the lakes.

As the old man talked, Alan realized he recognized this "life" and knew in advance its incidents. Gazing at the old man, Alan felt an exultation leap and throb within in him. The life old Burr was relating was the life of Munro Burkhalter, one of the few people on Corvet's list about whom Alan had been able to obtain full information!

When his watch ended, Alan sped below and got out the clippings left by Corvet and the notes of what he himself had learned in his visits to the home of these people. His excitement grew as he pored over them. He found that with their aid, he could account for all the lives of which old Burr had told him. Burr's "lives" might not be his own, yet neither were they fictions. They—their incidents at least—were quite real. They were woven from the lives of those upon Corvet's list!

Alan felt his blood beating fast in his temples. How could Burr have known these incidents? Who could he be to know them all? To what other man could all of them be known? Was old Burr . . . . Benjamin Corvet?

Alan could give no certain answer to that question. He could not find any definite resemblance in Burr's placid face to the picture of Corvet which Constance had shown him. Yet, as regarded his age and his physical characteristics, there was nothing to make his identity with Benjamin Corvet impossible. Sherrill or others who had known Benjamin Corvet well might be able to find resemblances which Alan could not. And, whether Burr was or was not Corvet, he was undeniably someone to whom the particulars of Corvet's life were known.

Alan telegraphed that day to Sherrill, but when the message had gone doubt seized him. He awaited eagerly the coming of whoever Sherrill might send and the revelations regarding Corvet which might come then, but at the same time he shrank from the thought of that revelation. He himself, he knew, had become wholly of the lakes now and from now on his life, whatever its future, would be concerned with the lakes. Yet he was not of them in the way he would have wished to be. For the moment, he was no more that an ordinary seaman. For an ordinary seaman, his message seemed presumptuous.

Benjamin Corvet, when he went away, had tried to leave his place and power among lakemen to Alan. He, refusing to accept what Corvet had left until Corvet's reason should be known, had felt obliged also to refuse friendship with the Sherrills. When revelation came, would it make possible Alan's acceptance of the place Corvet had prepared for him, or would it leave him where he was? Would it bring him nearer to Constance Sherrill, or would it set him forever away from her?

17

"Colder some tonight, Conrad."

"Yes, sir."

"Straits freezing over, they say." The skipper glanced out and smiled confidently but without further comment. After a few moments, he left the wheelhouse to go down to the car deck to observe the men who, under the direction of the mate, were locking the lugs under the car wheels as the trains came aboard. The wind, which had risen with nightfall to a gale off the water, whipped snow with it which swirled and back-eddied around the switching cars into the great, gaping stern of the ferry.

Officially, and to chief extent in actuality, navigation now had closed for the winter. Further up the harbor, beyond *Number 25*, glowed the white lanterns marking two vessels moored and laid up until spring, and another was still in the active process of laying up. Marine insurance, as regards all ordinary craft, had ceased. The Government at sunrise, five days before, had taken the navigational lights from the Straits of Mackinac, from Ile-aux-Galets, from north

Manitou, and the Fox Islands, and the light at Beaver Island had but five nights more to burn.

As the captain went below, Alan followed, and as he walked aft between the car tracks he saw old Burr, who had no particular duty when the ship was in dock. Alan saw old Burr step ashore and head toward the steamer that was laying up, watching with absorption the work going on. Alan followed Burr ashore.

There was a tug a little further along, with steam up and black smoke pouring from its short funnel. Old Burr observed this craft, too, and moved up a little nearer. Alan, following him, came opposite the stern of the freighter, where the snow let through enough of the light from the dock to show the name *Stoughton*. It was, Alan knew, a Corvet, Sherrill and Spearman ship. He moved closer to old Burr and watched him more intently.

"What's the matter?" he asked, as the old man stopped.

Looking down at the tug, old Burr he shook his head. "They're crossing," the wheelsman said aloud, but more to himself than Alan. Then, jerking his head toward the *Stoughton*, "They're laying her up here, and then they're crossing to Manitowoc on the tug."

"What's the matter with that?" asked Alan.

Burr drew up his shoulders and ducked his head down as a gust blew. It was cold—very cold indeed—in that wind, but the old man had on a mackinaw, and out on the lake Alan had seen him on deck coatless in weather almost as cold as this.

"It's a winter storm," Alan cried. "And it's like December fifth, but today's the 15th."

"That's right," Burr agreed. "That's right."

The reply was absent, as though Alan had stumbled upon what Burr had been thinking, and Burr had no thought yet to wonder at it.

"And it's the *Stoughton* they're laying up, not the . . . " He stopped and stared, giving Burr an opportunity to supply the word. When the old man did not, Alan repeated his prompt: "Not the . . ."

"No," Burr agreed again, as though Alan had actually spoken the name. "No."

"It was the *Martha Corvet* you laid up, wasn't it?" Alan quickly said. "Tell me, that time on the fifth—it was the *Martha Corvet,* wasn't it?"

Burr jerked away; Alan caught him again, and with physical strength detained him. "Wasn't it that?" he demanded. "Answer me! It was the *Martha Corvet!*"

The wheelsman struggled; he seemed suddenly terrified, and instead of weakening him, the terror supplied him with infuriated strength. He threw off Alan for an instant and started to flee back toward the ferry. This time Alan let him go, only following him to make sure that old Burr returned to *Number 25.*

Watching Burr until he was safely aboard the ferry, Alan then turned and headed back to the *Stoughton.*

Work of laying up the big steamer had been finished, and in the snow-filled dusk the men of her crew were coming ashore. Boarding, Alan went to the captain's cabin, where he found the *Stoughton's* master making ready to leave the ship. The captain, a man of forty-five or fifty, reminded Alan vaguely of one of the ship-masters who had been in Spearman's office when Alan first went there in the spring. If he had been there, he showed no sign of recollection of Alan now, but good-humoredly looked for him to state his business.

"I'm from *Number 25,*" Alan introduced himself. "This being a Corvet, Sherrill and Spearman ship, do you know Mr. Corvet when you see him, sir?"

"Know Ben Corvet?" the captain repeated. The manner of the young man from the carferry told him it was not an idle question. "Yes, I know Ben Corvet. I haven't seen him much in late years."

"Will you come with me for a few minutes then, Captain?" Alan asked. As the skipper stared at him and hesitated, Alan explained, "Mr. Corvet has been missing for months. His friends have said he's been away somewhere for his health, but the truth is, he's been missing. There's a man I want you to look at, Captain . . . if you used to know Mr. Corvet."

"I've heard of that." The captain moved alertly now. "Where is he?"

Alan led the master to the ferry. Old Burr had left the car deck, but they found him on the way to the wheelhouse.

The *Stoughton's* skipper stared. "That's the man?" he demanded.

"Yes, sir. Remember to allow for his clothes and his not being shaved, and that something has happened to him."

The *Stoughton's* captain followed to the wheelhouse and spoke to Burr. Alan's heart beat rapidly as he watched the conversation. Once or twice the skipper seemed surprised, but it was plain that his first interest in Burr had quickly vanished. Then he returned to Alan indulgently.

"You thought that was Mr. Corvet?" he asked, amused.

"You don't think so?" Alan asked.

"Ben Corvet like that? Did you ever see Ben Corvet?"

"Only his picture," Alan confessed. "But you looked strange when you first saw Burr."

"That was a trick of his eyes. They did give me a start. Ben Corvet had just that sort of trick of looking through a man."

"And his eyes were like that?"

"Yes, but Ben Corvet couldn't look like that!"

Alan prepared to go on duty. He would not let himself be disappointed by the skipper's failure to identify old Burr. The skipper had known immediately at sight of the old man that he was the one whom Alan thought was Corvet, and he had found definite resemblance. It might well have been only the impossibility of believing that Corvet could have become like this which had prevented fuller recognition. Mr. Sherrill undoubtedly would send someone more familiar with Ben Corvet, who might better be able to make allowances.

Alan went to his post as the steam whistle of the switching engine, announcing that all the cars were on board, was answered by a blast from the ferry. On the car decks the trains had been secured in place, and because of the roughness of the weather, the wheels had been dogged down on the tracks with additional chains, as well as with the blocks and chains usually used. Orders now sounded from the bridge, and the steel deck began to shake with the reverberations of the engines. The dock lines were taken in, the rails on the fantail of the ferry separated from the rails on the wharf, and clear water showed between. Alan took up his slow pace as lookout from rail to rail across the bow, straining his eyes forward into the thickness of the snow-filled night.

Because of the severe cold, the watches had been shortened. Alan would be relieved from time to time to warm himself, and then he would return to duty again. Old Burr at the wheel would be relieved and would go on duty at the same hours as Alan. Benjamin Corvet! The fancy reiterated itself to him. Could he be mistaken? Was that man, whose eyes turned alternately from the compass to the bow of the ferry as it shifted and rose and fell, be the same who had sat in that lonely chair turned toward the fireplace in the house on Astor Street? Were those hands, which held the steamer to her course, the hands which had written to Alan in secret from the little room off his bedroom, and which pasted so carefully the newspaper clippings concealed in the library?

Regularly at the end of every minute, a blast from the steam whistle sounded, and for a while, signals from the shore answered. For a few minutes the shore lights glowed through the snow. Then the lights were gone, and the eddies of the gale ceased to bring echoes of the signals. Steadily, at sixty-second intervals, the blasts of *Number 25*'s warnings burst from the whistle; then those too stopped. Although *Number 25* was cutting across the lanes of all ordinary lake traffic, with ordinary navigation closed the position of every other ship on the lake was known to the officers, and formal signals were not thought necessary. The great ship was on the lake alone. Flat ice floes, driven by wind and wave, had windrowed in their course. The ship was capable of maintaining two-thirds its open water speed even running through solid "green" ice two feet thick. As it met these obstructions, its undercut bow rose slightly and then crushed down and to the sides, hurling, pounding and scraping ice beneath the keel and along the black, steel sides of the ship.

Alan could hear and feel the hull resounding to the buffeting as it hurled floes away, and more came, or the wind threw them back. The water was rushing high—higher than Alan had experienced seas before. The wind, smashing almost straight across the lake from the west, with only a gust or two from the north, was throwing up the water in great rushing ridges on which the bow rose jerkily up and up, suddenly to fall, as the support passed on, with the next wave washing nearly to the rail.

Alan faced the wind with mackinaw buttoned about his throat, and to make certain of his hearing, his ears were left unprotected. They numbed frequently, and he would draw a hand out of the glove to warm them. The windows of the pilot house had been dropped, as the snow had gathered on the glass, and at intervals, as he glanced back, he could see old Burr's face as he switched on a dim light to look at the compass. The strange placidity which usually characterized the old man's face had not returned to it since Alan had spoken with him on the dock. Now its look was intent and queerly drawn.

Was old Burr beginning to remember—remember that he was Benjamin Corvet? Alan did not believe it could be that, as time and again he had spoken Corvet's name to him without effect. Yet there must have been times when, if he were actually Corvet, he had remembered who he was. He must have remembered who he was when he wrote directions to someone to send those things to Constance Sherrill. Then a strange thought came to Alan: Had he written them to himself? Had there been a moment when he had been so much himself that he had realized that he might not be himself again, and so had written the order which he had later obeyed?

This certainly would account for the package's having been mailed from Manitowoc, and for Alan's failure to find out who had mailed it.

It would account too for the unknown handwriting on the wrapper, if someone on the ferry had addressed the package for the old man. He must inquire whether anyone among the crew had done that.

What could have brought back that moment of recollection to Corvet, Alan wondered; the finding of the things he had sent? What might bring back another such moment? Would his seeing the Sherrills again—or Spearman—act to restore him?

For half an hour Alan paced steadily at the bow. The storm was increasing noticeably in fierceness; the wind-driven snowflakes had changed to hard pellets which cut and stung the face, and it was growing colder. From a cabin window came the blue flash of the wireless, which had been silent after notifying the shore stations of their departure. It had commenced again; this was unusual. Something still more unusual followed at once. The wind and waves which had been hitting the ship from dead ahead, were now coming in on the port side, and *Number 25*, still pitching with the thrust through the seas, was now also beginning to roll. This meant, of course, that the ship had changed course and was heading almost due north. It seemed to Alan that the engines were faster, and the deck vibrated more. He had not heard the orders for these changes and could only speculate as to what they might mean. His relief came after a few minutes more.

"Where are we heading?" Alan asked.

"Radio," the relief announced. "The *H. C. Richardson* calling; she's up by the Manitous."

"What sort of trouble?"

"She's not in trouble; it's another ship."

"What ship?"

"No word as to that."

Alan, not delaying to question further, went back to the cabins.

These stretched aft, behind the bridge, along the upper deck, some twenty or more on each side of the ship. The ship had accommodations for almost a hundred passengers, but on this crossing, only a few of the cabins were occupied. Alan had noticed some half dozen men among the passengers—business men, no doubt, obliged to make the crossing. There was also a Catholic priest, probably returning to some mission in the North. He had seen no women among the passengers. A small group of passengers was gathered now at the door of the wireless cabin, which was one of the row on the starboard side. Stewards stood with them and the cabin maid. Inside, bending over the table with the radio equipment, was the operator, with the second officer beside him.

The violet spark was rasping, and the operator, his earphones strapped over his head, strained to listen. He got no reply, evidently, and he worked his key again. Now, as he listened, he wrote on his pad.

"You get 'em?" someone cried. "You get 'em now?"

The operator continued to write. The second mate, reading, shook his head. "It's only the *Richardson* again."

"What is it?" Alan asked the officer.

"The *Richardson* heard four blasts of a steam whistle about an hour ago when she was opposite the Manitous. She answered with the whistle and turned toward the blasts. She couldn't find any ship." The officer's reply was interrupted by some of the others. "Then a few minutes ago they heard the four long again . . . They'd tried to pick up the other ship with the radio before . . . . Yes we got that here . . . Tried again and got no answer . . . But they heard the blasts for half an hour . . . They said they seemed to be almost beside the ship once . . . But they didn't see anything. Then the blasts stopped . . . sudden, cut off short in the middle as though something happened . . . She was blowing distress all right . . . The *Richardson*'s searching again now . . . Yes, she's searching for boats."

"Anyone else answered?" Alan asked.

"Shore stations on both sides."

"Do they know what ship it is?"

"No."

"What ship might be there now?"

The officer could not answer that. He had known where the *Richardson* must be, but he knew of no other ship likely to be there in this season. The spray from the waves had frozen upon Alan; ice gleamed and glinted from the rail and from the deck. His shoulders drew up in a spasm. The *Richardson*, they said, was looking for boats. How long could men live in little boats exposed to that gale and cold?

He turned back to the others about the radio cabin, and the glow from within showed him faces as gray as his. It lighted a face on the opposite side of the door—a face haggard with dreadful fright. Old Burr jerked about as Alan spoke to him, and then he moved away. Alan followed him and seized his arm.

"What's the matter?" Alan demanded, holding on to him.

"The four blasts!" the wheelsman repeated. "They heard the four blasts!" he iterated it once more.

"Yes," Alan urged. "Why not?"

"But where no ship ought to be; so they couldn't find the ship!"

Terror had seized the old man. He freed himself from Alan and went forward.

Alan followed him to the quarters of the crew, where night lunch for the men relieved from watch had been set out, and took a seat at the table opposite him. The louder echoing of the steel hull and the roll and pitching of the vessel, which set the table and its dishes swaying, showed that the sea was still increasing, and that they were now meeting heavier ice. At the table men estimated that *Number 25* had now made some twenty miles north of its course, and must therefore be approaching the neighborhood of where the distress signals had been heard. They speculated uselessly as to what ship could have been in that part of the lake and made the signals. Old Burr took no part in this conversation, but listened to it with frightened eyes, and presently got up and went away, leaving his coffee unfinished. *Number 25* was blowing its steam whistle again at the end of every minute.

Alan, after taking a second cup of coffee, went aft to the car deck. The roar and echoing tumult of the ice against the hull here drowned all other sounds. The thirty-two freight cars, in their four long lines, stood wedged and chained and blocked in place. They tipped and tilted, rolled and swayed like the stanchions and sides of the ship, fixed and secure. Jacks on the steel deck under the edges of the cars kept them from rocking on their trucks. Men paced watchful between the tracks, observing the movement of the cars. The cars creaked and groaned, as they worked a little this way and that. The men moved quickly with sledges and drove the blocks tight again, or took an additional turn on the jacks where needed.

As Alan ascended and went forward to his duty, the increase in the severity of the gale was very evident; the thermometer, the wheelsman said, had dropped below zero. Ice was making rapidly on the hull of the ship, where the spray, flying thicker through the snow, was freezing as it struck.

The deck was all ice now underfoot, and the rails were swollen to great gleaming slabs which had grown together. A parapet of ice rose at the bow, and all about the vessel swirling snow shut off everything from view. A searchlight flared from the bridge but pierced that screen not a ship's length ahead nor on the beam before the glare dimmed to a glow. It served to show no more than the fine, flying pellets of the storm. Except for the noise of the wind and the water, there had been no echo from beyond that screen since the shore signals had been lost behind.

Now a low, far-away sound came down the wind. It maintained itself for a few seconds, ceased, and then came again, and continued at uneven intervals longer than the timed blasts of *Number 25*'s whistle. It might be the horn of some struggling sailing vessel, braving the seas in spite of the storm and the close of navigation. At the end of each interval of silence, the horn blew twice now. The echo came abeam, passed astern and was heard no more. How far away it had been, Alan could only guess; being away to windward, the sailing vessel had probably not heard the whistle of *Number 25* at all.

Alan saw that old Burr, who was on his way to the wheelhouse, was stopping to listen too. For several minutes the old man would stand motionless; then he'd come on again, then stop again to listen. There had been no sound for quite five minutes now.

"You hear 'em?" Burr's voice quavered in Alan's ear. "You hear 'em?"

"What?" Alan asked.

"The four blasts! You hear 'em now? The four blasts?"

Burr was straining as he listened. Alan stood still, but no sound came to him except the noise of the storm. "No," he replied. "I don't hear anything. Do you hear them now?"

Burr stood beside him without making reply. The searchlight, which had been pointing abeam, shot its glare forward, and Alan could see Burr's face in the dancing reflection. The man had never more plainly resembled the picture of Benjamin Corvet. That which had been in the picture, that strange sensation of something haunting him, was upon this man's face—a thousand times intensified. But instead of distorting the features away from all likeness to the picture, it made it grotesquely identical.

And Burr was hearing something—something distinct and terrifying. He seemed not surprised, but rather satisfied that Alan had not heard. He nodded his head at Alan's denial, and without reply to Alan's demand, he stood listening. Something bent him forward, and he straightened. Again the something came, and again he straightened. Four times Alan counted the motions. Burr was hearing again the four long blasts of distress. But there was no noise but the gale. "The four blasts!"

He recalled old Burr's terror outside the radio cabin. The old man was hearing blasts that were not blown.

Burr moved on and took the wheel. He was a good wheelsman, and his touch made the vessel seem steadier on her course, and she steamed easier when the old man steered. His illusions of hearing could do no harm, Alan considered; they were only of concern to Burr and to him.

Alan, relieving the lookout on the bow, stood on watch again.

The ferry thrust on alone, and in the wireless cabin, the light burned steadily. They had been able to get the shore stations again on both sides of the lake and also the *Richardson*. As *Number 25* had worked northward, the *Richardson* had been working north too, under the impression that the vessel in distress, if it had headway, was moving in that direction. By its position, which the *Richardson* gave, the stricken vessel was about twenty miles away.

Alan fought to keep his thought all to his duty. They must be now nearly at the position where the *Richardson* last had heard the four long blasts. Searching for a ship or for boats in that snow seemed almost hopeless. With sight even along the searchlight's beam shortened to a few hundred yards, only accident could bring *Number 25* up for rescue. Only chance could carry the ship to where the shouts— or blasts of distress if the wreck still floated and had steam—would be heard.

Half numbed by the cold, Alan stomped and beat his arms about his body. The sweep of the searchlight in the circle about the ship had long ago become monotonous, and purely mechanical, like the blowing of the whistle. Alan stared patiently along the beam as it turned through the sector where he watched. They were meeting frequent and heavy floes, and he gave warnings of these by hails to the bridge; the bridge answered and when possible the steamer avoided the floes; when it could not do that, it cut through them. The windrowed ice beating and crushing under the bows took strange, distorted, glistening shapes. Now another shape appeared before them. Where the glare dissipated to a bare glow in the swirling snow, he saw a vague shadow. The man moving the searchlight failed to see it, for he swung the beam on. The shadow was so dim, so ghostly, that Alan sought it again before he hailed. He could see nothing now, but he was surer, somehow, that he had seen it.

"Something dead ahead, sir!" he shouted back to the bridge.

The bridge answered the hail as the searchlight pointed forward again. A gust carried the snow in a fierce flurry which the light failed to pierce. From the flurry suddenly, silently, spar by spar, a shadow emerged—the shadow of a ship. It was a steamer, Alan saw, a long low-lying old vessel without lights, and without smoke from the funnel slanting up just forward of the after deck house. It rolled in the trough of the sea. The sides and all the lower works gleamed in ghostly phosphorescence. It was refraction of the searchlight beam from the ice sheathing all the ship, Alan's brain told him. But the sight of that soundless, shimmering ship materializing from behind the screen of snow struck a tremor through him.

"Ship!" he hailed. "Ahead! Dead ahead, sir! Ship!"

The shout of quick commands echoed to him from the bridge. Underfoot he could feel a new tumult as the engines instantly stopped, then began backing down, full astern. But Number 25, instead of shearing off to right or left to avoid collision, steered straight ahead. The struggle of the engines against the momentum of the ferry told Alan that others, too, had seen the gleaming ship, or had at least heard the hail.

The skipper's instant decision had been to put to starboard, as Alan had heard him bawl to the wheelsman, "Hard over!" Yet, although the screws turned full astern, Number 25 steered straight on. The flurry was blowing before the bow again, and back through the snow the ice-shrouded shimmer ahead retreated. Alan leaped away and up to the wheelhouse.

Men were struggling there—the skipper, a mate, and old Burr, who held the wheel. He doggedly grasped it as if in a trance, and his arms rigidly held Number 25 to her course. The skipper struck him and beat at him while the mate tugged at the wheel.

Burr, finally torn from the wheel, made no resistance to the skipper's blows, but the skipper, in his frenzy, struck him again and knocked him to the deck.

Slowly, steadily, the ship responded to her helm, now. The bow pointed away and the beam of the ferry closed in on the beam of the silent steamer. They were very close now, so close that the search-light, which had turned to keep on the other vessel, now shot above its shimmering deck and lighted only its spars.

As the water rose and fell between them, the ships sucked closer together. *Number 25* shook with effort, seeming to oppose with all the power of its screws some force that was fatally drawing it on towards the other vessel. Then, as the water fell again, the ferry seemed to slip and be drawn toward the other vessel. They mounted crests together, side by side, and crashed, recoiled, and crashed again. The second crash threw all who had nothing to hold on to flat upon the deck. Then the ferry slid by, and the silent steamer vanished in the snow astern.

Gongs boomed below, and through the new confusion and the cries of men, orders began to be audible. Alan, scrambling to his knees, put an arm under old Burr, half raising him, and Burr's form struggled up. The skipper, who had knocked Burr away from the wheel, ignored him now. The old man, dragging himself up and holding to Alan, was staring with terror at the screen of snow behind which the other vessel had now disappeared. His lips moved.

"It was a ship!" he said. He seemed to be speaking more to himself than to Alan.

"Yes," Alan replied. "It was a ship, and you thought . . ."

"It wasn't there!" the wheelsman cried. "It's . . . it's been there all the time, all night, and I'd . . . I'd steered through it ten times, twenty times, every few minutes; and then . . . that time it was a ship!"

Alan's excitement grew greater, and he seized the old man again.

"You thought it was the *Miwaka*!" Alan exclaimed. "The *Miwaka*! And you tried to steer through it again."

"The *Miwaka*!" old Burr's lips reiterated the word. "Yes; yes . . . the *Miwaka*!"

He struggled, writhing with some agony not physical. Alan tried to hold him, but now the old man was beside himself with dismay. He broke away and started aft. The captain's voice recalled Alan to

252

himself, as he was about to follow, and he turned back to the wheel-house.

The mate was at the wheel. He shouted to the captain about following the other ship; neither of them had seen sign of anyone aboard it.

"Derelict!" the skipper thought. The mate was swinging *Number 25* about to follow and look for the ship again; and the searchlight beam swept back and forth through the snow. The blasts of the steam whistle, which had stopped after the collision, burst out again. As before, no response came from behind the snow. The searchlight picked up the silent ship again. It had settled down deeper now by the bow, Alan saw. The blow from *Number 25* had robbed it of its last buoyancy, and it was sinking. It dove down, then rose a little—sounds came from it now—sudden, explosive sounds; air pressure within hurled up a hatch; the tops of the cabins blew off, and the stem of the ship slipped down deep again, stopped, then dove without recovery this time, as the stern, upraised with the screw motionless, met a high wave, and went down with it and disappeared.

No man had shown himself; no shout had been heard; no small boat was seen or signaled.

The second officer, who had gone below to ascertain the damage done to the ferry, came up to report. Two of the compartments, those which had taken the crush of the collision, had flooded instantly, and the bulkheads were holding—only leaking a little, the officer declared. Water was coming into a third compartment, that at the stern, and the pumps were fighting the water there. The impact had sprung seams elsewhere, but if the after compartment did not fill, the pumps might handle the rest.

Soddenness already was coming into the response of the ship to the lift of the waves. The ferry rolled less to the right as she came about, beam to the waves, and she dropped away more dully and deeply to the left; the ship was listing to port and the lift of the ice-heaped bow told of settling by the stern. Slowly, *Number 25* circled about, her engines holding bare headway. Alan heard that the radio was sending word to the *Richardson* and to the shore stations of the finding and sinking of the derelict and the damage done to the ferry. Whether that damage was yet described in the dispatches as disaster, Alan did not know. The steam whistle, which continued to roar, maintained the single, separated blasts of a ship still seaworthy and able to steer and even give assistance. Alan was at the bow again on lookout duty, ordered to listen and look for small boats.

He gave to that duty all his conscious attention. Through his thought, whether he willed it or not, ran a riotous exultation. As he paced from side to side and hailed and answered hails from the bridge, and while he strained for sight and hearing through the gale-swept snow, the leaping pulse within him repeated, "I've found him! I've found him!"

Alan's mind no longer held the possibility of doubt that old Burr was Benjamin Corvet, since the old man had made plain to him that he was haunted by the *Miwaka*. Since that night in the house on Astor Street, when Spearman shouted that name to Alan, everything having to do with the secret of Benjamin Corvet's life had led, so far as Alan could follow it, to the *Miwaka*. All the change, which Sherrill described but could not account for, Alan had laid to that. Only Corvet could have been so haunted by that ghostly ship, and there had been guilt of some awful sort in the old man's cry. Alan had found the man who had sent him away to Kansas when he was a child, who had supported him there and then sent for him; who had disappeared at his coming and left him all his possessions and his heritage of disgrace; who had paid blackmail to Luke, and who had sent Captain Stafford's watch and the ring which came with it—the wedding ring.

Alan pulled his hand from his glove and felt in his pocket for the little band of gold. What would that mean to him now, and what of that was he to learn? And, as he thought of that, Constance Sherrill came more insistently before him. What was he to learn for her, his friend and Benjamin Corvet's friend, whom he, Uncle Benny, had warned not to care for Henry Spearman, and then had gone away to leave her to marry him?

For she was to marry him, Alan had read.

Cold terror suddenly closed over him. Would he learn anything from Benjamin Corvet now that he had found him? Only for an instant—a fleeting instant—had Benjamin Corvet's brain become clear as to the hallucination. Consternation had overwhelmed him then, and he struggled free to attempt to mend the damage he had done.

More serious damage than first reported! The pumps certainly must be losing their fight with the water in the port compartment aft, as the bow was steadily lifting and the stern was sinking. The starboard rail, too, was raised, and the list had become so sharp that water washed the deck abaft the forecastle to port. And the ship was pointed dead into the gale now. Long ago she had ceased to circle and steam slowly in search for boats. She struggled with all her power against the wind and the seas, a desperate insistence throbbing in the thrusts of the engines, for *Number 25* was now fleeing—fleeing for the western shore. She dared not turn to the nearer eastern shore to expose that shattered stern to the seas.

Four bells beat behind Alan; it was two o'clock. Relief should have come long before, but no one came. He was numbed now; ice from the spray crackled on his clothing when he moved, and it fell in flakes upon the deck. The stark figure on the bridge was that of the second officer, so whatever was happening below—that which was sending strange, violent, wanton tremors through the ship— was serious enough to call the captain below and cause him to abandon the bridge at this time! The tremors, quite distinct from the steady tremble of the engines and the thudding of the pumps, came again. Alan, feeling them, jerked up and stamped and beat his arms to regain sensation. Someone stumbled toward him from the cabins now, a short figure in a great coat. It was a woman, he saw as she hailed him—the cabin maid.

"I'm taking your place!" she shouted to Alan.

"You're wanted . . . everyone's wanted on the car deck! The cars . . ."

The gale and her fright all but strangled her voice, and she struggled to speak. "The cars . . . !" she managed to shout at last. "The cars . . . The cars are loose!"

18

Alan ran aft along the starboard side, catching at the rail as the deck tilted; the sounds within the hull, and the tremors following each sound came to him more distinctly as he advanced. Taking the shortest way to the car deck, he turned into the cabins to reach the passengers' companionway. The noises from the car deck, no longer muffled by the cabins, clanged and resounded in terrible tumult; with the clang and rumble of metal rose shouts and roars of men.

To liberate and throw overboard heavily loaded cars from an endangered ship was so desperate an undertaking and so certain to cost life, that men attempted it only in final extremities, when the ship must be lightened at any cost. Alan had never seen the effect of such an attempt, but he had heard of it as the fear which sat always on the hearts of men who navigate the ferries—cars loose on a rolling, lurching ship! He was going to that now.

Two figures appeared before him, one half supporting, half dragging the other. Alan sprang and offered aid, but the injured man called to him to go on; others needed him. Alan went past them and down the steps to the car deck. Half-way down, the priest whom he had noticed among the passengers stood staring aft, a tense, black figure. Beside him other passengers were clinging to the handrail and staring down in awestruck fascination. The lowest steps had been crushed back and half torn up; some monstrous, inanimate thing was battering about below, but the space at the foot of the steps was clear at the moment. Alan leaped over the ruin of the steps and down onto the car deck.

A giant iron casting six feet high and yards across weighing tons, tumbled and ground before him. It was this which had swept away the steps. He had seen it, with two others like it, on a flat car that had been shunted upon one of the tracks on the starboard side of the ferry, one of the tracks on his left now as he faced the stern. He leaped upon and over the great casting, which turned and spun with the motion of the ship as he vaulted it. The car deck was a pitching and swaying slope; the cars near him were still on their tracks, but they tilted and swayed dangerously from side to side; the jacks were gone from under them; the next cars already hurled from the rails, their wheels screaming on the steel deck, clanging and thudding together in their couplings.

Alan ran aft between them. All the crew who could be called from deck and engine room and firehold were struggling at the fantail, under the direction of the captain, to throw off the cars. The mate was working as one of the men, and with him was Benjamin Corvet. The crew must already have loosened and thrown over the stern three cars from the two tracks on the port side, as there was a space vacant, and as the train charged into that space and the men threw themselves upon it, Alan leaped with them.

The leading car—a box car, heavily laden—swayed and shrieked with the pitching of the ship. Corvet sprang between it and the car coupled behind; he drew out the pin from the coupling, and the men with pinch bars attacked the car to isolate it and force it aft along the track. It moved slowly at first, and then leaped its length; sharply with the lift of the deck, it stopped, toppled toward the men who, yelling at one another, scrambled away. The hundred-ton mass swung from side to side; the ship dropped swiftly to starboard, and the stern went down; the car charged, and its aftermost wheels left the deck; it swung about, slewed, and jammed across both port tracks. The men attacked it with dismay; Corvet's shout called them away and rallied them farther back; they ran with him to the car from which he had uncoupled it.

It was a flat car laden with steel beams. At Corvet's command, the crew ranged themselves beside it with bars. The bow of the ferry rose to some great wave, and with a cry to the men, Corvet pulled the pin. The others thrust with their bars, and the car slid down the sloping track. Corvet, caught by some lashing of the beams, came with it. The car crashed into the box car, splintered it, turned it, shoved it, and thrust it over the fantail into the water; the flat car telescoped into it and was dragged after, taking Corvet with it. Alan leaped upon it and catching at Corvet, freed him and flung him down to the deck, then leaped free just before the car reached the edge. A cheer rose as the car cleared the fantail, dove and disappeared.

Alan clambered to his feet. Corvet was already back among the cars again, shouting orders; the mate and the men who had followed him before leaped at his commands. The lurch which had cleared the two cars together had jammed others away from the rails. They hurtled from side to side, splintering against the stanchions which stayed them from crashing across the center line of the ship; rebounding, they battered against the cars on the outer tracks and crushed them against the side of the ship. The wedges, blocks, and chains which had secured them banged about on the deck, useless; the men who tried to control these cars, dodging as they charged, no longer made attempt to secure the wheels. Corvet called them to throw ropes and chains to bind the loads which were letting go; the heavier loads—steel beams, castings, machinery—snapped their lashings, tipped from their flat cars, and thundered down the deck. The cars tipped farther, turned over; others balanced back; it was upon their wheels that they charged forward, half riding one another, crashing and demolishing, as the ferry pitched; it was upon their trucks that they tottered and battered from side to side as the deck swayed. Now the stern again descended; a line of cars swept for the fantail, Corvet's cry came to Alan through the screaming of steel and the clangor of destruction. Corvet's cry sent men with bars beside the cars as the fantail dipped into the water; Corvet, again leading his crew, cleared the first of those madly charging cars and ran it over the stern.

The fore trucks fell and, before the rear trucks reached the edge, the stern lifted and caught the car in the middle; it balanced, half over the water, half over the deck. Corvet crouched under the car with a crowbar; Alan and two others went with him; they worked the car until the weight of the end over the water tipped it down; the balance broke, and the car tumbled and dived. Corvet, having cleared another hundred tons, leaped back, calling to the crew.

They followed him again, unquestioning, obedient; Alan followed close to him. It was not pity which stirred him now for Benjamin Corvet, nor was it bitterness, and it certainly was not contempt. Of all the ways in which he had fancied finding Benjamin Corvet, he had never thought of seeing him like this.

Perhaps for only a flash, but the great quality of leadership once possessed by Corvet had returned to him in this desperate emergency, which he had created. How much or how little of his own condition Corvet understood, Alan could not tell. It was clear only that he comprehended that he had been the cause of this catastrophe, and in his fierce will to repair it not only disregarded all risks to himself, but summoned up from within him—and was spending— the last strength of his spirit. But he was spending it in a losing fight.

He got off two more cars, but the deck only dipped lower, and water washed farther and farther up over the fantail. New avalanches of iron descended as box cars burst open; monstrous dynamo drums, broad-banded steel wheels and splintered crates of machinery battered about. Men, leaping from before the charging cars, got caught in the murderous melee of iron and steel and wheels; men's shrill cries came amid the scream of metal. Alan, tugging at a crate which had struck down a man, felt aid beside him, and turning, he saw the priest whom he had passed on the stairs. The priest was bruised and bloody, and this was not his first effort to aid. Together they bent their backs and lifted an end of the crate. Then Alan stepped back, and the priest knelt alone, his lips repeating the prayer for absolution.

Screams of men came from behind, and the priest rose and turned. He saw men caught between two wrecks of cars crushing together, and there was no moment to reach them. He stood raising his arms to them, his head thrown back, calling to them as they died, the words of absolution.

Three more cars at the cost of two more lives the crew cleared, while the sheathing of ice spread over the steel inboard, and dissolution of all cargo became complete. Cut stone and motor parts, chassis and castings, furniture and beams, swept back and forth, while the cars, burst and splintered, became monstrous missiles hurtling, sidewise, aslant, recoiling. Yet men, though scattered singly, tried to stay them by ropes and chains while water washed higher and higher. Dimly, far away, drowned out by the clangor, the steam whistle of *Number 25* was blowing the four long blasts of distress. Alan heard the sound now with indifferent wonder. Destruction lay within the ship, within this car deck, where the ship had loosed on itself all elements of its own annihilation. Who could possibly aid it from without? Alan caught the end of a chain which Corvet flung him and, though he knew it was useless, carried it across from one stanchion to the next.

Something sweeping across the deck caught him and carried him with it. It brought him before the coupled line of trucks which hurtled back and forth where the rails of track three had been. He was hurled before them and rolled over. Something cold and heavy pinned down upon him, and toward him the car trucks came. Before them, something warm and living—a hand and bare arm catching him quickly and pulling at him, dragged him a little further on. Looking up, Alan saw Corvet beside him, who, unable to move him farther, was crouching down there with him. Alan yelled at him to leap, to twist aside and get out of the way, but Corvet only crouched closer and put his arms over Alan. Then the wreckage came down upon them, driving them apart. As the moment stopped, Alan could still see Corvet dimly by the glow of the incandescent lights overhead, and the truck separated them. It bore down on Alan, holding him motionless, and on the other side, it crushed down upon Corvet's legs.

He turned over as far as he could, and spoke to Alan. "You have been saving me, so now I tried to save you," he said simply. "What reason did you have for doing that? Why have you been keeping by me?"

"I'm Alan Conrad of Blue Rapids, Kansas," Alan cried out to him. "And you're Benjamin Corvet! You know me; you sent for me! Why did you do that?"

Corvet made no reply to this. Alan, peering at him underneath the truck, could see that his hands were pressed against his face and that his body shook. Whether this was from some new physical pain from the movement of the wreckage, Alan did not know. He lowered his hands after a moment, and then he did not heed Alan or seem even to be aware of him.

"Dear little Connie!" he said aloud. "Dear little Connie! She mustn't marry him—not him! That must be seen to. What shall I do, what shall I do?"

Alan worked nearer to him. "Why mustn't she marry him?" he cried to Corvet. "Why? Ben Corvet, tell me! Tell me why!"

From above him, through the clangor of the cars, came the four blasts of the steam whistle. The indifference with which Alan had heard them a few minutes before had changed now to a scourge of terror. When men had been dying about him in their attempts to save the ship, it had seemed a small thing for him to be crushed or to drown with them and with Benjamin Corvet, whom he had found at last. But Constance! Recollection of her was stirring in Corvet the torture of his will to live. Alan struggled and tried to free himself. As well as he could tell by feeling the weight above him confined—but was not crushing—him. But what gain for her if he only saved himself and not Corvet too? He turned back to Corvet.

"She's going to marry him, Ben Corvet!" he called. "They're betrothed; and they're going to be married, she and Henry Spearman!"

"Who are you?" Corvet seemed only with an effort to become conscious of Alan's presence.

"I'm Alan Conrad, whom you used to take care of. I'm from Blue Rapids. You know about me. Are you my father or what? What are you to me?"

"Your father?" Corvet repeated. "Did he tell you that? He killed your father."

"Killed him? Killed him, how?"

"Of course," said the old man. "He killed them all . . . all. But your father . . . he shot your father. He shot him through the head!"

Alan recoiled inside. A vision of Spearman came before him, as he had first seen him—cowering in Corvet's library in terror at an apparition. *". . . and the bullet hole above the eye!"* So that hole had been made by the shot Spearman fired which had killed Alan's father! Alan peered at Corvet and called to him.

"Father Benitot!" Corvet called in response—not to Alan's question, but to something that question stirred. "Father Benitot!" he appealed. "Father Benitot!"

Someone, drawn by the cry, was moving wreckage near them. A hand and arm with a torn sleeve showed; Alan could not see the rest of the figure, but by the sleeve he recognized that it was the mate.

"Who's caught here?" he called down.

"Benjamin Corvet of Corvet, Sherrill and Spearman, ship owners of Chicago," Corvet's voice replied deeply, fully. There was authority in it and wonder too—the wonder of a man finding himself in a situation which his recollection cannot explain.

"Ben Corvet!" the mate shouted in surprise. He cried it to the others, those who had followed Corvet and obeyed him during the hour before and had not known why. The mate tried to pull the wreckage aside and make his way to Corvet, but the old man stopped him. "The priest, Father Benitot! Send him to me. I shall never leave. Send Father Benitot."

The word was passed without the mate moving away. The mate, after a minute, made no further attempt to free Corvet; that indeed was useless, and Corvet demanded his right of sacrament from the priest who came and crouched under the wreckage beside him.

"I am not Father Benitot. I am Father Perron of L'Anse."

"It was to Father Benitot of St. Ignace I should have gone, Father!"

The priest got a little closer as Corvet spoke, and Alan heard only voices now and then through the sounds of clanging metal and the drum of ice against the hull. The mate and his helpers were working to get him free. They had abandoned all effort to save the ship, and it was settling. And with the settling, the movement of the wreckage imprisoning Alan was increasing. This movement made useless the efforts of the mate; it would free Alan of itself in a moment, if it did not kill him; it would free or finish Corvet too. But he, as Alan saw him, was wholly oblivious of that now. His lips moved quietly, firmly, and his eyes were fixed steadily on the eyes of the priest. His strong will and determination was trying desperately to hold death at bay until he could bare his soul in confession.

19

The message, in blurred lettering and on flimsy tissue paper of a carbon copy—that message which had brought tension to the offices of Corvet, Sherrill and Spearman and had brought Constance and her mother downtown where further information could be more quickly obtained—was handed to Constance by a clerk as soon as she entered her father's office. It had already been read to her over the telephone. Now she read it herself:

"4:05 A.M. Frankfort Wireless Station has received following message from *Number 25*: 'We have Benjamin Corvet, of Chicago, aboard.' "

"You've received nothing later than this?" she asked the clerk.

"Nothing regarding Mr. Corvet, Miss Sherrill," the clerk replied.

"Or regarding . . . . Have you obtained a passenger list?"

"No passenger list was kept, Miss Sherrill."

"The crew?"

"Yes; we have just received the names of the crew." He took another copied sheet from among the pages and handed it to her, and she looked swiftly down the list of names until she found that of Alan Conrad.

Her eyes filled, blinding her, as she put the paper down, and then took off her coat. She had been clinging determinedly in her mind to the belief that Alan might not have been aboard the ferry. Alan's message, which had sent her father north to meet the ship, had implied plainly that someone whom Alan believed might be Uncle Benny was on *Number 25*, and she had been fighting these last few hours against the conviction that therefore Alan must be on the ferry too.

As the clerk went out, she stood by the desk looking through the papers which he had given her.

"What do they say?" her mother asked.

"Wireless signals from *Number 25*," she read aloud as she composed herself, "were received from the shore stations at Ludington, Manitowoc and Frankfort until about four o'clock when . . . "

"That would be about six hours ago, Constance."

"Yes, Mother, when the signals were interrupted." Then Constance read on:

"The steamer *Richardson*, in response to whose signals *Number 25* made the change in her course which led to disaster, was in communication until about four o'clock. The Frankfort station picked up one message shortly after four, and the same message was recorded by the carferry *Manitoulin* in the southern end of the lake. Subsequently all efforts to call *Number 25* failed of response until 4:35, when a message was picked up by Manitowoc, Frankfort, and the *Richardson*. Information, therefore, regarding the fate of the ferry up to that hour received here, consists of the following . . ."

Constance stopped reading aloud and looked rapidly down the sheet and then over the next. What she was reading was the carbon copy of the report prepared that morning and sent to Henry's apartment, which he had not as yet seen. It did not contain, therefore, the last that was known, which she now continued to read:

"After 4:10, shore stations and *Richardson* sent repeated signals to *Number 25*. 'Are you in danger?' 'Shall we send help?' 'Are you jettisoning cars?' 'What is your position?' No replies were received.

"The *Richardson* continued to signal, 'Report your position and course; we will stand by,' at the same time making full speed toward last position given by *Number 25*.

"4:35: No other message has been received from *Number 25* by *Richardson*. Manitowoc and Frankfort both picked up the following: 'SOS. Are taking water fast. SOS. Position probably twenty miles west N. Fox. SOS.' The SOS has been repeated, but without further information since."

Constance picked up the later messages, received in response to requests to transmit to Corvet, Sherrill and Spearman copies of all signals concerning *Number 25* which had been received or sent. She sorted out from them those recorded after the last hour mentioned in the report she had just read.

"4:40: Manitowoc is calling *Number 25*, '*Number 26* is putting north to you. Keep in touch.'

"4:43: *Number 26* is calling *Number 25*, 'What is your position?'

"4:50: *Richardson* calling *Number 25*, 'We must be approaching you. Are you giving whistle signals?'

"4:53: *Number 25* replying to *Richardson*, 'Yes, will continue to signal. Do you hear us?'

"4:59: Frankfort calling *Number 25*, 'What is your condition?'

"5:04: *Number 25* replying to Frankfort, 'Holding bare headway; stern very low.'

"5:10: *Number 26* calling *Number 25*, 'Are you jettisoning cars?'

"5:14: Petoskey calling Manitowoc, 'We are receiving SOS. What is wrong?' 'Have not previously been in communication with shore stations or ships.'

"5:17: *Number 25* calling *Number 26*, 'Are throwing off cars; have cleared eight; work very difficult. We are sinking.'

"5:20: *Number 25* calling *Richardson*, 'Watch for small boats. Position doubtful because of snow and course changes; probably due west N. Fox, twenty to thirty miles.'

"5:24: *Number 26* calling *Number 25*, 'Are you abandoning ship?'

"5:27: *Number 25* replying to *Number 26*, 'Second boat just getting away with passengers; first boat smashed. Six passengers in second boat, two injured crew, cabin maid, boy and two men.'

"5:30: Manitowoc and Frankfort calling *Number 25,* 'Are you abandoning ship?'

"5:34: *Number 25* replying to Manitowoc, 'Still trying to clear cars; everything is loose below.'

"5:40: Frankfort calling Manitowoc, 'Do you get anything now?'

"5:45: Manitowoc calling *Richardson,* 'Do you get anything? Signals have stopped here.'

"5:48: *Richardson* calling Petoskey, 'We get nothing now. Do you?'

"6:30: Petoskey calling Manitowoc, 'Signals became faint and failed entirely about 5:45, probably by failure of ship's power supply. Operator appears to have remained at key. From 5:25 to 5:43 we received disconnected messages as follows: " 'Have cleared another car . . . they are sticking to it down there . . . engine-room crew is also sticking . . . hell on car deck . . . everything smashed . . . they won't give up . . . sinking now . . . we're going . . . stuck to end . . . all they could . . . know that . . . hand it to them . . . have cleared another car . . . sink . . . SO . . . M'aidez! M'aidez!" Signals then ceased.' "

Constance knew that in French, *M'aidez* meant "Save me." The radio operator, who must have been of French descent, and was echoing cries the early explorers and voyageurs had brought to the Great Lakes three hundred years before—cries that well may have been heard aboard the *Griffin* when she was lost in 1679. It was not a distress call to ships or shore, as that call had already been made by the SOS. Rather, it was the cry of one who knows he is beyond human help and is about to die. In the final, fleeting, flash of a second, he perceives that there is Someone out there to help him, the infinite creative intelligence, from which all creation evolves.

Down through the centuries fighting men in battles have learned this, and even the most ardent atheist, not having the benefit of spiritual faith, learns this as well when the cold hand of death rests upon his shoulder. The wireless operator, from his heritage and

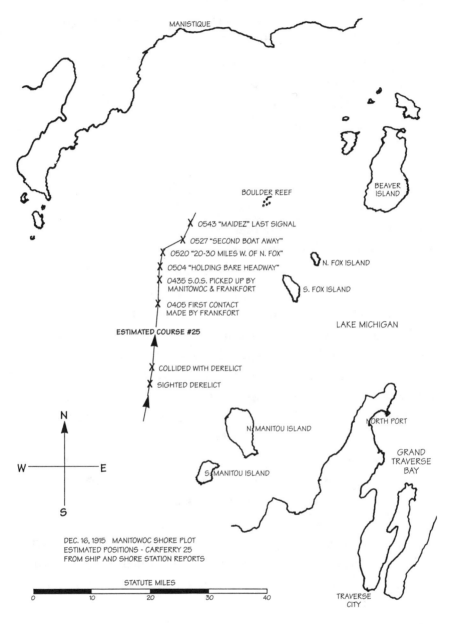

MANISTIQUE

BOULDER REEF

BEAVER
ISLAND

0543 "MAIDEZ" LAST SIGNAL

0527 "SECOND BOAT AWAY"

0520 "20-30 MILES W. OF N. FOX"

N. FOX ISLAND

0504 "HOLDING BARE HEADWAY"

0435 S.O.S. PICKED UP BY
MANITOWOC & FRANKFORT

S. FOX ISLAND

0405 FIRST CONTACT
MADE BY FRANKFORT

ESTIMATED COURSE #25

LAKE MICHIGAN

COLLIDED WITH DERELICT

SIGHTED DERELICT

N

W   E

S

N. MANITOU ISLAND

NORTH PORT

GRAND
TRAVERSE
BAY

S. MANITOU ISLAND

DEC. 16, 1915 MANITOWOC SHORE PLOT
ESTIMATED POSITIONS - CARFERRY 25
FROM SHIP AND SHORE STATION REPORTS

STATUTE MILES

0   10   20   30   40

TRAVERSE
CITY

D. A. JOHNSTON

knowledge of a young Nazarene carpenter who gave his life on a pagan Roman cross some nineteen hundred years before, and then was resurrected as history shows, may well have been prepared for this, as shown by his "M'aidez" call.

There was no more than this. Constance let the papers fall back on the desk, and looked at her mother. Mrs. Sherrill loosened her fur collar and sat back in her chair. Constance quickly shifted her gaze, and trembling with head erect, she walked to the window and looked out. The meaning of what she had read was quite clear; her mother was formulating it.

"So they are both lost, Mr. Corvet and his . . . son," Mrs. Sherrill quietly said.

Constance did not reply, either to reject or concur in the conclusion. There was not anything that was meant to be merciless in that conclusion; her mother simply was crediting what probably had occurred.

Constance could not in reason refuse to accept it too, yet she was refusing it. She had not realized, until these reports of the wireless messages told her that he had gone, what companionship with Alan had come to mean to her. She had accepted it as something that somehow would always exist—a companionship which might be interrupted often but always to be formed again. It amazed her to find how firm a place he had found in her world among those close to her, and with whom she must always be intimately concerned.

Her mother arose and came over beside her. "May it not be better, Constance, that it has happened this way?"

"Better?" Constance cried, before she controlled herself.

It was only what Henry had said to her months ago when Alan had left her in the North in the search which had resulted in the finding of Uncle Benny: "Might it not be better for him not to find out?"

Henry, who could hazard more accurately than anyone else the nature of that strange secret which Alan must now have "found out," had believed it. And now her mother, who at least had lived longer in the world than she, also believed it. There came before Constance the vision of Alan's defiance and refusal to accept the stigma suggested in her father's recital to him of his relationship to Mr. Corvet.

There came to her sight of him as he tried to keep her from entering Uncle Benny's house when Luke was there, and then her waiting with him through the long hour and his dismissal of her; his abnegation of their friendship. And at that time his disgrace was indefinite. Last night had he learned something worse than he had dreaded?

The words of his telegram took for her more terrible significance for the moment. "Have someone who knew Mr. Corvet well enough to recognize him even if greatly changed meet . . . ."

Were the broken, incoherent words of that message the last that she would hear of him, and of Uncle Benny? "They are sticking to it . . . . down there . . . . they won't give up . . . . they have cleared another car . . . . sink . . . ."

Had it come as the best way for them both?

"The *Richardson* is searching for boats, Mother," Constance returned steadily, "and *Number 26* must be there too by now."

Her mother looked to the storm. Outside the window which overlooked the lake from two hundred feet above the street, the sleet-like snow was driving ceaselessly. All over the western basin of the Great Lakes, as Constance knew—over Huron, over Michigan and Superior—the storm was established. Its continuance and severity had claimed a front page column in the morning papers. Duluth that morning had reported eighteen below zero and fierce snow. At Marquette it was fifteen below, and there was driving snow at the Soo and Mackinac, and at ports along both shores. She pictured little boats, at that last moment getting away from the ferry laden with injured and exhausted men. How long might those men live in open boats in a gale and with cold like that? The little clock on her father's desk marked ten o'clock. Those men had now been in the boats for nearly five hours.

Constance knew that as soon as anything new was heard, it would be brought to her, but with a word to her mother, she went from her father's office down the corridor into the general office. A hush of expectancy held this larger room. The clerks moved silently and spoke to one another in low voices, and she recognized in a little group of men gathered in a corner of the room some officers of Corvet, Sherrill and Spearman ships. Others among them, whom she did now know, were seamen, too—men who knew Ben Corvet and who, on hearing he was on the ferry, had come in to learn what more was known. The businessmen and clubmen, friends of Corvet's later life, had not heard yet.

There was a restrained, professional attentiveness among these lakemen, as of those in the presence of an event which any day might happen to themselves. They were listening to the clerk who had compiled the report, who was telephoning now, and Constance listened too, to learn what he might be hearing. He put down the receiver as he saw her.

"Nothing more, Miss Sherrill," he reported. "The *Richardson* has advised that she reached the reported position of the sinking about half-past six o'clock. She is searching but has found nothing."

"She'll keep on searching, though?"

"Yes; of course."

"It's still snowing there?"

"Yes, Miss Sherrill. We've had a message from your father. He has gone on to Manistique, as it's more likely that wreckage or survivors will be brought in there."

The telephone switchboard beside Constance suddenly buzzed, and the operator, plugging in a connection, said: "Yes, sir; at once," and through the partitions of the private office on the other side, a man's heavy tones came to Constance. That was Henry's office, and the voice was his, but it sounded so strange that she waited for an instant before saying to the clerk, "Mr. Spearman has come in?"

The clerk hesitated, but the voice from the other side of the partition had made reply superfluous. "Yes, Miss Sherrill."

"Did you tell him mother and I are here?"

The clerk considered again before deciding to reply in the affirmative. There was evidently some trouble with the telephone number which Henry had called; the girl at the switchboard was apologizing in frightened panic, and Henry's voice, loud and abusive, came more plainly through the partition. Constance started to give an instruction to the clerk; then, as the abuse burst out again, changed her plan and went to Henry's door and knocked. Whether no one else knocked in that way or whether he realized that she might have come into the general office, she did not know, but at once his voice was still. He made no answer and no move to open the door, so after waiting a moment, she turned the knob and went in.

Henry was seated at his desk facing her, his big hands before him and one of them holding the telephone receiver. He put it down slowly as he watched her with steady, silent, aggressive scrutiny. His face was flushed a little, but not much; his hair was carefully brushed, and there was something about his clean-shaven appearance and the set of his perfectly fitting coat, one not usually worn to business, which seemed studied.

He did not rise; only after a moment he recollected that he had not done so and came to his feet.

"Good morning, Connie," he said. "Come in. What's the news?"

There was something strained and almost menacing in his voice and in his manner which halted her. In some way, she felt, she—or her presence at that moment—was disturbing him. It frightened him, she would have thought, except that the idea was a contradiction—Henry frightened? But if it was not that, then what emotion was it that now controlled him?

The impulse which had brought her into his office went from her. She had not seen or heard from Henry directly since before Alan's telegram had come late yesterday afternoon.; she had heard from her father only that he had informed Henry; that was all.

"I've no news, Henry," she said. "Have you?"

She closed the door behind her before moving closer to him. She had not known what he had been doing since he had heard of Alan's telegram, but she supposed that he was in some way cooperating with her father, particularly since word had come of the disaster to the ferry.

"How did you happen to be here, Connie?" he asked.

She made no reply but gazed at him, studying him. The agitation he was trying to conceal was not entirely consequent to her coming in on him; it had been ruling him before. It had underlain the loudness and abuse of his words which she had overheard. That was no capricious outburst of temper or irritation; it had come from something which had seized and held him in suspense, in dread—in dread. There was no other way to define this impression to herself. When she had opened the door and come in, he had looked up in dread, as though preparing himself for whatever she might announce. Now that the door shut them in alone, he approached her with arms offered. She stepped back, avoiding his embrace, and he stopped at once but quite close to her.

That she detected faintly the smell of liquor about him was not the whole reason for her drawing back. He was not drunk; he was quite himself so far as any influence of that was concerned. Long ago, when he was a young man on the boats, he had drunk a good deal, as he had confessed to her once, but he had not done so for years. Since she had known him, he had been among the most careful of her friends; it was for "efficiency" he had said. Drinking now was simply a part—indeed, only a small part—of the subtle strangeness and peculiarity she marked in him. If he had been drinking now, it was, she knew, no temptation, no capricious return to an old appetite. If not an appetite, then it was for the effect . . . to brace himself. Against what? Against the thing for which he had prepared himself when she came upon him?

As she stared at him, the clerk's voice came to her suddenly over the partition which separated the office from the larger room where the clerk was receiving some message over the telephone. Henry straightened, listened. As the voice stopped, his great, finely shaped head sank between his shoulders, and he fumbled in his pocket for a cigar. His big hands shook as he lighted it, without word of excuse to her. A strange feeling came to her that he felt what he dreaded approaching and was no longer conscious of her presence.

She heard footsteps in the larger room coming toward the office door. Henry was in suspense as a rap came at the door. He whitened and took the cigar from his mouth and wet his lips.

"Come in," he summoned.

One of the office girls entered, bringing a white page of paper with three or four lines of purple typewriting on it which Constance recognized must be a transcript of a message just received.

She moved forward at sight of it, forgetting everything else, and he took the paper as though he did not know she was there. He merely held it until the girl had gone out, and even then stood folding and unfolding it, and his eyes did not drop to the sheet.

The girl had said nothing at all, but seeing her had excited Constance, for she had obviously not been a bearer of bad news. Constance, being certain she had brought some sort of good news, moved nearer to Henry to read what he held. He looked down and read, but silently to himself.

"What is it, Henry?" Constance asked.

He had drawn the sheet away from her as he began to read, and now he recovered himself and gave the paper to her. In that instant Constance braced for the worst, thinking she must have deceived herself the instant before about the possibility of good news. But the message stimulated what remained of hope.

"8:35 A.M. Manitowoc, Wisc," she read. "The schooner *Anna S. Solwerk* has been sighted making for this port. She is not close enough for communication, but two lifeboats, additional to her own, can be plainly made out. It is believed that she must have picked up survivors of *Number 25*. She carries no wireless so is unable to report. Tugs are going out to her."

"Two lifeboats!" Constance cried. "That could mean that they all are saved or nearly all, doesn't it? Doesn't it, Henry?"

He apparently had read some other significance into it, she thought, because his face betrayed dismay. Perhaps, she thought, with his greater understanding of conditions in the storm, he had been able to find no hope in what had been reported. That he might be dismayed by news that men were saved simply did not occur to her at once. When it did come now, it went through her first in a flash of incredulity.

"Yes," he said to her. "Yes."

He went out of the room to the outer office, and she followed him to the door and watched him. He went to the desk of the girl who had brought him the bulletin, and Constance heard his voice, strained and queerly unnatural. "Call Manitowoc on long distance and get the harbormaster. Get the names of the people the *Solwerk* picked up."

Constance retreated into the room as he returned. He did not want her there now, and for that reason she meant to remain. If he asked her to go, she intended to stay. But he did not ask her to go, although it was obvious in every word he spoke to her and in every moment of their silent waiting that he wanted her to go away, that he wanted to escape her, but dared not go about that freely.

The feeling of this flashed into her mind and left her stupefied. Henry and she were waiting for word of the fate of Uncle Benny and Alan, and they were waiting opposed! She was no longer doubting this as she watched him. She was trying to understand. The telephone buzzer under his desk sounded, and she drew close as he took up the receiver.

"Manitowoc?" he said. "I want to know what you've heard from the *Solwerk* . . . . You heard me? . . . The men the *Solwerk* picked up. Have you the names yet? . . . The *Benton?* . . . Oh, I understand! All from the *Benton.* I see! . . . No; never mind their names. How about *Number 25?* Nothing more heard from them?"

Constance had caught his shoulder while he was speaking and

now she could feel the release from strain going through him—the tension draining away. She felt it; she heard it in his tones; she saw it in his eyes.

"The steamer *Number 25* rammed proves to have been the *Benton,*" he told her. "The men are all from her. They abandoned her in the small boats, and the *Solwerk* picked them up before the ferry found her."

He was not asking her to congratulate him upon the relief he felt; he had not so far forgotten himself as that. But it was plain to her that he was congratulating himself. Before it had been fear—fear, she was beginning to understand, that those on the ferry had been saved. She shrank a little away from him. Benjamin Corvet had not been a friend of Henry's. They had quarreled; Uncle Ben had caused trouble. Yet, she could think of nothing that could explain the fear Henry betrayed at the possibility that Uncle Ben should be found safe. Henry had not welcomed Alan, and now Henry was hoping that Alan was dead.

Henry's words to her in the North, after Alan had seen her there, came back to her now: "I told that fellow Conrad not to keep stirring up these matters about Ben Corvet . . . . Conrad doesn't know what he'll turn up, and I don't know either. But it's not going to be pleasant." Only a few minutes ago she had still thought of these words as spoken only for Alan's sake and for Uncle Ben's. Now this fear could not be for their sake; it was for Henry's own. Had all the warnings been for Henry's sake too?

Horror and amazement flowed in upon her with her realization of this in the man she had promised to marry, and he seemed to appreciate the effect he was producing upon her. He tried obviously to pull himself together. He could not do that fully, but he managed to reflect an assertive manner over her.

"Connie," he said to her, "Connie!"

She drew back from him as he approached her; she was not yet consciously denying his right. What was controlling him, what might underlie his hope that they were dead? She could not guess, and she could not think or reason about that now. What she felt was only overwhelming desire to be away from him where she could think objectively. For an instant she stared at him, all her body tense, then, as she turned and went out, he followed her, again calling her name. But seeing the seamen in the larger office, he stopped, and she understood he was not willing to impose himself upon her in their presence.

She crossed the office swiftly, and in the corridor she stopped to compose herself before she met her mother. She heard Henry's voice speaking to one of the clerks, and she flushed hotly with horror. Could she be certain of anything about him now? Could she be certain even that news which came through these employees of his would not be kept from her, or only so much given to her as would serve Henry's purpose, thereby enabling him to conceal from her the reason for his fear? She pushed the door open.

"We can go home now, Mother, if you wish," she said steadily.

Her mother arose at once. "There is no more news, Constance?"

"No; a schooner picked up the crew of the ship the ferry rammed; that is all."

She followed her mother, but stopped in the ante-room beside the desk of her father's secretary, and asked: "Are you going to be here all day, Miss Bennet?"

"Yes Miss Sherrill."

"Will you please try to see personally all messages about the men on *Number 25* which come to Corvet, Sherrill and Spearman, or to Mr. Spearman, and telephone them to me yourself?"

"Certainly, Miss Sherrill."

When they had gone down to the street and were in the car, Constance leaned back and closed her eyes. She feared her mother might wish to talk with her. The afternoon papers were already out with the news of the loss of the ferry; Mrs. Sherrill stopped the car and bought one, and Constance looked at it only enough to make sure that the reporters had been able to discover nothing more than she already knew. The newspaper reference to Henry was only as to the partner of the great ship owner, Benjamin Corvet, who might be lost with the ship.

She called Miss Bennet as soon as she reached home, but nothing more had been received. Toward three o'clock, Miss Bennet called her, but only to report that the office had heard again from Mr. Sherrill. He had wired that he was going on from Manistique and would cross the Straits from St. Ignace; messages for him were to be addressed to Petoskey.

He had given no suggestion that he had news, and there was no other report except that vessels were still continuing the search for survivors because rumor from the L'Arbre Croche area was that the drum had been beating "short." The superstitious were certain that some of the men from *Number 25* yet survived.

Constance thrilled at what she heard. She did not believe in the drum, at least she had never thought she believed in it, but she stirred to the idea of its being true. If there was a drum, and if it was beating, she was glad it was beating short. It was apparently, at least, serving to keep the lakemen alert. She knew that the report of the legendary drum would not have played any part in her father's movements, for he, of course, did not believe in the legend. His move was plainly dictated by the fact that, with the western gale, drift of the ferry and any survivors would be toward the eastern shore.

A little later, as Constance stood at the window, gazing out at the snow on the lake, she drew back suddenly out of sight from the street, as she saw Henry's roadster appear out of the storm and pull up before the house.

She had been apprehensively certain that he would come to her some time during the day. He had been too fully aware of the effect he made upon her not to attempt to remove that effect as soon as he could. As he got out of the car, shaking the snow from his great fur coat and cap, looking up at the house before he came in and not knowing he was being observed, she saw something very much like triumph in his manner.

Her pulses stopped, and then raced, at seeing this air of triumph. It meant that if he brought good news, it would be good news for *him*, and it must then be bad news for her. She waited in the room where she was, and heard him in the hall speaking to Simons as he took off his coat, after which he appeared at the doorway. The strain he was under had not lessened, she could see, or rather, if she could trust her feeling at sight of him, it had lessened only slightly, and at the same time his power to resist it had too been lessening. His hands and even his body shook; but his head was thrust forward, and he stared at her aggressively, as he had obviously determined in advance to act toward her as though their relationship had not been disturbed.

"I thought you'd want to know, Connie," he said, "so I came right out. The *Richardson's* picked up one of the boats from the ferry."

"Uncle Benny and Alan Conrad were not in it," she returned; the triumph she had seen in him told her that.

"No; it was the first boat put off the ferry, with the passengers and cabin maid, and some injured men from the crew."

"Were they . . . alive?" her voice hushed tensely

"Yes; that is, they were able to revive them all, but it didn't seem possible to the *Richardson's* officers that anyone could be revived who had been exposed much longer than that; so the *Richardson's* given up the search, and some of the other ships that were searching have given up too, and have gone back on their course."

"When did you hear that, Henry? I was just talking with the office."

"A few minutes ago; a news wire got it before anyone else; it didn't come through the office."

"I see; how many were in the boat?"

"Twelve, Connie."

"Then all the vessels up there won't give up yet!"

"Why not?"

"I was just talking with Miss Bennet, Henry; she's heard again from the other end of the lake. The people up there say the drum is beating, and it's beating short still!"

"Short!"

She saw Henry stiffen. "Yes," she said swiftly. "They say the drum began sounding last night, and that at first it sounded for only two lives; it's kept on beating, but still is beating only for four. There were thirty-nine on the ship—seven passengers and thirty-two crew. Twelve have been saved now, so until the drum raises the beat to twenty-seven there is still a chance that someone will be saved."

Henry made no answer; his hands fumbled purposelessly with the lapels of his coat, and his bloodshot eyes wandered uncertainly. Constance watched him with wonder at the effect of what she had told. When she had asked him once about the drum he had professed the same skepticism which she had; but he had not held it; and he was not holding it now. The news of the drum had shaken him from his triumph over Alan and Uncle Benny, and over her. It had shaken him so that, although he remained with her for some minutes more, he seemed to have forgotten the purpose of reconciliation with her which had brought him to the house. When a telephone call took her out of the room, she returned to find him gone to the dining room; she heard a decanter clink there against a glass. He did not return to her again, but she heard him go. The front door closed behind him, and the sound of his car starting came. Then alarm, stronger even than that she had felt during the morning, came upon her.

She dined, or made pretense of dining, with her mother at seven. Her mother's voice went on and on about trifles, and Constance did not try to pay attention. Her thought was following Henry with ever sharpening apprehension. She called the office in midevening, as she knew it would be open to receive messages and reports on what was happening up North. A clerk answered; no other news had been received; then she asked Henry's whereabouts.

"Mr. Spearman went north this afternoon, Miss Sherrill," the clerk informed her.

"North? Where?"

"We are to communicate with him this evening in Grand Rapids; after that, Petoskey."

Constance could feel the rapid beating of her heart. Why had Henry gone, she wondered; not certainly to aid the search. Had he gone . . . to hinder it?

20

Constance went up to her own rooms; she could hear her mother speaking to one of maids on the same floor, but for her present anxiety, her mother offered no help and could not even be consulted. Nor could any message she might send to her father explain the situation to him. She was throbbing with determination and action, as she found her purse and counted the money in it. She never in her life had gone alone on an extended journey, much less been alone on a train overnight. If she spoke of such a thing now, she would be prevented; no occasion for it would be recognized, and she would not be allowed to go, even if properly accompanied. She could not, therefore, risk taking a handbag from the house; so she stuffed nightgown and toilet articles into her muff and the roomy pocket of her fur coat. She gained the street and turned westward at the first corner to a street car which would take her to the railway station.

There was a train to the North every evening. She knew it was not such a train as ran in the resort season, and she did not know the exact time of its departure, but she would be in time for it. The manner of buying a railway ticket and of engaging a berth on the Pullman sleeper were unknown to her—there had always been servants to do these things—but she watched others and did as they did. On the train, the berths had been made up, and people were going to bed behind some of the curtains. She procured a telegraph blank and wrote a message to her mother, telling her she had gone north to join her father. When the train had started, she gave the message to the porter, directing him to send it from the first large town at which they stopped.

She left the light burning in its little niche at the head of the berth, but had no expectation that she could sleep. Shut in by the green curtains, she drew the covers up about her and stared upward at the paneled face of the berth overhead. Then new, frightened distrust of the man she had been about to marry flowed in upon her and became all her thought.

She had not promised Uncle Benny that she would not marry Henry. Her promise had been that she would not engage herself to that marriage until she had seen Uncle Benny again. Uncle Benny's own act—his disappearance—had prevented her from seeing him, and for that reason she had broken her promise, and from its breaking, something terrifying, threatening to herself had come. She had been amazed at what she had seen in Henry, and she was appreciating now that, strangely, in her thought of him there was no sense of loss to herself. Her feeling of loss, of something gone from her which could not be replaced, was for Alan. She had admiration for Henry, pride in him; had she mistaken what was merely admiration for love? She had been about to marry him; had it been only his difference from other men she knew that had made her do that? Unconsciously to herself, had she been growing to love Alan?

Constance could not yet fathom Henry's part in the strange circumstances which had begun to reveal themselves with Alan's coming to Chicago, but Henry's hope that Uncle Benny and Alan were dead was beginning to make that clearer. She lay without voluntary movement in her berth, but her bosom was heaving with the thoughts which came to her.

Twenty years before some dreadful event had altered Uncle Benny's life. His wife had known—or had learned—enough of that event so that she had left him. It had been assumed by both Constance and her father that it must have been some intimate and private event.

They had been confirmed in believing this, when Uncle Benny, in madness or in fear, had gone away and left everything he possessed to Alan Conrad. But Alan's probable relationship with Uncle Benny had not been explanation. She saw now that it had even been misleading. For a purely private event in Uncle Benny's life—even terrible scandal—could not make Henry fear, and could not bring terror of consequences to himself. That could be only if Henry was involved in some peculiar and intimate way with what had happened to Uncle Benny. If he feared Uncle Benny's being found alive and feared Alan's being found alive too, now that Alan had found Uncle Benny, it was because he dreaded explanation of his own connection with what had taken place.

Constance raised her window shade slightly and looked out. It was still snowing, and the train was running swiftly among low sand hills, snow covered and only dimly visible in the dark. Beyond them, at times, she had glimpses of the lake, and she imagined she could hear the steady roar of its surf above the rhythmic noises of the train. The lake! Out there, maybe Alan and Uncle Benny were still struggling for their lives against bitter cold and ice and rushing water. She must not think of that.

Uncle Benny had withdrawn himself from men, and he had ceased to be active in his business and delegated it to others. This change had been strangely advantageous to Henry. Henry had been hardly more than an ordinary seaman then. He had been a mate—the mate of one of Uncle Benny's ships. Quite suddenly he had become Uncle Benny's partner. Henry had explained this to her by saying that

Uncle Benny had felt madness coming on him and had selected him as the one to take charge.

But Uncle Benny had not trusted Henry. He had been suspicious of him, and he had quarreled with him. How strange it was then that Uncle Benny should have advanced and given way to a man he could not trust!

It was strange, too, that if—as Henry had said—their quarrels had been about business, Uncle Benny had allowed Henry to remain in control.

Their quarrels had culminated on the day that Uncle Benny went away. Afterward Uncle Benny had come to her and warned her not to marry Henry, and then he had sent for Alan. There had been purpose in these acts of Uncle Benny's. Had they meant that Uncle Benny had been on the verge of making explanation—that explanation which Henry feared—and that he had been . . . prevented? Her father had thought this. At least he thought that Uncle Benny must have left some explanation in his house. He had told Alan that, and had given Alan the key to the house so that he could find it. Alan had gone to the house . . . .

In the house Alan had found someone who had mistaken him for a ghost, a man who had cried out at sight of him, something about a ship—about the *Miwaka*, the ship of whose loss no one had known anything except by the sounding of the drum. What had the man been doing in the house? Had he too been looking for the explanation—the explanation that Henry feared? Alan had described the man to her, and that description had not had meaning for her before, but now remembering that description, she could think of Henry as the only one who could have been in that house! Henry had fought with Alan there! Afterwards, when Alan had been attacked on the street, had Henry anything to do with that?

Henry had lied to her about being in Duluth the night he had fought with Alan. He had not told her the true cause of the quarrels with Uncle Benny. He wished her to believe that Uncle Benny was dead when the wedding ring and watch came to her—the watch which had been Captain Stafford's of the *Miwaka*! Henry had urged her to marry him once. Was that because he wished the security that her father—and she—must give her husband when they learned the revelation which Alan or Uncle Benny might bring?

If so, then that revelation had to do with the *Miwaka*. It was the *Miwaka* that Henry had cried out to Alan in the house. And what about the names of the next of kin of those on the *Miwaka* that Uncle Benny had kept? These things were beginning to explain to her something of the effect on Henry of the report that the drum was telling that some on Ferry *Number 25* were alive, and why he had hurried north because of that. The drum, the superstition said, had beat the roll of those who died with the *Miwaka*—had beaten for all but one! No one of those who accepted the superstition had ever been able to explain that; but Henry could! He knew something more about the *Miwaka* than others knew. He had encountered the *Miwaka* somehow, or encountered someone saved from the ship, and he knew, then, that one had been spared as the drum had told! Who had that one been? Alan? And was he now among those from *Number 25* for whom the drum had not yet beat?

She recalled that on the day when the *Miwaka* was lost, Henry and Uncle Benny had been on the lake in a tug. Afterwards, Uncle Benny had grown rich, and Henry had attained advancement and wealth. Her reasoning had brought her to the verge of a terrible discovery. If she could take one more step forward in her thought, it would make her understand it all. But she could not yet take that step.

In the morning, at Traverse City, she got a cup of coffee and some toast in the station eating house, before changing to a daycoach. It had grown still more bitterly cold; the wind which swept the long brick platform of the station was arctic, and even through the double windows of the daycoach she could feel its chill. Grand Traverse Bay was frozen across. Frozen, too, was Torch Lake, and to the north of that, snow-covered ice marked the chain of little lakes known as The Intermediates. The towns and villages lay under drifts, and the white of the rolling fields was broken only by leafless trees or blackened stumps. It had stopped snowing, however, and she found relief in that; searchers on the lake could see small boats now—if there were still small boats to be seen.

To the people in her Pullman sleeper, the destruction of the ferry had been only a news item competing for interest with other reports in the newspapers. Today, to the people in the daycoach, it was an intimate and absorbing thing. They spoke by name of the crew as of persons whom they knew. A white lifeboat, one man told her, had been seen south of Beaver Island, and another said there had been two lifeboats. They had been far off from shore, but according to the report cabled from Beaver, there had appeared to be men in them; the men—her informant's voice hushed slightly— had not been rowing. Constance shuddered. She had heard of things like that on the quick-freezing fresh water of the lakes—small boats adrift crowded with men sitting upright in them, ice-coated, frozen, lifeless!

Petoskey, with its great hotels closed and boarded up, and its curio and other shops closed and locked, was blocked with snow. She went from the train directly to the telegraph office. If Henry was in Petoskey they would know where he could be found, as he would be keeping in touch with them. The operator in charge of the office knew her, and his manner became still more deferential when she asked after Henry.

Mr. Spearman, the man said, had been at the office early in the day; there had been no messages for him. He left instructions that any which came were to be forwarded to him through the men who, under his direction, were patrolling the shore for twenty miles north of Little Traverse, watching for boats. The operator added to the report she had heard on the train. One lifeboat and perhaps two had been seen by a farmer who had been on the ice to the south of Beaver; the second boat had been far to the south and west of the first one; tugs were cruising there now. It had been several hours, however, after the farmer had seen the boats before he had been able to get word to St. James, the town at the north end of the island, so that the news could be cabled to the mainland. Fishermen and seamen, therefore, regarded it as more likely, from the direction and violence of the gale, that the boats, if they continued to float, would be drifted upon the mainland rather than that they would be found by the tugs.

Constance asked about her father. The operator told her that Mr. Sherrill and Mr. Spearman had been in communication that morning. Mr. Sherrill had not come to Petoskey, but had taken charge of the watch along the shore at its north end. It was possible that the boats might drift in there, but men of experience considered it more probable that the boats would drift in farther south where Mr. Spearman was in charge.

Constance crossed the frozen edges of the bay by sledge to Harbor Point. The driver mentioned Henry with admiration and with pride in his acquaintance with him. It brought vividly to her the recollection that Henry's rise in life had been a matter of personal pride to these people, lending luster to them and their neighborhood. Henry's influence here was far greater than her own or her father's. If she were to move against Henry or show him distrust, she would have to work alone. She could enlist no aid from these people. And her distrust now had deepened into terrible dread. She had not been able before this to form any definite idea of how Henry could threaten Alan and Uncle Benny; she had imagined only vague interference and obstruction of the search for them; she had not foreseen that he could so readily assume charge of the search and direct, or misdirect, it.

At the Point she discharged the sledge and went on foot to the house of the caretaker who had charge of the Sherrill cottage during the winter. Getting the keys from him, she let herself into the house. The electricity had been shut off, and the house was darkened by shutters, but she found an oil lamp and lit it. Going to her room, she unpacked a heavy sweater and woolen cap, and a short fur coat—winter things which were left there for use when they sometimes opened the house out of season—and put them on. Then she went down and found her snowshoes and the winter boots she wore with them. Stopping at the telephone, she called the long distance operator and asked her to locate Mr. Sherrill, if possible, and advise him she was heading on up the shore and that he was to move south along the shore so that they would meet. She put on her boots, and then went out and fastened on her snowshoes.

It had grown late. The early December dusk—the second dusk since the small boats had put off from *Number 25*—darkened the snow-locked land. The wind from the west cut like a knife, even through her fur coat. The pine trees moaned and bent, with loud whistlings of the wind among their needles; the leafless elms and maples crashed their limbs together; above the clamor of all other sounds, the roaring of the lake came to her, the booming of the waves against the ice, the shattering of floe on floe. No snow had fallen for a few hours, and the sky was even clearing; ragged clouds scurried before the wind and, opening, showed the moon.

Constance moved westward and then north, following the bend of the shore. The figure of a man appeared vaguely in the dusk after she had gone about two miles—one of the shore patrols, pacing the ice hummocks of the beach and staring out toward the lake. When she approached, he seemed surprised at seeing a girl—but less surprised once he recognized her. Mr. Spearman, he told her, was to the north of them on the beach somewhere, but he did not know how far. He assured her that there were men stationed all along the shore. And about a mile farther on, she came upon a second man, and about the same distance beyond she found a third, but she did not stop.

Her legs ached now with the unaccustomed travel on the snow-shoes, and the cold, which had only been a piercing chill at first, was stopping all feeling, and almost stopping thought as well. When clouds covered the moon, complete darkness came, and then she could go forward only slowly, or would have to stop and wait. But the intervals of moonlight were growing longer and increasing in frequency. As the sky cleared, she went forward quickly for many minutes at a time, straining her gaze westward over the tumbling water and the floes. It came to her with terrifying apprehension that she must have advanced at least three miles since she had seen the last patrol. She could not have passed anyone in the moonlight without seeing him, and in the dark intervals she advanced so little that she could not have missed one that way either.

She tried to go faster as she realized this, but now travel had become more difficult. There was no longer any beach. High, precipitous bluffs, which she recognized as marking Seven Mile Point, descended here directly to the hummocked ice along the water's edge. She fell many times, traveling upon these hummocks, and there were strange, treacherous places between them where, except for her snowshoes, she would have broken through. Her skirt was torn; she lost one of her gloves and could not stop to look for it; she fell again and sharp ice cut her ungloved hand and the blood froze upon her finger tips. She did not heed any of these things.

She was horrified to find that she was growing weak, and that her senses were becoming confused. She mistook at times floating ice, metallic under the moonlight, for boats; her heart beat fast then while she scrambled part way up the bluff to gain better sight and so ascertain her mistake. Deep ravines at places broke the shores, and following the bend of the bluffs, she got into these ravines, and only learned her error when she found that she was departing from the shore. She had come in all, perhaps eight miles, and fatigue was overtaking her. Other girls, she assured herself, would not have weakened like this. They would have had strength to make certain no boats were there, or at least to get help. She had seen no houses; those, she knew, stood back from the shore, high upon the bluffs, and were not easy to find, but she scaled the bluff now and looked about for lights. The country was wild and wooded, and the moonlight showed only the white stretches of the shrouded snow.

She descended to the beach again and went on. Her gaze continued to search the lake, but now, wherever there was a break in the bluffs, she looked toward the shore as well. At the third of these breaks, the yellow glow of a window appeared, marking a house in a hollow between snow-shrouded hills. She turned eagerly that way, but she could go only very slowly now. There was no path, or if there was one, the snow drifts had covered it. Through the drifts a thicket projected; the pines on the ravine sides overhead stood so close that only a silver trace of the moonlight came through, and beyond the pines, birch trees, stripped of their bark, stood black up to the white boughs.

Constance climbed over leafless briars and through brush and came upon a clearing perhaps fifty yards across, roughly crescent shaped, as it followed the configuration of the hills. Dead cornstalks above the snow showed plowed ground; beyond that, a little black cabin huddled in the further point of the crescent, and Constance gasped with disappointment as she saw it. She had expected a farm house, but this was plainly not even that. The framework was of logs or poles which had been partly boarded over, and above the boards and where they were lacking, black building paper had been nailed secured by big tin discs. The rude, weather-beaten door was closed. Smoke came from a pipe stuck though the roof.

She struggled to the door and knocked, and receiving no reply, she beat upon it with both fists.

"Who's there?" she cried. "Who's there?"

The door opened then a very little, and the frightened face of an Indian woman appeared in the crack. The woman had evidently expected someone—someone she feared, it seemed, for she was visibly relieved when she saw Constance. She threw the door open wider, and bent to help unfasten Constance's snowshoes. Having done that, she led her in and closed the door.

Constance looked swiftly around the single room of the cabin. There was a cot on one side; there was a table, home carpentered; there were a couple of boxes for clothing or utensils. The stove, a good range once in the house of a prosperous farmer, had been bricked up by its present owners so as to hold fire. Dried onions and yellow ears of corn hung from the rafters, and on the shelves were little birch bark canoes, woven baskets, and porcupine quill boxes of the ordinary sort for the summer trade.

Constance recognized the woman now as one who had come to Harbor Springs to sell such things, and who could speak fairly good English. The woman clearly had recognized Constance at once.

"Where is your man?" Constance had caught the woman's arm.

"They sent for him to go to the beach. A ship has sunk."

"Are there houses near here? You must run to one of them at once. Bring whoever you can get, and if you can't do that, tell me where to go."

The woman stared at her stolidly, and moved away.

"None near," she said. "Besides, you could not get somebody before someone will come."

"Who is that?"

"He is on the beach . . . Henry Spearman. He comes here to warm himself. It is nearly time he comes again."

"How long has he been up here?"

"Since before noon. Sit down. I will make you tea.."

Constance gazed at her; the woman was plainly glad of her coming.

Her relief—relief from that fear she had been feeling when she opened the door—was very evident. It was Henry, then, who had frightened her.

The Indian woman set a chair for her beside the stove, and put water in a pan to heat; she shook tea leaves from a box into a bowl and brought a cup.

"How many on that ship?" the Indian woman asked.

"Altogether there were thirty-nine," Constance replied.

"Some saved?"

"Yes; a boat was picked up yesterday morning with twelve."

The woman seemed to make some computation which was difficult for her.

"Seven are living then," she said at last.

"Seven? What have you heard? What makes you think so?"

"That is what the drum says."

The drum! There was a drum then! At least there was some sound which people heard, which they called a drum, for the woman had heard it.

The woman shifted, checking something upon her fingers, while her lips moved; she was not counting, Constance thought; she was more likely aiding herself in translating something from Indian numeration into English.

"Two, it began with," she announced. "Right away it went to nine. Sixteen then . . . that was this morning very early. Now, all day and tonight, it has been giving twenty. That leaves seven. It is not known who they may be."

She opened the door and looked out. The roar of the water and the wind, which had come loudly, increased, and with it the wood noises. The woman was not looking about now, Constance realized; she was listening. The drum! Blood prickled in her face and forehead, and in her finger tips. The drum was heard only, it was said, in time of severest storm, and for that reason it was heard most often in winter. It was very seldom heard by anyone in summer, and she was of the summer people.

Sounds were coming from the woods now. Were these reverberations the roll of the drum? Her voice was uncontrolled as she asked the woman:

"Is that the drum?"

The woman shook her head. "That's the trees."

Constance's shoulders trembled convulsively. When she had thought about the drum—and when she had spoken about it to others, who themselves had never heard of it—they always had said that, if there were such a sound, it was the trees. She herself had heard those strange wood noises, terrifying sometimes until their source was known—wailings like the cry of someone in anguish, which were caused by two crossed saplings rubbing together; thunderings, which were only some smaller trees beating against a great hollow trunk when a strong blew from a certain direction. But the Indian woman must know all such sounds well, and to her the drum was something distinct from them.

"You'll know the drum when you hear it," she said.

Constance grew suddenly cold. For twenty lives, the woman said, the drum had beat. That meant to her, and to Constance too now, that seven were left. Indefinite, desperate denial that all from the ferry must be dead—that denial which had been strengthened by the news that at least one boat had been adrift near Beaver—altered in Constance to conviction of a boat with seven from the ferry, seven dying, perhaps, but not yet dead! Seven out of twenty-seven! The drum had beat for them in little groups as they had died. When it beat again, would the toll go beyond this score?

The woman drew back and closed the door; the water was hot now, and she made the tea and poured a cup for Constance. As she drank it, Constance was listening for the drum; the woman too was listening. Having finished the tea, Constance returned to the door and reopened it; the sounds outside were the same. A solitary figure appeared moving along the edge of the ice—the figure of a tall man walking on snowshoes; moonlight distorted the figure, and it was muffled too in a great coat which made it unrecognizable. He halted and stood looking out at the lake and then, with a sudden movement, strode on. He halted again, and now Constance could see that he was not just looking, he was listening as she was. And he was not merely listening; his body swayed and bent to a rhythm, as if he were counting something he could hear. Constance strained her ears, but she could hear no sound except that of the waters and the wind.

"Is the drum sounding now?"

"No."

Constance gazed again at the man and found his motion quite unmistakable; he was counting, and if it was not something that he heard—or thought he heard—then he was recounting and reviewing within himself something that he had heard before, some irregular rhythm which had become much a part of him that it sounded now continually within his brain so that, instinctively, he moved in cadence with it. He stepped forward again now, and turned toward the house.

Her breath caught as she spoke to the woman. "Mr. Spearman is coming here now!"

Her impulse was to remain where she was, but realization came to her that there might be advantage in his not seeing her until he arrived, so she reclosed the door and drew back into the cabin.

Part
Six

Revelations

21

Noises of the wind and the roaring of the lake made inaudible any sound of his approach to the cabin. She heard his snowshoes, however, scrape the cabin wall as, after taking them off, he leaned them beside the door. He thrust the door open and then came in. He did not see her at first, and as he turned to force the door shut again against the wind, she watched him quietly. She understood at once why the Indian woman had been afraid of him. His face was bloodless, yellow and swollen looking, and his eyes were blood-shot. His lips were strained to a thin, straight line.

He saw her now and started, and as though sight of her confused him, he looked away from the woman and then back to Constance before he seemed certain of her.

"Hello!" he said tentatively. "Hello."

"I'm here, Henry."

"Oh! You are! You are!" He stood drawn up, swaying a little as he stared at her; whiskey was on his breath, as it became evident in the heat of the room, but whiskey alone could not account for this condition in which she now found him. Neither could it conceal that condition; some turmoil and strain within him made him immune to its effects.

She had vaguely realized on her way up here what that strain within him must be. Guilt of some awful sort connected him, and had connected Uncle Benny, with the *Miwaka*—the lost ship for which the drum had beaten the roll of those lost with it.

Now dread of revelation of that guilt had brought him here, near to the drum. He had been alone on the beach some twelve hours, the woman had said, listening and counting the beats of the drum for another ship, and fearing the survival of someone from that ship. Guilt was in his thought now, wracking him, tearing at his soul. And there was something more: that something she had seen in him when he first caught sight of her. It was fear—fear of her, Constance Sherrill.

He was fully aware, she now understood, that he had in a measure betrayed himself to her in Chicago, and he hoped to cover up and to dissemble that betrayal with her. For that reason she was the last person in the world whom he wished to find here now.

"The point is," he said heavily, "why are you here?"

"I decided to come up last night."

"Obviously." He uttered the word slowly and with care. "Unless you flew. Who came with you?"

"No one; I came alone. I expected to find Father at Petoskey, but he hadn't been there, so I came here."

"After him?"

"No; after you, Henry."

"After me?" She had increased the apprehension in him, and he considered and scrutinized her before he ventured to go on. "Because you wanted to be up here with me, Connie?"

"Of course not!"

"What's that?"

"Of course not."

"I knew it!" he moved menacingly. She watched him quite without fear; fear was for him, she felt, not for her. Often she wished that she might have known him when he was a young man, and now in a way, she was aware that she was having that wish. Under the surface of the man whose strength and determination she had admired, all the time had been this terror—this guilt. If Uncle Benny had carried it for a score of years, Henry had it within him, too. This had been within him all the time!

"You came up here about Ben Corvet?" he challenged.

"Yes . . . no!"

"Which do you mean?"

"No."

"I know then. For him, then . . . eh. For him!"

"For Alan Conrad? Yes," she said.

"I knew it!" he repeated. "He's been the trouble between you and me all the time!" She made no denial of that; she had begun to know during the last two days that it was so.

"So you came to find him?" Henry went on.

"Yes, Henry. Have you any news?"

"News?"

"News of the boats!"

"News!" he iterated. "News tonight? No one'll have more'n one news tonight!"

From his slow, heavy utterance, a quality of terrible satisfaction betrayed itself. His eyes widened a little as he saw it strike Constance, and then his lids narrowed again. He had not meant to say it that way; yet for an instant, satisfaction to him had become inseparable from the saying. This was followed by fright—the fright of just what he had said and what she had made of it.

"He'll be found!" she defied him.

"Be found?"

"Some are dead," she said, "but not all. Twenty are dead, but seven are not."

She looked for confirmation to the Indian woman, who nodded: "Yes." He moved his head to face the woman, but his eyes, unmoving, remained fixed on Constance.

"Seven?" he echoed. "You say seven are not! How do you know?"

"The drum has been beating for twenty, but not more!" Constance said. Thirty hours before, when she told Henry of the drum she had done it without belief herself, and without looking for belief in him.

But now, whether or not she yet believed or simply clung to the superstition for its shred of hope, it gave her a weapon to terrify him; for he now believed—believed with all the unreasoning horror of his superstition and the terror of long-borne and hidden guilt.

"The drum, Henry!" she repeated. "The drum you've been listening to all day on the beach—the one that sounded for those lost with the *Miwaka*; sounded, one by one, for all who perished! But it didn't sound for him! It's been sounding again, you know; but again, it doesn't sound for him, Henry, not for him!"

"The *Miwaka*! What do you mean by that? What's that got to do with this?" His swollen face was thrust forward at her; there was threat against her in his tense muscles and his bloodshot eyes.

She did not shrink back from him, or move, and now he was not waiting for her answer. Something—a sound—had caught his attention. Once it echoed, low in its reverberation, but penetrating and quite distinct. It came, so far as direction could be assigned to it, from the trees toward the shore, but it was like no forest sound. Distinct too was it from any noise of the lake. It was like a drum! Yet when the echo had gone, it was a sensation easy to deny—a hallucination, that was all. But now, low and distinct it came again, and as before, Constance saw it catch Henry, and hold him. His lips moved, but he did not speak; he was counting. "Two," she saw his lips form.

The Indian woman passed them and opened the door, and now the sound, louder and more distinct, came again.

"The drum!" she whispered, without looking about. "You hear? Three, I've heard. Now four! It will beat twenty, and then we will know if more are dead!"

The door blew from the woman's hand, and snow, swept up from the drifts of the slope, swirled into the room. The draft blew out the flame of the lamp in a smoky streak up the glass chimney and snuffed it out. The moonlight painted a rectangle on the floor, and showed a green, shimmering world outside. Hurried spots of clouds shuttered away the moon for moments, casting shadows which swept raggedly up the slope from the shore. The woman seized the door and, tugging it about against the gale, she slammed it shut. She did not try at once to light the lamp.

The sound of the drum was continuing, the beats a few seconds apart. The opening of the door outside had seemed to Constance to make the beats come louder and more distinct, but the closing of the door did not seem to muffle them again. "Twelve," Constance counted to herself. The beats seemed to be quite measured and regular at first, but now Constance knew that this was only roughly true, as they were beating now in rhythm rather than at regular intervals. Two came close together and there was a longer wait before the next; then three sounded before the measure—a wild, leaping rhythm. She recalled having heard that the strangeness of Indian music to civilized ears was its time. The drums beat and rattles sounded in a different time from the song which they accompanied; there were even, in some dances, three different times contending for supremacy.

Now this seemed reproduced in the strange, irregular sounding of the drum. She could not count those beats with any certainty. "Twenty . . . twenty-one . . . twenty-two!" Constance caught her breath and waited for the next beat. The time of the interval between measures of the rhythm passed, and still only the whistle of the wind and the undertone of water sounded. The drum had beaten its roll, and for the moment was done.

"Now it begins again," the woman whispered. "Always it waits and then it begins over."

Constance let go her breath; the next beat then would not mean another death. Twenty-two had been her count, as nearly as she could count at all, and the reckoning agreed with what the woman had heard. Two had died then, since the drum last had beat, when its roll was twenty. This was two more than before, and that meant that five were left! Yet Constance, while she was appreciating this, strained forward, staring at Henry. She could not be certain, in the flickering shadows of the cabin, of what she was seeing in him; still less, in the pounding heart and heavy breathing that it brought. But still it turned her weak, then spurred her with a vague and terrible impulse.

The Indian woman lifted the lamp chimney waveringly and scratched a match, and with unsteady hands, lighted the wick. Constance caught up her woolen hood from the table and put it on. Her action seemed to call Henry to himself.

"What are you going to do?" he demanded.

"I'm going out."

He moved between her and the door. "Not alone, you're not!"

His heavy voice had a deep tone of menace in it; he seemed to consider and decide something about her. "There's a farm house about a mile back; I'm going to take you over there and leave you with those people."

"I will not go there."

He swore. "I'll carry you then."

She shrank back from him as he lurched toward her with hands outstretched to seize her; he followed her, and she avoided him again. If his guilt and terror had given her mental ascendancy over him, his physical strength could still force her to his will, and realizing the impossibility of evading him or overcoming him, she stopped.

"Not that!" she cried. "Don't touch me!"

"Come with me then!" he commanded; and he went out the door, laid his snowshoes on the snow and stepped into them, stooping and tightening the straps; he stood by while she put on hers. He did not attempt again to put hands upon her as they moved away from the little cabin toward the woods back of the clearing, and he went ahead, breaking the trail for her with his snowshoes. He moved forward slowly. Had he wished, he could travel three feet to every two that she could cover, but he seemed to be wishing for delay rather than speed. They reached the trees; the hemlock and pine, black and swaying, shifted their shadows on the moonlit snow; bare maples and beeches, bent by the gale, creaked and cracked. The wind, which wailed among the branches of the maples, hissed loudly in the needles of the hemlocks; snow swept from the slopes whirled and drove about them, and she drew it in with her breath.

All through the woods were noises; a moaning came from a dark copse of pine and hemlock to their right, rose and died away; a wail followed—a whining, whimpering wail—so like the crying of a child that it startled her. Shadows seemed to detach themselves, as the trees swayed, to tumble from the boughs and scurry over the snow; they hid, as one looked at them, then darted on and hid behind the tree trunks.

Henry was barely moving, and now he slowed still more. A deep, dull resonance was booming above the wood; it boomed again and ran into a rhythm. No longer was it above; at least it was not only above; it was all about them—here, there, to right and to left, before, behind—the booming of the drum. Doom was the substance of that sound that was beating the roll of those lost on the lake. Could there be, abiding in the forest, a consciousness which counted the roll? Constance fought the mad feeling that it brought. The sound must have some natural cause, she repeated to herself—waves washing in some strange conformation of the ice caves on the shore, wind reverberating within some great hollow tree trunk as within the pipe of an organ. But Henry was not denying the drum now!

He had stopped in front of her, half turned her way; his body swayed to the booming of the drum, as his swollen lips counted its soundings. She could see him plainly in the moonlight, and she drew nearer to him as she followed his count. "Twenty-one . . . ," he counted. ". . . Twenty-two . . . !" The count continued. ". . . Twenty-four . . . twenty-five . . . twenty-six . . . !"

Would he count another?

When he did not, her pulse, which had halted, leaped with relief as comprehension rushed through her. It was thus she had seen him counting in the cabin, but so vaguely that she had not been certain.

He moved on again, descending the steep side of a little ravine, and she followed. One of his snowshoes caught in a protruding root, and instead of slowing to free it with care, he pulled it violently out, and she heard the dry, seasoned wood crack. He looked down, swore, and seeing the wood was not broken through, went on. As he reached the bottom of the slope, she jumped downward from a little height behind him and crashed down upon his trailing snowshoe just behind the heel. The rending snap of the wood came beneath her feet. Had she broken through his shoe or snapped her own? She sprang back, as he cried out and swung in an attempt to grasp her. He lunged to follow her, and she ran a few steps away and stopped. At his next step, his foot entangled in the mesh of the broken snowshoe, and he stooped, cursing, to strip it off and hurl it from him. Then he tore off the one from the other foot, threw it away and lurched after her again, but now he sank in above his knees and floundered in the snow. She stood for a moment while the half-mad, half-drunken figure struggled toward her along the side of the ravine, and then she ran to where the tree trunks hid her from him, but where she could look out from the shadow and see him. He gained the top of the slope and turned in the direction she had gone. Assured then, apparently, that she had fled in fear of him, he started back more swiftly toward the beach. She followed, keeping out of his sight among the trees.

To twenty-six, he had counted . . . to twenty-six, each time! That told that he knew one was living among those who had been on the ship! The drum—it was not easy to count with exactness those wild, irregular leaping sounds; one might make of them almost what one wished—or feared! And if, in his terror here, Henry made the count twenty-six, it was because he knew—knew—that one was living! Which one? It could only be one of two to dismay him so. There had been two on the ferry whose rescue he had feared; only two who, living, he would let die on this beach which he had chosen and set aside for his patrol, while he waited for them to die.

She forced herself on unsparingly as she saw Henry gain the shore and, believing himself alone, hurry northward. She went with him, staying among the trees, paralleling his course. On the windswept ridges of the ice where there was little snow he could travel for long stretches faster than she, and as she struggled to keep even with him, her lungs were seared by the cold air and she gasped for breath. But she could not rest; she could not let herself be exhausted. Minute after merciless minute she raced him thus. And then, suddenly, she made out a shape, a dark shape, stretched out on the ice ahead—a human figure! A man, in a mackinaw, half covered by snow. Beyond, still farther out at the edge of the ice, she could see something which might have been fragments of a lifeboat being tossed up and down where the waves thundered and gleamed at the edge of the floes.

Henry quickened his pace, and she desperately quickened hers, leaving the shelter of the trees and scrambling down the steep pitch of the bluff, shouting, and crying aloud. Henry whirled and, seeing her, stopped. She raced past and got between him and the form on the ice. Then she turned and faced him.

Now that she was there to witness what he might do, defeat— defeat of whatever frightful purpose he had—was his. In his realization of that, he burst out in oaths against her. He advanced, but she stood, confronting, defiant. He swayed slightly in his walk, then and swung past and veered away, leaving behind the form on the beach and continuing on along the icy hummocks toward the north.

Constance ran to the crumpled, snow-covered figure of the man in the mackinaw and cap; his face hidden partly by the position in which he lay and partly by the drifting snow. Before she swept the snow away and turned him to her, she knew that he was Alan.

She cried to him, and when he did not answer, she shook him. But she could not rouse him. Praying in wild whispers to herself, she opened his jacket and felt within his clothes. He was still warm.

At least he was not frozen within! And . . . and now she felt some stir of his heart! She tried to lift him, to carry him, then to drag him. But she could not. He fell from her arms into the snow again, and she sat down, pulling him onto her lap and clasping him to her.

She must find aid, she must get him to some house, she must take him out of the terrible cold; but she dared not leave him! Might Henry return, if she went away?

She arose and looked about. Far up the shore she saw his figure rising and falling in his flight over the rough ice. A sound came to her too, the low, deep reverberation of the drum beating once more along the shore and in the woods, and out on the lake, and it seemed to her that Henry's figure, in the stumbling steps of his flight, was keeping time to the wild rhythm of the drum.

She stooped to Alan and covered him with her coat, then left to get help, no longer afraid that Henry would return.

22

"So this isn't your house, Judah?"

"No, Alan; this is an Indian's house. It is Adam Enos' house. He and his wife went somewhere else when you needed this."

"He helped to bring me here then?"

"No, Alan. They were alone here—she and Adam's wife. When she found you, she came here for help and they brought you here—more than a mile along the beach. Two women!"

Alan choked as he put down the little porcupine quill box which had started this line of inquiry. Whatever questions he had asked of Judah or of Lawrence Sherrill these last few days had brought him very quickly back to her.

Moved by some intuitive certainty regarding Spearman, she had come north; she had not thought of peril to herself; she had struggled alone across dangerous ice in the storm—a girl brought up as she had been!

She had found him—Alan!—upon the beach, his life almost extinguished. She and the Indian woman, Wassaquam had just said, had brought him along the shore. How had they managed that?

They had somehow got him to this house, which in his ignorance of exactly where he was on the mainland, he had thought must be Wassaquam's. She had gone to get help . . . . His eyes closed and his throat closed up, and his eyes filled as he thought of this.

In the week during which he had been cared for here, Alan had not seen Constance; but there had been a peculiar and exciting alteration in Sherrill's manner toward him, he felt. It was something more than mere liking for him that Sherrill had shown, and Sherrill had spoken of her to him as "Constance," not, as he had always called her before, "Miss Sherrill" or "my daughter." Alan had dreams which had seemed impossible of fulfillment, of dedicating his life and all that he could make of it to her; now Sherrill's manner had brought to him something like awe—something quite incredible.

When he had believed that disgrace was his—disgrace because he was Benjamin Corvet's son—he had hidden, or tried to hide, his feeling toward her. He knew now that he was not Corvet's son, because Corvet had said that Spearman had shot his father. But he could not be certain yet who his father was or what revelation regarding himself might now be given. Could he dare to betray that he was thinking of Constance as . . . as he could not keep from thinking? He dared not without daring to dream that Sherrill's manner meant that she could care for him, and that he could not presume. What she had undergone for him—her venture alone up the beach and that dreadful contest between her and Spearman—must remain circumstances which he had learned, but from which he could not yet draw conclusions.

He turned to the Indian.

"Has anything more been heard of Spearman, Judah?"

"Only this, Alan; he crossed the Straits the next day on the ferry there. In Mackinaw City he bought liquor at a bar and took it with him, and asked about trains into the northwest. He has gone, leaving all he had. What else could he do, Alan?"

Alan crossed the little cabin and looked out the window over the snow-covered slope, where the bright sun was shining. It was very still out there; there was no motion at all in the pines toward the ice-bound shore, and the shadow of the wood smoke rising from the cabin chimney made almost a straight line across the snow. Snow had covered any tracks there had been upon the beach where those who had been in the boat with him had been found dead. He had known this must be; he had believed them beyond aid when he had tried for the shore to summon help for them and himself. The other boat, which had carried survivors of the wreck, blown farther to the south, had been able to gain the shore of North Fox Island. As these men had not been so long exposed before they were brought to shelter, four men lived. Sherrill had told him their names; they were the mate, the assistant engineer, a deck hand and Father Perron, the priest, who had been a passenger but who stayed with the crew until the last. Benjamin Corvet had perished in the wreckage of the cars.

As Alan went back to his chair, the Indian watched him and seemed not displeased.

"You feel good now, Alan?" Wassaquam asked.

"Almost like myself, Judah."

"That is right then. It was thought you would be like that today."

He looked at the long shadows and at the height of the early morning sun, estimating the time of day. "A sled is coming soon now."

"We're going to leave here, Judah?"

"Yes, Alan."

Was he going to see her then? Excitement stirred him, and he turned to Wassaquam to ask that, but suddenly he hesitated and did not inquire.

Wassaquam brought the mackinaw and cap which Alan had worn on *Number 25*, and he took the new blankets furnished by Sherrill from the bed. They waited until a farmer appeared, driving a team hitched to a low, wide-runnered sled. The Indian settled Alan on the sled, and they drove off.

The farmer looked frequently at Alan with curious interest. The sun shone down, dazzling, and felt almost warm in the still air. Wassaquam, with regard for the frostbite from which Alan had been suffering, bundled up the blankets around him, but Alan pushed them down reassuringly. They traveled south along the shore, rounded into Little Traverse Bay, and the houses of Harbor Point appeared among their pines. Alan could see that these houses were snow-covered and boarded up without sign of occupation, but he saw the Sherrill house was open; smoke rose from the chimney, and the windows winked with the reflection of a red blaze within.

He was so sure this was their destination that he started to throw off the robes.

"Nobody there now," Wassaquam indicated the house. "At Petoskey; we go there."

The sled proceeded across the edge of the bay to the little city, and even before leaving the bay ice, Alan saw Constance and her father; they were walking at the waterfront near the railway station, and they came out on the ice as they recognized the occupants of the sled.

Alan felt himself alternately weak and roused to strength as he saw her. The sled stopped, and as she approached he stepped down. Their eyes encountered, and hers looked away; a sudden shyness, which sent his heart leaping, had come over her. He wanted to speak to her, to make some recognition to her of what she had done, but he did not dare to trust his voice, and she seemed to understand that. He turned to Sherrill instead.

An engine and tender coupled to a single car stood at the railway station.

"We're going to Chicago?" he inquired of Sherrill.

Not yet, Alan . . . to St. Ignace. Father Perron . . . the priest, you know . . . went to St. Ignace as soon as he recovered from his exposure. He sent word to me that he wished to see me at my convenience. I told him that we would go to him as soon as you were able."

"He sent no other word than that?"

"Only that he had a very grave communication to make to us."

Alan did not ask more. At mention of Father Perron he had seemed to feel himself once more among the crashing, charging freight cars on the ferry and to see Benjamin Corvet, pinned amid the wreckage and speaking into the ear of the priest.

Father Perron, walking up and down on the docks close to the railway station at St. Ignace, where the tracks end without bumper or blocking of any kind above the waters of the lake, was watching south directly across the Straits.

It was mid-afternoon and the ice-breaker *Ste. Marie*, which had been expected at St. Ignace about this time, was still some four miles out.

During the storm of the week before, the floes had jammed into that narrow neck between the great lakes of Michigan and Huron, and it was said that the Straits were ice-filled to the bottom. The *Ste. Marie* and her sister ship the *St. Ignace* had plied steadily back and forth breaking up the ice, as they ferried passengers and freight back and forth across the Straits.

Through a stretch where the ice-crusher now was, the floes had changed position, or new ice was blocking the channel, as the *Ste. Ignace*, having stopped, was now backing, and her funnels shot forth fresh smoke as she charged ahead. The priest clenched his hands as the ship met the shock of her third propeller—the one beneath her bow, which sucked the water out from under the floe and left it without support. She met the ice barrier, crashed some of it aside, and then she broke through, recoiled, halted, charged, climbed up the ice and broke through again. As she drew nearer now in her approach, the priest walked back toward the railway station.

It was not merely a confession which Father Perron had taken from the lips of the dying man on *Number 25*, it was an accusation of crime against another man as well. The confession and accusation both had been made, not only to gain forgiveness from God, but to right terrible wrongs as well.

If the confession left some things unexplained, it did not lack confirmation; the priest had learned enough to be certain that it was no hallucination of madness. He had been charged definitely to repeat what had been told him to the persons he was now about to meet, so he watched expectantly as the *Ste. Marie* made its landing. A train of freight cars was on the ferry, and a single passenger coach was among them, and the switching engine brought this off first. A tall, handsome man appeared on the platform. Father Perron thought it must be Mr. Sherrill, with whom he had communicated. The young man from *Number 25* followed him, and then the two helped down a young and beautiful girl. They recognized the priest by his dress and came toward him at once.

"Mr. Sherrill?" Father Perron inquired.

Sherrill nodded, taking the priest's hand and introducing his daughter.

"I am glad to see you safe, Mr. Stafford." The priest had turned to Alan. "We have lots to be thankful for, you and I!"

"I am his son, then! I thought it must be so."

Alan trembled at the priest's sign of confirmation. There was no shock of surprise in this; he had suspected ever since August, when Captain Stafford's watch and the wedding ring had so strangely come to Constance, that he might be Stafford's son. His inquiries had brought him at that time to St. Ignace, as Father Perron's had brought him now, but he had not been able to establish proof of any connection between himself and the baby son of Captain Stafford—the baby born in that town.

He looked at Constance, as they followed the priest to the automobile which was waiting to take them to the house of old Father Benitot, whose guest Father Perron was; she was very quiet. What would that grave statement which Father Perron was to make to them mean to him—to Alan? Would further knowledge about that father whom he had not known, but whose blood was his and whose name he must now bear, bring pride or shame to him?

A bell was tolling somewhere, as they followed the priest into Father Benitot's small, bare room, which had been prepared for their interview. Father Perron went to a desk and took from it some notes which he had made. He did not seem, as he looked through these notes, to be refreshing his memory; rather he seemed to be seeking something which the notes did not supply; for he put them back and reclosed the desk.

"What I have," he said, speaking more particularly to Sherrill, "is the terrible, not fully coherent statement of a dying man. It has given me names . . . also it has given me facts. But isolated. It does not give what came before or what came after, therefore it does not clearly explain. I hope that, as Benjamin Corvet's partner, you can furnish what I lack."

"What is it you want to know? Sherrill asked.

"What were the relations between Benjamin Corvet and Captain Stafford?"

Sherrill thought a moment. "Corvet," he began, "was a very able man. He had insight and mental grasp . . . and he had the fault which sometimes goes with these abilities, a hesitancy of action. Stafford was an able man too, considerably younger than Corvet."

Sherrill paused a few moments and then continued. "We, ship owners of the lakes, have not the world to trade in, Father Perron, as they have upon the sea; if you observe our great shipping lines you will find that they have, it would seem, apportioned among themselves the traffic of the lakes; each line has its own connections and its own ports. But this did not come through agreement, rather it came through conflict; the strong have survived and made a division of the traffic; the weak have died. Twenty years ago, when this conflict of competing interests was at its height, Corvet was the head of one line, Stafford was head of another, and the two lines had very much the same connections and competed for the same cargoes."

"I begin to see!" Father Perron exclaimed. "Please go on."

"In the early 'Nineties both lines still were young; Stafford had, I believe, two ships; Corvet had three."

"So few? Yes; it grows clearer!"

"In 1894, Stafford managed a stroke which, if fate had not intervened, might well have ensured the ultimate extinction of Corvet's line or its absorption into Stafford's. Stafford gained as his partner Franklin Ramsdell, a wealthy man whom he had convinced that the lake traffic offered chances of great profit. This connection supplied Stafford with the capital, lack of which had been hampering him, as it was still hampering Corvet. The new firm—Stafford and Ramsdell—projected the construction, with Ramsdell's money, of a number of great steel freighters. The first of these was the *Miwaka*, a test ship whose experience was to guide them in the construction of the rest. It was launched in the fall of 1895, and was lost on its maiden voyage with both partners aboard."

After clearing his throat, Sherrill went on. "The Stafford and Ramsdell interests could not survive the deaths of both owners and disappeared from the lakes. Is this what you wanted to know, Father Perron?"

The priest nodded. Alan leaned tensely forward, watching; what he had heard seemed to have increased and deepened the priest's feeling over what he had to tell and to have aided his comprehension of it.

"His name was Caleb Stafford," Father Perron began. "This is what Benjamin Corvet told me when he was dying under the wreckage on the ferry:

" 'He was as fair and able a man as the lakes ever knew,' Corvet said to me. 'I had my will of most men in the lake trade in those days, but I could not have my will of him. With all the lakes to trade in, he had to pick out for his that traffic which I had already chosen for my own. But I fought him fair, Father, I fought him fair, and I would have continued to do that to the end.

" 'I was at Manistee, Father, at the end of the season—December fourth, 1895. The ice had begun to form very early that year and was already bad; there was cold and a high gale. I had laid up one of my ships at Manistee, and I was crossing that night on a tug to Manitowoc, where another was to be laid up. I had still a third one lading in the Northern Peninsula at Manistique for a last trip which, if it could be made, would mean a good profit from a season which so far, because of Stafford's competition, had been only fair. After leaving Manistee, it grew still more cold, and I was afraid the ice would close in on her and keep her where she was, so I determined to go north that night and see that she got out. None knew, Father, except those aboard the tug, that I had made that change.

" 'At midnight, Father, to westward of the Foxes, we heard the four blasts of a ship in distress—the four long blasts which have sounded in my soul ever since! We turned toward where we saw the steamer's lights; we went nearer and, Father, it was Stafford's great new ship—the *Miwaka*! We had heard two days before that she had passed the Soo; we had not known more than that or where she was. She had broken her new shaft, Father, and was intact except for that, but helpless in the rising sea she was adrift . . . .' "

The priest broke off his account of Corvet's confession and interjected his own exclamation. "The *Miwaka*!" he said. "I did not understand all that that meant to him until just now . . . the new ship of a rival line, success of which for him meant failure and defeat!"

The priest paused momentarily, satisfying himself that he understood. "There is no higher duty," he continued, "than the rescue of those in peril at sea. He, Benjamin Corvet, swore to me that at the beginning none upon the tug had any thought except to give aid. A small line was drifted down to the tug and to this a hawser was attached which they hauled aboard. There happened then the first of those events which led those on the tug into doing a great wrong. He—Benjamin Corvet—had taken charge of the wheel of the tug. Three men were handling the hawser in ice and washing water on the stern. The whistle accidentally blew, which those on the *Miwaka* understood to mean that the hawser had been secured, so they drew in the slack; the hawser tightened unexpectedly and caught and crushed the captain and deckhand of the tug and threw them into the water.

"Because they were short-handed now on the tug, and also because consultation was necessary over what was to be done, the young owner of the *Miwaka*, Captain Stafford, came down the hawser onto the tug after the line had been put straight.

"Captain Stafford went to the wheelhouse, where Benjamin Corvet was, and they consulted. Then Benjamin Corvet learned that the other owner, Ramsdell, was aboard the new ship as well—Ramsdell, the man whose money you have just told me had built this ship and was soon to build others. I did not understand before why learning that affected him so much.

" 'Stafford wanted us,' Benjamin Corvet said, 'to tow the *Miwaka* on down the lake; I would not do that, but I agreed to tow him to Manistique.

" 'The night was dark, Father—no snow, but frightful wind which had been increasing until it now sent the waves washing clear across the tug. We had gone north about an hour, when low upon the water to my right I saw a light, and I heard the whistling of a buoy which told me that we were passing nearer than I would have wished, even in daytime, to windward of Boulder Reef. There are, Father, no people on that reef, and its sides of ragged rock go straight down forty fathoms into the lake.

" 'I looked at the man with me in the wheelhouse—Stafford—and hated him! I put my head out of the wheelhouse door and looked back at the lights of the great new ship following straight and safe at the end of its towline. I thought of my two men who had been crushed and lost by the clumsiness of those on board that ship; and how my own ships had a name for never losing a man, and how that name would be lost because of the carelessness of Stafford's men! And the sound of the shoal brought an evil thought to me. Suppose I had not happened across his ship; would it have gone upon some reef like this and been lost? I thought that if now the hawser should break, I would be rid of that ship and perhaps the owner who was on board as well. We could not pick up the tow line again so close to the reef. The steamer would drift down upon the rocks—' "

Father Perron hesitated an instant. "I bear witness," he said solemnly, "that Benjamin Corvet assured me—his priest—that it was only a thought, that the evil act it suggested was something he would not do or even think of doing. But he spoke something of what was in his mind to Stafford, for he told me, 'Father, I said to Stafford that "I must look like a fool to you to keep towing your ship!"'

"They stared, he told me, into one another's eyes, and Stafford grew uneasy, as he answered, 'We'd have been all right until we got help, if you'd left us where we were!' He, too, listened to the sound of the buoy and of the water dashing on the shoal. 'You are taking us too close,' he said, 'too close!' He went aft then to look at the tow line."

Father Perron's voice ceased; what he had to tell now made his face whiten as he arranged his thoughts and memory. Alan leaned forward a little and then, with an effort, sat straight. Constance turned and looked at him, but he dared not look at her. He felt her hand warm upon his; it rested there and then moved away.

"There was a third man in the wheelhouse when these things were being spoken," Father Perron continued, "the mate of the ship which had been laid up at Manistee."

"Henry Spearman," Sherrill supplied.

"That is the name. Benjamin Corvet told me of the man that he was young, determined, brutal in nature sometimes, and set upon getting position and wealth for himself by any means. He watched Corvet and Stafford while they were speaking, and he, too, listened to the shoal until Stafford had come back. Then he went aft.

" 'I looked at him, Father,' Benjamin Corvet said to me, 'and I let him go—not knowing. He came back and looked at me once more, and again went to the stern. Stafford had been watching him as well as I, and he sprang away from me now and scrambled after him. The tug leaped suddenly; there was no longer any tow holding it back, for the hawser had parted; and I knew, Father, the reason was that Spearman had cut it!

" 'I rang for the engine to be slowed, and I left the wheel and went aft; a struggle was going on at the stern of the tug; a flash came from there and the cracking of a shot. Suddenly all was light about me as, aware of the breaking of the hawser and alarmed by the shot, the *Miwaka* had turned its searchlight on the tug. The cut end of the hawser was still on the tug, and Spearman had been trying to clear this when Stafford attacked him; they fought, and Stafford struck Spearman down. He turned and cried out against me—accusing me of having ordered Spearman to cut the line. He held up the cut end toward Ramsdell on the *Miwaka* and cried out to him and showed by pointing that it had been cut. Blood was running from his hand with which he pointed, for he had been shot by Spearman; and now again and a second and third time, from where he lay upon the deck, Spearman fired. The second of those shots killed the engineer who rushed out where I was on deck; the third shot went through Stafford's head. The *Miwaka* was drifting down on the reef; her whistle sounded again and again the four long blasts. The fireman, who had followed the engineer up from below, fawned on me! I was safe, he said; I could trust Luke—Luke would not tell! He too thought I had ordered the doing of that tragedy.

" 'From the *Miwaka*, Ramsdell yelled curses at me, threatening me for what he thought that I had done! I looked at Spearman as he got up from the deck, and I read the thought that had been in him; he had believed that he could cut the hawser in the dark, none seeing, and that our word that it had been broken would have as much strength as any accusation Stafford could make. He had known that to share a secret such as this with me would 'make' him on the lakes; for the loss of the *Miwaka* would cripple Stafford and Ramsdell and strengthen me; and that he could make me share with him whatever success I made. But Stafford had surprised him at the hawser and had seen.

" 'I moved to denounce him, Father, as I realized this; I moved— but I stopped! He had made himself safe against accusation by me!

No one ever would believe that he had done this except by my order, if he should claim that; and he made plain that he was going to claim just that. He called me a fool and defied me. Luke, my own man—the only one left on the tug with us—believed it! And there was murder in it now, with Stafford dying there on the deck and with the certainty that all those on the *Miwaka* could not be saved. I felt the noose as if it had already been tied about my neck! And I had done no wrong, Father! I had only thought wrong!

" 'So long as one lived among those on the *Miwaka* who had seen what had been done, I knew I would be hanged; yet I would have saved them if I could. But in my comprehension of what this meant, I only stared at Stafford where he lay and then at Spearman, and I let him get control of the tug. The tug, whose wheel I had lashed, heading her into the waves, had been moving slowly. Spearman pushed me aside and went to the wheelhouse; he sent Luke to the engines, and from that moment Luke was his. He turned the tug around to where we still saw the lights of the *Miwaka*. The steamer had struck the reef, and hung there for a time. Spearman had the wheel, and Luke, at his orders, was at the engines. We held the tug off and we beat slowly to and fro until the *Miwaka* slipped off and sank. Some had gone down with her, no doubt, but two boats got off, carrying lights. They saw the tug approaching and cried out and stretched their hands out to us, but Spearman stopped the tug. They rowed toward us then, but when they got near, Spearman moved the tug away and then again stopped. They cried out again and rowed toward us; again he moved the tug away, and then they understood and stopped rowing and cried curses at us. One boat drifted far away, and we knew of its capsizing by the extinguishing of its light. Those in it who had no lifebelts and could not swim, sank first. Some could swim, and for a while they fought the waves.' "

Alan, as he listened, ceased consciously to separate the priest's voice from the sensations running through him. His father was Stafford, dying at Corvet's feet while Corvet watched the deaths of the crew of the *Miwaka*. The deaths of all those aboard but one . . . a child floated with a life belt among those struggling in the water whom Spearman and Corvet were watching die, and Corvet plucked him out to safety . . . .

Was it memory of that which now had come to him? No. Rather, it was a realization of all the truths which the priest's words were bringing together and arranging rightly for him. He, a child, saved by Corvet from the water because he could not bear witness, seemed to be on that tug, sea-swept and clad in ice, crouching beside the wounded form of his father while Corvet stood aghast . . . .

Corvet, still hearing the long blasts of distress from the steamer which was gone, still hearing the screams of the men who were drowned. Then, when all who could tell were gone, Spearman turned the tug toward Manitowoc . . . .

Now and again the priest's voice became audible to Alan.

Alan's father died in the morning. All day they stayed out in the storm, avoiding vessels. They dared not throw Stafford's body overboard or that of the engineer, because if found, the bullet holes would have aroused inquiry. When night came again, they had taken the two ashore at some wild spot and buried them. To make identification harder, they had taken the things that they had with them and buried them somewhere else.

The child—Alan—Corvet had smuggled ashore and sent away. Later, he told Spearman the child had died.

"Peace . . . rest!" Father Perron said in a deep voice. "Peace to the dead."

But for the living there had been no peace. Spearman had forced Corvet to make him his partner; Corvet had tried to take up his life again, but had not been able. His wife, aware that something was wrong with him, had learned enough so that she had left him. Luke had come and come and come again for blackmail, and Corvet had paid him. Corvet grew rich; those connected with him prospered; but with Corvet lived always the ghosts of those he had watched die with the *Miwaka*—of those who would have prospered with Stafford except for what he had done. Corvet had secretly sought and followed the fate of the kin of those people who had been murdered to benefit him; he found some of their families destroyed; he found almost all poor and struggling.

And though Corvet paid Luke to keep the crime from disclosure, yet Corvet swore to himself to confess it all and make such restitution as he could. But each time that the day he had appointed with himself arrived, he put it off and paid Luke again and again. Spearman knew of his intention and sometimes kept him from it. But Corvet had made one close friend; and when that friend's daughter, for whom Corvet cared now most of all in the world, had been about to marry Spearman, Corvet defied the cost to himself, and he gained strength to oppose Spearman. So he had written to Stafford's son to come; he had prepared for confession and restitution; but, after he had done this and while he waited, something seemed to break in his brain; too long preyed upon by terrible memories, and the ghosts of those who had gone, and by the echo of their voices crying to him from the water, Corvet had wandered away; he had come back, under the name of one of those whom he had wronged, to the lake life from which he had sprung. Only now and then, for a few hours, did he have intervals when he remembered all; in one of these lucid intervals he had dug up the watch and the ring and other things he had taken from Captain Stafford's pockets, and had written to himself directions of what to do with them, against the time his mind again failed.

And for Spearman, strong against all that assailed Corvet, there had always been the terror of the legendary drum—the drum which had beat short for the *Miwaka*, the drum which had known that one was saved! That story came from some hint which Luke had spread, Corvet thought; but Spearman, born near the L'Arbre Croche home of the legend, believed the drum had known and had tried to tell; all through the years Spearman had dreaded this, and the sound which had tried to betray him.

So it was by the drum that, in the end, Spearman was broken.

The priest's voice had stopped, as Alan slowly realized. He heard Sherrill's voice.

"It was a trust that he left to you, Alan; I thought it must be that—a trust for those who suffered by the loss of your father's ship. I don't know yet how it can be fulfilled; we must think of that."

"That's how I understand it," Alan replied.

Fuller consciousness of what Father Perron's story meant to him was flowing through him now. Wrong, great wrong there had been, as he had known there must be; but it had not been as he had feared, for he and his father had been among the wronged ones. The new name that had come to him—he knew what that must be: Robert Alan Stafford; and there was no shadow on it. He was the son of an honest man and a good woman; he was clean and free; free to think as he was thinking now of the girl beside him; and to hope that she was thinking so of him.

Through the tumult in his soul he became aware of physical feelings again, and of Sherrill's hand put upon his shoulder in a cordial, friendly grasp. Then another hand, small and firm, touched his, and he felt its warm, tightening grasp upon his fingers; he looked up; and his eyes filled and hers, he saw, were brimming, too.

They walked together, later in the day, up the hill to the small, white house which had been Caleb Stafford's. Alan had seen the house before, but not knowing then whether the man who had owned it had or had not been his father, he had merely looked at it from the outside. There had been a small garden filled with flowers before it then; now the yard and roofs were buried in deep snow. The woman who came to the door was willing to show them through the house; it had only five rooms. One of those on the second floor was so much larger and pleasanter than the rest that they became quite sure it was the one in which Alan had been born, and where his young mother soon afterward had died. They were very quiet as they stood looking about.

"I wish we could have known her," Constance said.

The woman, who had shown them about, had gone to another room and left them alone.

"There seems to have been no picture of her and nothing of hers left here that anyone can tell me about; but," Alan choked, "it's good to be able to think of her as I can now."

"I know," Constance said. "When you were away, I used to think of you as finding out about her and . . . and I wanted to be with you. I'm glad I'm with you now, though you don't need me any more!"

"Not need you!"

"I mean . . . no one can say anything against her now!"

Alan drew nearer to her, trembling.

"I can never thank you . . . I can never tell you what you did for me, believing in . . . her and in me, no matter how things looked. And then, coming up here as you did . . . for me!"

"Yes, it was for you, Alan!"

"Constance!" He took her in his arms. She let him hold her; then, still clinging to him, she put him a little away.

"The night before you came to the Point last summer, Alan, he . . . he had just come and asked me again. I'd promised, but that evening when we drove to his place and . . . there were sunflowers there. I knew that I couldn't love him."

"Because of the sunflowers?"

"Sunflower houses, Alan, they made me think of . . . you. Do you remember?"

"Remember!"

The woman was returning to them now, and perhaps it was just as well; for not yet, he knew, could he ask her all that he wished; what had happened was too recent yet for that. But to him, Spearman—half mad and fleeing from the haunts of men—was beginning to be like one who had never been; and he knew she shared this feeling. The light in her deep eyes was telling him already what her answer to him would be; and life now stretched forth before him, full of love and happiness and hope.

THE   END